The sunshine streaming in through his uncovered windows made the highlights in her shiny hair glow, and he itched to run his fingers through all those dark and reddish strands.

He tried to think of a word to describe it and couldn't. *Brown* was too plain a term to describe all that lustrous silk.

"What color is your hair?" Oh man, had he actually asked that out loud? What was wrong with him?

"What?" She gave him a quizzical look.

Liam shrugged and hoped his face wasn't as flushed as it felt. "Meg has a thing about people calling her hair red and I, uh, just wondered if you had a name for your color like she does."

She ran a hand over her hair. "It's chestnut. Why?"

Liam nodded, but didn't answer her question. He'd embarrassed himself enough for one day. "Are you planning on telling me why you're here?"

She rubbed her hands on her thighs and drew in a deep breath. "I know we decided this summer was no strings attached, but—"

"About that, Ellie, I—"

"I'm pregnant."

Baby Bombshell Surprise

CARRIE NICHOLS
&
MELISSA SENATE

Previously published as *His Unexpected Twins* and *Detective Barelli's Legendary Triplets*

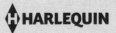

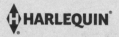

Recycling programs for this product may not exist in your area.

ISBN-13: 978-1-335-97693-2

Baby Bombshell Surprise
Copyright © 2020 by Harlequin Books S.A.

His Unexpected Twins
First published in 2019. This edition published in 2020.
Copyright © 2019 by Carol Opalinski

Detective Barelli's Legendary Triplets
First published in 2018. This edition published in 2020.
Copyright © 2018 by Melissa Senate

All rights reserved. No part of this book may be used or reproduced in any manner whatsoever without written permission except in the case of brief quotations embodied in critical articles and reviews.

This is a work of fiction. Names, characters, places and incidents are either the product of the author's imagination or are used fictitiously. Any resemblance to actual persons, living or dead, businesses, companies, events or locales is entirely coincidental.

This edition published by arrangement with Harlequin Books S.A.

For questions and comments about the quality of this book, please contact us at CustomerService@Harlequin.com.

Harlequin Enterprises ULC
22 Adelaide St. West, 40th Floor
Toronto, Ontario M5H 4E3, Canada
www.Harlequin.com

Printed in U.S.A.

CONTENTS

Carrie Nichols grew up in New England but moved south and traded snow for central AC. She loves to travel, is addicted to British crime dramas and knows a *Seinfeld* quote appropriate for every occasion.

A 2016 RWA Golden Heart® Award winner and two-time Maggie Award for Excellence winner, she has one tolerant husband, two grown sons and two critical cats. To her dismay, Carrie's characters—like her family—often ignore the wisdom and guidance she offers.

Books by Carrie Nichols

Small-Town Sweethearts

The Marine's Secret Daughter
The Sergeant's Unexpected Family
The Scrooge of Loon Lake

Visit the Author Profile page at Harlequin.com for more titles.

His Unexpected Twins

CARRIE NICHOLS

In loving memory of my cousin
Captain Donald "Chuck" Elliott
of the Springfield (MA) Fire Department.

Chapter 1

"How about that new guy from—"

"No." Ellie Harding paused mid-slice in the sheet cake she was dividing into equal squares to scowl at her friend's attempts at matchmaking.

Meg McBride Cooper stood on the opposite side of the rectangular table, a stack of plain white dessert plates cradled against her chest. Ellie and Meg were volunteering at the payment-optional luncheon held weekly in the basement of the whitewashed clapboard church on the town square in Loon Lake, Vermont.

"I don't need or want help finding a date," Ellie said, and considering what she'd survived in her twenty-seven years, going solo to a friend's wedding shouldn't even be a blip on her radar. Did her friends think she couldn't find a date on her own? Memories surfaced of how she'd sometimes been treated after her cancer diagnosis. She knew her friends didn't pity her, but experiencing being pitied behind her back as well as to her face as a child had made her more sensitive as an adult.

Ellie pushed aside memories and went back to slicing the chocolate frosted cake with vigorous strokes. Heck, guys called her. Yep. They called all the time. *Slice*. They called when they needed a shortstop for a pickup softball game or a bowling partner. *Slice*. One even called last month, asking if she had a phone number for that new X-ray tech. *Slice*.

Meg plopped the plates onto the table with a *thunk* and gnawed on her bottom lip as she gazed at Ellie. Yeah, Meg was feeling guilty and wanted to confess something.

"Spill it," Ellie ordered.

"Now, don't get mad, but…" Meg sighed. "I asked Riley if he knew anyone who might be interested in being your date for the wedding."

"Uh-oh. Is Meg trying to set you up with arrestees…again?" A fellow volunteer, Mary Carter, came to stand shoulder to shoulder with Ellie, another sheet pan clutched in her hands. Mary was the future bride in question and a transplant to their close-knit central Vermont community, but she had jumped into town life and activities with enthusiasm. "Really, Meg, don't you think Ellie can do better than a felon? I'm sure if I asked, Brody could contact one of his old army buddies. I'll tell him to only choose ones that have never been arrested."

Meg rolled her eyes. "I'm sure asking Brody won't be necessary, Mary."

"Just in case…" Mary set the cake next to the stack

of plates. "Ellie, what are your feelings on speeding tickets, because—"

"Oh, for heaven's sake," Meg interrupted and made an impatient sound with her tongue.

Ellie stifled a giggle at their antics but couldn't decide if she was grateful or annoyed. Now that her two besties had found happily-ever-afters, they seemed to think it their sworn duty to get her settled, too. So what if she hadn't found Mr. Right yet? Between long shifts as a nurse in the ER and studying for a more advanced degree, she led a full, busy life, thank you very much.

Mary winked at Ellie. "At least *I'm* not trying to set her up with someone who's been arrested."

"As I've told both of you already, that guy wasn't under arrest." Meg planted her hands on her hips. "He just happened to be in the building and Riley recruited him for a police lineup, that's all there was to it. No crime. No arrest."

Ellie continued to slice the cake. "If there was no crime, why was there a police lineup?"

"I meant *he* didn't commit a crime."

Mary slanted a look at Ellie. "Please correct me if I'm wrong, but didn't the witness identify him?"

"Mary," Meg huffed. "You're not helping."

"Sorry," Mary said, but her grin told a different story.

Ellie sucked on her cheeks to stifle a laugh, grateful to be off the hot seat, even temporarily. She appreciated her friends' concern but she wasn't a project. At times like this, Meg conveniently forgot she hadn't dated anyone for five years until Riley Cooper came back to town after serving in the marines in Afghanistan. Ellie decided not to point that out because her friends meant well. And she didn't want to turn their attention—and matchmaking attempts—back to her.

Meg blew her breath out noisily, disturbing the wisps of curly red hair that had escaped her messy ponytail. "I've explained this to you guys like a thousand times already. It was a case of mistaken identity. I swear."

"Uh-huh, sure." Mary laughed and elbowed Ellie. "Ooh, maybe Riley can get the sheriff's department to start an eligible bachelor catch-and-release program."

"You guys are the worst," Meg grumbled, and began laying out the plates.

"Yup, the absolute worst, but you love us, anyway." Ellie grinned as she plated cake slices.

"Yeah, it's a good thing— Ooh, Ellie, how about that oh-my-God-he's-so-gorgeous guy coming down the stairs? If I wasn't hopelessly in love with Brody…" Mary bumped shoulders with Ellie and motioned with head.

Ellie's gaze followed Mary's and her heart stuttered. *Liam McBride.* What was he doing at the luncheon? She'd had a serious crush on Meg's brother since…well, since forever. At four years older, Liam had seen her as an annoying kid and had treated her accordingly. By the time she'd matured enough for him to notice, she'd been "his kid sister's friend" for so long she doubted it registered that she was a grown woman.

"What? Who? Where?" Meg whirled around and made a sound with her tongue against her teeth. "That's Liam."

"Liam?" Mary's eyes widened. "You mean that's—"

"Ellie's date for the wedding." Meg swiveled back, clapping her hands together, her mouth in a wide smile. "It's perfect."

"What? No." Ellie took a step back, shaking her head and holding up the knife as if warding off marauding zombies. She could accept matchmaking between friends. Even being relegated to Liam's friend zone would be acceptable, but begging for a pity date? *Nuh-uh.* Not gonna happen. No way. "Absolutely not."

"No... *No?*" Mary glanced at Liam again and snapped back to Ellie, looking at her as if she were insane for refusing. "I don't know why you wouldn't want—"

"Because he's Meg's brother." Ellie sneaked another glance at the sexy six-foot-two hunk of firefighter strutting toward them.

From his chronically disheveled dark brown hair and broad shoulders to his slim hips, long legs and that touch of confident swagger, Liam McBride oozed pheromones. And Ellie longed to answer their alluring call by throwing herself at his feet, but good sense, not to mention strong self-preservation instincts, prevailed. Thank God, because she didn't relish getting stepped on by those size 13 Oakley assault boots. To him, she was his little sister's friend. The girl who used to make moon eyes at him, the teen who blushed and stuttered every time he talked to her. When she'd been diagnosed with cancer in her teens, one of her first thoughts had been that she might never get to kiss Liam McBride.

"Be right back," Meg threw over her shoulder and rushed to meet her brother as he crossed the room.

"Oh, my. I mean, I had no idea," Mary whispered, leaning closer to Ellie. "Whenever she mentioned her brother, I was picturing a male version of Meg. You know...vertically challenged, wild red hair, freckles."

Ellie burst out laughing, but drew in a sharp breath

when Liam's head snapped up. His gaze captured hers and his lips quirked into an irresistible half grin. The air she'd sucked in got caught in her chest. Why did he have to be so damn sexy? As if handsomeness had been handed out unchecked on the day he received his looks.

"Liam takes after their dad," she whispered to Mary. And not just in physical appearance.

Ellie knew Liam and his dad had buried themselves in work when Bridget McBride got sick. Firefighting was an admirable profession, but relationships needed care and feeding, too. All Ellie had to do was look at her parents to understand the cost when one partner checked out emotionally during a life-threatening situation. She might have survived the cancer that had plagued her childhood, but her parents' close relationship hadn't. As an adult she knew the guilt she'd carried throughout her teen years was irrational, but that didn't stop it from gnawing at her whenever she saw her parents together. What happened to them proved no relationship was immune to life's challenges.

So she'd admire the sexy firefighter, and if given the chance, she'd take that secret Make-A-Wish kiss, but she'd keep her heart and hopes for the future far, far away from Liam McBride.

"Heart? You listening?" she asked sotto voce before sneaking another longing glance at Liam.

Liam's footsteps had faltered at that distinctive laugh. *Ellie Harding.* Her laughter, like her honey-brown eyes, sparkled and drew him in whenever she was close. Today, her long, shiny dark hair was pulled back and secured with one of those rubber band thingies his sister and niece favored. He shook his head and tried to force his thoughts into safer territory. As his sister's friend, Ellie was off-limits, a permanent resident of the no-dating zone. It was a good thing they lived three hours apart so he wasn't faced with temptation on a regular basis. The last time he'd seen her was at his nephew's christening, nearly nine months ago.

The fact that she'd had cancer as a child and could have died had nothing to do with his resistance to her charms. Nothing at all. He'd hate to think he was that shallow, despite knowing the destruction illness left in its wake.

No. His reluctance was because messing with a sibling's friend could have nasty consequences. He and his best friend, Riley Cooper, were just patching up a huge rift in their friendship. Riley had broken the bro code and Liam's trust by getting Meg pregnant before deploying to Afghanistan and disappearing from her life. But all that was in the past. His sister was crazy in love with Riley, who'd come back, taken responsibility for his daughter and convinced Meg to marry him. Riley was also the reason for the glow of happiness in his sister's eyes these days.

So he'd buried the hatchet, and not in Riley's privates as he'd longed to do once upon a time. He was even spending saved vacation time in Loon Lake to help his brother-in-law renovate. Meg and Riley were outgrowing their modest cottage-style home after the birth of their second child, James.

His gaze met Ellie's and objections scattered like ashes. Damn, but off-limits would be a lot easier if she weren't so appealing. Why some guy hadn't scooped her up by now was a mystery. He almost wished one had and removed temptation. *Almost*. Something he kept buried deep and refused to explore railed against the picture of Ellie married to a random dude, forever out of reach. Except out of reach was where she needed to stay, because he'd filled his quota of losing people. From here on out, his heart belonged to his job. *Stay back three hundred feet, Ellie Harding.*

"Liam, what are you doing here?" Meg asked.

"I'm here to help Riley with your addition, remember?"

"I mean here…at the luncheon."

"When you weren't home, I remembered you volunteered here on Thursdays." He shrugged. "So, here I am."

She grinned and looped her arm through his. "You have no idea what perfect timing you have."

Then she began guiding—yeah, more like frog-marching—him across the church basement toward Ellie of the twinkling eyes and engaging laugh.

Liam's indrawn breath hissed through his teeth. "Uh-oh."

"You're the answer to our problem," Meg said in a too-bright tone, and squeezed his arm.

"Huh, that's new." He gave her a side-eye look. "Usually you're accusing me of being or causing the problem."

Meg's expression was calculating, as if sizing him up for something. *Crap.* He knew that look and nothing good ever came from it. Now that she was happily married, she seemed to think everyone should be. Living three hours away, he'd managed to avoid her less-than-subtle hints that it was time he settled down. He loved his sister and was happy to help with the interior finishing work on her new home addition, but he wasn't about to let her manipulate him into any sort of permanent relationship. Even if the intended target had the most beautiful golden eyes he'd ever seen.

He made a show of looking around. "Where's Riley? Why isn't your husband here solving your problems? Isn't that what he's for?"

"Nah, he can't help with this one, so enjoy being the solution for once, brother dear." Meg stopped at the table where Ellie and an attractive dark-haired woman about the same age were dishing out slices of chocolate cake.

"Meg tells me you need me to sample that cake." He winked at Ellie, who blushed. His breath quickened at her flushed features. *Friend zone*, he repeated to himself, but his mind kept conjuring up unique and enjoyable ways of keeping that pretty pink color on her face.

Meg tugged on his am, acting like her seven-year-old daughter, Fiona. "First, agree to our proposition, then you can have cake."

Ellie was shaking her head and mouthing the word *no*. Obviously whatever Meg had in mind involved her. Despite his wariness, he was intrigued.

Meg was nodding her head as vigorously as Ellie was shaking hers. "Ellie needs a date for Mary's wedding."

"I do not. Don't listen to her. This was all your sister's harebrained idea." Ellie dumped a piece of cake onto a plate and it landed frosting side down. She cursed and he cleared his throat to disguise his laugh.

"But Liam is going to be in town, so it's perfect," Meg said.

He winced. Tenacious was Meg's middle name. Another reason to keep Ellie in that friend zone. He'd have to live with the fallout into eternity.

"Hi, I'm Mary. The bride." The raven-haired woman

set aside the slice with the frosting side down and thrust out her hand. "And you're welcome to come to my wedding with—" she glanced at Ellie "—or without a date."

He untangled his arm from Meg's and shook hands. "Thanks, I—"

"Oh, look. They need help at the pay station," Meg said, and scooted away.

"Nice meeting you, Liam. I'd love to stay and chat, but I promised to help in the kitchen." Mary disappeared as quickly and efficiently as his sister.

"Cowards," Ellie muttered, and shook her head. "Look, I'm not hitting you up to be my date for the wedding. I'm fine going by myself."

He nodded. Ellie was smart and independent, but that didn't mean she wanted to go to a wedding alone if everyone else was paired up. They could go as friends. And if he happened to hold her close as they danced… He shook his head, but the image of Ellie in his arms wouldn't go away. Huh, Meg wasn't the only tenacious person today. And damn if Meg hadn't once again manipulated him. "Are you saying you don't want to go with me? I've been known to behave myself in public."

Ellie raised her eyebrows, but her eyes glinted with mischief. "That's not what I've heard."

"Lies and exaggerations. Don't believe a word you hear and only half of what you see." He pulled a face.

"Uh-huh, sure." She laughed and went back to dishing out cake.

Her laugh washed over him and he arranged the plates so the empty ones were closer to her. People had begun lining up at the other end of the string of tables, but no one had reached the dessert station yet. He took advantage and hurried to Ellie's side of the table. He could help hand out the cake. Yeah, he was a regular do-gooder and it had nothing to do with standing next to Ellie and breathing in her light, flowery scent. "Why don't you want to go to this wedding with me?"

Ellie shook her head. "I'm not looking for a pity date."

He sighed. If she knew where his thoughts had been, she wouldn't be saying that. Besides, it wasn't like a real date because they'd be friends hanging out together. As simple as that. "So how do I appeal to your better nature and get you to take pity on me?"

"What? No. I meant…" she sputtered, her face turning pink again. She made what sounded like an impatient noise and put the last slice of cake on a plate.

He shouldn't, but he enjoyed seeing her flustered and if he was the cause, all the better, because she certainly had that effect on him. "How did you do that?"

She looked up and frowned. "Do what?"

He could get lost in those eyes. *Focus, McBride.* He cleared his throat and pointed to the last cake square on the plate. "You made those come out even."

A smile spread across her face and she glanced around before leaning close. "It's my superpower."

"I'm intrigued," he whispered, but he wasn't referring to cake or plates.

She straightened and turned her attention to a woman who appeared in front of them. "Hello, Mrs. Canterbury. Cake?"

After the woman had taken her cake and left, he bumped his hip against Ellie's. "Whaddaya say, Harding, help a guy out. Do your good deed for the month and come to this wedding with me?"

She narrowed her eyes at him. "Why? So I can perform CPR on the women who faint at your feet?"

Liam threw his head back and laughed. He spotted Meg watching them, a smug expression on her face. He'd deal with his sister later. Maybe he could interest Fiona in a drum set or buy James, who would be walking soon, a pair of those annoying sneakers that squeaked.

Except he was intrigued by the idea of going with Ellie, so he gave her what he hoped was his best puppy-dog face. "Please. I hear it's the social event of the season."

"Oh, brother," she muttered and rolled her eyes.

Why had it suddenly become so important for her to say yes? He should be running the other way. Ellie didn't strike him as the sort of woman who did casual, and that's all he was looking for—with Ellie or anyone. Keep it light. No more wrenching losses. But that damn image of holding her while dancing, their bodies in sync, sometimes touching, wouldn't go away.

"How long are you staying in Loon Lake?"

Her question dragged him away from his thoughts and he frowned. "Exactly when is this wedding?"

"You missed the point. That was my attempt at changing the subject," she said, and greeted an elderly woman shuffling past.

Liam smiled at the woman and tried to hand her a dessert.

The woman shook her head and held up a plate loaded with meat loaf, potatoes and green beans. "Gotta eat this first, son."

Liam nodded, put the dessert back on the table and turned his head to Ellie. "I'll be here for a month."

"Goodness gracious, son, it won't take me that long to eat," the woman said before meandering off to find a seat.

Ellie giggled, her eyes sparkling with amusement, and he couldn't look away. *She's Meg's friend. Are you forgetting about cancer and how much it hurts to lose someone?* Sure, she was in remission, but there was a reason that term was used instead of *cured.* In his mother's case, the remission didn't last. Ellie was off-limits for so many reasons. But that message was getting drowned out. "So, you'll go with me to this wedding?"

"Look, Liam, I appreciate the offer, but—"

He leaned closer, dragging in her scent, and tilted his head in the direction of his sister. "It might shut her up for a bit. Let her think she got her way."

"Hmm." Ellie sucked on her lower lip for a second, then shook her head. "Nah. It'll just encourage her."

"It'll throw her off the scent if we hang out for a bit. We'll know that's all we'd be doing, but she won't." He'd lost his ever-lovin' mind. Yup, that must be the explanation for pursuing such an idiotic suggestion.

Ellie smiled and continued to hand out the cake. Although she had fewer freckles than she had as a kid, she still had a sprinkling of them high on her cheekbones and the bridge of her nose. He wouldn't have thought freckles could be sexy, but on Ellie they were, and he had to fight the urge to count them by pressing his fingertips to each one. Or better yet, his tongue.

"But we won't really be dating?" she asked during a lull in the line of people.

"Did you want to date?" What the hell was he doing asking such a loaded question? He handed out the last piece of cake to an elderly man in a Red Sox baseball cap.

"Meg means well, but it might be nice to take a break from her matchmaking efforts." She picked up the plate with the frosting-side-down slice and held it up. "Split?"

"Sure." He reached for the fork she offered. His fingers brushed hers as he took the utensil and their gazes met. "Thanks. Looks delicious."

Her cheeks turned pink, making the tiny freckles stand out even more. As if they were begging for someone—him—to run their tongue along them. He cleared his throat and jabbed his fork in the cake.

"So, whaddaya say, Harding, do we have a deal?"

She shrugged. "Sure, McBride, why not?" Someone called her name and she turned away to leave but said over her shoulder, "We'll talk."

He set the fork on the empty plate and watched her disappear into the kitchen. She never did answer his question about wanting to date. Not that it mattered, because they would be hanging out. No dating. No relationship. Nice and safe: the way he preferred it.

Chapter 2

"Check out the guy who just walked in." Stacy, the triage nurse on duty, elbowed Ellie.

Ellie looked up from the notes she'd been studying to glance out the large glass window into the emergency waiting area. Her heart sped at the sight of Liam dressed in jeans and a dark blue Red Sox championship T-shirt approaching them. She hadn't seen him since the community luncheon two days prior, but he hadn't been far from her thoughts. If Stacy hadn't spotted him first, Ellie might have wondered if he was figment of her overactive imagination.

Ignoring Stacy's obvious curiosity, Ellie opened the door to the triage area. "Hey, what are you doing here?"

"Hey, yourself." He gave her that sexy half grin that threatened to leave her in a puddle.

Janitorial, mop up triage, please.

She clutched the clipboard across her chest as if it could protect her vital organs like a lead apron during X-rays. "Everything okay?"

"Heard you'd be getting off soon." He shrugged. "Thought you might like to grab some supper with me."

In the little office, Stacy cleared her throat, but Ellie ignored her.

Was he asking her on a date? "And where did you hear my shift was ending?"

"I asked Meg." He put his hands into his front pockets and hunched his shoulders forward. "So, how about some supper?"

A pen dropped, followed by a sigh. Stacy was probably memorizing every word and detail of the encounter to pass along later in the cafeteria.

Ellie shuffled her feet. Was she going to do this? *Repeat after me: "not a real date."* "Sure. I've got some extra clothes in my locker. If you don't mind waiting while I change."

From the sound of it, Stacy was rearranging files on her desk, and evidently, they were fighting back.

Ellie grinned and turned around. "Stacy, have you met my friend Meg Cooper's brother, Liam?"

Stacy stepped forward and stuck out her hand. "Pleased to meet you, Liam."

"Let me get changed. I'll be right back," Ellie said while Stacy and Liam shook hands.

Stacy laughed. "Don't rush on my account."

Despite Stacy's comment, Ellie hurried to her locker. Had this been Liam's idea or was Meg somehow behind this? After changing into jeans and a short-sleeved cotton sweater, she undid her hair from the braid and brushed it out. Even if this wasn't an honest-to-goodness date, she wanted to look her best. She fluffed her hair around her shoulders and applied some cherry lip gloss and went in search of Liam.

Hands shoved in his back pockets, Liam stood in front of the muted television in the waiting area. He turned as she approached and smiled broadly. "I gotta say, Harding, you clean up nicely."

"Not so bad yourself, McBride." She put her purse strap over her shoulder and waved to Stacy through the window. The triage nurse was with a patient but glanced at Liam and back to Ellie with a grin and a thumbs-up.

"I thought we'd take my truck and I can bring you back here for your car," Liam said as the automatic doors slid open with an electronic *whoosh*.

A light breeze was blowing the leaves on the trees surrounding the parking lot. A thunderstorm earlier in the day had broken the heat and humidity, making the evening warm but comfortable.

"Sounds good." *Sounds like a date.*

Using his key fob to unlock his truck, he approached the passenger side and opened the door for her. "Riley says that new hard cider microbrewery on the town square has great food."

"They do. Best burgers in town, if you ask me." She sucked on her bottom lip as she climbed into his truck. Everyone in Loon Lake knew Hennen's Microbrewery was the place to hang out with friends, while Angelo's was the restaurant you brought your date to. So, not a date. *At least we cleared that up.*

Once she was in the passenger seat, he shut the door and strolled around the hood of the truck. He climbed in and settled himself behind the wheel.

"Yeah, Meg mentioned that Angelo's has added a

dining patio but—" He started the truck and music from the Dropkick Murphys blasted from the speakers. Leaning over, he adjusted the volume. "Sorry about that."

His movements filled the front seat with his signature scent. She was able to pick out notes of salty sea air, driftwood and sage. Thinking about his aftershave was better than trying to figure out what he'd been about to say about Angelo's. Okay, color her curious. "You were saying something about Angelo's new patio."

He checked the mirrors and the backup camera before leaving the parking spot. "Hmm…oh, yeah. Meg said during the winter you can see across the lake to their house from the patio."

Serves you right for asking. "That's cool."

He cleared his throat. "She was going on and on about how romantic the new patio was with something called fairy lights."

Not exactly subtle, Meg. Ellie fiddled with the strap of her purse. "Yeah, they've got small trees in ceramic pots scattered around with tiny LED lights strung around the trunks and branches. Very pretty, with lots of atmosphere."

The air in the confined space felt supercharged with something…awareness? Chemistry? She couldn't be sure, couldn't even be sure that he felt it, too. Maybe this was all in her head. All one-sided, like it had been in her childhood.

He glanced at her for a second before bringing his attention back to the road. "So, you've been to Angelo's patio?"

Was he trying to get information on her social life or lack thereof? "No, but Mary and Meg have both been."

She huffed out her breath. "Believe me, I've heard all about it."

He reached over and laid his hand over hers. "Sounds like I may have to take up the challenge to be sure you get to experience this patio, too."

Her heart did a little bump, but she laughed, hoping to brazen through. "You signing me up as their new janitor, McBride?"

He squeezed her hand and brought it to his chest. "You wound me, Harding. I was thinking more along the lines of the waitstaff. I can see you in a white blouse and a cute little black skirt."

"Glad we cleared that up." She laughed for real this time. Date or not, there was no reason she couldn't enjoy being with Liam. Even if anything that could happen with Liam had nowhere to go. They didn't live in the same town. And then there was the whole thing with Liam having used his job to avoid dealing with his emotions. Even his sister couldn't deny that truth. But that didn't mean she couldn't enjoy hanging out with him while he was here. Having a life-threatening illness like lymphoma had taught her she didn't want to die with regrets if she could help it. After enduring chemo coupled with radiation, she'd been in remission for almost nine years, a good chunk of time, and her oncologist was optimistic but the experience had changed her outlook on life.

"How are the renovations coming?" she asked.

He squeezed her hand and put it back on her lap. "Is this you changing the subject?"

"So you *can* take a hint."

He jokingly muttered something about respect for her elders but launched into an amusing story about framing out the new master bedroom closet at Meg and Riley's place.

"That house is going to be awesome once the addition is finished."

He made a hum of agreement. "Yeah, I guess she made the right choice moving here."

"She said you had tried to get her to move into one of your rentals." She hadn't seen Liam's place, but she knew he owned one of those iconic Boston three-family homes commonly referred to as "three-deckers" by the locals. He'd purchased it as a bank foreclosure and had been remodeling it ever since, according to Meg. Ellie knew it was Liam's pride and joy.

"I did, but she's always loved this town and that vacation home. Even all the repairs it needed didn't deter her. My sister can be stubborn."

Ellie laughed. "Yeah, so I noticed."

"But I gotta say, she made the right choice for her." He stopped for a red light.

"What about you?" The words were out before she could prevent them.

He turned his head to look at her. "Me? I'm exactly where I belong."

Yeah, that's what she thought. And like Meg, he was happy where he lived.

Swallowing, she pointed out the windshield. "Green light."

She glanced at Liam's strong profile. Could *she* be happy in Boston? "No regrets" included trying new things, new places.

Hey, Ellie, aren't you getting a little ahead of yourself? This wasn't even a real date.

The route along Main Street took them past a few

rectangular, early-nineteenth-century gable-roofed houses gathered around the town green. Some of the stately homes had been repurposed as doctors' offices, an insurance agency and an attorney's office, but some were still single-family residences.

The manicured common space boasted a restored white gazebo that doubled as a bandstand for concerts and picnics in the summer. Homes soon gave way to brick-fronted businesses, and the white Greek Revival church where they held the weekly lunches. With its black shutters and steeple bell tower, the church anchored the green at one end.

No doubt the town was picturesque, but she recalled how, when she was sick, the women of Loon Lake had worked year-round to keep the Hardings' refrigerator full of casseroles and sandwich fixings. In the summer, the men had made sure their lawn was mowed. In the winter, the men plowing for the town had been careful to keep the end of their driveway relatively clear.

He pulled the truck into one of the angled parking spots in front of the pub-style restaurant. "I'm assuming you've been here before, since you said you liked the burgers."

"Yeah, I've been a few times with some of the people from work."

He turned the engine off and opened his door. Ellie opened hers and was getting out when he came around to her side. He put his hand under her elbow to steady her as she scrambled out. His touch sent sparks up her arm...straight to her core.

You'd better be listening, she cautioned her heart. *Liam and I are hanging out, nothing more.* Unlike Angelo's, this wasn't a romantic date place. Since this wasn't a date, she had no right to feel disappointed. And she certainly had no right to be using or thinking the word *romantic* in context with anything she and Liam did.

They strolled across the sidewalk to the entrance, his hand hovering over the small of her back, not quite touching. How was she supposed to read the mixed signals he was sending? Maybe it was all her fault for trying to read things into his actions and words that weren't there. *Your fault because you wanted this to be a date and it's a let's-hang-out night.* She swallowed the sigh that bubbled up.

He turned his head toward her as they made their way toward the restaurant. "Something wrong with Hennen's?"

Had he picked up on her confusion? She shook her head. "No. It's fine."

"Hey, I'm not such a guy that I don't know what 'fine' in that tone of voice means." He held the glass entry door open.

After stepping inside, she glanced up at him, her eyebrows raised. "And what does 'fine' mean?"

The outer door shut, leaving them alone in the restaurant's vestibule. A small table with a bowl of wrapped mints and stack of takeout menus stood off to one side. Muffled sounds—music, conversations and clinking of dishware—came from beyond the inner door.

"I'm thinking it means there's something wrong and I'm expected to figure it out." His light blue eyes darkened.

Lost in those eyes, she had to swallow before she could speak. "And have you figured it out?"

"No, but I have an idea how to fix it." He took a step toward her, his intense gaze on her lips.

"Oh? You can fix it without even knowing what it is?" All thoughts of why she was even upset flew out of her head. Liam's sexy and oh-so-kissable lips took up all available space.

"Uh-huh," he said, and lowered his head. "I was thinking of kissing it and making it all better."

She noisily sucked in her breath. Were they really going to do this? Here of all places?

"Are you in?" His voice was hoarse, his expression hopeful as his gaze searched hers.

She rose on her tiptoes, placed her hands on either side of his face, pulling him close enough she smelled breath mints. "Does this answer your question?"

He dipped his head until his lips latched onto hers. The kiss was gentle, probing but firm. Her sigh parted her lips and his tongue slipped inside. The kiss she'd been waiting for her entire life was even better than she'd thought possible. It was sexy enough to send heat to her most sensitive areas and yet sweet enough to bring tears to her eyes. *Make-A-Wish, eat your heart out.*

She wanted it to last forever, but cooled air and noise from the restaurant blasted them as the inner door opened. Someone cleared their throat and Liam pulled away so quickly she swayed. His hands darted out, coming to rest around each side of her waist and lingering for a moment before dropping away.

"Ellie?" a familiar voice inquired.

Liam stepped aside and she came face-to-face with Brody Wilson. She groaned inwardly. As if getting caught kissing in public wasn't embarrassing enough, it had to be by someone she knew, someone who would tell his fiancée, Mary, who would tell Meg. Trying to salvage the situation, Ellie plastered a smile on her face, which was probably as red as the ketchup on the tables inside.

"This is, uh…a surprise." She turned toward Liam. "Have you two met?"

Brody juggled a large white paper bag into the other hand, then reached out to shake. "We met very briefly at Meg and Riley's wedding."

"Speaking of weddings, you must be the groom." Liam shook hands. "I met the bride a couple days ago."

"Yes, Mary mentioned that." Brody nodded, his assessing gaze darting between them.

"Are Mary and Elliott with you tonight?" Ellie glanced through the glass door to the restaurant.

"No. They're at home." He held up the bag. "I stopped to grab burgers on my way back from checking in on Kevin Thompson."

"Checking on Kevin?" Ellie touched Brody's arm. "Did something happen?"

Kevin Thompson was a local youth who could have headed down the wrong path if not for Loon Lake's caring residents. Ellie knew Riley and Meg had encouraged Kevin to stay in school, and Brody and Mary had boosted his self-confidence by having him interact with the kids at their summer camp for children in foster care.

The camp had been Mary's dream. When she and Brody became a couple, they'd started a nonprofit and made her dream a reality. Their farm on the edge of town was the perfect spot.

Brody nodded. "Yeah, he sprained his wrist yesterday."

"Oh, no. Wasn't he your helper for the carnival preparations?"

Brody sighed. "With Riley working on their house and picking up overtime hours, I hate to ask him, but I may have to if we're going to be ready on time."

Liam quirked an eyebrow at her. "What's this about a carnival?"

"I help out with a childhood cancer survivor group," Ellie said. "We counsel survivors and those going through treatment. Plus, every year we put on a carnival as a fun activity for the kids." She enjoyed giving back to a group that had been so helpful when she'd needed it. "We have as much fun as the kids and it's important for them to see they can get through sometimes grueling treatments and enjoy life."

"What sort of help do you need?" Liam asked Brody.

Brody stroked his chin with his free hand. "Mostly muscle and someone to assemble wooden booths. You good with a hammer?"

Liam bobbed his head once. "Sure. I'd be happy to help out."

The inner door opened and Brody stepped aside to let a couple pass through. "Ellie, why don't I give you a call later and we can make arrangements."

"That sounds good. You might want to get home before those burgers get cold or you'll be in trouble with Mary."

"Yeah, we don't want that." Brody laughed and winked.

Liam's hand found the small of Ellie's back as if magnetized. He licked his lips at the cherry taste that lingered on them. What had he been thinking, kissing her like that in public? Yeah, no thinking involved. Ellie's presence tended to scramble his thought process.

A hostess inside the restaurant greeted them and led them to a booth.

"Thank you for offering to help out with the carnival," Ellie said as she slid into the seat. "You're here working with Riley and now spending off-time working some more. Hardly seems fair."

He sat across from her. "Are you going to be there?"

"Yeah. I always help out," she said, and picked up the colorful menu.

Normally he'd run a mile from reminders of the disease that claimed his ma. Just thinking about cancer made his skin crawl, but he could man up and do this. For Ellie. "Then I'm in."

She gave him a big smile and flipped open the menu. Yeah, that smile was worth giving up a few hours to help some kids. He should regret the kiss but he didn't, couldn't regret something that felt so damn good. With that kiss, tonight felt more like a date, despite him being careful not to turn it into one.

He'd decided to keep things casual with Ellie because being in remission was no guarantee the cancer couldn't return. Nothing like wanting his cake and eating it, too, or in this case, wanting his Ellie and none of the burdens of a real relationship. How the hell was he going to make this work?

"Do you want to?"

Ellie's question brought him back with a jolt. Had he said any of that aloud? "Huh?"

She *tsk*ed. "I asked if you wanted to split an appetizer."

Before he could answer, someone called her name.

Two men in EMT uniforms approached their booth. Liam frowned at the way they strutted over to Ellie's side. The tall one appeared to be around Ellie's age, while the shorter, dark-skinned one was older.

"Sorry, Ellie, we didn't mean to interrupt your date," said the older one.

She glanced over at Liam. "Oh, we're just—"

"On a date but it's no problem." What the hell prompted him to say that? He was still striving for control, for keeping his feelings casual. If they'd run into two of Ellie's female friends, would he have made the same claim? If he were a better man he'd know the answer. Since he didn't, that put him in the "not a better man" category.

"We're not staying, just picking up our supper, and noticed you in here while we were waiting," said the younger guy.

"I'm glad you came to say hi," Ellie said. "This is my friend Liam. Liam, this is Mike and Colton. As you can plainly see by their uniforms, they're EMTs. It just so happens Liam is a firefighter."

Liam shook hands with both men, applying a bit of pressure with the younger one, Colton, whose intense gaze had been on Ellie since they'd come over to the table. Yeah, more juvenile than a better man would behave, that's for sure.

"We missed you at the softball game last weekend," Colton said to Ellie, but gave Liam the once-over as he said it, as if Liam had prevented Ellie from playing.

Ellie rested her elbows on the table, lightly clasping her hands together. "Sorry I missed it. Did you win?"

"No. We got clobbered." Colton shook his head and scowled. "That's why we need you."

Mike backhanded his partner on the arm. "Looks like our order's up."

Colton nodded but didn't take his eyes off Ellie. "The cops challenged us to another game to raise money for a K-9 unit. You in?"

"Sure." Ellie smiled and nodded. "Give me a call when you get a time and place."

Liam bit down on the urge to tell the guy to get lost already. If Colton was interested, why hadn't *he* taken her to the new patio at Angelo's? *Pot? Kettle. You brought her here instead of trying to get reservations at Angelo's.*

"Some of the guys were talking about getting a bowling night together." Colton mimed holding a phone. "I'll give you call."

"Hey, man, you can't pick her up while she's on a date with someone else," Mike said, and attempted to pull his partner away from the table.

"Sheesh, I wasn't picking her up, just asking if she was interested in bowling. It's for charity," he grumbled, but turned back and grinned at Ellie. "See ya, Els."

Els? What the...? Liam ground his back teeth as the two EMTs walked away. "He was definitely trying to pick you up."

Ellie rolled her eyes. "Yeah, right. Colton called a couple months ago asking if I had the number of the new X-ray tech."

So this Colton was a player? Well, he could go play in someone else's sandbox. He and Ellie were...what? Hanging out to get Meg off their case did not a relationship make.

"Believe me, he was hitting on you," Liam insisted.

She glanced over at the two men leaving the restaurant.

"Maybe it didn't work out with the X-ray tech," Liam muttered, and shook the menu open with a snap.

"Maybe." She shrugged and set her menu down.

Did she have feelings for this Colton? He pretended to be interested in the menu's offerings. "That Mike guy—"

"Stop right there. You're not going to try to tell me he was hitting on me." She heaved a deep sigh. "Mike's happily married. He has a beautiful wife and two sweet daughters, all of whom he adores."

Before he could say anything more about either EMT, a petite waitress with a short blond bob and an eyebrow piercing came over to the table.

"Hi, I'm Ashley, and I'll be your server tonight," she said, and rested her hand on the table near his.

"I'll have a bacon cheeseburger and onion rings," Ellie told the waitress.

Ashley nodded and scribbled on her pad without taking her eyes off him. He echoed Ellie's order because he'd been too busy fending off her would-be suitor to read the menu.

"*Now* who is getting hit on?" Ellie said in a dry tone as she watched the perky blonde sashay across the room.

"Who? The waitress? She looks barely old enough to be serving drinks." He sipped his water. "And we were talking about you. Colton was definitely hitting on you."

She made a derisive sound blowing her breath through her lips. "I find that hard to believe."

He shook his head. Did she not know the effect she had on guys? That megawatt smile that made her eyes sparkle created a pull, one he couldn't deny. So why wouldn't any other guy feel the same? "What? Why would you say that?"

"Because guys don't see me like that. All they see is a shortstop for their softball team or a bowler for charity."

"I don't know who put that idea in your head, but it's simply not true. And I'm a guy, so I should know." Damn. Why did he say that? If she liked this Colton dude, saying things like that might give her ideas.

She snorted. "I don't see you putting the moves on me."

"What if I were to put a move on you?"

"Yeah, right," she sputtered, and shook her head.

He let it drop, but began calculating how many moves he could make in thirty days.

Chapter 3

Several times during the day on Friday, Liam considered excuses to get out of helping Ellie with her carnival. Last weekend had been the anniversary of his mother's death from stage 3 breast cancer that had spread. The years had muted the pain, but he wasn't looking forward to all the reminders because it also reminded him of his friend and mentor, Sean McMahan. During Liam's year as a probationary firefighter, Sean had taken him under his wing and they'd become close. Cancer had claimed Sean eighteen months after Bridget McBride. And yet he couldn't—wouldn't—let Ellie down, so that evening, he accompanied her to the church where they were setting up for the carnival. He'd insisted on giving her a ride when she mentioned meeting him there. Generosity didn't enter into his offer; ulterior motives did. He wanted to see if she'd planned on coming or going with that EMT Colton, but her eager acceptance of his offer reassured him.

Liam resisted reaching for Ellie's hand as they descended the stairs to the brightly lit basement. The place buzzed with the sounds of hammering, chatter and laughter. The scent of raw wood and paint permeated the air.

"I promised to paint some of the signs and to help Mary corral some of the younger kids. We're providing nursery services to our volunteers," Ellie said with a touch on his arm. "I'll talk to you later."

Brody waved Liam over and wasted no time putting him to work constructing a booth for one of the carnival games. Brody gave him a rough sketch of what it was supposed to look like. After helping with Meg and Riley's renovations, this would be a cinch.

As Liam got busy laying out the precut wood Brody had supplied, a towheaded boy of around ten came to stand next to him. The boy shuffled his feet but didn't speak.

Liam picked up the first pieces. "Hey, there, I'm Liam. What's your name?"

"Craig." The boy glanced at his paint-stained sneakers. "Are you Miss Ellie's fireman?"

The pencil in Liam's hand jumped and messed up the line he'd been marking. *Calm down. He's a kid asking a question, not making an observational statement.* "I'm a fireman."

The boy's gaze rested on Liam. "I always wanted to be one."

Liam's heart turned over at the look of wistfulness on the boy's face. Did this kid have cancer? Or was he one of the survivors? The boy's choice of words hadn't gone unnoticed. "Have you changed your mind about it?"

Craig shook his head. "Nah. But my mom gets a worried look on her face when I talk about becoming a fireman…like she wants me to pick something else. She's been like that ever since my cancer."

"You still have lots of time to decide what you want to be when you grow up." What the heck was he supposed to tell the kid? Liam glanced around but everyone was busy building or shooing young ones back into one of the side rooms being used as a nursery.

The boy shrugged. "Yeah, the doctors say I'm in remission, but my mom still worries."

Liam knew how the kid's mom felt. He worried about losing more people to cancer, including Ellie, but he couldn't say that to the boy. "Do you think you could help me get this put together? I could use the extra hands."

Craig's face lit up as he vigorously nodded his head. "I sure would."

"Okay." Liam handed him a peanut butter jar full of nails. "You can hand me the nails when I ask."

The kid looked disappointed so Liam rushed to explain. "That way, I don't have to stop and grab one each time. This will go a lot faster with your help. And I'll be happy to answer any questions you have about firefighting as we work."

Craig seemed to consider it. "I just wish my mom wouldn't get that scared look when I talk about being a fireman."

"Well, you're still a little young to join. Maybe by the time you're old enough, your mom will feel better about you becoming a firefighter."

"I hope so. Does your mom worry?"

Had Bridget McBride worried when he joined the fire department? If she had, she'd kept it hidden. Of course, following in his dad's footsteps may have made a difference. He honestly didn't know if she worried because she'd never said so. "She might have."

"My mom says it's dangerous." The boy pulled his mouth in on one side.

Liam put his hand out for a nail. "I won't lie and say it isn't, but that's why you attend the fire academy for rigorous training and learn all you can about the job before getting hired. Even after you get hired, you're on probation."

"Huh?"

Liam resisted the urge to ruffle Craig's hair. Chances are the kid would be insulted. "It means you're still learning from the older guys."

Craig carefully laid a nail on Liam's outstretched palm. "You gotta go to school to be a fireman?"

"You sure do. Lots to learn about fires and staying safe." He hammered the boards together. At least with firefighting you had training and were in control of the equipment. It wasn't as if you could train for cancer. And doctors and others were in charge of the equipment to fight it, leaving you helpless. "We do all that training so we know exactly what to do to make it less dangerous. I can talk to the crew here in Loon Lake and see about taking you on a tour of the fire station. Maybe see what it's like to sit in one of the rigs."

Craig pulled out another nail. "That would be awesome. Thanks."

Liam nodded. "Sure thing. I'll talk to some of the guys."

"Miss Ellie says you're in Boston." Craig scrunched up his face. "How come?"

Liam took the nail. "That where I live, and my dad and his dad before him were on the Boston Fire Department. That's why I joined up."

"My dad's a lawyer. Is your dad still a fireman?"

"No, he's retired." Even after several years, it still felt weird to say that. Liam always thought Mac would be one of those guys who stayed until they carried him out the door. Had his dad let Doris talk him into retirement? He liked his dad's new wife. It had been awkward at first, seeing him with someone other than his mom, but now he was glad they'd found happiness together.

"What about your mom? Can you ask her? Maybe she can talk to mine and tell her it's okay."

Liam shook his head and swallowed. "I'm afraid not, buddy. My mom died."

"Cancer?"

"Yeah."

The boy nodded, looking much older than he should have. "That's a—" He broke off and glanced around. "That sucks."

"It does." Liam bit back a laugh. What had the kid been about to say? He caught that because he'd had to watch his language around his niece, Fiona.

"But Miss Ellie says you can't live your life afraid because you had cancer or you wouldn't have a life."

Liam began cleaning up after Craig left. He'd have to track down some of the guys at the Loon Lake station and see if they could arrange something for Craig. Maybe even something for the boy's mom to set her mind at ease. Ellie had said how she'd had to fight her parents' need to smother and hover even after she'd been in remission for the golden five-year mark. Her words, as repeated by Craig, kept coming back to him. *You can't live your life afraid because you had cancer or you wouldn't have a life.*

"I wanted to thank you for pitching in." A deep voice behind him caught Liam's attention.

He turned to Brody Wilson. "Hey, man, no problem. Glad to help."

Brody chuckled. "And earning Ellie's gratitude probably doesn't hurt, either."

Liam couldn't deny he liked putting that light in Ellie's golden eyes. "Looks like you have your hands full." Liam tipped his chin toward the curly-haired toddler chasing another boy around under Mary's watchful eye. Earlier, Brody had been chasing after his active son.

"Yeah, Elliott's a handful. When he's not sleeping, he's full speed ahead. He has no neutral." Brody's love and pride were evident in his voice and the expression on his face as he watched his son.

Liam knew from Ellie that Brody had adopted Mary's young son from her previous relationship with his half brother, Roger, who had wanted nothing to do with the baby. Elliott may have been rejected by his biological father, but Brody's love for the boy was obvious. "He's got lots of space to work off that energy. Meg tells me you've got a lot going on out at your farm. Some sort of camp for foster kids to come and enjoy fresh air and animals."

Brody laughed. "Yeah, believe it or not, I had picked that particular place thinking I wanted quiet and isolation."

Liam didn't know much about Brody except what

he'd heard from Meg or Ellie. But the guy had been through some nasty stuff during his time in the army, so his wanting someplace to nurse wounds, even the unseen kind, was understandable. "Funny how that sometimes works. What happened?"

"Mary and Elliott happened." Brody's expression went all soft. "I know it sounds corny, but they made me want to do what I could to make this a better world."

Brody had that same look Riley got when he talked about Meg. Ha, maybe it was something in the Loon Lake water. "And so you started the camp?"

"Camp Life Launch started as Mary's idea, but I guess you could say I took it and ran with it. Some of the guys I served with in the army are pitching in and we've even talked about doing something for returning veterans who might want to help with the kids or simply be surrounded by nature. You'd be surprised how calming watching the night sky or a pair of alpacas snacking on carrots and enjoying the sunshine can be."

Liam nodded and an idea struck him. Something Craig had said. "Sounds like something these kids might benefit from, too. Ellie says it can be hard for them to just be children, even after the cancer is under control."

Brody wiped a hand over his mouth. "You might have something there. The older ones might even enjoy volunteering as counselors to younger ones, show 'em life-after-cancer stuff. Kevin and Danny, those two boys your sister and brother-in-law were helping out, have turned into a valuable resource helping with some of our youth campers. I'll definitely talk to Mary about it."

Just then, Brody's curly-haired boy toddled up to

Liam. "Alley-oop," he said, thrusting his arms up and balancing on his toes.

"Alley-oop?" Liam shook his head and looked to Brody for help.

Brody chuckled and ruffled his son's hair. "Sorry, big guy, I don't think Liam understands Elliott Speak."

The boy bounced on his toes. "Alley-oop, alley-oop."

Brody glanced at Liam and laughed. "He's saying 'Elliott, up.' He's asking you to pick him up."

"Oh, okay, that I can do." Liam bent down and picked up the smiling toddler. He settled Elliott on his hip. "Have you been trying to keep up with the other kids? I think James is more your speed since he's still new to this whole walking gig."

"Won't be long before James will be running around, too." Brody laughed as he leaned over and chucked his son's chin. "Mary and I have started discussing giving this guy a brother or sister. We've been immersed in getting Camp Life Launch going this past year but things are settling down."

"Alley Daddy." The boy bounced up and down in Liam's arms.

"Yeah, that's your dad." Liam hung on to the agile toddler. Warmth spread across his chest at the feel of the toddler's sturdy weight in his arms. Holding Elliott had him thinking of what it would be like to have his own family. "You want to go back to him now?"

Elliott gave Liam a grin and pointed. "Alley Daddy."

Liam handed him over to Brody and the toddler threw his arms around Brody's neck.

"Alley Daddy." The toddler rubbed his face on Brody's shirt.

"I sure am, big guy." Brody rubbed the boy's back and turned to Liam. "He hasn't mastered his name yet."

Liam laughed. "I just got Fiona to say Liam and now James is calling me Meem."

"Meg is practically glowing these days. I'm so glad to see her happily settled."

"Yeah, I guess Riley has been good for her."

"Well, I know Mary and Elliott are the best thing that's ever happened to me." Brody shook his head as if in wonderment. "And I have a feeling this camp will be, too. If you ever want to stop by, feel free. Although I can't promise we won't put you to work."

"I may just do that," Liam said. Brody had the same glow of happiness as Meg. Would he ever be so lucky as to find such contentment? An image of Ellie came to mind and even the specter of her cancer returning couldn't chase it away.

"Thanks again for all the help. You should come back on carnival night and see everyone enjoying all your hard work."

Brody strolled over to Mary, who waved to Liam. Brody said something to her and leaned down and gave her a kiss.

"Hey, I see you're fitting right in." Ellie came to stand next to him.

"Fitting in?"

"Talking to Craig. He's been wanting to meet you ever since I told him I knew a real live fireman." Ellie hooked her arm through his. "Of course I was referring to your dad, but I guess you'll do."

"Hey." He drew his brows together and scowled, but his lips twitched with the need to grin.

"Did he ask about the job?"

"Yeah. He said his mom was trying to talk him out of it, but he's kinda young for her to be worried already." Liam leaned down and filled his nose with her scent.

"Things change when kids get cancer, and his mom has had a tendency to hover since his diagnosis. Fire-fighting can be considered a dangerous job."

Sure, but unlike cancer, *he* was in charge. "Yeah, I told him about all the training and safety equipment. I'd love to try to set something up locally if he wanted to visit the firehouse."

"That's really sweet of you. Thanks." She squeezed his arm. "What were you and Brody talking about?"

"He was telling me about the summer camp they've set up at their farm. When he said they had youths who'd turned their lives around act as counselors, I suggested kids like Craig might be interested in something like that, too. Maybe even act as advisers or counselors to children still going through that."

Her eyes widened. "You did that?"

"Yeah, why?" He tried to shrug it off, but the fact that she seemed pleased made his stomach swoop like it had on the day he'd shed his probie status with the department.

"I think that's a great idea. Thanks so much for suggesting it to Brody." She gave him a strangely amused smile.

Warmth rose in his face. How could he have been so oblivious? "You've already suggested it to him?"

She patted his chest. "Doesn't mean it's not a great idea, and I appreciate you taking an interest."

He grunted. "Are you patronizing me?"

She looked genuinely hurt and he regretted his accusation.

"Absolutely not," she said before he could apologize. "Mary and Brody offered to give me a ride home so you won't have to go out of your way to take me back. Your sister's place is in the other direction."

"I brought you. I take you home," he said, and scowled.

"Okay." She checked her watch. "It's still early. How about if I make some popcorn and we watch a movie? That is, if…if you want to."

He draped an arm over her shoulder. "I'd love to."

Ellie tried to contain her excitement as Liam drove them to her place from the church. How was Liam supposed to see her as an adult if she acted and sounded like her teen self around him? She'd even been sitting on the steps to her place waiting for him when he picked her up. *Way to go*, she scolded herself. Except he'd said yes to popcorn and a movie. And now she probably had a big goofy grin on her face.

They pulled into her driveway and drove past a rambling log home more suited to *Architectural Digest* than Loon Lake. Although she hadn't been inside she knew the floor-to-ceiling windows in the back offered a breathtaking view of the lake. The motion-sensitive lights came on as Liam's truck approached the three-car garage where she rented the upstairs apartment. Despite living here for six months, she had yet to meet the absent owner of the impressive main house. Her rental was handled through a management company.

Liam pulled his truck next to her car. "Am I blocking anyone if I park here?"

"No. It's fine. The log home's owner is still absent."

He hopped out of his truck. "Who owns it?"

"That's the big Loon Lake mystery." She started up the stairs to her apartment. Partway up, she turned to him. "There's a rumor it belongs to Thayer Jones, that ex-hockey player who grew up here. But no one really knows. Even Tavie Whatley doesn't know for sure."

Liam laughed. "Then it really is a mystery."

Warmth flowed through her at his laugh. "Yeah, I didn't think it was possible to do anything in this town without Tavie knowing all the details."

Seventysomething Tavie Whatley ran Loon Lake General Store and much of the town from her perch behind the cash register. She and her husband, Ogle, were not only fixtures in the community but the force behind many of its charitable endeavors. Brody jokingly called Tavie Loon Lake's benevolent dictator.

She unlocked her door and they entered her small but efficient kitchen. She loved the light gray bottom cabinets, porcelain farmhouse-style sink and open shelving above a wooden countertop. A breakfast bar divided the kitchen from the living area. Off the living room was a short hall leading to her bedroom and the bathroom.

"I'd give you a tour, but this is really it—other than the bedroom..." She cleared her throat. Why did showing Liam her bedroom feel so awkward? Her bed was made and there wasn't a stuffed animal in sight: an adult bedroom. Huh, did she want to avoid reminders she was an adult and old enough to be sexually active? "How about some popcorn?"

"Sounds good. Need help?"

"Thanks. I got it covered." She handed him the remote. "You pick something while I get it." She pulled out her glass microwave popcorn maker, glancing at him sprawled on her sofa. *Don't get any ideas*, she cautioned herself. They were hanging out, sitting together and watching a movie. She set the microwave timer and looked over at him again. She swallowed. When had her couch gotten so small?

Liam was flipping through the movies on her paid streaming subscription. "What do you feel like watching?"

"How about that new action movie with what's-his-name?"

He turned his head to give her one of his sexy half grins. "Are you psychic? That's the one I've been wanting to see."

She laughed. "Just another example of my super-powers."

The timer on the microwave dinged and she removed the glass popper. She poured the popcorn in the bowl and salted it. Handing Liam the bowl, she plopped down next to him.

"How about this one?" He clicked on a movie selection. "It's got what's-his-name in it."

She tossed a popped kernel at him, but he caught it in his mouth and grinned as he chewed. He set the bowl on the coffee table and leaned closer.

She couldn't be sure who moved first, but their lips found each other in a sweet kiss that held the promise of more. All thoughts of movies and actors flew out of her head. He angled his face closer and she—

The music for the movie startled her and she abruptly pulled away. "Sorry."

"I'm not," he said, brushing her hair off her cheek and tucking it behind her ear.

He leaned back on the couch and pulled her into his side. She cuddled next to him and tried to concentrate on the movie, but it wasn't easy with his body warm against hers and his luscious scent surrounding her.

As the credits rolled he set the empty popcorn bowl on the end table next to the couch and picked up a book that had been on the table.

"This looks like a textbook."

"Yeah, working on my advanced nursing degree."

He nodded. "So you can finally move away from Loon Lake?"

"What? Absolutely not." She wasn't about to abandon the people who'd been there for her and her family when they'd needed it. "I like living in Loon Lake."

He flipped through some of the pages. "Will you be able to use the new degree at the hospital?"

"I suppose I could, but they'll be breaking ground soon on a skilled nursing facility and I'm hoping to work as a nurse practitioner there. If I time it right, I will have my gerontology degree when they finish construction."

"Skilled nursing facility?"

Ellie grinned. "A nursing home."

"Is that nurse speak?" he asked and wiggled his eyebrows.

She rolled her eyes. "C'mon, you're not turned on by nurse speak, are you?"

"Only if you're the one speaking it." He put the book back and settled against the cushions. "Sounds like you have it planned out."

"I want to help the people I've grown up with. Give back to a community that gave so much to me. I haven't forgotten how everyone rallied around when I was sick." Damn. She hadn't meant to bring up the past like that. She glanced at him out of the corner of her eye.

When he didn't comment but put an arm around her shoulder, she relaxed against him. "What about you? I heard you're determined to follow in your dad's footsteps at the fire department."

He nodded. "That's the plan. I should hear if I made captain soon. My dad was one of the youngest captains and I'm hoping to follow suit."

"So we haven't convinced you yet that Loon Lake is a great place to live?" She tried to keep her tone light, but she needed to hear him say it so maybe her stupid heart would get the message.

"Are you kidding?" He shook his head as he toyed with her hair. "The Loon Lake firehouse is part time. If not for guys who are willing to work in the department on their days off from full-time jobs, Loon Lake FD would be an all-volunteer one."

"And that's bad why?" Her body tensed on behalf of the guys she knew who worked for the town.

"It's not bad. It's how most small towns are able to afford full-time protection," he said. "But it's not what I want."

She swallowed. Yeah, that's what she thought. Riley Cooper and Brody Wilson might have embraced small-town life, but Liam evidently didn't feel like he could do the same.

Chapter 4

Liam turned off his truck and grabbed a pizza box off the passenger seat before climbing out. It had been three days since he'd helped with her carnival. He glanced up at a curtain blowing in an open window in the upstairs apartment and inhaled a deep, satisfied breath. Ellie was in there.

Ellie had texted to thank him for arranging for Craig's visit to the firehouse in Loon Lake. When he replied, he'd suggested supper and she'd offered to cook for him. He'd responded that he knew she'd been on her feet all day in the ER and offered to bring pizza.

He was halfway up the stairs when her door opened and she stood silhouetted in the doorway. As if she'd been waiting for him, as if she'd been as eager to see him.

Don't make this more than it is, he cautioned himself. They were simply friends hanging out. Nothing more.

"Hey, there," she said, and grinned.

Dressed in a T-shirt and shorts that showcased her long, slender legs, she got his blood pumping.

He reached the small landing at the top of the stairs. She was barefoot and for some reason that had him struggling to drag in air. Who knew bare feet were sexy? To him, they'd previously only been necessary for walking. He stood mute in front of her, thinking about her purple-painted toenails until her welcoming smile slipped and her brows gathered into a frown.

Mentally kicking himself, he forced words past his dry lips. "Hey, yourself."

Yeah, a real smooth talker, McBride.

She held out her hands for the box. He passed it over but didn't let go of his end. Tugging the cardboard toward him brought her closer. He leaned over and gently brushed his lips against hers. After thinking about her all day, he couldn't resist and the kiss couldn't get out of hand with the box between them. He had this whole situation under control.

She sucked in air when they pulled apart. "Wha- what was that for?"

Yeah, what was that for? "It was meant as a greeting between two friends."

Something passed over her face, something he couldn't interpret and only noticed because he'd been staring at her.

"Well then, c'mon in…friend." She took the pizza and went inside.

He wiped his feet on her welcome mat before entering the kitchen. She set the pizza on the counter next to a bottle of wine and stood on her toes to reach up to grab plates from the open shelving. Her T-shirt rode up and revealed a swath of creamy skin above her butt. He picked up the bottle of wine to keep from reaching out and running his fingers along that exposed skin to see if it was as soft and smooth as it looked.

"I have beer in the fridge. If you prefer that over wine." She came down flat on her feet and tilted her head toward the stainless steel refrigerator.

"Thanks. I prefer beer." He forced himself to look away.

She set the plates on the counter and pulled her shirt back down. "A cheap date. Nice to know."

"Me, cheap?" He picked up the wine again. "Ellie, this is two-buck Chuck."

"But it was such a good month." She set napkins on the plates.

He bumped shoulders. "We talkin' last month?"

"Pfft. And you're such a connoisseur?" She pushed back.

"Hey, I've been down the wine aisle at Whole Foods."

When she rolled her eyes, he leaned down and gave her a quick kiss on the end of her nose.

"Wha-what was that one for?"

"For being so impertinent." He licked his lips before continuing. "Now that we've gotten that out of the way, let's eat. I'm starved."

To hide the color he was certain had blossomed on his cheeks, he buried his head in her refrigerator and pretended to look for the beer. He grabbed a longneck bottle.

"Yes, um…well…" She cleared her throat. "The breakfast bar or the couch? Your choice."

"Is this like Angelo's, where I can pick inside or patio dining?" What was that kiss all about? He twisted the cap off his beer and tossed the top into her recycling bin. This was Ellie and they were hanging out. He wasn't supposed to be thinking about her exposed skin or those tiny freckles or how shiny her hair looked. Or how he wanted to keep on kissing her until she was breathless.

"Exactly like Angelo's...if you don't count the lack of fairy lights, table service or cannoli." She nodded her head several times. "Couch or kitchen?"

"Couch sounds okay. That's what I do at home." He picked up the box and she trailed behind with the plates and napkins. "And what's this no-cannoli business?"

She set the stuff on the coffee table and snapped her fingers. "Actually, I do have some. Let me take them out of the freezer so they can defrost while we eat the pizza."

He set the box down next to the plates. "Frozen cannoli?"

She huffed out a breath. "Really? You gonna be a cannoli snob, too?"

He lifted his hands up as if surrendering, the beer dangling from his fingers. "I'll allow it since you haven't had Mike's."

"Mike's?" She went back to the kitchen area and took the cannoli out of the freezer, setting the package on the counter with a *clunk*.

"It's a bakery in the North End of Boston and totally worth fighting wicked traffic to get there." He took a sip of beer and set the bottle down. "I'll bring you some real cannoli the next time I come back."

"Thanks, but in the meantime we'll have to make do with Trader Joe's." She came back and sat on the couch.

He lowered himself onto the cushion next to her, close but not enough to crowd her. Or to tempt him into doing something he might regret. But she'd been into that vestibule kiss, his inner voice reminded him.

She flipped open the cover on the pizza, filling the room with the scent of fresh dough and pepperoni. Grabbing a plate, she set a slice on it and handed it to him.

"And you said there wouldn't be any table service," he said as he folded the piece in half and took a bite.

"I haven't had a chance to talk to Craig, but I hear he was on cloud nine after his visit to the fire station. Thank you again for arranging it."

"Happy to do it." Especially since it had given him another excuse to hang out with Ellie. He set his plate down. "Almost forgot. Craig made me promise to show this to you."

He pulled his phone out of a pocket and thumbed through his pictures until he came to the one of the youngster fitted out in bunker gear and handed it to her.

"Will you look at that. How did you manage this?"

He shrugged, but he loved making her eyes shine like a freshly polished fire engine. "I remembered the guys talking about another house getting their hands on reasonably authentic bunker gear in miniature for a Make-A-Wish recipient. I contacted the firehouse that arranged it and they put me in touch with the people they'd used."

She leaned over and kissed his cheek. "Thank you."

"Sure. My pleasure. He seemed like a nice kid." Damn but he wanted to turn his head so his lips were on hers.

She took another slice and put it on her plate but left it on the low table in front of them.

"Where'd the remote go? I always keep it here on the coffee table." She pointed to the exact spot where it had been until he'd picked it up.

"Were you referring to this?" He held up the remote, trying not to laugh at her expression.

She tried to grab it, but he managed to keep it out of reach. Her shirt pulled up when she lifted her arm, exposing her stomach. Once again, his body tightened at the sight. He did his best to temper his reaction. If he wasn't careful, she'd know *exactly* what she was doing to him.

"I just want to see what's on your watch list," he told her, pointing the remote and chuckling, hoping to cool his rioting hormones. "Let's see what we've got here. Wait a sec, what's all this sappy romance— Oomfff."

She'd blindsided him by making a dive for the remote, but he reacted by pulling it farther out of reach, and she landed across his lap and chest. She struggled to sit up but he put his arm around her, trapping her where she was. Her honey eyes darkened as he lowered his head. He felt her tense, but then she melted against him once his lips touched hers. Her lips tasted like cherry. He kissed his way across her jawline, nipped her earlobe and touched his tongue to the spot where her neck and shoulder met.

Suddenly, "Bohemian Rhapsody" began blaring from the kitchen.

He lifted his head. "What the…?"

"My phone," she said in a breathless tone.

He pulled away, feeling equal measures of relief and annoyance. What was he doing messing with Ellie? She was Meg's friend…*his* friend. *Way to screw up friend-ships, dumbass.*

The air in the room suddenly felt thick. It was hard to breathe, as if the oxygen had been vacuumed out. The phone continued to blast the unmistakable tune.

He managed to suck in some air. "Going with a classic?"

That was so not what he'd wanted to say, but the things he wanted to say were probably best left unsaid.

"It's a classic for a reason," she shot back, using her hands and elbow to scramble off his lap. Thankfully that elbow missed his important bits.

He shifted and adjusted his jeans. *That was a close call…*

Ellie went into the kitchen, arguing with herself whether the interruption was a good thing. It wasn't as if she'd ever aspired to be a booty call. And he'd pulled back in a hurry, so maybe it had been a good thing that he'd gotten freaked out. She grabbed her phone and checked the caller ID. Craig's mom. Was she calling to thank her for introducing her son to Liam? Talk about irony.

Ellie listened to the woman on the other end, but her gaze and her attention was on Liam, whose attention was on the television. Had he, like her, gotten caught up in the moment?

After accepting the gratitude and telling her she'd pass that on to Liam, Ellie disconnected the call. She tugged on the hem of her T-shirt and went back into the living area.

"That was Craig's mom. She said she can't thank you enough for arranging everything for him. The kid-sized bunker gear was the icing on the cake. She said she's having trouble getting him to take it off." She picked up her plate and sank back against the cushions. "We should finish the pizza before it gets cold."

He cleared his throat and picked up the remote again. "I see you've got *Seinfeld* on your list. Wanna watch some of those episodes?"

"Sounds like a plan. Have—have you ever seen the show?"

"No, but I've heard a lot about it. Another classic for a reason?"

"Probably." Were they going to ignore what happened? "Do we need to…uh, talk about…"

When he frowned, she waved her hand back and forth between them.

He sat forward a little, resting his elbows on his knees. "Do *you* need to?"

She shrugged. Did she want to discuss it or ignore it?

He straightened up and touched her shoulder. "This wasn't a booty call, if that's what you're worried about."

Worried or hoping? She huffed out a laugh. "If it was, it would've been a first."

"C'mere." He pulled her next to him and draped an arm over her shoulder. "Let's see what this show is all about."

"Sounds like a plan." She smiled and snuggled against him. "Catching up on our pop culture knowledge. There's talk about Hennen's starting a trivia night."

"We'll be an unstoppable force."

She liked the way he used "we" so casually. Tonight might be eating pizza and cannoli while watching classic television, but she would cherish this time spent with Liam. It wasn't what they were doing but being together that mattered.

When the episode ended, he turned his head. "Is there a path to the lake?"

"Yes, and not only a nice path, there's a small gazebo with a swing. I sometimes go down there in the evenings to unwind. Letting nature surround me is calming."

He rubbed his chin. "Yeah, that's what I was thinking…a nice night to be surrounded by…uh, nature."

She bumped his shoulder. "You are so full of it."

"Is it working?" He wiggled his eyebrows.

She heaved a sigh, but she loved that the awkwardness after the kiss had dissolved. "Let me get my shoes on and grab a sweater."

"A sweater? Ellie, it's August."

"For your information, I don't have the same amount of body mass that you do to keep me warm and sometimes it gets cool down by the water…even in August."

"Then go bundle up." He tilted his head toward the mess on the coffee table. "I'll pick this stuff up and put the leftovers in the refrigerator."

"A sweater is not bundling up," she muttered as she scooted off the couch but turned back. "Thanks for cleaning up."

In the bedroom, she pulled on her sneakers and grabbed a cardigan sweater from her bureau drawer.

"Do you have your key?" He touched her arm as she started to pull the door shut.

"We're only going down to the lake."

"But it's—"

"Loon Lake," she interrupted.

He gave her a look. "Please tell me you don't do this when you're alone."

"I don't usually go alone to the lake after dark. I love listening to the loons, but if I open my windows I can hear them from the safety of my bedroom since those windows face the lake."

Landscape lights lit the crushed shell path and the dog-day cicadas serenaded them from the surrounding trees.

"Meg loves listening to the loons at night as they settle in and call for their mates to join them," Ellie said as they made their way toward the water.

"Yeah, my mom was the same. She used to drag us kids down to the water's edge in the evenings."

Ellie reached for his hand and squeezed. "I know you both miss her."

When she would have pulled her hand away, he held on.

"Yeah, as a kid I grumbled when she insisted on boring stuff like walks to the lake to stand around and listen. She said we were making memories and that someday I would understand. I would give anything now to tell her I understand." He sighed. "I never told her."

"I don't think your mother expected you to thank her, Liam. She probably didn't thank hers, either. But she passed on that experience by giving you a happy, secure childhood. Just as you'll do for your kids."

"Pfft. I know I disappointed her by choosing the fire academy over college."

"I'm sure she wanted you happy in your career." Her heart went out to him, reacting to the sadness in his tone. How could he not know this?

When he made a disparaging sound, she stopped and turned toward him. Most of his face was in the shadows but she didn't need to see his expression to feel his skepticism. "It's true. She told my mom how proud she was of how much you helped with Meg and Fiona."

He shrugged. "It isn't hard to love Fiona."

"But you put your life on hold to help out so Meg could finish her degree." She longed to make him understand, wipe away the self-reproach she heard in his voice.

"Put my life on hold?" He huffed out a mirthless laugh. "All I did was move out of a sparsely furnished apartment to move back home. Not exactly a big sacrifice."

"You did it to help. That meant a lot."

"When Meg finally confessed about the pregnancy, my mom had it all worked out that she'd babysit while Meg finished college. But then Ma got sick and Meg was ready to drop out. I couldn't let that happen. Mom had already been disappointed when I joined the department before completing my degree."

"So why can't you believe how proud she was of you for doing that for your sister?" Her hand still in his, she tugged on his arm.

He sighed. "It's not so much believing as wishing I had done more for her."

"As someone who has had cancer, take it from me— it eased her mind about Meg and Fiona. That means a lot."

"Yeah?"

"Yeah."

They came to the small gazebo and sat side by side on the wooden swing that hung from the rafters of the ceiling. He still had her hand in his. Using his feet, he set the swing in motion.

"You have a sweet deal here. How did you find out about the apartment?" he asked.

"I was on duty when an estate agent passed through the ER. He heard me talking with some of the other nurses about trying to find a rental apartment. He gave me his card and said to call him. At first I thought it might be a scam but Meg and Riley came with me to check it out. Other than being a bit farther out of town than I'd like, it's perfect."

He glanced around. "It's quiet. Has the owner ever shown up?"

"Not yet. They were still doing the interior work on the main house when I moved in. So it honestly hasn't been completed for all that long."

"Have you been inside?"

"Before they finished up, some of the workmen let me take a tour."

"Do you think you'll stay here for a while?"

"For now, yeah. When I was growing up we lived next door to my cousins and I loved it. Especially as an only child, it was nice to have playmates. My cousins and I are still very close today. If I ever get married and have kids, I'd love to live close to family, let our kids grow up together." She left out the part of dreaming about living with him and a couple of kids next door to Meg.

Jeez, live in your head much? No wonder you don't have an active dating life.

"If?" He turned to look at her. "What's this 'if' business? You planning to dedicate yourself to your career?"

"No. I'd love to get married, but first someone has

to ask me, and I'm still not convinced I'll be able to get pregnant." She hated to admit it, but that fact alone sometimes held her back. What if she met a nice guy who wanted kids and she wasn't able to give him that?

"Because of the cancer?"

"Because of the treatments but yeah…because of the cancer. The doctors say it's possible, but possible and probable are two different things."

"Then I hope it happens if that's what you want."

"I've learned not to dwell on things out of my control." She shrugged. "Besides, there's other ways. Since becoming friends with Mary, I've given a lot of thought to fostering or at least helping out with their summer camp once they get the cancer survivors part going."

"Yeah, that seems like a worthwhile project. Whoever thought that up must be a genius."

She laughed. "I thought so, too."

Chapter 5

"Hey, Els, got any plans for tonight?"

The day after sharing pizza with Liam, Ellie had been on her way out of the hospital after her shift, but turned as Colton caught up to her. He and Mike had brought in a suspected heart attack just as her shift ended. Luckily, her replacement was already on duty for the night and she was able to leave.

She raised her brow. "Why? Did you lose the X-ray tech's phone number?"

"Aw, c'mon, you're not holding that against me, are you?" He stopped in front of her with a sheepish grin.

"No, but aren't you working?" she asked. Colton was a great-looking guy. One most women would be happy to date. But he had one big flaw. He wasn't Liam.

"My shift ends in an hour. Maybe we could—"

He was interrupted by "Bohemian Rhapsody." For

once, she didn't mind the interruption when she saw her caller was Liam.

"Sorry." Ellie pulled the phone from the front pocket of her purse. "Excuse me but I need to get this."

She had a pang of guilt but reminded herself that Colton had asked her for another woman's phone number. "Hey."

"Glad I caught you. Have you left the hospital yet?"

"No. Is there something wrong?"

"Nothing wrong. I simply hoped to catch you before you got all the way home. My dad and Doris arrived this afternoon and we're having an impromptu family cookout. Whaddaya say, Ellie, will you come?"

"But if it's family…" She was acutely aware of Colton watching her.

"You're family. Just say yes. You know you want to."

She clutched the phone tighter. Of course she wanted to say yes, but feared she was opening herself to more heartache. She glanced down at her scrubs. They were clean but they were still scrubs. "I'm not dressed for—"

"Did I mention it's a cookout?"

Could she pass up spending time with Liam? "Okay. What can I bring?"

"Just your cute self."

Colton's radio squawked and he held up his hands as if in surrender. "Gotta run. Catch you later."

Ellie waved as the EMT trotted away.

"Who's that with you?" Liam asked.

"Colton."

"The EMT?"

She nodded, then realized Liam couldn't see her. "Yeah, they brought in a patient as my shift was ending."

"So I'll see you in a bit?"

"I'm on my way."

Liam pocketed his phone and walked across the yard to his sister's place. He glanced at his watch. How long would it take for Ellie to get here from the hospital? What if Colton distracted her? He stumbled over a small exposed root in Meg's yard.

Meg glanced up from putting condiments, utensils and plates on the picnic table. "Is Ellie coming?"

"Yeah. She was just leaving the hospital." He shoved his hands in his jeans.

Inviting Ellie had been Meg's idea. That's right. All Meg's idea. He had this thing with Ellie under control. Although she didn't say anything, Meg had a smug smile on her face.

Yeah, the joke was on her because he and Ellie were just hanging out, throwing her off the scent. "Got any cold beer, sis?"

Meg tilted her head toward the house. "In the refrigerator. Get me one while you're at it and don't shake it."

He rolled his eyes. "I'm not twelve."

She rolled her eyes right back at him. "No, you just act like it."

"Yeah, yeah. Keep it up and you can fetch your own beer."

"And you can get in your truck and drive to the store and get your own." She planted her hands on her hips.

A screen door banged shut.

Mac McBride stood on the porch, arms folded over his chest. "Exactly how old are you two?"

"She started it."

"He started it."

Doris emerged from the house and stopped beside Mac, who put his arm around her.

The looks they gave each other seemed to say broken hearts did mend. Liam shook his head at the thought. Avoiding all that pain in the first place sounded like a better course of action.

His dad's new wife—he had trouble thinking of Doris as a stepmother—had been a widow who'd lost both her husband and only child to a drunk driver. And yet she'd found happiness again with his dad, and showered Fiona and James with as much grandmotherly love as his own mother would have. For that, and for his sister's sake, he was glad his dad and Doris had taken another chance. Since Mac's retirement, they'd purchased a Class A motor home and spent months at a time traveling.

Doris handed James's baby monitor to Meg. "He's sound asleep. Since he had supper he may sleep through the night at this point."

"Thanks for helping." Meg hugged Doris.

"My pleasure. I need to finish my pasta salad. Want to help?" Doris turned to Mac.

"I'd love to help." Mac grinned. Turning to his kids, he scowled. "Can I count on you two to behave?"

"Tell him that."

"Tell her that."

Doris slipped her hand in Mac's. "Let's get while the getting is good."

After they'd gone into their motor home, which they had parked in the side yard, Meg set the baby monitor on the picnic table and sat down on the bench. "Whaddaya think? Don't come a-knockin' if this van's a-rockin'."

"Eww." Liam shuddered. That was one picture he didn't want in his head.

"You're welcome." Meg gave him a toothy grin. "Hey, I thought you were getting a beer."

"I—" He stopped as a Subaru pulled into the long driveway. "Ellie's here."

Instead of going into the house, he swerved and headed toward where Ellie was parking her car. Meg snorted a laugh and Liam slowed his steps. He was greeting a friend, that's all, like he might greet Nick Morretti, the engineer driver on his shift, or any one of the other guys. *And when was the last time you wanted to plant a kiss on Nick?*

He opened Ellie's car door. "Hey. Glad you could come."

"Thanks." She swung her legs out and stood.

Reaching down, he took Ellie's hand as she stepped out. He looked up in time to see Meg's smirk. Canting his head to one side, he crossed his eyes at her. Meg responded by sticking out her tongue.

"That your dad's?" Ellie pointed to the motor home parked off to the side.

"Yeah, that's Matilda."

"He named it?" She laughed. "I love it."

He could listen to that laugh for the rest of his life. He took a step back and cleared his throat. Where did that come from? They were hanging out while he was in Loon Lake. Friends. Period.

Meg wandered over. "Ellie, glad you could come. My brother was just getting us beers. Would you like one?"

He winked at Ellie. "Or how about some cheap wine?"

"Hey." Meg shook her head. "Have you no manners?"

Ellie laughed. "It's okay. It's an inside joke."

Liam frowned. *Inside joke.* Isn't that what couples shared?

Friends could share them, too, he assured himself.

Ellie turned around as tires crunched on the gravel. A county sheriff's vehicle drove up and parked behind her Subaru. She waved to Riley, who flashed the emergency vehicle lights in response.

"You didn't tell me the cops were hot on your tail." Liam draped an arm over her shoulder as they walked toward the picnic table. "You led them right to us."

Ellie grinned. "Hmm…maybe Riley came up with a few more felons for me to date."

"Am I ever going to live that down?" Meg groaned and walked past them, heading toward Riley.

"What have I missed here?" Liam demanded, his gaze bouncing between Ellie and Meg.

Meg turned back, shaking her head. "It's nothing. All a misunderstanding."

"Just before you showed up at the church luncheon, Meg was trying to fix me up with some guy Riley arrested," Ellie told him. "She seemed to think he'd make a great date for Mary's wedding."

Liam scowled. "What? Why would—"

"Like she said, a misunderstanding," Ellie said, and explained what they were talking about.

Riley had gotten out of the car and Meg threw her arms around his neck and kissed him.

"Guys. Could you save that, please? You have company." Liam waved his arms as if directing airliners to the gate.

Ellie shook her head. The man had no clue how fortunate he was to have a family so openly affectionate. Even her aunts, uncles and cousins were more subdued in her parents' company, perhaps because they remembered how much things had changed during the cancer treatments, especially when her future had been uncertain.

Riley glanced around. "Where is everyone? I was led to believe we were having a big family get-together."

Riley kept his arm around Meg's waist as they strolled over to stand next to the picnic table. Riley grabbed some chips out of the bag Meg had brought out earlier.

"James is napping after having a meltdown and your daughter has another—" Meg checked her watch "—five minutes of house arrest."

"Uh-oh." Riley grimaced. "Would I be wrong if I assumed those two things are related?"

"And now for the *Reader's Digest* version." Meg grabbed the last chip in Riley's hand. "Fiona yelled at James because he threw her brand-new Barbie into the toilet when she left the lid up. James lost his balance and fell on his butt, but I think the tears were because his beloved big sister was mad at him."

Riley winced as he reached into the bag for another handful of chips. "Please tell me he didn't flush."

"Thankfully, no. We sent in G.I. Joe to do a water rescue." Meg giggled and turned to Liam and Ellie. "See all the fun you guys are missing out on?"

Liam took a seat on the picnic bench. "I'm sure if

Ellie and I were in charge, we'd have it all under control, sis."

Meg rolled her eyes. "You are so clueless, brother dear. Right, Ellie?"

Ellie smiled and nodded. What would it be like to be a permanent member of this affectionate family? She sat on the bench next to Liam. She had to keep reminding herself they were hanging out so Meg wouldn't continue her matchmaking.

"Hey, two against one." Liam gently squeezed Ellie's shoulder. "Riley, some help here."

"Don't look at me." Riley held his hands up in surrender and leaned over to kiss Meg again.

"Jeez, guys, please." Liam brought his open palm toward his face and turned his head.

Riley laughed, giving Meg a noisy, smacking kiss. "Where are Mac and Doris?"

"They're in the motor home. Preparing the pasta salad." Meg made air quotes as she said it.

Liam groaned and buried his head in his hands, his elbows on the picnic table. Riley snorted with laughter.

"What's so funny?" Ellie asked.

"Ever since catching his dad doing the morning-after walk of shame, Liam doesn't like thinking about what his dad and Doris might really be doing." Riley clapped Liam on his shoulder.

Liam lifted his head, giving Meg an accusing look. "You told him."

"Of course. He's my husband." Meg put her arm through Riley's.

"Well, no one's told me." Ellie tugged on Liam's arm.

Liam shot Meg a you're-so-gonna-pay-for-this look. "It was after I'd moved to my Dorchester place. Meg was still living with Dad and had asked to borrow something. I don't even remember now what she wanted—that's probably my attempt to block the whole incident from my memory. Anyway, I stopped by wicked early one morning before my shift to drop it off. I was in the kitchen when Dad was letting himself in the back door wearing the previous day's clothes and looking way too satisfied for my peace of mind."

Liam closed his eyes and shook his head. Ellie laughed, enjoying spending time with the McBrides and being reminded some families laughed and teased and loved openly. Her parents were still subdued, as if joking around and having fun was asking for trouble. They might not have always been as boisterous as some families, but enough that she missed the love and laughter when they disappeared.

Riley gave his shoulder a push. "Think of it this way, McBride—Mac's still got it at his age."

Liam looked appalled. "Why would I want to think about that?"

"Face it. We're gonna be that age someday." Riley leaned down and kissed Meg's forehead. "I need to change out of this uniform."

"Is Fiona allowed out of jail?" Riley asked on his way into the house.

"Yes, tell her she can come out but Mangy needs to stay in the house or he'll be pestering us while we eat."

"You left the dog with her?" Riley shook his head. "Not much of a punishment if she got to keep her dog with her."

Meg shrugged. "I felt bad about her new doll."

"Was it ruined?" Riley frowned.

"No, but now it's tainted. Forever destined to be Toilet Barbie."

Mac and Doris came out of the motor home and crossed the yard. Doris set a large covered Tupperware container on the picnic table.

"Ellie, I'm so glad you were able to join us," Doris said, and gave her a motherly hug.

Ellie returned the hug. "Thanks for including me."

"Of course, dear, why wouldn't we?"

Ellie caught Liam's frown in her peripheral vision. Had including her been Meg's doing? She needed to be careful, or she would find herself with a one-way ticket to Heartbreak Ridge.

Chapter 6

Ellie checked her watch. Liam would be arriving soon to pick her up for Brody and Mary's wedding. She'd spoken to him several times over the phone in the week since the family cookout, but they'd both been too busy working to get together. At least that was the excuse he'd used, and she'd accepted it.

A car door slammed and Ellie contorted herself into another unnatural position but still no luck. That damn zipper was unreachable, despite all her valiant efforts. Footsteps on the stairs signaled that Liam was getting closer. No getting around asking for his help. Sighing, she opened the door and stepped onto the landing.

Liam looked up and paused partway up the stairs, mouth open and feet on different steps. He wore a deep charcoal suit, white shirt and royal blue tie. She couldn't decide which was sexier—Liam in a suit and tie or

Liam in his red suspenders and turnout pants. *How about Liam in nothing at all?* a little voice asked, but she quickly pushed that away.

With all the excess saliva, Ellie had to swallow twice to keep from drooling. "Liam…" Was that breathless croak coming from her?

"Wow, look at you." He shook his head and continued up the stairs.

She'd splurged on a cream-colored dress with a scoop neck, gathered waist and sheer organza overlay from the waist down. The bright blue embroidered flowers on the dress made a bold statement, but the royal blue peep-toe platform high heels screamed *sexy*.

He came to a halt in front of her. "Are you sure we need to go to this wedding?"

"Why do you think I bought this dress and these shoes?"

"To impress me?" His tone was hopeful.

You better know it. "Ha! You wish. Come in."

"Oh, I wish for a lot of things. Want to hear some of them?" His mouth quirked up on one side.

"I'd love nothing better, but I don't want to be late for Mary's wedding." She did her best to keep her tone light and teasing as she stepped back inside. "However, I do need a favor from you."

Once they were inside her kitchen, she pulled her hair over her shoulder on one side and presented him with her back. "Can you zip this up the rest of the way?"

He made a noise that sounded like it was part groan, part growl.

She glanced over her shoulder. "Problem?"

He shook his head and swallowed, his Adam's apple

prominent. "I'm just not used to having wishes granted so quickly."

A low, pleasant hum warmed her blood. "Helping me zip up was on your list?"

He snapped his fingers and made a face. "That's right. You said 'up.' Every time you say 'up,' I hear 'down' in my head for some reason."

"And what is this? Opposite day?" Thinking about his easing her zipper down gave her sharp palpitations.

"A guy can hope." His fingers caressed the skin exposed by the gaping zipper.

She drew in her breath. Was she going to do this? "Of course, I will need help *after* the wedding."

His light blue eyes darkened and glinted. "Anytime you need help getting undressed I'm your man."

"Good to know." She cleared her throat. "Now could you zip me up? *U-P.* Up."

He complied and rearranged her hair, pressing a finger to a spot near her collarbone. "You have a freckle right there."

"I do?" She'd always disliked her freckles, but it didn't sound as if Liam felt the same.

She turned her head toward him as he leaned over her shoulder. He cupped her chin to angle her face closer and kissed her. The kiss was hot and yet sweet, full of unspoken promises, a combination that had her blinking back tears of happiness.

Though neither one mentioned the kiss during the ride to the church, Ellie couldn't help replaying it. After the simple wedding ceremony, they drove to the far end of the lake in Ellie's Subaru for the reception, so she wouldn't have to climb into his truck in her dress and heels.

"This place is gorgeous," Ellie remarked as she and Liam walked across the parking lot toward the covered outdoor pavilion overlooking the lake. Flickering chandeliers hung from the A-frame log ceiling, and the tables, draped in white cloths, had flower centerpieces surrounded by votive candles.

"Is this what you would call romantic?" Liam had his palm planted firmly on the small of her back as they entered the venue.

She laughed and looked up at him. "Yes. Brody said he wanted Mary to feel like a fairy princess on her wedding day."

He gave a low whistle. "You're telling me Brody planned all this?"

"What? You don't think guys can be romantic?" She enjoyed teasing him, especially when he took the bait. "That's like the ultimate aphrodisiac to a woman. She'll pick the romantic guy every time."

He scratched his scalp. "Huh…"

"Relax." She grinned. "Brody came to Meg and me, and we suggested trolling Pinterest for ideas and put him in touch with people who could make it happen."

"Who knew you could be such a tease?" His mouth crooked at the corner.

"It's the shoes." She angled her foot from one side to the other.

"Are they imbued with special powers?" His eyes glinted as he admired her heels.

"They must be because they're holding your interest."

"You've always held my interest, Ellie."

Ellie wanted to believe him, but thinking like that

was going to get her heart broken for sure. They were just joking around talking like that. Weren't they?

"Hey, wait up, you two," Meg called as she and Riley crossed the parking lot toward them.

Ellie let go of their conversation as they fell into step with the other couple and entered the wedding reception. During the meal, Ellie did her best to ignore Meg's calculating grin every time she looked at them.

When the music started, Liam held out his hand and invited her to dance. Having him hold her as they danced was even better than she imagined…and she'd done copious amounts of imagining over the years. Her current fantasies regarding Liam were very adult.

"What you said back at your place…" he began, and tightened his hold on her as they swayed to the music, "about needing help getting undressed…"

"Whoa." Even with the shoes he was taller and she had to look up to meet his gaze. "When did unzipping my dress turn into undressing me?"

He wiggled his eyebrows. "Huh, I guess my brain was connecting the dots."

"It was connecting something, all right," she said, but cuddled closer to him until they were barely moving.

"Ellie?" he whispered, his breath tickling her ear. "You need to know I'll only be here for another week, maybe less. Riley and I are almost finished with the reno."

"I always knew you weren't staying in Loon Lake." It hurt, but it was the truth and she'd accepted that.

"I wanted to be totally up-front about that."

"I'm a big girl. I'm not expecting this every time I get involved with someone." She waved her hand around at the wedding reception. And that was true, but she hadn't exactly been involved with a lot of guys. "Sometimes I just want to have fun."

Ellie couldn't help thinking dancing with Liam at the reception was like a prelude to what was coming next. After seeing the happy couple off to their honeymoon, she and Liam held hands as they walked to Ellie's car.

They didn't talk much on the way back to her place but the sexual tension was palpable—at least on her end. She threw a couple furtive glances at Liam, but his concentration seemed to be on driving. What if he didn't want this? She hated the thought of throwing herself at him if—

"Ellie?" He reached for her hand and enclosed it in his much larger one.

Oh, God. Was he going to tell her he changed his mind? Was he thinking of a way to let her—

"I hear you all the way over here."

"But I didn't say anything."

"But you were busy thinking it."

"Guilty," she admitted.

He angled a glance at her. "Are you having second thoughts?"

"Are you?"

"No, but I will respect your wishes."

"Then I'm wishing you'd drive a little faster. Pretend you're on your way to a fire."

"Fire?" He lifted an eyebrow. "More like a conflagration." Liam pulled the car into her driveway and glanced over at her as he parked the car. "Still with me?"

"Absolutely."

He took her hand as they climbed the stairs. Once inside her apartment, he kicked the door shut and took her into his arms. He brushed the hair off her cheeks with his thumbs. "Sweet, sweet Ellie, I'm praying you want this as much as I do."

More than you could ever imagine. "Yes."

He rained kisses along her jaw and neck; when he got to her collarbone, he paused.

"I've been thinking about these freckles all damn day," he said, and pressed his lips along her skin, followed by his tongue.

She shivered, and with a low growl he swept her up into his arms and carried her into the bedroom, where he pulled her dress up and over her head, dropping it to the floor at his feet. Laying her gently on the white comforter, he spread her hair around her head.

Easing over her, he caressed the exposed skin on her hip. "Look at what we have here."

She lifted her head. "My surgery scar?"

"Nope. More freckles, but these were hiding from me all this time," he said, and bent down to kiss above her hip.

Her nipples hardened as his hand neared her breasts, making her shiver. She sucked her breath in when his fingers found her breast and kneaded the flesh. He rubbed his palm over her hardened nipple through the lace.

Wanting more, wanting his mouth where his hand was, she arched her back to press closer to him.

He ran his fingertips along the top of her bra and sent shivers along her nerve endings. She pressed closer and he pushed the bra down, freeing her breasts.

"Finally," she moaned.

He chuckled. "Is that what you wanted?"

"I was ready to do it myself."

He made a tutting noise with his tongue. "I never knew you were so impatient."

"Only with you."

"Then maybe you'll like this," he said, and lowered his head and covered her nipple with his mouth. His tongue made twirling motions around the bud. At her sharp intake of breath, he began to suck gently. The moist heat of his mouth made her tremble with need.

When he lifted his mouth and blew lightly on the wet nipple, she nearly shattered right then and there. With clumsy fingers, she unbuttoned his shirt, needing to touch his bare skin.

He lifted his gaze to hers, his eyes glittering with something raw and primitive. Something she'd never seen in him before, and it thrilled her. She hadn't finished unbuttoning his shirt, but he simply pulled it over his head and tossed it on the floor. Standing up, he shed his pants and boxer briefs, then slowly lowered himself back down on the bed.

She pressed her lips against the warm, smooth skin on his chest; he tasted tart and salty.

His mouth brushed over hers in a light, caressing kiss that had her wanting to plead for more. He slid a hand under her nape and drew her closer.

She closed her eyes as his lips moved in gentle urgency over hers. Her blood felt like high-octane fuel racing through her body. Every thudding beat of her heart had her wanting him more and more, until her desire rose to a feverish pitch. She could feel a tension building within her in a push-pull sensation, leaving her hot and moist in a need for the full possession of her body by his.

His tongue demanded entry to her mouth and she

opened with a moan of pleasure as it danced with hers, cavorting back and forth, sliding and caressing.

His hand covered one of her breasts and sent shock waves down to her toes. With his other hand behind her he unclasped her bra and tugged it aside. Once again his mouth claimed her breast, his mouth sucking the nipple and teasing it with his teeth. Her other breast begged for the same attention and she ground her hips against him.

When his mouth touched the other nipple she thought she would explode from the pleasure and the longing. He gave that one the same attention, licking, sucking and nipping at the rigid nipple. As he lifted his mouth and blew on the nipple again, her hips twitched and bucked toward his erection.

All her nerve endings humming and sizzling, she reached up and twined her arms around his neck. She pulled him down, reveling in the way his weight felt on top of her. He kissed her with a searing hunger, as if he'd been waiting for her all his life. He feasted on her mouth like a starving man.

His mouth left hers and he trailed sweet, tantalizing kisses over her shoulders, stopping to kiss the freckles on her collarbone, then moved again to her breasts. He drew his tongue lightly across the underside of her breasts and toward her belly button. He kissed a spot on her hip and let his tongue drift over the elastic waist of her cream lace bikinis. She arched her hips up and buried her hands in his disheveled hair.

His breath flowing over her created goose bumps on her flesh and a mind-numbing sensation in her pleasure-fogged brain. Just when she felt she couldn't stand it a moment longer, he touched the spot that had been begging for attention and she exploded.

She'd barely come back to earth when a foil packet rustled and she reached up to take the condom, saying, "Let me."

He handed the packet to her, his eyes dark with desire and gleaming with anticipation.

His gaze locked on hers and held her in an erotic embrace before he thrust into her. He withdrew and thrust again, more deeply this time, all the while watching her, his blue eyes blazing with a light that should have blinded her. The depth of their connection shocked her, heated her from the inside out each time he filled her.

The need began to spiral to life within her for a second time and all thought was lost; she could only feel, drowning in sensation. He increased the pace as she tried to reach for her release. They both fell into the abyss at the same time, their heavy breathing the only sound in the room.

Liam climbed back into bed after taking care of the condom and pulled Ellie into his arms. He was still processing what they'd just shared. Somehow it transcended mere sex. That fact should scare him, but he was feeling too boneless and satisfied to worry.

She sighed and snuggled closer, resting her head on his chest. "That was…"

"Yeah, it was." He kissed the top of her head and rubbed his hand up and down her arm.

"I never knew freckles could be sexy." She caressed his chest.

He twined his fingers through hers. "You better believe it."

"I always hated them."

"And now?"

She giggled. "I guess they aren't so bad."

"What was the scar from?"

"Surgery."

"For the cancer?"

"Indirectly. They moved my ovaries aside to decrease the chances of becoming infertile due to the treatments."

"I guess the treatments can be as destructive in their own way as the cancer." He squeezed her hand. "So did the operation work?"

"I won't know until I start trying, but like I said, it's possible. Why?" She moved her head back to look at him.

Her silky hair brushing against his chest wasn't helping his current condition. "I don't have any more condoms with me."

"And I don't have— Oh, wait!" She sat up. "Would glow-in-the-dark ones work?"

What was his Ellie doing with glow-in-the-dark condoms? Was there even such a thing? "Ellie, what the…"

She grinned. "Leftovers from Mary's bridal shower."

He shook his head. "Do I even want to know?"

She leaned over and kissed him. "Probably not."

His body won out over his good sense. "Where are these condoms?"

She reached into the nightstand and held up a foil-wrapped strand.

He rolled his eyes. "Ellie, this better not ever become a topic of conversation at a future family gathering, like my dad's morning-after walk of shame."

"I wouldn't dream of it," she told him as they came together again.

* * *

Liam awoke with Ellie pressed against him, her back to his front, his arm around her waist as if he'd been afraid of her escaping while he slept. Where the heck had such a crazy thought come from?

Glow-in-the-dark condoms aside, he couldn't remember the last time—if ever—he'd been this affected. He tried to tell himself it was because they had become friends. It wasn't as if he had developed deeper feelings.

He and Ellie were hanging out while he was here and if that involved some sex, so be it. They were adults. They'd acted responsibly. Yeah, okay, the condoms had been unique but they'd used them. Responsible. He could go back to Boston, to his regular life, with memories of their jaw-dropping sex. He—

His phone began to buzz. Not wanting to wake Ellie, he slipped out of bed and found it in his pants. Going into the kitchen area, he answered the call from Chief Harris.

Several minutes later, he ended the call. He puffed up his cheeks and slowly released the trapped air.

"Who was that?"

He turned to face Ellie. She wore a very unsexy fleece robe but knowing she was probably naked underneath threatened to send his blood pooling below his waist. He did his best to shove those thoughts aside. Unlike Ellie, he hadn't stopped to put anything on before answering the phone.

"Liam?"

"It was my chief. Some of the guys are out sick and he was asking if I could cut my vacation a few days short. Guys are reaching their max for working extra shifts."

She huddled deeper into her robe. "So you need to go back today?"

"Yeah." He rubbed his chest at the sudden restricting tightness from the thought of leaving Ellie behind. Of Ellie becoming involved with someone like Colton. A guy who had the temerity to call her asking for another woman's phone number. Surely Ellie was smarter than that. "I need to jump in the shower and collect my stuff and let my sister know."

She smiled but it didn't reach her honey-gold eyes. "While you're in the shower, I'll make some breakfast."

He went to her and kissed her forehead. "Thanks. I—"

She waved her hand and stepped back. "We both knew it was temporary."

Chapter 7

Finishing his twenty-four-hour shift, Liam checked his watch as he headed out of the redbrick firehouse located in a densely populated area of South Boston.

"Got a hot date waiting for you at home?" Nick Morretti, the driver engineer on Liam's shift, caught up to him.

"I have last night's episode of *Around the Horn* waiting for me on my DVR." Liam stopped and turned to hold the door open. He hadn't had a date in the two months he'd been home from Loon Lake. Two months since he'd last seen Ellie. Last held Ellie. It wasn't as if they'd broken up, because there was nothing to break. They'd had fantastic sex after the wedding; that's all. No regrets. No recriminations. It all sounded very civilized. So why did it feel so shabby? *We both knew it was temporary.*

"Thanks." Nick grabbed the door and followed Liam outside. "When you gonna take that plunge and settle down? You ain't gettin' any younger."

Liam shook his head. "Have you been talking to my sister?"

Nick laughed and fell into step beside Liam as they went into the early-morning October sunshine of the parking lot. "Don't want you missing out on all the good stuff that comes with marriage and kids."

"Face it, Morretti, you're just jealous because I get to go home and watch sports highlights in my under-shorts." Yeah, the exciting life of a thirtysomething bachelor.

Nick laughed. "Is that what floats your boat these days, McBride?"

"It beats fishing a Barbie out of the toilet," he shot back. It did, didn't it?

Nick huffed out his breath. "Damn. When did Gina tell you about that?"

Liam barked out a laugh and tossed his gym bag into the bed of his pickup. "I was talking about my sister's kids, but do tell."

"And put you off marriage and kids? No way." Nick fished his keys out of his pocket. "Your sister, she's got what, two now?"

"And another on the way." Liam shook his head. "I swear all she and Riley have to do is look at each other and bam, I'm an uncle again. That's why I took all that vacation time up there in Vermont a couple months ago. I was helping Riley with an addition to their place. Only I didn't think they were going to need it quite this soon."

Nick opened the driver's door to a soccer mom–style SUV and climbed in. Sticking his head out the window, he wiggled his eyebrows. "And I suppose that attractive nurse I heard about was an entertaining perk."

Liam's fist tightened around his key fob and the truck's alarm beeped. Ellie wasn't a *perk*. She was... what? Some summer fun? Why did that have to sound so shabby? He wouldn't have thought that with any-one else.

He lifted his chin to acknowledge Nick's departing wave and climbed into his truck. He was bushed from taking extra shifts at a part-time station, but working had helped keep his mind off Ellie. That's the expla-nation he was going with. A decent few days of unin-terrupted sleep and he'd be back to his old self, stop wondering what Ellie was doing. And he'd stop thinking about her honey-gold eyes, the way her hair smelled like flowers he didn't know the name of, and stop tasting the cherry flavor of her lip gloss on his tongue. Yeah, sports highlights, breakfast and stop mooning over Ellie sounded like a workable plan.

Ellie drew her knees up to her chest and bounced her feet on the concrete stoop of Liam's three-decker in the Dorchester section of Boston. A perfect example of the city's iconic multifamily housing units, the col-orful home towered above her, looking like three small homes neatly stacked one on top of the other. The large bay windows curving around the right side of the build-ing reminded her of a castle turret. No moat, but the roots from the lone tree in front of Liam's house had cracked and lifted the sidewalk as if trying to escape its concrete jungle. Poor tree.

God, first a car commercial last night and now a stu-pid tree. She swiped at a useless tear with the back of her hand. Damn her hormones for running amok and turning her into a crier. If this kept up much longer, she'd have to learn better coping skills. Not to mention perfecting those before Liam arrived home.

She inhaled and stretched her neck to glance up and down the quiet street. Why hadn't she called or texted first? Just because he was completing a twenty-four-hour shift this morning didn't mean he'd come straight home. He might stop off somewhere to eat or... She hugged her knees tighter. Or he might be with another woman at her place. She closed her eyes and swallowed against a fresh wave of nausea. What if he was bringing a woman home? After all, it had been eight weeks since their— Her chest tightened painfully as she searched for the right word to describe what they'd had. What had it been? A fling? An affair? Friendship with benefits?

Sighing deeply, she turned her head toward the glossy chestnut-stained front door behind her. What if there was a woman in there right now also waiting for Liam to come home? She made a choking sound before turning to face the street again.

No, there couldn't be, because if *she* saw a strange woman on her front porch for thirty minutes, she'd open the door and demand to know what was going on. However, it would serve her right for not calling ahead if there was another woman. She'd have to laugh it off and say something like, "I was in the neighborhood and..."

"Yeah, like he's gonna buy that," she muttered. Heck, Meg hadn't believed her lame excuse when Ellie had asked about Liam's work schedule. Curiosity had been evident in Meg's expression, but for once she didn't meddle. Not that it mattered, because Ellie wouldn't be able to hold Loon Lake gossip off for very much longer.

She could tell the people she worked with were already getting suspicious by the looks they gave her.

She sighed and rested her forehead on her knees. Short of abandoning her family, friends, job, future plans and everything she held dear in Loon Lake, swallowing her pride to confront Liam was inevitable. Of course, showing up with no prior notice might not be the best way to begin this particular conversation. Lately her head had been elsewhere, but she needed to do this in person. This wasn't something that could be handled in a text or even a phone call.

The low rumble of a truck engine alerted her and she sat up and braced her shoulders as a late-model gray pickup turned onto the street and slowed. *Liam.* And he was alone. Thanking whatever lucky stars she had left, she stood and shook her legs to straighten her jeans.

Liam maneuvered his truck into a parallel spot two houses away. She swallowed hard as he shut off the engine. The door slammed shut.

"Here goes nothing," she whispered, and stepped away from the front stoop.

He walked around the back of the truck and she drank in all six feet two inches. Still dressed in his uniform of navy blue pants and matching shirt with the red and bright yellow Boston Fire Department patch, he looked as though he'd just stepped off a beefcake charity calendar. The only things missing were his turnout pants with those sexy red suspenders. Her mouth watered at that seductive image. At least something other than nausea was making her mouth—

"Ellie?"

"It's me," she said with forced brightness and a fake smile.

He frowned. "Is something wrong? Meg, the kids… or you? You haven't—"

"No. No." She waved her hands in quick, jerky movements. *Scare the poor man, why don't you?* Yeah, she should've warned him of her visit but what would she have said if he'd asked why she was coming? For all she knew, he'd moved on from this summer. Unlike her. "Everyone is fine. Sorry. I should have called ahead but…"

He lifted his arms and embraced her in a welcoming hug. She threw her arms around him, gathering strength from his solid warmth. Wait…was he sniffing her hair? His arms dropped away before she could decide and she let go, despite the desire to hold tight. No clinging. She was an adult and could take care of herself. This trip was to deliver news. That's all.

She glanced back at the front door. No outraged woman bursting out demanding an explanation. One less thing to fret about. A small victory but she'd take it. "I, uh… I hope I'm not interrupting anything."

He draped an arm over her shoulder, gave her a quick shoulder hug and let go. "Nah, I just got off work."

"I know. I mean… I checked with Meg before I came." She scuffed the toe of one red Converse sneaker against the concrete. Doing this on his front porch was not an option. She sighed and motioned with her head toward the house. "You gonna invite me in, McBride?"

He pulled out his cell phone. "Sure, Harding, just let me tell the Playboy bunnies inside to exit through the back."

She rolled her eyes. "Yeah, right. Getting them to hide your porn stash is more like it."

"Ouch." He pocketed his phone with a devastating

grin, then motioned for her to go onto the porch ahead of him.

"I won't take up too much of your time." *Just long enough to change your whole life.*

On the porch, she stood to the side so he could unlock the door. He smelled faintly of garlic and tomato sauce. "You on kitchen duty?"

"Why? Do I smell like an Italian restaurant?" He lifted his arm, sniffed his sleeve and laughed, his eyes crinkling in the corners, the wide grin deepening those adorable grooves on either side of his mouth.

Ellie's toes curled. Score one for her newly heightened sense of smell. Except she didn't need to go where his sexy laugh and her rioting hormones wanted to take her. This trip wasn't about that. And once she told him why she'd come, he wouldn't be interested, either. "You never did bring me any cannoli from that Italian bakery you told me about."

"Mike's?" His light blue eyes flashed with mischief. "Sorry, Harding, but even if I'd gotten some, believe me, they would not have made it all the way to Vermont in the same truck as me."

God, but she'd missed him. She was such a sucker for that teasing glint in his eyes, but nevertheless she made a disparaging noise with her tongue. "McBride, it's a three-hour drive."

"Exactly," he said with a firm nod and a wink. "Sorry, but you'll have to make do with frozen."

She gave him a playful shoulder punch before following him into the inner hallway. A stairway led to the upper units on the left and the entrance to the ground floor unit was on the right. Liam unlocked his door and pushed it open, lifting his arm so she could scoot under.

No sexy heels today to add an extra three inches to her five feet three inches.

Flooded with morning sunlight from the large bay windows, the living room was standard, no-frills bachelor fare, with a brown distressed leather couch and matching recliner facing a giant flat-screen television with an elaborate sound system. Two empty beer bottles, a pizza box and wadded-up napkins littered the coffee table along with an array of remote controls. A sneaker peeked out from under the couch. The sunny room, even the clutter, was like a comforting arm around her shoulder and it warmed her. She could do this.

He cleared his throat. "Sorry about the mess."

"It's a wonderful space. I love these windows. They give you so much natural light." She set her purse on the couch.

"Thanks. Meg says if I had some taste, this place could be great." He tossed his keys on the coffee table and glanced around. "She calls my decorating style the 'under arrest' method…everything lined up against the walls as if waiting to be frisked and handcuffed."

Ellie laughed, picturing Meg chastising him. "Sisters."

A new and unfamiliar awkwardness rushed in to fill the silence. Had sex messed with their friendship? Had he moved on? It was not like they'd made any promises to each other or anything. Ellie rubbed the pad of her thumb over her fingers and swallowed another, more urgent, wave of nausea.

"I guess you're—"

"Would you like—"

Bitterness coated her tongue, making it curl in warning. If she didn't get to a bathroom—stat—she was going to throw up all over Liam's glossy wood floor. She covered her mouth with her hand, barely managing to gag the word, "Bathroom?"

His brow furrowed as he turned and pointed. "Down the hall. First door on the left."

She stumbled into the bathroom, slammed the door and dropped to her knees in front of the toilet. Hugging the bowl, she threw up the breakfast she'd convinced herself to eat before driving to Boston. Yuck. It would be a long time before she could eat oatmeal again…if ever.

Well, there was one bright spot to this whole debacle. At least he hadn't had a woman with him.

Pacing the hall outside the bathroom, Liam calculated ambulance response times against how quickly he could drive her to Brigham and Women's Hospital in midmorning traffic. Listening to Ellie being sick brought back memories of his ma spending hours puking in the bathroom after endless rounds of chemo. The word *cancer* blocked his field of vision like flashing neon. No, that was silly, Ellie had been in perfect health eight weeks ago. God forbid, but what if she was in Boston for an appointment at the Dana-Farber Cancer Institute? No, Meg would have said—

He flung the door open with such force it banged against the wall and bounced back, hitting his arm.

Ellie sat hunched over the bowl and he knelt down beside her. "My God, Ellie, what's wrong? Should I call paramedics? Or I could—"

She held up her hand and croaked out, "No," before the retching began again.

He pulled her hair away from the porcelain with one

hand and rubbed her back with the other. Things he could've—should've—done for his ma but hadn't because he was busy burying his head in the sand, convinced she would beat the cancer. His chest tightened, but with the ease born of practice, he shoved unwelcome emotions aside. He refused to fall apart. If he could run into a smoke-choked inferno, he could handle this. Right? "Tell me what's wrong."

She flushed the toilet, sat back and wiped her mouth with the back of her hand.

He reached up and grabbed a towel off the sink. "Here."

"Thanks." She wiped her mouth and hands before giving the towel back. "I'm okay now."

A chill ran through him and he searched her face as if he would find an answer there. "Are you sure?"

She nodded vigorously and began to rise. He tossed the towel aside, put his hand under her elbow and helped her up.

"May I?" She motioned toward the sink.

He sidestepped to give her a little more room to maneuver, but she was pale and sweating so he was going to be a jerk and stay close, even if he had to crowd her personal space. He didn't want her passing out on him. She turned on the faucet, captured water in her cupped hand and rinsed her mouth. He leaned past her for the discarded towel and mentally kicked himself for not going to Vermont to visit her. Why had he fought his own instincts to call or text her on a daily basis? Yeah, that wouldn't have made him look needy or anything.

She splashed water on her face and he handed her the towel. After she dried her face, he offered his bottle of mouthwash. She glanced from the uncapped plastic bottle in his hand and back to him, a frown creasing her brow.

He shrugged. "What? I lost the cap. Swig it."

"You're such a guy," she muttered.

"And I'm sure you meant that in the kindest possible way." He grinned, relaxing because the bantering was familiar, comfortable, easy to handle. That was his Ellie and— Wait. What was this "his Ellie" stuff about?

She rolled her eyes but raised the bottle to her lips.

Folding his arms across his chest, he watched while she rinsed her mouth and spit into the sink. Now that her skin had lost its previous pallor, she looked more like the Ellie he'd left in Vermont, the healthy one. His friend. The one he just happened to—

He shifted his stance and turned his thoughts away from Ellie's eyes and upturned nose with the light smattering of freckles. He'd put himself back out there in the dating world soon and life would return to normal. That's what he wanted, wasn't it?

"Do you mind?" She bumped him with her hip. "A little privacy, please."

She also had freckles on that hip. *What are you doing?* Thinking about Ellie's skin was not the first step in getting back to normal. "Can I get you something to eat?"

Those honey eyes widened. "Really? You're talking food after my little display?"

Damn she was right, but he needed something to do. Standing around feeling helpless was not something he enjoyed. He needed to be productive. "Hmph, coffee then."

She shuddered.

What the heck? Ellie loved her morning coffee. Now

she was scaring him. "Since when don't you like coffee?"

She glared at him. "Oh, I don't know, maybe since I just threw up what I had this morning."

Yeah, that was a lame question, but he hated not knowing what was wrong. "Fair enough. What would you like?"

"Got any decaf tea?"

Unfolding his arms, he stepped away. "I think I still have some from…"

"From who?"

"From Meg. The last time she was here she wanted decaf, so she bought a box." He frowned at her sharp tone. From the moment he'd seen her sitting on his front steps, she'd thrown him off-balance. "What, Ellie, do you think there's a woman in the closet waiting for you to leave?"

Her eyes narrowed but she didn't say anything. He ground his teeth. Damn, why couldn't he just keep his big mouth shut? Because she was hiding something from him. He just knew it and he didn't like it. Nor did he like the way he wanted to pull her into his embrace, bury his face in her soft hair and let her sweetness take his mind off the restlessness that had plagued him these past two months.

He sighed into the strained silence, regretting his remark. Maybe if he had visited her since their time in Loon Lake, he'd know what was going on with her and there wouldn't be this weird vibe between them. "I'll go check and see if I have any tea bags."

"Thanks. I'll be out in a minute." She shut the door behind him with a soft *snick*.

He found the tea in a cupboard and put some water on

to heat. While he waited for the water to boil, he stuck a pod in his coffee maker. Sleep was probably out of the question so he might as well enjoy some caffeine. Why she had come was a mystery, but something told him Ellie wasn't there to renew their friends-with-benefits arrangement. A morning filled with fantastic sex was looking less and less likely.

Ellie appeared in the doorway as he poured boiling water into a mug with her tea bag. As always when he saw her, his heartbeat sped up. It would appear her red sneakers had a similar effect on his libido as those sexy bright blue heels from the wedding. Like that wasn't messed up or anything.

His gaze rose to her face to take in the pink nose and shiny eyes. His stomach tumbled. Oh, Christ, had his tough-as-nails ER nurse Ellie been crying? Had he caused that with his thoughtless comment? What the hell was wrong with him saying stupid stuff like that, to Ellie of all people? She was the last person he wanted to hurt with a careless remark.

"Your tea." He handed her the hot mug, but what he really wanted was to shake her and demand she tell him what was going on. Or to grab her close and never let her go. Keep her safe forever. But keeping her safe was impossible because cancer didn't respect how much or how many people cared.

She wrapped her hands around the chipped ceramic as if warming them. "Thanks."

"I'm…uh…" What was wrong with *him*? This was Ellie and they'd talked endlessly for hours when they weren't—*hey, remember, we're not going there.* "I hope you like that kind. Meg bought it."

"This is fine." She jiggled the bag up and down. "Got any milk?"

"Let me check." He pulled the milk out of the refrigerator and sniffed the open carton. "Yeah, I do."

Her sudden laughter sent a tingle along his spine. He'd missed that laugh, her unique view of the world, her friendship. Okay, that's what was wrong with him. Ellie hadn't been just a sexual partner like others but a true friend. Relieved to find a reasonable explanation for the way he'd been feeling, he grinned. "We can go in the living room and sit."

"Yeah, that furniture looks more…comfortable."

His gaze landed on the wicked ugly collapsible card table and metal folding chairs from his dad's basement that doubled as a dining set. Not that he ever once dined on it. Eating takeout in front of the TV was more his style. Cooking for the guys while on shift was different from preparing something just for himself. "I haven't gotten around to doing much in here yet."

Her golden eyes sparkled. "Why? Did the couch or recliner resist arrest?"

"Took me a while to read them their rights." His mood was buoyed by the shared moment. Yeah, he'd missed that wacky humor of hers.

"You should get Meg to help with the decorating." She dropped her used tea bag into the wastebasket in the corner. "She's done a fantastic job with her kitchen and the new addition. The entire place really."

"I think she's got her hands full at the moment with being pregnant again. They didn't waste much time after James was born." He was happy for his sister, but seeing Meg so settled had him looking more closely at his own situation. And he didn't always like what he saw. But that was crazy, because as he'd told Nick, he was doing exactly what he pleased. He had a full life.

Ellie clucked her tongue. "She's happier than I've ever seen her. I hope you didn't say anything stupid like that to her face."

He picked up his coffee and followed her into the living room. "It wouldn't do any good if I did. As she's been telling me since she was five I'm not the boss of her."

"No, but she respects your opinion." She sat back on the couch but scooted forward when her feet dangled above the floor. "Besides, you like Riley."

He plopped down in the recliner. "I do as long as I don't have to think about what he and my sister get up to."

"Or your dad and Doris?"

He groaned and shook his head. "At least they're not popping out kids as proof."

She took a sip of her tea and set it on the table next to the couch. The sunshine streaming in through his uncovered windows made the highlights in her shiny hair glow, and he itched to run his fingers through all those dark and reddish strands. He tried to think of a word to describe it and couldn't. *Brown* was too plain a term to describe all that lustrous silk.

"What color is your hair?" Oh, man, had he actually asked that out loud? What was wrong with him?

"What?" She gave him a quizzical look.

He shrugged and hoped his face wasn't as flushed as it felt. "Meg has a thing about people calling her hair red and I, uh, just wondered if you had a name for your color like she does."

She ran a hand over her hair. "It's chestnut. Why?"

He nodded, but didn't answer her question. He'd embarrassed himself enough for one day. "Are you planning on telling me why you're here?"

She rubbed her hands on her thighs and drew in a deep breath. "I know we decided this summer was no strings attached, but—"

"About that, Ellie, I—"

"I'm pregnant."

Chapter 8

Ellie winced. She hadn't meant to blurt it out like that, but he'd been acting strangely. Not that she could blame him, considering her showing up unannounced and then madly dashing to the bathroom. She could imagine him thinking the worst but that question about her hair color… What was that about? She shifted in her seat and glanced over at him. "Liam?"

He stared at her, his eyes wide, his mouth open, his breathing shallow. She'd imagined all sorts of scenarios during the drive to Boston, including him being stunned and angry, surprised and excited. The latter one was the one she preferred but not the most reasonable. *You left out the one where he declares his undying love and proposes.* Yeah, pregnancy hormones might be messing with her, but she was still tethered to reality. She'd been flummoxed to learn she was pregnant. Imagine poor Liam.

At least she knew now the cancer treatments hadn't rendered her sterile. Of course this wasn't the way she would've planned starting her family. Did wanting to be happily married first make her a prude?

"Are you going to say anything?" she asked, unable to stand the silence a moment longer.

He sprang from his chair as if galvanized by the sound of her voice, and came to sit next to her on the couch, crowding her space. He took her hand in his and rubbed his free one over his face. "Are you sure? Did you take a test? See a doctor?"

She tilted her head, lowered her chin and gave him the *are you kidding me* look. "Hello? Nurse Ellie here."

"Oh. Right." He closed his eyes and pinched the bridge of his nose. "This is… I mean… We… I… You…"

"Yeah, we did, but nothing is one hundred percent. Not even glow-in-the-dark condoms." Maybe Liam was as fertile as his sister. Of course now might not be the best time to point out that observation. Maybe someday they'd be able to get a chuckle or two out of it.

"Have you been to a doctor yet?" he asked.

"Not yet. I wanted to tell you before I went. In case you wanted to…to be involved…" Her voice trailed off.

Then she drew in a breath and plunged in with her prepared speech. "Look, I get that this is a lot to take in, but I want you to know I'm not going to force you to do anything you don't want. I have a good job and a great support system with family and friends in Loon Lake and—"

"Have you told anyone yet?"

"What? Why? Tell me why you would ask me something like…like… Liam?" Her voice had risen with each word; blood rushed in her ears.

He lifted their entwined hands and pressed them close to his chest. "Christ, Ellie, don't look at me like that. I figure you must've already come to a decision or you wouldn't even be here now telling me about the baby." He pulled her closer so she was practically on his lap. "Besides, you know me better than that. I know the ability to have children has been a concern of yours, and knowing how much you love kids, I'm sure you want them."

Relief washed through her and she nodded against his chest, the faint garlic aroma making her empty stomach rumble. Really? Food at a time like this? *You'd rather be thinking about sex?* "So why did you ask if I'd told anyone?"

He rubbed his thumb over her palm. "I was there when it happened, so I should be there when you tell your parents. At least I assume you're planning to tell them."

For the first time since coming to Boston, she was able to take a deep breath and released it with a laugh. Relief, or maybe it was oxygen, making her giddy. "I know it's early to be telling people but what happened in your bathroom is only a part of what's been happening. I either avoid my family for another month or tell them why I'm so tired, dizzy and pale. I don't want my mom thinking the cancer has returned. And it's not something I will be able to hide for very long from my family."

"You'd be surprised. I remember Meg hid it for as long as she could." He squeezed her shoulder.

"Your sister's situation was different. Meg was nineteen, still living at home, and Riley had left town, possibly forever. I'm twenty-seven, employed and, if that's not enough, I happen to know where you live." Why in heaven's name was she arguing with him? She should be ecstatic and yet she was…what? Disappointed because he hadn't pledged his love? This was Liam. Over the summer he had become not just a lover but also a friend. Still, he wasn't the most emotionally available guy she knew. Supportive was good. Supportive worked.

"I don't know about your parents, but my dad has this tone of voice…" He leaned against the couch cushions, drawing her back with him. "Makes me feel twelve all over again when he uses it."

"My mom…she gets this look." She blinked. Damn, but she'd never been a crier. She was smart, practical Ellie, a cancer survivor. A survivor who decided she wanted a fling with the deliciously sexy fireman who also happened to be a friend. She'd wanted to experience something a little wild, maybe even a little wicked. Of course she should have known better than to fall for her temporary fling. "I guess I'm a total failure at this fling business. Not getting pregnant must be like, what, number one on the no-no list?"

"A rookie mistake." He brushed his knuckles across her back.

She blew the hair off her forehead. "A big one."

He gently tucked those stray hairs behind her ear. "I'm sure your dad will be more likely to lay the blame on me."

She sat up straighter and pulled away so she could look at him. "I'll talk to my dad, make him understand that forcing someone into ma—into something they don't want isn't a solution."

He untangled himself and stood up, looking at her with that little half grin. "Wanna explain that to Mac, too?"

"I'm sure your dad will be fine." She huffed out a mirthless laugh. "He dotes on Fiona and James. He loves being Grampa Mac. And he has to know at your age that you're, uh, sexually active."

"Did you want to tell Mac while I'm here in Boston?"

"My dad and Doris are on another one of their jaunts in their motor home and not due back until next week." He stopped pacing and perched his butt against the windowsill. "I do need to tell Meg. If she finds out before I tell her, she'll never let me hear the end of it. What about you?"

"I'll tell my parents and since we'll be telling Meg, I'd like to tell Mary before she hears it from someone else. We've become good friends since she's moved to town. I can call her or stop by the farm."

Liam chuckled. "Meg likes to complain about Loon Lake gossip reaching me down here, but she's usually the one to call and tell me stuff. She claims that she's doing it before the chatter reaches me."

"You can still change your mind about coming with me to talk to my parents." She was giving him an out but prayed he wouldn't take it.

"No, I want them to know I'm not some random guy that got you—"

"Gee, McBride, thanks a lot." She wasn't about to confess to Liam how few guys she'd been intimate with…ever. And this wasn't how she'd imagined she'd feel when having a baby. Instead of celebrating with the man she loved, this was beginning to feel more like triage. She scooted off the sofa to go and stand in front of him.

"What? I only meant—"

"I know what you meant." She sighed but couldn't help leaning into his warmth. "That's the problem."

"I know you don't sleep around. What I'm saying is I need to face your dad. Apologize and—"

Her gaze clashed with his. "Liam? Zip it."

"Right."

"So, we need to break the news to my parents and Meg. Is…" She cleared her throat and took a step back, needing space before asking this next question. Correction, she needed space before receiving his answer. "Is there anyone else you might need to tell?"

"Like? Oh, you mean…" He straightened up and away from the windowsill and took a step, closing the distance she'd put between them. "There hasn't been another woman since…there's no other woman."

She released the breath she'd been holding. That tidbit warmed her more than she would've imagined. "Me, either."

"That's because I'm irreplaceable." He flashed her one of his devilish, intensely sexy smiles.

She gave him a backhanded slap on the arm, but she couldn't wipe the silly grin off her face. Or the relief from her heart.

Liam scrubbed his scalp vigorously as he lathered the shampoo and tried not to think, but Ellie's *I'm pregnant* was stuck on an endless loop in his head. No question he needed to step up and be there for Ellie and their child. He ducked his head under the shower spray and rinsed. Ellie would be a great mom. Exhibit one: she wasn't hiding in the bathroom using taking a quick shower as an excuse to build up much-needed defenses.

On a scale from an unplanned pregnancy to Ellie's cancer returning, the pregnancy was less scary every time, but that didn't mean he wasn't scared. Being a dad had been a nebulous idea for the future. Not on today's to-do list.

When he'd seen Ellie waiting for him on his steps, it had taken all his willpower to remain casual, to not confess how much he'd missed her, to not tell her how many times he'd thought about her. The hug he'd given her had been meant as platonic, two friends greeting each other, but the moment she'd been in his arms, he'd wanted her with an intense ache. And it hadn't been all physical. He could handle simple lust but this felt like more. More than he wanted to admit or accept.

Angry with himself for dwelling, he snapped the faucet off, grimacing when the building's ancient pipes rattled and groaned at his careless treatment. He stepped out of the shower, snatched a towel from the rack and dried off, dressing in jeans and a long-sleeve pullover shirt.

He grabbed a pair of socks and went back in his living room, where he found Ellie seated on the couch, watching television and looking relaxed. But the trash was gone from the coffee table, the remotes were lined up like soldiers, except for the one in her hand, and both of his sneakers sat by his recliner. Yeah, Ellie liked organization and structure.

"You didn't have to clean." He scooped up his sneakers and sank into the chair.

"I'd hardly call throwing a pizza box away cleaning." She waved her free hand in a dismissive gesture, but she was white-knuckling the remote in the other.

Before he could think of something to say, she prattled on. "Did you know that there's a nonprofit organization that studies and ranks tall buildings? Evidently they give out awards or something. Who would have thought to give awards to skyscrapers?"

She continued her one-sided discussion while he pulled the socks on.

"Isn't that interesting?" She peered at him, an expectant expression on her beautiful face.

"Uh-huh." He stuffed his feet into his beat-up running shoes, all the while trying to figure out where she was going with all this skyscraper talk.

She thrust out her lower lip. "You're not even listening."

He met her accusing glare and tried not to smile at her being indignant on behalf of inanimate objects. He longed to take that plump lower lip between his teeth and nip it so he could then soothe it with his tongue and then— Whoa. What happened to not going there?

"Liam?"

"I'm listening…honest…nonprofit…tall buildings… awards. See? But I fail to understand why you're sounding like the Discovery Channel all of a sudden." Where was all this going? Had he missed something?

"Would you prefer I sit here and cry?" She set the remote on the table and sniffed.

"God, no. Tell me more about these awards. They sound fascinating." He crowded beside her on the couch. When he put his arm around her, she leaned into his side and he rested his cheek on her hair. Her chestnut hair. Now he needed the name of the flowers it smelled like, but he damn sure wasn't going to ask her—at least not today. Her subtle scent surrounded him like whirling smoke. "I told you, I'm not going anywhere and I'm gainfully employed. That has to count for something."

She sniffed. "But you only wanted a short fling."

He tightened his embrace. Ellie would demand, and deserved, more than what he could give to this relationship, but he had to try if they were going to be parents. "But we're friends. We'll be friends having a baby."

"Have you forgotten you live here in Boston, and I live in Vermont?" She sighed, a sound filled with frustration.

Ellie wasn't a quitter and neither was he. It would take some adjusting, but they could work this out. "Now that you've mentioned it, there's plenty of room in—"

She pulled away. "Forget it. I'm not moving in with you."

Huh, that stung. Way more than he would've thought. And definitely more than he liked. Especially since that wasn't what he'd been suggesting. "I wasn't asking. My second-floor tenant is—"

"No, thanks. I wouldn't like the commute to work or the high city rents." She shot him a sour look.

"I haven't said anything about charging you rent."

"And I don't want to be responsible for putting you in a financial bind. Don't you need both rents to make the mortgage?"

Yeah, losing a rent would make it tough, but he wasn't about to admit that to her. "You let me worry about that."

How were they supposed to work things out if she kept throwing up roadblocks? He tried to pull her back against him, but she resisted. Was she upset because he hadn't asked her to move in with him? "In case you hadn't noticed, Boston has hospitals."

"Why do I have to be the one to move?" she sputtered. "Vermont has fire departments."

In Vermont, he wasn't in line for a promotion. In Vermont, he wasn't a fourth generation firefighter. Loon Lake was a part-time house. He needed full time with benefits. And the smaller the battalion, the longer it took to rise in the ranks. "They're not the Boston Fire Department."

"Oh, excuse me." She scowled. "Vermont might not have the honor of having the first fire department in the nation, but they know how to fight fires in Vermont. Last I heard they'd traded in their horses for shiny red trucks."

"I'm a fourth-generation Boston firefighter. It's a tradition that might continue with…" He glanced at her still-flat stomach. Would there be a fifth generation?

She placed a hand over her abdomen as if protecting it from him. "And maybe she won't want to be a firefighter."

"She?" All thoughts of their argument flew out of his head. He swallowed hard. How could a simple pronoun make his stomach cramp? "You already know it's a girl?"

"No, but I couldn't continue to say 'it,' so I started saying she. I figure I have a fifty-fifty shot at being right." She leaned back against the cushions, her expression smug.

"I see." By next year at this time, there'd be a new little person in his life, one he'd be responsible for and—He pushed those thoughts aside. One problem at a time. "So, you'll think about moving here?"

"Nope," she said.

Argh. Why was she being so stubborn? That would be the perfect solution. *You mean perfect for you.* He blocked out the accusing voice in his head. "Why not? Your skills would transfer to any of the emergency rooms here and you could probably earn more, too."

"But I wouldn't be happy. I like living in Loon Lake. I like where I am, the people I work with." She crossed her arms over her chest.

"But didn't you say you were looking for a new job?" He seized on what he could to convince her while trying to ignore the way her crossed arms pushed up her chest.

"Those plans are up in the air for now." She patted her stomach. "It may take me a bit longer to finish the degree."

Guilt jabbed him. Here he was, trying to get her to do what he wanted to make life easier for him, without giving any thought to how this affected her plans. Was he that selfish? "Is there anything I can do?"

"Not unless you want to carry this baby for a while." She raised her eyebrows at him.

"Would that I could." His gaze went to her stomach. "But if you were upstairs, I could feed you, help you study."

She shook her head. "And don't you think having us living right upstairs would cramp your style? It might be hard to explain to your dates."

"There won't be any dates. I already told you there hasn't been anyone since…well, there hasn't been anyone else." He hated admitting his self-imposed drought, but maybe the reassurance would help change her mind. *That's mighty big of you, McBride. When did you get to be such an—*

"But that doesn't mean there won't be. You're not planning on being celibate the rest of your life, are you?" She raised her eyebrows at him.

Hell no. Huh, might be best to keep that to himself for now. He had better survival instincts than to continue any talk about sex, even if that's what he'd been hoping for when he'd spotted her on his front steps. And how had this conversation deteriorated into a discussion of his sex life? Ellie had an uncanny ability to know what he was thinking and...yeah, best not dwell on that. She might be ignoring their chemistry, but it still sparked, at least for him. Although this might not be the best time to point that out. "How about we just get through telling the necessary people our news for now?"

"Sounds like a plan. I drank the rest of your milk."

"Oh-*kaay*..." The abrupt change of topic was enough to give him whiplash, but he'd take it. "We can go to the corner store and get more."

Her face brightened. "How far is it? This looks like a nice neighborhood to take a walk."

She wanted to take a walk? Hey, it was better than sitting here, *not* talking about sex. "Speaking of walking, where's your car? I didn't notice it out front."

Her gaze bounced away. "That's because it's not exactly out front."

"Oh? There are usually spots this time of the day. For instance, there was the one I took." He knew where this was going and he was going to enjoy taking it there. Teasing Ellie and watching her eyes spark always made him want to lean over and—huh, maybe this wasn't such a good idea.

"Well...there was only one and I thought... I thought—"

"Are you telling me you can't parallel park?" He leaned closer.

She scooted off the couch and went toward the bay windows. "Hey, it's not my fault. It's genetics. I'm missing the parallel parking gene."

"Genetics?" He stood and followed, as if tethered by invisible rope. "So does that mean this deficiency can be passed on? Isn't that something you should have warned me about?"

"Sorry?" She sucked on her bottom lip.

"Eh." He bit the inside of his cheek, trapping a smile. "Too late now. C'mon. Let's go to the corner store for milk." He puffed out his chest. "And while we're at it, I'll pull your car closer if you want, since I'm in possession of this awesome gene."

"Oh, brother." She rolled her eyes. "This corner store wouldn't by any chance have sandwiches or a deli?"

Was she serious? "You're hungry?"

"Starved."

"But I thought…" Liam tried to remember what Meg had been like when she was pregnant with Fiona and James, but his sister had hidden it or he'd been too blind to notice. Yeah, he was good at ignoring the obvious. Like with his ma. "If you say you're hungry, then I'll feed you."

She shook her head. "Yeah, not with what you've got on hand. I checked."

"You rummaged through my cupboards?" Was she really that hungry?

She scrunched up her nose. "Yes, Mother Hubbard, and I hate to break it to you, but they're pretty bare."

Who cared about what his kitchen cabinets did or

did not contain when that pert, freckled nose was begging to be kissed?

"McBride?"

"Huh?" He shook his head, trying to get back on topic. He blamed his self-imposed eight-week period of celibacy for his lack of concentration.

She pointed to her mouth. "Food?"

It was his turn to wrinkle his nose. "You're serious about wanting to eat?"

"Oh, you mean because of the…in the bathroom?" She tilted her head toward the hallway and pulled a face.

He needed to proceed with caution if he wanted to avoid an argument or, worse, hurting her feelings. "You snapped at me for even suggesting coffee."

She fiddled with the neck of her sweater. "Yeah, about that… I lied. Sorry. The smell turns my stomach. I haven't been able to drink it or smell it for the past few weeks."

He glanced at the mug he'd set on the floor next to his recliner. "Do you want me to get rid of mine?"

Her eyes widened. "You mean you'd do that for me?"

"Of course." The coffee was probably cold by now, anyway. No great loss. He could make another cup when they got back from the store.

"That's so sweet," she gushed. "I can't tell you how much that would mean…you giving up coffee for the next seven months."

Wait…what? He opened his mouth but was incapable of forming words.

She patted his chest and hooted with laughter. "Sucker."

Yeah, he'd walked right into that one, but Ellie's

laugh was worth it. Ellie made a lot of things worth it. He couldn't imagine going through this with anyone but her.

Chapter 9

Ellie pondered the situation as they made their way to the corner store. His offer to be present when she broke the news to her parents had surprised and pleased her, and yet at the same time disappointed her. Had she expected more or were her hormones messing with her? Regardless, she had to admit she yearned for an admission that he'd missed her as much as she had him and that he regretted the no-strings-attached part of their arrangement. She needed to remember her vow to stay rooted in reality. *Learn to want what you have, not wish for what you don't.* Even if he'd proposed marriage, she wouldn't have accepted. She didn't want to end up like her mother with a kitchen table that had a lazy Susan but no one to use it. No shared meals or lively conversations. Now, her parents sat in front of the TV so they didn't have to talk and slept in separate bedrooms. They were like ghosts rattling around in the same house. Things hadn't been like that before her diagnosis and Ellie carried the burden of guilt. If she hadn't gotten cancer, would her mom and dad still be that loving, demonstrative couple she remembered from her pre-cancer days? The thought of doing something like that to her own child chilled her.

Instead of dwelling on a past she couldn't change, she pushed aside depressing thoughts to admire the differences and similarities in the homes lining the narrow street. Front porches and columns were common, although some had ornate railings and trim while many of the homeowners had boxed in the rococo trim using vinyl siding. She glanced back at Liam's and admired how his had only original details...except one. "How come yours is the only one with an external fire escape?"

"I'm the only fireman on the block."

Before she could comment, an elderly woman wearing a burgundy sweatshirt that said World's Greatest Grandma came toward them, dragging a fully loaded fold-up shopping cart.

Liam approached the woman. "Good morning, Mrs. Sullivan, looks like you could use some help getting that up your steps."

"Morning, Liam. I'm not the doddering old woman you seem to think, but since you're here..." She opened the gate on a chain-link fence surrounding a three-decker painted the same red and cream as Liam's.

"It's not your age but your beauty that attracts me, Mrs. Sullivan." He took the shopping cart from her.

"Oh, you are so full of it today, Liam McBride." She

leaned around him and smiled at Ellie. "Is that because you have this lovely young lady with you?"

"You wound me, Mrs. Sullivan, I assure you I'm totally sincere." He picked up the cart and set it on the wooden porch of the home.

Ellie's stomach tingled at Liam's solicitous behavior toward the older woman. It confirmed what she'd always known about his character.

"Aren't you going to introduce me?" The older woman clucked her tongue.

"Of course. Ellie Harding, this is Mrs. Sullivan." He motioned between the women.

"Fiddle faddle, I told you to call me Barbara." The woman poked him. "A pleasure to meet you, Ellie."

Ellie shook hands with the woman. "Same here."

"I haven't seen you around here before," the older woman said.

Ellie smiled at Barbara Sullivan. "That's because I live in Vermont. Loon Lake."

"Ah, that explains why Liam was gone so much this summer." The woman grinned and poked him again. "And here you were, telling me you were helping your sister."

He raised his hands, palms out. "I was. I helped them add a new master suite and family room."

"Why didn't you say something about Ellie when I tried to set you up with my granddaughter Chloe?"

He wanted her to live upstairs so he could take care of her? Yeah, right. And how would Chloe feel about a third or fourth wheel? Or maybe he wasn't interested in this Chloe because of their summer fling. Realistic? Maybe not, but it helped her to keep smiling at Chloe's grandmother.

"Shame on you for not telling me you already had someone in Vermont," the woman continued.

"That's because I—"

"We're not—"

Mrs. Sullivan looked from one to the other. "Uh-huh. Usually I see him and he's running or jogging or some such thing to keep fit for the ladies. You're not running today, Liam? But I guess if you've already been caught…"

"I'm not running because—" His brow knit and he hooked his thumb in Ellie's direction. "She's crap at keeping up."

"Apparently I'm crap at parallel parking, too," Ellie muttered. She didn't want to think about Liam and other women. And she certainly didn't want someone insinuating that she'd "caught" Liam as if she'd deliberately set a trap by getting pregnant.

"Don't worry about it, dear. I've lived on this street for fifty years and never learned to parallel park." Barbara Sullivan winked at Ellie.

"You don't own a car," Liam pointed out.

The woman shot him an affronted look. "What's that got to do with it?"

Liam heaved an exaggerated sigh. "Apparently nothing. Do you need help getting your shopping inside?"

"No, but thank you. Now you and your Ellie enjoy your walk." The older woman made a shooing motion.

"She seems nice," Ellie said as Liam shut the gate with a clang of metal.

Liam nodded. "Mmm, she is…for the most part."

"Sorry if she assumed that we were…well, that we were together." Good grief, why was she apologizing? This baby wasn't an immaculate conception—even if that's what she'd love to be able tell her dad. Not to mention all the elderly ladies at the church next time she volunteered at the weekly luncheon. *Oh, grow up, those women were all young once.* "But then, we're going to have a baby so I guess you can't get more to-gether than that."

He frowned. "Are you saying—"

"I'm not saying anything. Like I said—huh, well, I guess I am saying *something.*" *Damn hormones.* "But I'm not pressing you for anything."

"For God's sake, Ellie, I'll do my share."

The rational part of her brain, when it still worked, knew that expecting him to move would be as crazy as him expecting her to move. Offering her a place to live might solve the problem of distance for him, but being on the periphery of Liam's life was not what she wanted. She wanted to *be* Liam's life. She wanted what Meg and Riley, or Mary and Brody, had. Yeah, that right there was the problem. "That might be difficult since you'll be here and I'll be in Loon Lake."

"Careful." He placed a hand under her elbow and pointed to the uneven sidewalk.

"I'm pregnant, not blind." She cringed at her own waspish tone and blinked to hold back tears. Since when did she have the power to make people react or feel the way she wanted? If she had that power, she'd have put her parents' in-name-only marriage back together.

"But with my schedule, I can get ninety-six hours off, unless I take extra shifts. That's four days."

"I know how long ninety-six hours is." And she knew how long it took to drive from his place to hers. How in-volved could she honestly expect him to be? She might have regularly scheduled hours at her job but it wasn't as if she was always able to leave on time. Same for Liam if they got called out before quitting time; she knew he couldn't just leave.

He blew out his breath. "Are you trying to start a fight?"

"No." *Liar.* "Maybe."

He stopped, placed his hands on her shoulders and turned her to face him. His gaze scanned her face, his blue eyes full of concern. "What can I do to get your mind off fighting?"

An image popped into her head. Yeah, like she was going to suggest something like *that*. She chose option two. "You could try feeding me."

Was that disappointment on his face? Hmm, seems his mind had gone there, too. *Join the club.* But now was not a good time to muddle things with sex, her sensible half pointed out. But it could be so much fun, her daring half argued.

At the moment hunger was the deciding factor. Those cookies and milk she'd eaten while Liam was in the shower seemed like ages ago. "Is that pizza I smell?"

"There's a small place around the corner."

Her stomach growled. "Can we go there?"

"It's barely ten and that place is a grease pit." He frowned.

"And your point is?"

"Grease can't be good for…for—" his Adam's apple bobbed "—the baby."

"For your information, grease is a food group." Despite her insistence, a pizza didn't hold the same appeal as it had a few minutes ago. And yet a feeling of dissatisfaction made her persist. "Are you going to feed me or not?"

"Fine. We can go to there if you really want or we can go to the store and get milk, some stuff for sandwiches and maybe some fruit or salad."

She already regretted acting so disagreeable. Why did being with Liam again make her feel so contrary? She was blaming her body's reaction to his touch. "Fruit and salad? Who are you and what have you done with the Liam I know?"

"Smart aleck." He dropped his hands, but not before giving her shoulders a gentle squeeze and dropping a kiss on the end of her nose.

She fell into step beside him. "Actually, sandwiches sound better than pizza."

He draped an arm around her shoulders. "If you insist on empty calories after sandwiches, I have some snickerdoodles from Meg and—"

"Had," she interrupted.

"Huh?"

"Had, as in past tense. I…uh, found them while I was tidying up. Why do you think I drank the rest of your milk?"

"Huh." He rubbed his chin. "I guess my cupboards weren't as bare as you claimed."

"Don't push it, McBride."

"I wouldn't dream of it, Harding."

A bell dinged and a cashier greeted them when they entered the neighborhood store, reminding Ellie of the Whatleys' Loon Lake General Store; Liam's offer of an apartment in his building flashed through her mind, but she just as quickly discarded it. They'd muddle through somehow, especially since their work schedules gave them both stretches with days off.

The cashier who'd greeted Liam by name as they entered immediately engaged him in a discussion of the baseball playoffs. Listening to the two debate a controversial ruling at second base, Ellie wandered to the rear of the store and a well-stocked deli.

"Morning." A woman with short dark hair and a Red Sox baseball cap stood behind the deli counter. She hitched her chin toward the front of the store. "You a friend of Liam's?"

"Something like that." *Friends who just happen to be having a baby.* Being friends with Liam was easy; resisting his crooked smile and quick wit was a different matter. Sleeping with him again would only complicate things. *But it sure would be fun.*

"What can I get you?" the clerk prompted, tightening the ties on her bibbed apron.

"Hmm…" Ellie's gaze traveled up and down the display case. She never knew what her stomach was going to accept. One minute she craved something, the next it made her gag. Her appetite was as mercurial as her moods.

"Liam's partial to the honey ham," the clerk suggested.

"Okay, that sounds good." At least he could eat it if her stomach revolted. "And some provolone."

Liam approached carrying a loaf of white bread and Ellie shook her head. "I'm not eating that."

He held the package up and eyed it. "What? You don't like bread now?"

She liked bread but was trying to eat healthy, or at least healthier. She was going to be someone's mom and needed to set a good example. "Don't they have whole wheat or twelve grain? Did you learn nothing from me this summer?"

"Yeah, I learned to hide my junk food," he said, and rolled his eyes.

A suspicious snickering sound came from the other side of the counter and Ellie glanced over. The woman's back was to them but her shoulders were shaking.

"Glad you find my being forced to eat healthier funny, Mrs. O'Brien," Liam said in a dry tone.

The woman turned around. "It's about time you settled down with a woman who is interested in taking good care of you, Liam."

"We're not—"

"Oh, we're just—"

The woman winked as she handed over two packages wrapped in white butcher paper. "I sliced it the way you like."

Liam was still stuffing his wallet into his back pocket after paying when Ellie poked into the bag and pulled out a package of chocolate-covered graham crackers. What the hell? He shook his head. She'd given him grief over some stupid bread and she was chowing down on more cookies. He made a mental note to ask Riley if pregnancy made women unreasonable.

Ellie stuck the package of cookies under her arm and held out her hands. "I can carry some of that."

He lifted the bags out of reach as they exited the store. "I got it."

She glanced back as they turned the corner onto his street. "See? That's why I could never move in upstairs."

He turned his head. What was she seeing that he wasn't? The street looked the same as it had when they'd arrived. "I don't follow what you're getting at."

"They assumed we were together."

"Umm…we were."

She shook her head vigorously. "I mean *together* together."

Maybe he was the one losing his mind. He chose silence.

"Once my pregnancy starts showing, people would be asking all sorts of questions and making assumptions."

"Assumptions? Like that we'd had sex?" Damn his big mouth. "C'mon, they'll do all that in Loon Lake."

"Yes, but, judgment or not, they'll also be there for me if I ever need help." Her lower lip came out in a pout.

Ooh, what he wanted to do with that sexy lower lip. Even in a pout, that mouth called to him. "This is Dorchester today, not in the 1950s. No one is going to judge you."

"That's what you think. How come you never went out with Mrs. Sullivan's granddaughter?" she asked as they passed Barbara Sullivan's three-decker.

"Because I have to live on this street." Evidently they were done talking about moving. He'd bide his time, but he wasn't giving up. Huh…he should be relieved she wasn't demanding all sorts of concessions from him, but the idea of her being so far away from him, in Vermont, annoyed him.

"But you said you always part on friendly terms with women you date. No harm, no foul," Ellie said.

"You wanna try explaining that to Grandmother Sullivan?"

She nodded. "Good point."

"And for your information, I'm not some sort of serial dater." However, he'd had enough relationships to understand the signals leading to the point where women began uttering accusations like "emotionally unavailable" and ended things before that happened. He liked to end on good terms. If the relationship progressed to the point of using those phrases, the inevitable parting could become acrimonious. He never wanted anything like that for himself and Ellie. Is that why he'd hesitated getting involved with her in the past? Of course the no-strings-attached thing hadn't exactly worked in his favor. He glanced at Ellie. Or had it? Could a child keep them together?

"You have to admit, you've dated a lot of women," she was saying.

"True, but they've been spread out over sixteen years. Never two at once and I never poached." Why did he feel the need to defend his dating history? He never had in the past.

They were back at his house and he shifted the bags so he could reach his keys.

Ellie reached over and grabbed a bag. "Here, let me take one of those."

Their fingers brushed and there was that spark he'd remembered but had tried to deny for the past two months. He needed to ignore it if he was going to put Ellie back into the friend zone. That was where she needed to be if they were going to work on a partnership for the sake of their child.

After lunch in the living room, Ellie brought her empty plate into the kitchen and paused in the doorway. Liam's hair had flopped over his forehead as he bent over to load the dishwasher and her fingers twitched with the need to brush it back. Their summer fling was over, and pregnant or not, she didn't have the right to touch him with such tenderness, as much as she ached to do so.

"I should leave soon to beat the traffic." She handed him her plate and grabbed another chocolate-covered graham cracker from the bag on the counter.

"Leave? Already?" He glanced up and frowned. "Why don't you stay tonight? You look beat."

"I'll be fine. I didn't plan to stay, so I didn't bring anything with me." She contemplated her cookie before taking a bite. The thought of packing an overnight bag had occurred to her, but she didn't like the message that would send. Whether to Liam or to herself, she wasn't sure. Maybe both.

"We can go and get you whatever you need. Boston happens to be a very cosmopolitan city. Stores, restaurants, hospitals—"

"Don't start with me." While she believed in co-parenting, living in such proximity to him without sharing his life would be impossible. She wanted it all. She was sick of being in the friend zone with guys. Was it too much to want one who saw her as a friend and a lover, a life partner, a guy whose heart sped up at the sight of her? Someone who was interested in something other than her bowling score or batting average? One who wouldn't bury himself in work when life got tough?

Her father used work to bury his emotions brought on by the uncertainty of her cancer. But blocking out his emotions meant he couldn't deal with his wife's, either. Ellie couldn't blame it all on her dad. She understood not everyone could handle all those emotions surrounding such a diagnosis. Of course, she also understood her mother feeling abandoned by the man who was supposed to be there for her in sickness as well as health. Trying not to take sides meant her own relation-ship with her parents was strained and not as close as it had once been.

He slammed the dishwasher door shut. "If you insist on going back this afternoon, I'm driving. I don't want you falling asleep at the wheel."

"Hello? I'm an ER nurse. I know better than that." If a brisk walk around the block didn't work, she would think of something that made her spitting mad. Angry people tended to be more alert. If that failed, she'd pull into the first rest area.

He leaned against the counter, his arms folded over his chest, his feet crossed at the ankles. "Either stay here with me tonight or I drive you back to Vermont. That's the deal."

She grabbed another cookie. She could argue with him, but what would that accomplish? And she really was dead on her feet and not looking forward to the drive to Loon Lake. Now that she'd delivered her news the nervous energy was gone, replaced with the usual afternoon fatigue. "But how will you get back?"

"One of the guys can drive my truck to pick me up."

"Were you able to get enough sleep on your shift?"

He nodded. "Yeah, a couple callouts but not bad."

"Okay, you can drive me back." Spending more time together was important if they were going to co-parent.

His head jerked back as he studied her. That dev-ilishly sexy grin appeared, the one that deepened the grooves bracketing his mouth. The one that threatened her resolve to not throw herself at him. The one she was powerless to resist.

When he opened his mouth, she pointed her cookie at him. "Don't crow. It's not attractive."

"Says you." He straightened up and pulled away from the counter, his light blue eyes gleaming with mischief. "Let me get some things so *I* won't get caught short spending the night."

"Fine, but if you stay at my place, you'll be sleeping on the couch," she called to his retreating back.

He turned and began walking backward. His low chuckle said he was remembering the things they'd done on her couch. Damn. Now she had all those images in her head.

Those pesky snippets were still playing like movie trailers in her head as they drove through the narrow, winding streets of Boston.

"What can I say to convince you to move here?" he asked.

Tell me you love me and can't live without me. Tell me I'm the most important person in your life. Tell me you're in this for the good times and *the tough ones.* "Nothing. It ain't gonna happen."

He glanced over at her as he took the on-ramp to the interstate and sped up to blend into traffic. "The upstairs apartments are just as nice as mine. You said you liked it and you could decorate any way you wanted."

"I'm sure it's very nice, but I want to stay in Loon Lake." There, she wouldn't have to watch Liam living his life with her on the periphery. In Boston, she'd be cut off from friends. If she were truly already a part of Liam's life, giving up Loon Lake wouldn't be that hard. But she wasn't and it mattered. "You said Meg picked Loon Lake to live in to raise Fiona. I want the same things for my child. I have nothing against where you live. Your street is very nice and if Mrs. Sullivan is anything to go by, the people are nice, too. But I enjoy small-town living for all its inherent problems."

"Okay, I won't press."

"Thanks," she said, but she had a feeling the subject wasn't dead, just dormant. But she'd enjoy the respite. "I love the idea of our child growing up close to Meg's kids."

He nodded and sighed. "There is that."

"Just think, another seven or eight years and Fiona will be able to babysit." Family ties were another reason to stay in Loon Lake. Her child would have ties to the town and its people the same way she did.

"Fiona babysitting. Lord help us all." He chuckled.

Ellie laughed and yawned. She settled back against the seat. It seemed like she ran out of steam every afternoon, no matter how much sleep she'd gotten the night before. And due to her pending trip, she hadn't gotten a whole lot last night.

Despite her pregnancy fatigue, her mind wouldn't turn off. Yes, she wanted to do what was best for her child and she was convinced Liam would be a wonderful father. Not to mention, the rest of the McBrides would surround her child with family and love.

Was it selfish to want some of that for herself, too?

Chapter 10

Liam had meant what he said. He wouldn't keep pressing her about moving, but he hated having two hundred miles between them. What was he supposed to do in an emergency? What if Ellie or his child needed him? He didn't want to be so far away from either of them.

He spared a quick glance over at his sleeping passenger and grinned. As much as he enjoyed Ellie's company, he was glad she was getting the rest she so obviously needed, judging by the circles under her eyes.

Yep, not letting her drive was the right decision. She'd make a great mother, and surely Ellie could undo anything he might inadvertently screw up. The enormity of the situation was sinking in and he must be getting used to the idea of being a father because he didn't panic each time the thought ran through his head. Well, that whole not-panicking thing was relative.

Before they'd left, he'd decided telling his sister right away made sense and Ellie had agreed. He'd hate for Meg to hear the news from someone else. Slowing Ellie's car, he turned onto the driveway to his sister's house.

The driveway leading to Meg and Riley's began as a shared driveway, then it forked off into two. Her home was set back about one hundred yards from the main road. The house was surrounded by towering trees on three sides, and if not for the other home across the front yard from theirs, Meg and Riley would be all alone in the woods. On the other side of the trees, the lake was visible only during winter.

A swing set, sandbox and bicycle leaning against the open porch announced this was a family home. At one time, Liam had urged Meg to go in with him to purchase the Boston three-decker, but she'd been adamant about wanting a real yard for Fiona and his wasn't much more than a postage stamp. He saw now that she'd made the right choice. Even before Riley returned to claim his small family, Meg had done the best thing for her and Fiona by moving here. Was that how Ellie felt?

He parked next to his sister's car and shut off the engine. Reaching over, he shook Ellie's shoulder. "Hey, sleepyhead, we're here."

Ellie blinked and sat up straight. She wiped a hand across her mouth and groaned. "Was I drooling?"

"Only the last hour or so." He took the key from the ignition.

"Why didn't you wake me?"

"Because then I couldn't razz you about drooling."

"Brat." She unbuckled her seat belt and scrambled out of the car. "Let's get this over with."

He got out and followed her onto the porch. Leaning down, he squeezed her hand and whispered, "Think of this as a practice run before we tell your parents."

Ellie had barely knocked when the front door was flung open and Meg, dressed in jeans and an oversize sweatshirt, greeted them.

"I thought I heard a car pull in." Meg gave Liam a questioning look as he hugged her and kissed her cheek. "This is a surprise."

"I hope we didn't come at a bad time," Ellie said. She was chewing her bottom lip.

"No, no. Come in." Meg waved them in and led them through the original cozy living room to the kitchen. "I hope you don't mind, but I have cookies in the oven and don't want them to burn."

Liam glanced around, surprised by the silence. With two kids and a dog, Meg and Riley's home was usually a lot more boisterous. "Where is everyone?"

"James is taking a nap and Riley had the day off, so he did the school run to get Fiona, and the dog jumped in the truck with him. He texted that they were going to stop at the lake to let Mangy and Fiona blow off some steam before coming home." Meg pulled out a cookie tin and set it on the table. "Sit."

Liam reached for the tin. "Snickerdoodles?"

"Manners much?" Meg swatted his arm. "Let Ellie have some first. These cookies are Riley and Fiona's favorites. They already gave me grief for taking half the batch to you last time I made them."

"I didn't forget, but *someone* got into my stash and ate the rest." He scowled at Ellie, doing his best to hide a grin.

Ellie glared back and pulled out a chair. "Hey, there weren't that many."

"Want some coffee to go with the cookies?" Meg asked, giving them quizzical looks.

"No," Liam practically shouted, remembering Ellie's aversion to the smell. Clearing his throat, he searched for a calmer tone. "No, thanks. Milk is fine."

Meg frowned but pulled a gallon of milk out of the refrigerator and reached into the cabinet for glasses.

Ellie sat down and grabbed a cookie while Liam poured milk for everyone.

Meg leaned toward Ellie. "I knew you were going to Boston, but you didn't tell me you were bringing trouble back with you."

Ellie broke a cookie in half and dipped it into her milk. "I didn't know he was coming. He insisted. You know how bossy he can get."

"You know I can hear you two," he grumbled before shoving a cookie in his mouth. Meg's body language told him she suspected something was up and they weren't going to be able to hold her off for much longer.

He swallowed his cookie and made eye contact with Ellie, checking to make sure she was ready. "We, uh, have something we need to tell you."

Meg did a fist pump. "What's up? I know how you clicked over the summer. You two getting married?"

Liam nearly choked on his milk. "No!"

"Ass." Meg punched his arm, sending milk sloshing over the top of his glass and onto his hand.

"Language?" Liam used a napkin to wipe off his hand and wet sleeve. He tried to act affronted but he regretted his knee-jerk answer. Looking at Ellie's face, he knew he shouldn't have said anything, even if that was his first reaction.

"You deserved it and the kids can't hear me." Meg turned to Ellie and shook her head. "I apologize for my—"

"It's okay," Ellie interrupted. "We don't have any plans like that."

Liam felt like the ass his sister had called him. Ellie was smiling, but her eyes were overly bright. Damn, he'd made her cry twice in one day. He reached across the table and touched Ellie's hand. "I didn't mean it the way it sounded."

"I know." Ellie cleared her throat. "I'm... That is, we're having a baby."

"A baby?" Meg's eyes grew wide. "Wow... Uh, I mean congratulations. That's...serious."

"Oh, we're not—"

"We aren't—"

"Uh, guys." Meg's gaze bounced from one to the other, shaking her head. "Having a baby together is pretty serious."

Seeing Ellie's flushed face, Liam sent his sister a nonverbal warning, hoping their sibling connection would say what he wasn't, even if he didn't know exactly what he was trying to say. "Yes, it's serious, but we're friends who will also happen to be parents together."

Meg nodded, but her expression screamed skepticism. "Does Dad know?"

Liam squeezed his eyes shut. "Not yet."

"At least you're in a better situation than I was when I had to confess," Meg said.

Liam groaned. "It's not like I can use my age as an excuse."

"He'll get over it. Doris has been a good influence on him and she'll be thrilled. She loves babies," Meg said, and turned her attention to Ellie. "I'm happy for both of you and excited to be an aunt. I never thought I'd have that honor. Riley's an only child and, well, Liam, he's—"

"Sitting right here, sister dear," he interrupted, raising his eyebrows.

Meg rolled her eyes. "I'm excited to be an aunt and for Fiona and James and this new baby to have a cousin."

Before Ellie could respond, Meg rushed on, "Too bad you won't be here in Loon Lake. We could be like pregnant sisters."

Ellie shook her head. "Oh, but I have no plans to move anywhere."

Liam ground his molars. Ellie's pregnancy wasn't planned but it was a reality and he didn't appreciate being shut out of major decisions, which might happen if Ellie stayed in Loon Lake. What other explanation was there for his caveman behavior around her?

Meg glanced at him with a *help me out here* look. He responded with a quick shake of his head.

"That's even better," Meg said. "We can be pregnant together. I think Mary and Brody are starting to think about giving Elliott a brother or sister. Wouldn't that be fun? Our kids could form their own play group."

Ellie pulled her hand free of Liam's. She leaned over and gave Meg a hug. "I'd love that. Our kids are going to be family and I want them to be close."

"Yeah, you're getting to be an old pro at this, sis," Liam said.

"Liam!" Ellie poked him with her elbow.

Meg laughed. "What can I say? Riley and I—"

"Riley and I what?" another voice came from the doorway to the kitchen.

Riley greeted Liam and Ellie as he walked over to Meg and leaned down to give her a kiss.

Meg put her arm around her husband's waist. "Where's Fiona?"

"Dang, I knew I forgot something." He leaned in for another kiss. When he finally pulled away, he said, "She's outside with the dog. Mangy's paws got all dirty and I didn't think you'd want muddy prints all over your floors."

"Mmm. Good call." Meg gave him a dreamy look.

Liam brought his hand up and covered his eyes. "Guys, company here."

Despite his joking complaints, something sharp poked him when he saw how happy his little sister was in her marriage. He was glad, he truly was, but seeing it made him realize what he was lacking. Could he and Ellie build that sort of life together? Whenever he imagined his future, Ellie was front and center.

"Oh, yes." Meg patted Riley's chest. "Wait until you hear Liam and Ellie's news. They're having a baby."

"Really? Congratulations." Riley clapped Liam on the back. "When's the big day?"

"Uh, we don't know yet… Ellie hasn't gone to the doctor." Liam looked to Ellie.

Riley shook his head. "I didn't mean the baby due date, I meant— Oomph."

Meg's jab to the ribs effectively silenced Riley, and she turned to explain. "Ellie and my brother are going to be…" She glanced at Liam but didn't wait for confirmation before saying, "They're going to be friends who have a baby together."

Before anyone could say anything else, Fiona burst into the kitchen. "Mommy, I taught Mangy to catch the Frisbee. 'Cept he won't bring it back to me."

"That can be lesson two," Meg said. "Did you tie him to the outdoor run before coming in?"

"Uh-huh, I tied him so he can't run away or run into the woods and get lost. Uncle Liam, I didn't know you were here. Where's your truck?" The redheaded dynamo, a mini Meg, barreled over to Liam and hugged him.

"I came with Nurse Ellie." He gave his niece a bear hug.

"Are you sick?" She tilted her head back and looked up at him.

He chucked her under her chin. "No, Ellie and I are friends, just like she and your mom are friends. We came in her car to visit you."

"How come you came to visit me?" she asked.

Liam laughed. "I meant—"

A baby's cry came from somewhere in the house.

"I'll go get him," Riley said.

"Thanks." Meg pulled him back with a hand on his shirt and gave him another kiss.

Fiona pointed at her parents. "Uh-oh, Mommy, you better be careful. Uncle Liam said all that kissing stuff is what leads to all our babies."

Liam groaned and rolled his eyes. The little blabbermouth. He just couldn't catch a break today.

"Oh, he did, did he?" Meg gave him a stern look. "Fiona, why don't you take Ellie outside and show her how you taught Mangy to catch the Frisbee. Maybe

Auntie Ellie knows how to make Mangy bring the Frisbee back."

Fiona scrunched up her face. "Aren't you and Uncle Liam coming?"

"Yes, we'll be out in just a minute."

Riley chuckled and clapped Liam on the shoulder before leaving the kitchen. "Good luck."

Liam watched Fiona take Ellie's hand as they went outside and wished like heck he was going with them.

Once the door shut behind them, he turned to his sister. "You gonna rip me a new one now?"

"Nope." Meg shook her head. "But I will say that how many kids Riley and I have is none of your business, just like whether or not you marry Ellie for the sake of *your* child is none of mine."

"Maybe we shouldn't have stayed for supper with my parents," Ellie said when Liam yawned as they drove to her apartment later that evening. He hadn't had the benefit of a nap as she had and he'd spent the better part of the afternoon chasing the dog to retrieve the Frisbee for Fiona to throw again. "I forgot you just came off a shift this morning."

After leaving Riley and Meg's, they'd stopped at her parents' home to break the news. Liam had suggested it, likening it to ripping off a bandage. Faster was better, he'd suggested. She would have preferred maybe another day to gather her courage but didn't want to take a chance they'd hear it from someone else.

But if she were honest, having to tell her parents she was pregnant hadn't been what bothered her the most about going to her childhood home. When they'd arrived, her father had been in his basement workshop, where he spent most of his time. As if he wasn't a part of what went on above those stairs. Her mom was in the stark white living room, where footprints didn't mar the carpet. Ellie could remember when the house was full of noise and clutter. No, it was the memories being dredged up. She could remember the laughter, the loving glances and tender touches between her parents before she'd gotten sick. She'd taken all of that for granted when she'd had it, thinking it would last forever. Now they were more like polite strangers. They'd remained married because her mother believed that's what you did. The marriage was in place but their relationship had withered and died.

"It's okay. Your mom's a good cook and I slept some last night. Plus, I have time to sleep before the extra shift I mentioned at supper." He glanced over at her and grinned. "Besides, I wasn't about to argue with your dad when he extended the invitation."

She picked at a hangnail. Despite her mom's initial concern over the fact that they had no marriage plans, she was looking forward to being a grandmother. Her dad had started to say something about the risk to her health but her mother shut him up with a stern look and a muttered "It's not our decision." When her dad had suggested Liam join him in the den while she helped her mom load the dishwasher she'd wanted to throw herself into the doorway to block their exit. And her objection wasn't solely because of her dad's sexist attitude toward chores. If she wanted to know something, she needed to ask. "What did my father say to you when you two went into the den?"

"Oh, you know…" He shrugged. "The usual guy talk."

She rubbed her chest. Had he already put her back into the *one of the guys* category? "You forget, I'm a woman." She managed a small laugh. "What's the usual guy talk?"

He took his eyes off the road to give her an assessing glance. "Whether or not the Patriots can go all the way again this year. You okay?"

"Fine." She glanced at the passing scenery as they drove across town. They might not be in any sort of committed relationship, but having a baby together was pretty important. Important enough to share things. "So you're going to tell me that you and my dad went into the den to talk about football?"

He blew out his breath. "It's all in the subtext."

Okay, so maybe they did talk sports. "So my dad didn't come right out and threaten your manhood?"

"Don't go there. Please." Liam winced and glanced down at his lap.

"Sorry," she said, and bit the inside of her cheek to keep from laughing.

"No, you're not." He huffed out his breath. "Your dad was subtle. He didn't drag out a shotgun to polish or anything like that. He did, however, stress that it was important for me to be an involved father and that included financial support. I assured him I'd do my share."

"My mother said maybe we should have started out a little slower, like maybe getting a dog first…see how that worked out." Her mother had been torn between rejoicing at having a grandchild and being concerned over her still-single status.

Liam chuckled. "There's still time…to get a dog, that is. I could check with Riley. I know he researched the one he got for Fiona so it wouldn't aggravate Meg's asthma."

"Yeah, Meg said he was careful before getting it."

"And then he went and spoiled it by letting Fiona name it Mangy."

She choked out a sob of half laughter. "How would we take care of it? With both our jobs, we—" She shifted in her seat. "Oh, God, Liam, how can we be parents if we can't even take care of a dog?"

He pulled into the driveway that led to her rental apartment, but didn't go all the way up to the place. Putting the car into Park, he grabbed her hand and gave it a supportive squeeze. "First of all, we don't have a dog, so quit worrying about a hypothetical situation. You're going to be a great mom. And we have plenty of time to work out the logistics."

"I'm going to be a single mother. Who knows if I'm going to be able to finish everything for my NP certification? That means I can't give up my current job." She hated that she sounded as if she were whining. Her job, while sometimes stressful, was something she enjoyed and it paid enough to support her and a baby; she had it a lot better than most. Plus Liam said he would be stepping up and she knew he was a man of his word. Poor Meg had had to do the single-mother thing for years before Riley came back into her life. Ellie knew Liam had done what he could to help Meg, but she'd still been alone at the end of the day.

"No one is asking you to give up your career goals. We'll work out our schedules."

She opened her mouth to ask how he could be so cavalier, but shut it without saying anything. He was being supportive and didn't need her finding fault. "You're right."

"What did you say?"

She huffed out a sigh. "I said you're right."

"Can I get that in writing?"

"Don't push it."

He laughed and squeezed her hand once more before letting go and driving the rest of the way to her place.

The motion-sensitive lights came on as they approached the three-car garage.

"Do you park in the garage?" Liam asked.

"I haven't been, because there's no inside access to the apartment. Of course, I may rethink that in the middle of winter if the owner of the main house still hasn't moved in."

Liam parked her Subaru and she led the way up the exterior stairs located on one side of the garage and unlocked the door. Her place was perfect for a single woman. But where would she put all the paraphernalia needed for a baby? Even a high chair would be a tight fit for the kitchen.

The *thump* of a duffel bag hitting the floor interrupted her thoughts, and hands came to rest on her shoulders as if he'd been able to follow her silent thoughts. She leaned back into Liam's warmth and strength.

"It's going to be okay," he said as his fingers massaged the kinks caused by the day's tension.

She tilted her head back and stared up at him. He had the beginnings of a five o'clock shadow. He'd let his facial hair grow out a bit on his four-day rotation, but he would have to be clean-shaven when he went back on duty to allow the secure suction his respirator needed.

She knew so many things about him and yet they now felt like mere details. "How come I'm the one freaking out and you're the voice of reason?"

His arms went around her and he leaned down and kissed the tip of her nose. "Just abiding by the rules."

"Rules?" She turned in the shelter of his arms. It felt so good to be there, to lean her head against his chest and listen to his steady heartbeat.

"I've decided only one of us is allowed to freak out at a time. I'm counting on you to be the voice of reason when I panic." He gave her a quick squeeze. "Whaddaya say? Deal?"

She hugged him but quickly stepped back, making sure the contact didn't last too long. Like ripping off a bandage. She didn't want him to think she was throwing herself at him—even if that was what she wanted to do. "Deal."

Chapter 11

Liam stooped to pick up his duffel from the kitchen floor. Ellie's message was clear that she'd put him back in the no-sex friend zone. But that was good...wasn't it? Friendship was what he'd been telling himself he wanted. Anything more than that meant opening up, making himself vulnerable, which he was pretty sure Ellie would demand, and he was just as sure he would refuse. How could he tell her his concerns about the threat of being left a single parent if the cancer returned? He'd look like a selfish chump saying something like that. Shaking his head at the thoughts dancing around in his head, he followed her into her living area.

Her apartment, around six hundred square feet, was half the size of his place. He remembered all the stuff his sister had needed for Fiona; there'd been baby gear everywhere in the traditional Cape Cod–style house he'd been sharing with his dad and sister. After his ma had been diagnosed, he'd moved back to his childhood home, ostensibly to help, but frankly he'd welcomed being closer to his family during that time. He'd bought his three-decker after his mother's death, hoping Meg would join him, but she'd insisted on moving to the family's vacation home in Loon Lake.

He glanced around. Where would Ellie put all the baby stuff? Ellie was compulsively neat and organized, even keeping her possessions to a minimum in the apartment to avoid clutter.

"Are you going to have enough room here?" If she intended to move, he and Riley could help, maybe even scrounge up a few other guys. She didn't need to be lifting things in her condition.

"You've stayed over before. It was never a—"

"No, I meant after the…" He swallowed. "After the baby comes."

"I told you already, I'm not moving into your upstairs apartment." She opened the linen closet next to the bathroom in the short hall leading to the bedroom.

"That's not why I said it." That was still his idea of the best scenario but he wasn't going to argue with her tonight. She looked tired and his conscience pricked him. Rest was what she needed. "If you decide to move to somewhere else in Loon Lake, Riley and I can help. I'm sure we can find plenty of people willing to do the heavy lifting for you."

She stepped back from the open closet, a stack of sheets and a blanket in her arms. "Right now, I'm not sure I have the energy to pack and move."

He lifted the bedding from her arms. Would the fact that she'd had cancer make a difference to the pregnancy? Could all that she'd gone through have an impact on her ability carry the baby safely to term? "Is that normal? Should we go to the doctor to be sure?"

"Fatigue is perfectly normal in the beginning."

"Like the throwing up?" He crushed the sheets in his grip.

"Yeah, I'm afraid that is, too." She frowned and snatched one of the sheets from his grasp. "Hopefully, both will improve in about a month. I understand the second trimester is actually rather pleasant. Don't you remember any of this from your sister?"

"Like I said, she was good at hiding it the first time and I didn't live with her the second time around." Or he was just that good at ignoring the obvious.

"Given the circumstances for her first pregnancy, I guess that makes sense." She reached for the sheet in his arms and began to put it on the couch. He set the rest of the bedding on the coffee table and began to help her.

"So you were serious when you said I had to sleep on the couch." He raised his eyebrows as he tucked the sheet between the cushions and the back of the couch.

"You can always sleep at your sister's, if she'll have you." Ellie slipped a pillowcase over the pillow.

Okay, she put him in his place. But hey, a guy could try. "I think it would get a little crowded."

"Crowded? I thought that's what the new addition was for." She punched the pillow.

He winced as he watched her treatment of his pillow. "I was thinking crowded more in terms of people and dog, rather than space."

Sighing, she fluffed the pillow out. "What do you think this place is gonna be like once we have a baby?"

"Why do you think I suggested moving into my upstairs apartment?" He regretted the words as soon as they found air. Pressing his point right now was counterproductive.

"Give it a rest, Liam." Ellie smoothed out a blanket over the sheet and arranged the pillow at one end of the sofa. "Well, good night. I hope you get a good night's sleep."

"So you're not going to take pity on me?" he called to her retreating back.

"That puppy-dog face of yours won't get you anywhere, McBride."

"Hey, you weren't even looking."

After she had shut the bedroom door, Liam stripped down to his boxer briefs and got between the covers on the sofa.

A short time later, he jackknifed into a sitting position and glanced around. He sat and listened to see what had awakened him up from a sound sleep. He was accustomed to sleeping around a dozen other guys during shifts at the fire station, so noises in the night didn't usually bother him.

"Are you okay?" he asked Ellie as she came down the short hall from her bedroom.

She nodded. "I got up to use the bathroom and decided to get a drink of water. I'm sorry if I woke you, but I'm not used to having someone here with me."

"It's okay. I just wanted to be sure you weren't sick again." And he wanted to say stuff, but he wasn't even sure what it was he wanted to say, let alone how to say it. And, man, wasn't that messed up?

She shook her head. "No. That's mostly in the mornings but that's not hard and fast."

He nodded. "That's good."

"Glad you think so." Her tone was dry.

Aw, man, could he not catch a break? "I didn't mean... I only meant—"

"You're making this way too easy." She thumped him on the shoulder and grinned.

"And yet you keep doing it," he grumbled, and rubbed his shoulder, but his actions were for effect. She wasn't angry and he was grateful. He certainly hadn't meant to piss her off. "I'm trying to be supportive."

"And I appreciate it, but you don't need to hover."

"I don't hover." And even if he did, who could blame him? Ellie was pregnant with his child. He was doing his best to hold it all together and not let his panic show.

"Well...good night. And sorry for waking you."

"Don't worry about it."

She went back into the bedroom and he sank down on the couch and punched the pillow. He had just stretched out when a noise had him opening his eyes. Ellie was standing next to the couch.

He sat up. "What's the matter?"

She chewed on her bottom lip. "Umm...that couch isn't very comfortable."

"I've had worse."

She reached out her hand toward him and he grabbed it. Still unsure of what was happening, he frowned. "Ellie?"

"I don't want to send the wrong signal but..." She tugged on his hand. She waved her free hand toward the bedroom. "We can share, right? I'm talking platonic."

Relief swept through him as he grabbed his pillow with his free hand and let her lead him to the bedroom. Spending the night in the same bed with Ellie, even in a platonic sense, was important. He couldn't pinpoint why. Too much had happened today to make sense of the jumble of emotions. He just knew he wanted to be as close as possible to her.

Ellie's first thought upon awakening was Liam. She lay in his arms and it wasn't a dream. Oh, yeah, she'd invited him to sleep in the bed. At the time she'd fallen asleep he'd been way over on his side of the bed and she on hers. Now they were huddled together in the middle as if their bodies had taken over while they slept.

Sighing, she burrowed closer, intent on enjoying the moment. This time of year, the mornings could be cool, so waking to warmth was unusual.

"Ellie?" he murmured near her ear.

"Mmm?" She huddled closer.

He cleared his throat. "Could you not do that?"

She moved again, shimmying closer, then scolding herself. What was she doing? She shouldn't tease unless she intended to follow through. Maybe sex wouldn't be a total disaster. After all, she couldn't get pregnant again. She shifted.

"Yeah, that," he groaned, his voice tight.

"Sorry." She scooted away and turned to face him. Did she want to do this? "Truly, I am sorry. That wasn't nice."

"Not unless you plan to—" His cell phone rang before he could finish. He heaved an exasperated sigh. "That's my dad's ringtone."

Ellie was already scooting to the other side of the bed. Interrupted or saved? She couldn't decide. "Then you'd better get it."

"Wait." Liam stopped her retreat to the other side of the bed with a hand on her arm.

She turned back to face him and he gave her a quick kiss. The mattress bounced a little as he got up. She got a good look at his broad back and fine butt encased in black cotton boxer briefs as he hurried into the living area.

Grabbing her robe and pulling it on, she followed him into the other room.

"Hey, Dad. What's up?" He listened and winced. "I should have known this would happen. We had planned to tell you when you got back. So we could do it in person."

Ellie couldn't hear the other end of the conversation but she imagined Mac being more hurt than angry if he'd heard the news from someone else.

Liam rolled his eyes when their gazes met and she smiled.

"Yeah, you did and I was but—" Liam nodded. "I will and yes, I was with her when we told her parents. Thanks. Talk to you soon."

He placed the phone back on the counter. Blowing out his breath, he rubbed a hand over his face.

"I take it your dad found out?"

He nodded and rubbed a hand across his face.

"Meg?"

"Fiona. Dad said at first he thought she was talking about Meg's pregnancy but Fiona clarified before Meg could get the phone away from her."

"Was he angry?" She felt bad that Mac had found out through someone else, but at least it was a family member.

Liam rubbed the back of his neck. "Not about us

not telling him. He understood the situation with them being out of town."

Yeah, Mac was a pretty reasonable guy. "Let me guess, he doesn't understand the friends-having-a-baby part."

Liam stabbed a finger in the air. "That would be the one."

She put her arms around his waist and gave him a loose hug. "Once the baby is here, he'll be thrilled."

"Yeah, I could hear Doris in the background saying congratulations." He hooked his arm around her waist, pulling her closer and kissing the top of her head.

His phone rang again. He dropped his arm and stepped away. "And that'll be my sister."

He picked up the phone and pointed the screen at her. "Told ya."

"Uh-oh." Ellie laughed.

Liam swiped his thumb and answered. "Well, if it isn't my blabbermouth sister."

Ellie was close enough to hear Meg apologizing on the other end.

"When has Fiona ever been able to keep a secret? She takes after someone else I know." He quirked a smile. "Yeah, you. As I've said before, it's like growing up with you all over again."

While he was talking with Meg, she pulled out ingredients to make breakfast. Most mornings she ate cereal but the thought didn't appeal, and since Liam was here, she decided on scrambled eggs and sausages.

Liam set his phone back down. "Do I have time for a quick shower before breakfast?"

"Sure."

After breakfast, he helped her clean up the kitchen.

"I noticed your tire pressure light was on so I thought I'd take your car to get some air in the tires and fill you up your gas tank."

"Okay." She found her purse and pulled out her wallet to reimburse him.

"Ellie." He shook his head. "Put that away."

"But…"

"No buts." He leaned over and kissed her forehead. "We're in this together."

Ellie stayed home to catch up on some studying for an upcoming exam. She wasn't sure if she'd be able to finish her degree requirements in time for her plans for getting a job at the proposed assisted living and nursing facility, but she still needed to keep up with the classes she was taking.

The money she'd been spending on school might be better spent on a bigger apartment. This one would be crowded with a baby. *There's always Liam's offer of one of his rentals*, an inner voice reminded her.

She frowned and rubbed her stomach, sending a silent apology to the new life growing inside. Was being stubborn going to mean her baby would ultimately suffer for her decisions? Or would getting involved with someone who coped with emotions by pulling away and burying himself in work be worse?

The apartment door opened and she slammed her book shut, realizing she hadn't really studied. "That took a while."

Liam closed the door behind him. "I got your oil changed, too."

"You didn't have to do that."

"Ogle insisted. Said it was time." Liam shrugged. "Who am I to argue?"

"Well, if Ogle wanted to do it."

"He's got some kid working for him that he said needed the experience."

"A kid? You and Ogle let a kid change my oil?" She frowned. Her tone carried a bit of annoyance, but she was touched by his actions on her behalf. It was the type of thing her dad did for her mom, even after the breakdown of their relationship; she suspected Mac had done it for Liam's mom and now for Doris. Ellie realized it was nice to have someone who had your back.

"Yeah, Kevin says hi." Liam chuckled and held up his hands in a self-protection stance.

She made a moue with her lips. "You shouldn't tease me when I'm hungry."

"Oh, no, do I have a hangry diva on my hands?" He put his arm around her shoulders and squeezed.

"Yes, you do. I slathered peanut butter on a banana for lunch, but it's worn off."

"Don't worry about it. I'm taking you out for..." Liam said and grinned. "An early supper."

"You are?" Her heart skipped a beat. *As in a date?* Here they were, having a baby and never actually been on a real date. That strange quasi-date at Hennen's when they'd run into Mike and Colton didn't count.

"I'm here, so we may as well hang out together."

Oh, but she yearned for more than hanging out. She wanted them to be a couple—a family—a real family. Maybe she should come right out and tell him what she wanted. How could you get something if you didn't ask for it? "Liam, I—"

"Maybe if we'd gone out more, we might not be in this situation," he interrupted.

Maybe now wasn't the time for confessions. She managed a little laugh. "You think?"

His blue eyes twinkled as he regarded her. "Nah, not really. I think it's payback from the universe for all the comments I make about Meg and Riley."

"I think it was a little more than that."

"Really?" He raised his eyebrows. "Maybe you need to show me…just so I'll know better in the future."

"Nice try, but you promised to take me out to supper and I'm starving." Not that she didn't want to explore that chemistry again, but hunger took precedence.

He sighed. "If I feed you, maybe we can revisit this discussion?"

She tilted her head from side to side as if sizing him up. "Perhaps."

"There's nothing more appealing than a decisive woman." He draped an arm around her shoulders and laughed. "So, when you're not tossing your cookies, you're hungry. Have I got that right?"

"It's not funny. Sometimes I feel as though I'm all over the map. One minute happy, the next crying. And food I used to love makes me sick just to think about it."

"I hate to disagree…especially with a pregnant woman but…" He gently rubbed his knuckles across the top of her head. "It's a bit funny from where I'm standing, but I will take you out to eat."

"Ha, you weren't exactly Mr. Calm-and-Collected when I was losing it in your bathroom."

He sighed. "You had me scared to death."

She knew he was probably thinking of his mother, so she didn't tease. "Sorry."

He gave her a smile that melted her heart. "Let's get some food in you before you become unbearable."

Scooting out from under his arm—even though it felt heavenly—she said, "Sounds like a plan."

He reached behind him and scooped up her car keys from the kitchen counter. "Ready?"

"You're driving?"

He jangled her keys and tilted his head. "No?"

"Fine, but quit messing with the presets on my radio."

"If you had decent music, I wouldn't be forced to listen to the radio." He shook his head, looking at her as if he pitied her.

She pushed him toward the door. "We won't listen to anything then. I'll serenade you."

"Oh, good Lord." He stopped dead in his tracks.

She plowed into him and swatted his freaking broad shoulders. "Hey!"

He chuckled and captured her hand and threaded his fingers through hers. "C'mon, let's go."

Chapter 12

Ellie hummed to herself the next morning as she pulled out a carton of eggs from the refrigerator. Liam had gotten out of bed and brought her saltine crackers to settle her stomach before jumping into the shower.

Having breakfast ready for him was a good way to repay the favor. She was dicing peppers and onions when her cell phone rang. She wiped her hands on the kitchen towel hanging over the oven handle before answering.

"Ellie, so glad I caught you." Meg sounded a little breathless.

"What's up?" Ellie frowned.

"I really hate to bother you on your day off, but do you think you could watch James for a couple hours today? Riley got called in to work and I'd already promised to help chaperone Fiona's class trip to the pumpkin patch."

"Sure." Ellie glanced at the clock on the stove. "Do I have time to shower and get dressed?"

"Of course. Thanks, I really appreciate this."

"No problem. I'll be there as soon as I can."

Liam appeared in the in the living area, his jeans unbuttoned and riding low on his hips, the band from his boxer briefs visible. He was shirtless, a towel thrown over his shoulder. "Did you get called in to work or something?"

"No. That was Meg. She asked if I could help her out." She swallowed as her gaze took in his gloriously bare chest, remembering how those muscles reacted to her touch.

"What does Meg need help with?"

Of course if he was on one of those calendars, then all women would be drooling over the six-pack abs and the dusting of hair that formed a V and disappeared under the waistband of his jeans. His dark hair was more disheveled than normal.

"Ellie? My sister?"

She forced her gaze upward and her thoughts on the conversation, but it wasn't easy. Liam wasn't musclebound like a weight lifter, but he was fit. Oh, boy, was he ever.

Clearing her throat, she explained, "Meg asked if I could watch James while she helps chaperone Fiona's class trip to the pumpkin patch."

He tossed the towel over the back of the chair and picked up a gray waffle-weave henley draped over the back of the couch. "What time does she need you?"

"As soon as I shower and dress." She checked her watch.

"Do you want some breakfast before we head over?" he said and pulled the shirt over his head.

Her heart rate kicked up. "Oh, you're coming with me?"

"Is that okay with you?" He grabbed his sneakers and sat on the sofa.

"Sure. I had already started on breakfast but I'd better jump in the shower instead."

He stuffed his feet into his sneakers. "What were you making?"

"The ingredients for omelets are on the counter."

He finished tying his laces and came to stand next to her. "Go get in the shower. I can handle omelets."

Liam drank a quick cup of coffee while Ellie was in the shower and rinsed the cup in the sink. He finished chopping the peppers and onions and set about making omelets. He was putting the plates on the breakfast bar when she came back from her shower. They ate quickly and Liam stacked the plates in the sink before they left.

Meg met them at the door, holding James on her hip, the dog at her side. The baby had a piece of a banana clutched in his fist. "Ooh, two for the price of one."

Liam bumped shoulders with Ellie. "You didn't say you were getting paid. Trying to get out of sharing with me?"

Meg led them through the small original living room into the new, expansive family room with large windows and patio doors looking into the woods at the back of the house. They didn't have a deck or patio yet, but Riley hoped to put one in soon.

"Yeah, good luck getting to those snickerdoodles before me," Ellie said, and smiled at James and gave him a kiss on the top of his head. "Hello there, little man."

He waved the banana around and showed her a toothy grin. The dog, an Aussiedoodle with reddish-brown curls, whined, his intent gaze on the fruit.

Meg wiped a piece of banana off his cheek. "He was just finishing his morning snack. I haven't had a chance to get him washed yet."

The baby thrust the smashed banana toward Liam. "Meem."

"Thanks, buddy, but I just ate."

"I can get him cleaned up." Ellie reached out and took James in her arms. "Looks like you're enjoying that nanner, bud."

Meg nodded. "Bananas are his new favorite snack."

He offered it to Ellie, but she shook her head, her lips clamped firmly together. James, imitating her by vigorously shaking his head, opened his fist and let the banana piece fall, but Mangy scooped it up in midair.

Meg laughed. "You guys might want to consider getting a dog."

Remembering how upset Ellie had gotten over the thought of taking care of a pet, Liam winced. He glared at his sister, shaking his head, but Meg threw him a puzzled look. His gaze went to Ellie, but evidently she was too busy talking to James to be upset.

Meg kissed James before Ellie took him to wash his hands and face. She turned to Liam. "What was that all about? Ellie likes dogs. So do you."

He swiped a hand over his face. "It's a long story."

"And I'm in a hurry. Any questions before I leave?"

Liam glanced at the flat screen he and Riley had

mounted to the wall. "As a matter of fact I do. Tell me again the channel number for ESPN on your television."

"I don't know." Meg picked up her purse and keys.

"How can you not know something that important?"

"Yeah, like I have time to watch television. By the time I get Fiona and James down for the night, I'm ready to crawl into bed myself, especially with Riley on nights." Meg patted her still-flat stomach. "At least by the time this one comes, he'll have enough seniority to get a day shift when one becomes available."

"Okay. Jeez. Sorry I asked." He threw up his hands in a defensive gesture but laughed when Meg held up a fist. "I'm sure I can find it."

Meg lowered her arm. "You'll have to find the remote first. It's James's new favorite thing now that he can lift up against the coffee table."

"Not exactly running a tight ship, are we, sis?" As soon as he said it, he realized his mistake. Meg would have plenty of opportunities to point out parenting errors to him in the near future.

She gave him a big, evil smile. "Oh, I am so going to enjoy picking on you when you have one running around."

"Ellie and I will have it all under control." *Nothing like compounding your mistakes.*

"Ha! I love it." Meg laughed and rubbed her palms together. "You are so clueless. I'd help you look for the remote, but I'm already running late."

"So much for sitting around watching sports highlights in my underwear," he muttered as he lifted couch cushions in his search for the remote. Each time he lifted a cushion Mangy stuck his shaggy head under it. He patted the dog's head as he pushed it out of the way so he could replace the cushion. "What you looking for, boy?"

The dog whined and stuck his nose in the space between the arm and the cushion, grabbing something.

Liam latched onto the dog's collar before he could scamper off with his treasure. He pried a set of plastic keys from the animal's mouth.

"What are you two doing?" Ellie stood in the doorway to the large family room, James perched on her hip. The baby spotted the dog and grunted and lunged, but Ellie managed to hang on.

"Mangy and I were looking for the remote and he found these." The dog sat and whined as his gaze followed Liam's hand. "Sorry, boy, I doubt these are yours."

"Here, you take James and I'll wash those keys off."

He shook his head. "If I set them down, the dog is going to run off with them."

She leaned down and put James on the floor. "You stay here with Uncle Meem while I take care of this."

"Don't start with that Meem stuff. I just got Fiona to say it correctly."

"Meem… Meem… Meem," James babbled as he crawled to the coffee table and pulled himself up. One hand rested on the table and the other stretched toward Liam.

Liam tossed the keys to Ellie and reached down to ruffle his nephew's hair. "Hey, buddy, not sure what you're talking about. Can you say 'Liam'?"

"Sorry, but I think you're going to be Uncle Leem or Meem for the foreseeable future. At least you won't have to worry about that with ours."

Liam looked up from his search for the remote. "Why not?"

Ellie clicked her teeth. "Because she will be calling you Daddy."

"Oh, yeah." He scratched his scalp and frowned. "What?"

"That's a scary thought, but I guess if my baby sister and Riley can do it, so can we." Had his dad gotten a mini panic attack thinking about being a parent before Liam was born?

"Can we?"

"You certainly can, you're an ER nurse. Of course you're qualified." Ellie was going to be great. He wished he had as much confidence in himself as he did her.

"Bet they wouldn't let me take home a baby if they knew how scattered I've been lately."

"I find that hard to believe." He jammed his fingers in the back of the couch. That damn remote had to be here somewhere.

She sank down next to James as he slapped his palm on the coffee table. "Believe it. I poured orange juice on my cornflakes last week."

"Run out of milk?" His searching fingers found something and he pulled out a tiny pink plastic hard-hat. What the...?

"No, I didn't run out of milk. I pulled out the OJ by mistake."

"What did you do?" He started to set the tiny toy on the coffee table but looked at James and decided against it.

"I threw them out and started over, but what's that got to do with it?"

"It proves you're good at problem solving, because I would have eaten them."

"You are such a guy."

He wiggled his eyebrows. "Glad you finally noticed. Aha, here's the remote."

Ellie rolled her eyes. "Give that hat to me and I'll put it in Fiona's room. It belongs to her Barbie Builder set."

"How do you know these things?" He put the cushions back on the sofa.

"It's a girl thing."

"Hey, James, how about we watch some sports? Make sure that father of yours is teaching you the right teams to root for." He scooped his nephew off the floor and sat down on the sofa with him.

"I think he's wet. Let me go get a fresh diaper."

Liam held James up in the air. "Now she tells me. Are you wet?"

The boy let out a string of baby giggles.

Ellie came back with a diaper and tub of wipes. "Want me to take him?"

"It's okay. I've changed Fiona's. May as well get some more practice in." He truly did want to be involved.

He put James on the blanket on the floor and unsnapped the baby's pants to get at the diaper. At least he remembered how to do that much from when Fiona was a baby. He removed the soggy diaper.

"Liam, wait! Put this over…"

He glanced up as Ellie launched what looked like a washcloth at him.

What the heck was she on about? He knew how to—

Something wet and warm squirted all over the front of his shirt.

He glanced down at his giggling nephew. "Why did he do that?"

Ellie had her fist pressed against her mouth and her shoulders were shaking. She cleared her throat. "It's something baby boys do."

"Why didn't you warn me?" After getting over being grossed out, he could appreciate the humor in it. And he couldn't be angry with an innocent—he glanced down at his giggling nephew. Huh, maybe not quite so innocent.

"I thought you knew. You said you'd changed diapers before," Ellie said.

"I changed Fiona's diaper a time or two and nothing like this ever happened." He shook his head.

"Girls are different but it can still happen."

"So, is there a trick to not getting wet?"

"I think the trick is to keep something over him like the old diaper or a cloth."

"Why would I know something like this?"

"You've never changed James's diaper before?" He shook his head and she continued, "Well, now you know. Look on the bright side, at least your face wasn't in the line of fire."

James began laughing and Liam put his palm over the baby's belly and tickled him. "You think that's funny? Now I'm going to have to wear one of your daddy's shirts and I'll make your mommy wash mine."

The baby giggled. "Meem."

He shook his head at James. There was so much he didn't know about babies and kids despite having spent a lot of time around his niece and nephew. Had his dad been nervous and clueless in the beginning? Maybe by the time his child was old enough to form memories of his or her childhood, he'd have a better handle on the whole parenting thing.

Once again, Ellie awoke to a cold, empty bed. She'd been doing that ever since Liam's friend Nick had picked him up three days earlier. She rolled over and rubbed her hand over the cool sheets. Liam had only slept over for a few nights, but she'd gotten used to having him here.

She had no idea when she'd see him again. He'd told her that during his time off he was taking an extra shift at one of the part-time stations. He apologized and explained that this had been planned for a while.

Sighing, she got up and pulled on her pink fleece robe against the apartment's early-morning chill. She paused to see if this was a morning sickness day. It wasn't. At least not yet. Of course her nausea didn't just strike first thing; sometimes it lasted all day or hit unexpectedly. Smells could trigger it, too.

The nausea had been getting worse but she knew the extra hormones that caused it kicked in around the eight-week mark, so it wasn't surprising.

Today was her first appointment with the obstetrician. She'd be going alone and part of that was her fault. She'd assured Liam that the checkup was just routine and it was, but now that she was faced with going alone, it felt…sad. It was still early in the pregnancy for the doctor to want an ultrasound. At least Liam wasn't missing out on something like that.

Buck up, Ellie, and quit your whining.

Liam had stepped up, but the fact that they lived

three hours apart wasn't going to change unless she moved to Boston. Pulling up stakes, leaving everything she knew and had worked for to move so she could live on the periphery of Liam's life, held no appeal.

"But I'm reserving the right to revisit this decision," she told her reflection as she brushed her hair before dashing out the door.

At the doctor's office, Ellie flipped through old magazines, kicking herself for not remembering to bring a book. Not that it mattered since she doubted she'd be able to concentrate any better on the latest spy thriller than she could this three-month-old *People* magazine. Too many things running through her head. Being in the medical profession at times like this was not helpful.

The blood tests scheduled for today might be routine, but this was *her* baby they were running tests on. That changed everything. She was doing this so she could be prepared, not because she suspected something was wrong. Intellectually she knew her chances of a successful pregnancy were the same as anyone else's, but emotions didn't always operate on facts. But the situation gave her some perspective on what her parents must've gone through when her cancer was diagnosed.

Would she be faced one day with her child having a life-threatening illness? Her hand covered her still flat stomach as sympathy for her parents filled her.

She glanced around the waiting room at the other women in various stages of pregnancy, some with partners, others alone like her.

Heaving a sigh, she tossed the magazine aside just as the inner door opened and the nurse called her name.

Ellie jumped up. At least doing something would be better than just sitting and waiting.

The nurse smiled. "Ellie, it's so good to see you again."

Ellie recognized the woman from hospital rotations during nursing school. "Kim Smith, right?"

"It's Dawson now." The nurse led her down a hallway.

"Mine's still Harding, but I guess you could see that from the chart." Ellie hated the warmth in her cheeks. Plenty of single women had babies these days. Even in Loon Lake.

"It's been a while." Kim stopped in front of a balance beam scale. "How have you been?"

"Is that a professional question or making conversation?"

"Both, I guess." Kim laughed. "Okay, hop up on the scale."

"I hate this part." Ellie sighed and glanced at her red sneakers. "Can I take these off first?"

"Really? At your first appointment." Kim clicked her tongue but grinned. "This is only the beginning."

Ellie glanced at her feet and debated, but giggled and toed her shoes off.

Kim marked her weight on the chart. "Okay, take a seat and we'll get blood pressure next."

"You should've done that *before* you weighed me." Ellie motioned toward the scale. "Having to get on that thing probably raised it."

Kim chuckled. "So you're feeling okay? No complaints?"

"I'm doing good, if you don't count the morning sickness that pops up at all hours and crying over the stupidest things." Ellie sat in the chair and rolled up her sleeve.

"I hear that. I carried sandwich bags and tissues in

my purse." Kim set the chart on the table. "Take a seat and we'll get your pressure, then some labs, but I guess you know the drill."

Ellie nodded. "Yeah, I know all this stuff like getting a patient's blood pressure is standard procedure, but when it's being done to you, it doesn't feel routine at all."

So far there was no need for Liam to be here for these mundane things. So why did she feel so bereft?

"Yeah, we don't always make the best patients, do we?" Kim adjusted the blood pressure cuff on her upper left arm. "You still like working in the ER?"

"I do, but I've been thinking of a change." Ellie laid her other hand over her stomach. "Especially now. Do you like this kind of nursing?"

"I'm sure it's not as exciting or interesting as the ER but the hours are easier. Plus, holidays and weekends off is nice for family life." Kim made notes on the chart as the Dinamap displayed her blood pressure.

Ellie nodded. From now on, she'd have someone else to take into consideration. Working twelve-hour shifts might not be feasible. She put out her arm but cringed when Kim came at her with the needle. Being a nurse didn't make getting stuck any easier.

"We should have the results back in one to two weeks." Kim marked the vials of blood. "And we'll just take a quick look today to verify the pregnancy and check for iron and vitamin levels. We'll need to get you started on prenatal vitamins."

After a week of denying her suspicions, Ellie had decided she needed to be proactive. "Yeah, I took some over-the-counter ones, but they don't have the same folic acid levels."

"I've got everything I need. It was good seeing you again." Kim opened the door and dropped the chart in the holder on the door. "The doctor should be in shortly."

Ten minutes felt like an eternity and Ellie was starting to get antsy when the door opened and Kim popped her head in. "The doctor has decided he'd like you to have an ultrasound. Fortunately, we can do one on-site. The tech will be in in just a minute to escort you back there."

Ellie's stomach twisted into knots. Not since being diagnosed with cancer had she felt so helpless. "Tell me what's wrong. Why do they want to do an ultrasound now? What can't wait?"

"Ellie, you of all people know I can't say anything." Kim shook her head. "Let's keep the imagination reined in," she added with a smile before closing the door.

Ellie glared at the closed door Kim had escaped through and wrung her hands. Was she overreacting? The way she saw it, she was allowed to do so. This was *her* baby, maybe her only chance to be a mom.

She should have said yes when her mother had offered to come. But she would've had to take off work and Ellie hated for her to use her PTO to come to a routine first exam. She had assumed the most exciting part would be to hear the baby's heartbeat. Except being alone with only her thoughts for company wasn't a good idea. She sat on her hands trying to keep them warm and swung her legs.

There was a quick rap on the door.

"Finally," she muttered. At least they'd be getting this show on the road. Despite Kim's advice, she'd let her imagination run roughshod over her rational self.

The door opened but instead of the ultrasound tech or the doctor, the receptionist stood in the doorway. "Someone is insisting on seeing you, but we can't let anyone back here without your permission."

Had her mother come, anyway? Who else could it be? The receptionist cleared her throat and Ellie nodded. "Yes, that's fine."

Before she could react, Liam loomed in the doorway, still in his dark blue BFD uniform. She blinked, but he didn't disappear. Liam was here! Oh, God, the news was so bad they called him. No wait, that was crazy. They hadn't done anything yet and he couldn't have gotten here in such a short time even if he'd been in town. Nothing had been wrong ten minutes ago... but was it now?

Chapter 13

She straightened and pulled her hands from under her thighs. "What are you doing here? How did you get here? How did you find me?"

He shut the door and crossed the small room in two strides. "I'm here because I was serious when I said wanted to be involved. I hit the road as soon as I got off shift this morning and I called Meg to ask where you'd be," he said, ticking off his answers by holding up his fingers. "I think that covers all your questions."

"You don't know how glad I am to see you." Ellie swallowed several times, trying to keep it together, fiercely holding back the tears burning at the back of her eyes. "Something isn't right."

He stood directly in front of her, then nudged himself between her legs until his thighs rested against the table. "What is it? What's wrong?"

"I don't know. It was supposed to be just a routine exam and labs but then...then..." She waved her hands in front of her, fumbling for words.

Without a word, he pulled her into the shelter of his arms and held her close. *She loved him.* She was in love with Liam. Not a schoolgirl crush. Not lust for a sexy-as-sin fireman. But soul-deep, forever love.

She snuffled against his chest. "Oh, Liam, what if something's wrong with our baby?"

His arms tightened into a bear hug. "Then we'll deal with it."

"Did..." He cleared his throat and loosened his hold. "Did they say what could be wrong?"

She shook her head and eased away from him enough so she could speak. "No, but they test for Down syndrome. But they won't have those results for at least a week. I don't know what this means."

He rubbed her back. "The receptionist didn't act like anything was wrong."

"She probably doesn't know and even if she did, they're not allowed to say anything." Next time she was faced with an angry relative demanding answers, she'd have a lot more sympathy.

"Ellie?" Kim opened the door. Her eyes widened when she spotted Liam, her gaze taking in his uniform. "Oh, I didn't know anyone had come with you."

Liam stepped away from Ellie and held out his hand. "Liam McBride. I arrived a bit late. I came after getting off shift this morning."

"Off shift?" She glanced at the Boston patch on his shirt and lifted an eyebrow. "As in Boston off shift?"

Liam nodded. "That's the one."

Ellie leaned to the side so she could see around Liam. "Liam's the...uh, baby daddy."

What a silly thing to call him, but it was the easiest explanation.

"Nice meeting you, Liam. I'm Kim. Ellie and I went through nursing school at the same time." Kim shook his hand. "They've got the ultrasound ready for you. It's just down the hall. Ellie, you can leave your things in here."

Kim glanced at Liam. "Umm...if you'll—"

"I want him with me," Ellie said, and reached for his hand.

Kim nodded. "Of course, I just thought he might want to wait here while we get you ready."

Liam paced the small room, waiting for the nurse to come and get him. His gut churned with every step. Was something wrong with Ellie? Or the baby?

Every time the word *cancer* tried to invade his brain, he shoved it aside and slammed the door. *One worry at a time, McBride.*

"Wait until they tell us," he muttered, and glared at the closed door.

He wanted to fling it open and demand they tell them something. He wanted to run to Ellie and hold her and make everything okay.

Thank goodness he'd listened to his gut, not to mention his conscience, when it told him he should be with Ellie. She had needed him. How could he have thought she didn't? Her assertion that it was just a routine exam had rung false because this was *their* baby. Nothing would be just routine for either of them. But this...

He couldn't imagine leaving her to go through this

uncertainty alone. He remembered his promise to be strong when she needed him to be. It looked like it would be his turn to be the strong one today.

The door opened and he resisted the urge to pounce on Kim and demand answers.

"We're ready for you," she announced cheerfully.

He followed the nurse to a room with complicated-looking equipment and a monitor on a rolling stand. Ellie lay on her back on an exam table with her knees up and a sheet draped over the bottom half of her body.

"This is Liam," Kim said to a technician.

The technician looked up. "Hi, I'm Sherrie."

"I'll leave you to it," Kim said. "Sherrie will take good care of you."

Sherrie smiled as she got her equipment ready. "You know we won't be able to determine the baby's sex yet."

"Yeah, that's not why we're here," Ellie told her.

The other woman nodded. "I wanted to get that out of the way so you won't be disappointed."

Liam went to stand next to Ellie and she reached for his hand.

The technician got out what looked like a wand and rolled a rubber sheath on it. Ellie squeezed his hand. He winked at her and she grinned, some of the tension melting away. He leaned close to her ear.

"I think it's a little too late to give me pointers now," he whispered.

She choked on a laugh.

"Okay, if you could relax for me now, Ellie," the technician said, and scooted the stool to the end of the exam table.

He laced his fingers through Ellie's and pulled her hand against his chest. Watching the monitor, he tried to make sense of what he was seeing. The technician's face gave nothing away. He'd bet they were trained to not reveal anything.

"I'm just going to call the doctor in." Sherrie stood and scooted out the door.

"Liam?" Ellie looked from the closed door and back to him. "I thought I saw—but her face was blank."

"Hey, hey, calm down." Brushing the hair back from her cheek, he tucked it behind her ear and cupped his palm against her jaw. He pressed his lips against her forehead. "You know yourself, technicians aren't allowed to tell you anything."

"They tell you good stuff like 'Oh, look, there's your perfectly healthy baby.'" Ellie sniffed. "If she went to get the doctor, that means something is wrong. Oh, Liam, I'm scared."

"Look at me." He leaned over so his face was directly in front of hers. "Whatever it is, we'll handle it together. I'm not going anywhere."

Tough talk from a guy who'd rather be feeling his way through thick smoke in an unfamiliar structure in danger of collapsing than to be here right now. Ellie's fear gutted him and his belly clenched.

A man with a thick thatch of gray hair hustled in and introduced himself. Liam shook hands but he couldn't hear the man's name above the roaring in his ears.

"Let's take a look and see what we have." Dr. Stanley put on a pair of glasses and settled on a stool in front of the screen.

"What is it?" Ellie asked in a hoarse voice.

The doctor slid his glasses onto the top of his head. "It appears there are two embryos."

Liam cleared his throat. "T-two?"

Dr. Stanley nodded. "Congratulations. You're having twins."

The man's words caused all the air to swoosh out of Liam's lungs. Wait...what? Twins? Was that even possible? *Of course it's possible, dumbass.*

"Thank you... I don't know what to say. I'm so relieved. Thank you," Ellie was saying to Dr. What's-His-Name. "Isn't wonderful, Liam? Liam?"

The doctor jumped up and pushed the rolling stool toward Liam. "Son, I think you need this more than I do."

Liam sank down, still trying to digest the information. Of course he was ecstatic that nothing was wrong...but two babies? At the same time? "You're sure?"

"Most definitely. It's too early to determine the sex yet, but I can tell you they're fraternal." The doctor slipped his glasses back down onto his nose to look at the monitor again. "Everything looks normal for twins. Of course with multiples, we'll want to monitor you a bit more closely, especially toward the end, but I see no reason for concern."

"With fraternal, we could have one of each," Ellie said. "Meg will claim we're trying to keep up with her."

Dr. Stanley glanced between them. "Well, if you don't have any questions, I'll have Kim give you some pamphlets on multiples and a prescription for prenatal vitamins."

"Thank you, Doctor, I'm just relieved everything is okay," Ellie said.

"Sorry if you had some anxious moments, but rest assured, everything appears normal." With a quick nod of his head, he stuck out his hand to Liam. "Congratulations again, son."

Liam shook hands with the other man, but if asked to describe him after he left the room, he wouldn't have a clue. It was as if he was experiencing the world through his respirator…his breathing loud in his ears while everything else was muffled.

"You look a little shell-shocked," Kim observed as she led him to the previous exam room while Ellie got cleaned up and dressed.

"I was just wrapping my head around one and now it's two…at once." His voice cracked on the last part.

Kim patted him on the shoulder. "Believe me, this isn't the first time I've seen that look. Before you leave, I'll put you in touch with the local support group for multiples."

"Support group for multiples…" Liam shook his head. "That's a thing?"

She chuckled. "Yup. Your reaction to the news is quite typical."

"Ellie should be back in a moment," Kim added and left.

He needed to hold it together for Ellie. Today's news was unexpected but he could handle it and keep everything under control. Sitting hunched forward with his elbows on his thighs, his mind raced at the thought of two babies. Would having twins put more of a strain on Ellie's body? Having her move to Boston seemed even more urgent now, but he knew better than to confront her. Ellie could be stubborn. He stared at his boots as if they could supply him with answers. Maybe he'd talk to Meg. This was a role reversal…asking his little sister for advice.

* * *

Standing next to Liam on Meg and Riley's porch, Ellie knocked on the door. Meg had insisted they come to supper while Liam was in Loon Lake. Ellie wasn't quite sure how she felt about Meg treating them as a couple. It wouldn't be long before the whole town was doing that, especially with Liam showing up in time for the ultrasound. The medical personnel couldn't say anything but that privacy didn't extend to the people in the waiting room. Liam showing up in his uniform hadn't gone unnoticed.

Waiting for Meg or Riley to answer, Ellie turned to Liam. "This feels like déjà vu."

He wiggled his eyebrows. "Yup. Déjà vu all over again."

She rolled her eyes but was glad he could joke. His face had drained of color when the doctor had told them she was expecting twins. He'd recovered quickly, but she could see he'd been putting on a happy face. Once the relief that nothing was wrong passed, the truth of her situation had started to sink in. She was going to be a single mother to twins. She wiped her clammy hands on the front of her jeans. Her initial relief that nothing was wrong had started to wear off and it was sinking in that the situation she thought she'd had under control this morning had done a one-eighty.

The door swung open and Riley greeted them with a sobbing James in his arms. "C'mon in. Sorry about this."

"Oh, no. What's wrong?" Ellie's heart ached for a now-hiccupping James. And for herself. She was going to have this, times two!

"He's crying because he's not allowed to play with Fiona's toys." Riley stood aside so they could enter.

"Worried about his masculinity?" Liam chuckled as he stepped into the living room.

Meg appeared and clucked her tongue at her brother. "It's a choking hazard. All those little pieces go in his mouth."

Liam glanced around. "Where is Fiona?"

"She had a half day of school and she went out to Brody and Mary's farm. She spent the afternoon entertaining Elliott so Mary could catch up on some paperwork. They'll bring her home later tonight."

James threw his arms toward Meg. "Mommy."

Riley ruffled his son's hair before handing him over to Meg. Turning his attention to his guests, he motioned with his head. "C'mon in and sit, you two. Supper isn't ready yet. We got a little behind with all the ruckus."

Ellie draped her jacket over the back of the sofa. "Can I help with anything?"

"Thanks, but I have it under control…for the moment." Meg laughed and tickled James's tummy and the baby burst into giggles. "But Riley can take my brother with him to help get the grill ready."

"Maybe we should give them our news first," Ellie said, and glanced at Liam.

Meg looked from one to the other. "More news? Does this mean you two are—"

"The news was from the doctor," Ellie interrupted. She didn't want Meg getting the wrong idea and starting a discussion she had no intention of engaging in.

"Is there something wrong?" Meg adjusted James on her hip. "Guys, you're scaring me."

"No, it's okay." Ellie put a hand over her stomach. "They said the babies are fine."

"Oh, well that's— Wait! Did you say *babies*? As in plural?" Eyes wide, Meg pointed to Ellie's stomach. "You mean…"

"Twins." Ellie couldn't help grinning. She was still riding high, grateful that nothing was wrong. At one point in her life she hadn't been sure she'd be able to have kids at all because of the cancer treatments. At the time of her treatment, being able to get pregnant didn't mean a whole lot but as she got older, having a baby became more important. Now to have two, while daunting, was a real blessing.

Meg shifted James and gave Ellie a one-armed hug. "I'm so happy for you. I know… Well, I just want you to know how happy I am."

When Meg pulled away, Riley gave Ellie a hug. "Congratulations."

"And you, too, bro." Meg gave Liam a quick hug. "Leave it to Liam to try to outdo me."

"I told you she would say that!" Liam scowled at his sister.

Meg sniffed and stuck her nose in the air. "Of course you'd have to be having triplets to catch up, or quad—"

"Bite your tongue," Liam grumbled.

Ellie raised her hand and waved it about. "Let's not forget I'm the one carrying these babies."

"Sorry." Meg laughed. "I'll settle for being an auntie twice over."

"Are there any twins in either of your families?" Riley asked.

"None that we know of. I asked my mom when I called to tell her the news," Ellie said.

"I'll bet she's excited," Meg said.

Ellie nodded. "She's already trying to decide what she wants to be called."

Meg laughed. "She may not get a choice. Fiona called Doris 'Mrs. Grampa Mac' for the longest time."

James pointed a finger at Liam. "Meem."

Everyone laughed and James bounced on Meg's hip, as if proud of having made everyone laugh.

Ellie's throat closed up and threatened to choke her. If, in the future, she and Liam weren't a couple, would he bring the children to McBride family gatherings without her? Would her kids come home and tell her how much fun they'd had? She blinked against the sudden burning in her eyes.

"Yeah, your kids seem to have a problem with names," Liam said, but the look he gave James made Ellie's insides feel all squishy. He might not believe it yet, but he was going to make a great dad.

"And I suppose yours won't?" Meg shot back. "You can call him anything you want, sweetie," she told James in a stage whisper. "Maybe when you get older, I can teach you a few other names."

Riley chuckled and clapped a hand over Liam's shoulder. "Maybe you'd better come help me get the steaks on the grill before you dig yourself an even deeper hole."

With the guys outside, Ellie helped Meg get James ready for bed.

"Pretty soon, we'll be doing this together to your kids," Meg remarked as she put pajamas on James.

"I have a feeling I'll be coming to you a lot for advice," Ellie told her.

Meg picked up her sleepy son and cuddled him. "I'll be here for you. You know that, right?"

"Of course, and I know Liam's going to be a great dad." And she did believe it.

"He will," Meg agreed, and gave James a small blanket with satin binding.

"Nigh-nigh." James hugged the ragged blanket to him and stuck his thumb in his mouth.

"Is it always this easy to get him to bed?"

Meg shook her head as she laid him in his crib. "I wish. No, he calls the security blanket his 'night-night.' I put him in his crib a few times when he was actually asking for his blanket."

Ellie went with Meg back to the kitchen to get the rest of the supper ready while the guys finished grilling the steaks.

Ellie was setting the bottles of salad dressing on the table when Liam came back in carrying a plate of foil-wrapped baked potatoes, Riley was behind him carrying a platter of grilled steaks.

"Hope you ladies are hungry," Riley said as he set the platter on the table.

Meg stepped behind Riley and put her arms around his waist. "For you, dear, always."

Liam made gagging sounds. "How are we supposed to eat now?"

"Can't you control him?" Meg asked Ellie.

Ellie shrugged it off with a grin, but her stomach clenched because she longed for what Meg had with Riley. Liam's pallor over having twins was fresh in her mind, along with the way he'd been fake-smiling on the porch. She needed a relationship that could withstand whatever life threw at them. Was that asking too much?

With a scrape of chairs, they all sat down and began dishing out the food.

"Will you be staying in your current apartment once the babies are born?" Meg asked as she passed the bowl of salad.

Ellie was hyperaware of Liam next to her. "For now. But twins changes things a bit. I had thought I could squeeze a crib into my place…but two?"

She was aware of him tensing and she rushed on, "I definitely want to look for a place in Loon Lake. Staying here is important to me."

In her peripheral vision she saw Liam press his lips together but didn't say anything.

Meg snagged a steak and put it on her plate. "Wouldn't it be awesome if you could buy that house next door?"

"But the property isn't for sale," Riley pointed out as he passed the platter of potatoes.

Meg nodded. "I know, but the owner has had trouble keeping it consistently rented. I'm not sure why."

"That's easy," Liam said. "It's because they have to live next to you, sister dear."

Meg pulled a face. "If you think you're safe because you're on the other side of the table, think again."

"Riley, have you no control over your wife?" Liam joked as he opened the foil on his baked potato.

Riley leaned over and kissed his wife. "Happy wife. Happy life. Right, dear?"

"Jeez, you've got him brainwashed," Liam grumbled, but he was grinning.

"Maybe he'd be interested in a long-term rental." Ellie put butter and sour cream on her potato. "Do you have his contact information?"

"I can call the agent. I think I still have her information somewhere from when I used to clean cottages between rentals," Meg told her.

"Thanks. I'd appreciate that." Ellie knew it was a long shot, but it was worth it to get in touch with the owner. Living next to Meg and Riley would be wonderful. Her children could grow up together with their cousins, as she had.

The table fell silent while everyone started eating.

"Are you here for three days now?" Riley looked across the table at Liam.

Liam shook his head. "Nah, I have to head back tonight."

"You do? Why?" Ellie chewed on her lower lip. She'd assumed Liam would be spending his off time with her. Didn't she have a right to expect that, after the news they'd just received? It wasn't every day you found out you were going to be parents to twins. She wanted to talk about it, maybe make some plans or even argue over names, something for him to show her he was in this with her. She blinked back tears. *Hormones*, she told herself.

His gaze searched hers. "Nick worked my part-time shift today and I promised to work his tomorrow."

She met his gaze and forced a smile. "I'm so glad you could come for the appointment today, but I hate that you have to drive back tonight already."

"It's okay. It was totally worth it." He touched her arm.

"Now who is making the googly eyes." Meg *tsk*ed. "But you're forgiven because finding out you're going to be a dad twice over doesn't happen every day."

Liam's knee was bouncing up and down under the

table and Ellie gently laid her hand on it. When he looked at her, she whispered, "My turn to be the calm one. Remember we said we wouldn't both freak out at the same time?"

The wink he gave her said he understood what she was doing and he put his hand over hers and squeezed, but it was as if he'd had his hand around her heart.

She blinked to clear her vision. She'd fallen in love with Liam. Sure, she hadn't had far to go, but now it was like a neon sign blinking in her head.

She swallowed, glancing around the table. What would happen to her if she moved to Boston and left behind her support system? And if she stayed in Loon Lake, could her and Liam's tenuous relationship withstand the stress of long distance? What if her cancer returned? Her heart clenched. What would happen to her children? Would another fight for her life cast a pall over this family as it had hers? Or, unlike hers, would they rally around and wrap her and the twins in their warmth?

Chapter 14

Ellie rubbed her back as she left the ER after her shift. Three days had passed since she'd seen Liam and she missed him. Ever since he found out about the babies a few weeks ago, they had been spending more time together. But talking over the phone wasn't the same. She stretched her neck, trying to work out the kinks. If she was this tired and sore now, what was going to happen over the next few months? The exhaustion should ease up in the second trimester but carrying twins had to be tiring, regardless of the month. What did she have at home to make for supper? She had to eat and she had to eat right, but sometimes she was too tired to go home and do much more than make a peanut-butter-and-Marshmallow-Fluff sandwich.

She and Liam had spoken every night since he'd left. They made small talk, and every night she stopped short of admitting her love. If she said the words, put them out there, would he use them to get her to move to Boston? Would he think she said them to wrangle a proposal or him uprooting his life? She didn't know the answer so she bit her tongue and didn't say anything.

In the corridor, she looked up and saw Liam leaning against the nurses' station. Surprise had her halting mid-stride. He was chatting up the nurses, who looked enraptured by whatever story he was telling. Before she could decide if she should be jealous, he glanced over and a huge grin split his face when he spotted her. The smile, the glint in his eyes, were for her and that knowledge filled her. She felt lighter in spite of her exhaustion.

"Sorry, ladies, but it looks like my date has arrived," he said, and stepped toward her.

Ellie said goodbye to the nurses and fell into step beside Liam as they left the hospital.

"What's this about me being your date?" She asked, torn between the prospect of going out with Liam or putting her feet up in front of the television. At this time of year it was dark when she left the ER, and going home suited her.

"I was talking about feeding you," he said, and stopped under a humming sodium vapor lamp near her car.

She looked up at him in the yellowish glow from the lights. "That sounds lovely but I confess I was looking forward to going home and not moving for at least twenty-four hours."

Would he take that as a rejection? She shivered and pulled her light jacket closer around her. The temperature had dropped along with the sun.

He put his arm around her shoulders and pulled her against his chest. "No problem. I brought things with me. We can go to your place and I'll cook while you put your feet up."

"I can't tell you how amazing that sounds." She burrowed closer to his warmth and rubbed her cheek against the soft cotton of his sweatshirt. He smelled like clean laundry.

"What were you planning on having if I hadn't shown up?" he asked, his voice rumbling in his chest.

"My old standby. A Fluffernutter," she said, referring to her craving for a peanut-butter-and-marshmallow sandwich. She pulled away enough to look up at him.

He quirked an eyebrow and his lips twitched. "On the appropriate whole-grain bread?"

"Um…" She stared at her feet.

He clicked his tongue against his teeth. "Shame on you, Ellie Harding. After all that grief you gave me."

She shrugged. "I know, but it's not the same if it's not on white bread."

"Well, if you can see your way clear to eat healthy, I brought stuff to make a stir-fry."

"That sounds wonderful. Thank you."

"Don't thank me until you taste it." He cleared his throat. "And I brought something special but you gotta eat the healthier stuff first."

"What? Are you practicing saying dad stuff?"

He laughed. "I have to start somewhere."

"About this dessert. Did you buy it or—"

He held up a finger. "I'm not saying anything except maybe a certain bakery might be involved."

She cuffed him on the shoulder. "Don't tease if you can't deliver."

"Wouldn't dream of it." He kissed the top of her head. "And believe me when I say I can deliver."

She rubbed her slightly rounded stomach. "I know you can."

"C'mon. Let's get you home so you can relax while I make supper."

"You must be tired, too, if you just came off shift."

"Yeah, but I wasn't on my feet the entire time like you and I'm not carrying around two extra people."

"But at the moment your turnout gear weighs more than these two." She pointed to her stomach.

"True, but I get to take it off at some point."

"You got me there." She laughed and rubbed her belly. "If they're wearing me out now, I can't imagine what it'll be like once they're born. I watch Mary's Elliott running around and I can't imagine two doing that at the same time."

"Just remember, you're not in this alone." He met her gaze. "You know that right?"

"Yes, I know that." She did, but part of the time he'd be nearly two hundred miles away. She didn't voice her thoughts. A lot of women had it worse. Meg had been alone until Riley returned from Afghanistan, and Mary had been a single mother with no help until she'd met Brody and they fell in love. Unlike Riley, who hadn't even known about his daughter for years, or Roger, who had rejected Mary and his son, Liam was willing to be involved. Sure, she'd vowed to live her life out loud, but there was that sticky thing called pride. Their children would tie her to Liam for a lifetime, regardless of whether or not they were a couple. If she admitted her feelings and he didn't return them, he might pity her.

She'd had enough of being pitied to last her a lifetime. It was one of those things that eroded self-esteem.

"Okay, let's get you home, warmed up and fed."

Liam followed Ellie to her place, the bags from the Pic-N-Save on the passenger seat. Before going to the hospital, he'd stopped at the local supermarket for ingredients. He wasn't much of a cook but he could do a simple stir-fry and rice. Glancing at the white bakery box with its bright blue lettering on the passenger-side floor, he grinned.

He pulled in behind Ellie's car and cut the engine. Scooping up the box, he stuck it in one of the bags and got out. His chest tightened as he followed her up the stairs. Being back in Loon Lake with her felt comforting, secure. But that was crazy. Why would he need comforting?

Following her into her kitchen, he set the bags on the counter. "Before I forget, someone named Lorena at the Pic-N-Save said to say hi."

Ellie laughed. "Did you tell her you were cooking supper for me?"

"She gave me the third degree as she rang up the stuff. I got the feeling if I said I was cooking for someone else, I was going to be in trouble."

"Small-town life," she said as she took off her jacket. "Let me go change and I'll help."

"Take your time. I got this." He began pulling things out of the bags.

"There's beer in the fridge if you want. Help yourself, I can't drink it," she said, and disappeared down the hallway.

He pulled the rice cooker off the shelf and dumped in

rice and water before plugging it in. Sipping on a long-neck, he began chopping the vegetables. He was slicing the beef when she came back into the kitchen area; when he looked up, his breath hitched in his chest. A strange combination of feelings, a confusing mixture of lust and fierce protectiveness, filled him. He'd experienced both before but never at the same time. This was like a punch to the gut.

"Liam?"

He blinked. "Huh?"

"What can I do?" she asked, frowning when he didn't respond.

"Just stand there and look beautiful." He winced when the casual, teasing tone he was going for fell short.

She sighed and shook her head. "That's hardly productive."

"Then tell me about your day." He poured oil in a pan and adjusted the burner.

She got dishes down and utensils from the drawer, telling him how the EMTs brought in a man having a psychotic episode. "Luckily, Riley and another deputy came in with him."

"Damn." He paused in the middle of adding the vegetables to the pan. He'd heard stories from EMTs about how volatile those situations could get. The thought of Ellie—his Ellie and their babies—caught in the middle of something like that chilled him. "Do you think the ER is the best place for you?"

She set the plates and utensils on the counter with a clatter. "What's that supposed to mean?"

"I know how these situations can go bad. You could've been hurt trying to defuse it." He stirred the vegetables and removed them from the pan once they'd started to soften.

She put her hand over her stomach. "These babies are very well protected at the moment."

"I wasn't talking about them. I was talking about you. You, Ellie, *you*." He pointed at her to emphasize his point, adding the thinly sliced meat to the pan to brown.

"I'm an adult. I don't need someone hovering."

"Since when is being concerned about your safety hovering?" He recalled the time Meg told him how Ellie had gotten beaned by a foul ball during a game to raise money for new water and ice rescue equipment for the EMTs. He took a sip of his beer and put the vegetables back in the pan with the meat. "And should you be playing softball?"

"Softball? It's October. What are you on about it?" She planted her hands on her hips and glared at him. "Oh, wait, I get it. We wouldn't even be having this conversation if I wasn't pregnant, would we?"

The rice cooker clicked from Cook to Warm. He shook his head. "I can't answer that because you are pregnant."

"I assure you, pregnant or not, I can and do take care of myself. I don't need you—"

He turned the burner off and put the meat and vegetables on a platter. "Your supper is ready. We should eat before it gets cold."

She opened her mouth and closed it again. He set the hot pan in the sink where it sizzled when the faucet dripped. With a strangled sound she went to him and put her arms around his waist, pressing her front to his back.

He grabbed her hands in his and turned around, putting her hands back at his waist, and held them there.

She looked up at him. "Why are we arguing?"

He shook his head. "I'm sorry if I worry about you. And I mean *you*. I'm not saying I'm not concerned over the babies, but it's you I think about, Ellie."

"That's good because I think about you, too, Liam." She gave him a squeeze. "And I appreciate you making me a healthy supper."

"Better than a peanut-butter sandwich?"

"Much."

"You haven't tried it yet." He wasn't much of a cook, but stir-fry was pretty easy and healthy.

After eating seated side by side at the breakfast bar, Ellie insisted on cleaning up while he found them something to watch on TV. He decided not to argue with her. Since he didn't do much of the cooking at the firehouse, the guys usually put him on cleanup.

Taking a seat on the couch, he picked up Ellie's pregnancy book from the cushion next to him. He opened the book to the place she had bookmarked.

"Ellie?" His voice sounded strained to his own ears.

She had a bookmark on the chapter about engaging in sex during the different stages of pregnancy. Well, well, well. So, did Ellie have this on her mind? Or was she simply reading the book cover to cover and happened to stop there?

"Ellie?"

"Hold your horses. I'm coming." She came into the living area carrying the bakery box and napkins. Her gaze went to the book in his hand and she stopped short, eyes wide, cheeks pink.

He held up the book. "Interesting reading."

She put the box of cannoli on the coffee table and sat down next to him on the sofa. "I'll take that."

"But I'm not done reading this fascinating chapter yet," he said, and winked.

She tried to pry the book out of his hands, but he was holding on tight.

"I think it's important we read this together. You know, share *all* aspects."

"That's because you're reading the chapter about sex."

"We could read it together," he offered.

She narrowed her eyes. "Just this one? Or all of it?"

"I guess if I was there for the good stuff, I should be there for the...uh, other stuff. Huh?" Leaving Ellie alone to handle all of this would be unforgivable and he liked to think he was better than that.

"Well..." She canted her head to one side as she studied him. "We could start with this particular chapter and then move on to some of the others."

He tossed the book onto the coffee table and jumped up.

She lifted an eyebrow. "No book? Does this mean you're going to wing it?"

His gaze bounced between her and the book. "Is there something special I should know?"

"Not really. I'm not that far along."

That was all he needed to know, as he placed his arm behind her knees and swept her high up into his arms.

"Liam! You're going to hurt yourself."

He grunted and staggered but kept her close in a firm grip. "Now that you mention it..."

"Hey, I haven't gained that much weight, especially with all the nausea."

"If you say so," he teased. He was enjoying the way her eyes sparkled.

"Brat. Put me down," she said, then looped her arms around his neck.

He shook his head as he headed toward the bedroom. "Momentum is on my side."

"Why are you even doing this?" She tightened her hold on him.

"What? You saying you aren't impressed?"

"Maybe if you weren't grunting so much."

He stepped into the bedroom and set her down gently. Straightening up, he put his hands on his back and made an exaggerated groaning sound.

She studied him with a sly smile. "I guess this means you won't be able to—"

He put his hands around her waist to fit her snugly against him. "Does that seem like I'm incapacitated in any way?"

She put her arms around him and nuzzled his neck. "Hmm… I might need further convincing." She kissed him. "Just to be sure."

"Mmm." He nibbled on her earlobe. "Should we get some of these clothes off?"

"Sounds like a plan," she said and pulled her sweatshirt over her head.

His gaze went to the small swell of her stomach. His babies were in there. Without conscious thought, he dropped to his knees and pressed his cheek against the taut skin.

Her hands were in his hair, her nails grazing his scalp as he put his arms around her. The moment might have started as sexy teasing but this was suddenly something more. He searched for words, but the tangle of emotions inside him prevented them from forming.

Her fingers tightened in his hair. "Liam?"

He might not have the words but he could show her what she meant to him.

Rising, he took her hand and led her to the bed, where he quickly disposed of the rest of her clothing.

He caressed her breasts and the areas around her nipples. "Have these gotten darker?"

"Yeah, it's increased pigmentation from..." She swallowed audibly. "Sorry, TMI?"

"You know I'm a sucker for nurse speak." He grinned, then sobered. "You're beautiful, Ellie."

She looked up at him. "And you have too many clothes on."

He reached around her and pulled the covers back. "Get in and I'll take care of that."

He left his clothes in a pile and slipped into bed, taking her into his arms.

Unlike the first time, when they'd both been so eager, he took this slow to demonstrate how much she meant to him. Even if he hadn't said the words.

Afterward, Liam settled her against him and rested his cheek against her silky hair. They worked as a couple and he dared to think about their future. Together.

Chapter 15

Ellie stepped out of the shower the next morning still glowing from the previous night's lovemaking. Dared she hope they had a future together? She smiled to herself as she grabbed a towel from the rack. He might not have come out with the words she longed to hear, but then neither had she.

Liam was taking her to Aunt Polly's, a local restaurant known for its pancakes. Maybe after that she'd—

All thoughts scattered as she felt a slight swelling under her left arm. She shook her head and swallowed back nausea. A swelling where the axillary lymph node was located wasn't good.

Of course there could be any number of non-lethal explanations but her mind insisted on taunting her with cancer. Fighting the urge to curl up in the fetal position on the floor, she wrapped herself in her ER nurse persona and called to Liam.

He popped his head in the doorway and his eyes widened and a grin spread across his face. His smile was her undoing and she choked back a sob.

"Ellie, my God, what is it? What's wrong?" He stepped inside her small bathroom.

"It's here." She lifted her left arm.

"What? What's there?" He stood in front of her.

"A lump…the axillary lymph node is enlarged," she whispered.

His gaze met hers. "Are you sure?"

"Of course I'm sure," she snapped.

He pulled her into his arms. "I only meant that we shouldn't panic. Maybe you bumped yourself."

"Don't you think I've been through all those excuses already? I think I would have remembered bumping myself under my arm. It's not sore or black and blue like a bruise." She buried her head in his chest while he rubbed her back.

They stood locked in the embrace, the only sound was that of a sports show coming from the television in the other room.

Sighing, she pulled away. "I'll need to get a biopsy."

Liam sucked in his breath. "Okay. Where and when do we get one?"

If only it was that easy… Well, it was, but those were the mechanics. The emotions that went along with it weren't. Especially now with her pregnancy. And Liam. Whatever they had was just beginning. She shook her head. Maybe her parents were right not to want— No! She refused to give in to defeatism. "You make it sound like ordering something off the internet."

His fingers were shaking when he reached out. Using his thumbs, he wiped the moisture from her cheeks. "I'm sorry. I only meant—"

"No, I'm sorry. I shouldn't take my anger out on you." She sighed. "Let me get dressed and I'll make some calls."

Sometimes being an ER nurse, not to mention a resident of a small town like Loon Lake, paid off. Ellie was able to get a biopsy scheduled for that afternoon with her oncologist.

Liam insisted on taking her to breakfast as planned, telling her sitting around and brooding wasn't doing either one of them any good. She appreciated his attempts at proceeding as normal. At the same time they annoyed her. But she had to eat for the sake of the babies so she agreed.

After the restaurant, Liam drove them to the doctor's office. He was by her side and yet…

She clung to his hand in the waiting room, but thoughts of her parents clamored in her mind. Was this how it started for them?

The oncologist, a kindly man in his fifties, carefully examined a cut on her forearm. "This could be our culprit."

"But it doesn't appear to be infected," Ellie told him.

"And maybe your immune system is doing its job and fighting it off." The doctor pushed his glasses on top of his head as he looked at her. "We'll do some tests just to be certain, but I don't want you to worry. We'll have the official results early next week."

Back at home, Ellie tried to take the doctor's advice and remain optimistic. She pretended to read her textbook while Liam fixed her toilet that kept running. She'd told him she'd put in a work order with the management company but he'd insisted. Not that she could blame him. Doing busywork was probably his coping strategy.

She heard him on his phone and soon he came out of the bedroom with his duffel bag: the one he used when going back and forth to Boston.

"What's going on?"

He looked up from his phone, a flush rising in his face. "I was asked to take an extra shift."

She'd heard him on the phone, though she hadn't heard it ring. Had he called looking for an excuse to escape? She immediately felt guilty for even thinking he'd do something like that.

He ran his hand through his hair, a muscle ticking in his cheek. "It's my job. Something I will need to support these babies."

"Are you sure you're not taking it to escape?" She hadn't meant to challenge him like that, but it hurt that he'd chosen work over her.

"Escape?" He scowled at her. "What the heck does that mean?"

She scuffed the toe of her sneaker on the rug. "Maybe it means that going to work is preferable to being trapped here with Cancer Girl?"

"Why would you even say something like that?"

"You see how my parents are. My dad used work to escape and look what it did to them."

"We're not your parents."

No, her parents were in a committed relationship.

When she didn't respond, he made an impatient motion with his hand. "The doctor said you won't have test results for three days at least. I'll be back once the shift is done. You make it sound like I'm deserting you."

You are! She swallowed and tried to remain calm but it was getting harder. Was this how her mom felt when her dad buried himself in work? Like he deserted her when she needed him? She resisted the urge to act childish by stamping her feet or using emotional blackmail by crying and carrying on. "You're absolutely right, Liam, but I also can't help feeling abandoned. I'm sorry and it might not be fair, but that's how I'm feeling right now. You didn't even consult me."

"I didn't realize I had to." He rubbed the back of his neck. "I'm going to work, not out partying, for crying out loud."

"I know it's irrational but feelings just are…they don't always subscribe to what's rational." It hurt to have him point out that they didn't even have enough of a relationship that he would consult her.

He heaved a deep sigh. "We're in this together."

She glanced at his duffel sitting by the door. "If you say so."

His gaze followed hers and he frowned.

"Could you have refused?"

"It's my job." He shook his head, his face a blank mask.

"My father had a job, too. I saw what my cancer did to my parents, to their relationship. For a while I blamed myself. I was convinced it was all my fault but now I know better. Cancer happened *to* me. I'm not my disease. And I'm sorry if you can't handle it, but that's not my fault."

"I'm not deserting you, Ellie," he said, and shook his head. "I need a little time and space to process all this."

"And that's fine. I understand that." She stuck out her chin. "I can give you time and space, but I refuse to be in a relationship with a ghost."

Three hours later, Liam walked into the station with Ellie's words echoing in his head. Leaving Ellie alone while she waited for the biopsy results was a cowardly move. But the emotions he'd been trying to deny had threatened to overcome him, so he'd run. He wouldn't blame Ellie if she hated him. He hated himself. By rules, the department couldn't force him to come back early but he hadn't said no. He hadn't said no because he'd panicked. From the moment he'd walked in on Ellie in the bathroom, he'd been unable to take a deep breath. His insides were a tangled black mass threatening to choke him. It was his ma, and to a lesser degree his friend and mentor Sean, all over again. He was going to lose Ellie and it was going to hurt more than the other two combined.

He went about his duties at the house by rote, his mind refusing to be calmed by the familiar routines.

Had he honestly believed being away from Ellie would make his black mass of emotions hurt less, make the panic disappear? Instead, being away increased the pain a thousand times over. He called to check in and they engaged in what could only be described as a stilted conversation.

Had he made the biggest mistake of his life by leaving?

He shook his head and threw the chamois cloth over his shoulder and stood back to check the shine on the engine he'd been polishing instead of watching a movie with the other guys.

"Chief wants to see you, McBride."

Liam nodded and tossed the chamois to the probie. "Have at it, Gilman."

What could the chief want? He hovered in the doorway to the office. "You wanted to see me?"

Al Harris stood up and held out his hand across the desk. "Let me be the first to congratulate you, Captain McBride."

It took a minute for the words to penetrate. Captain? Him? He'd done it. He made captain at a younger age than his dad.

He shook Chief Harris's hand and tried to feel something other than numb.

"You don't look like someone who has just accomplished a lifelong goal."

Yeah, why didn't he feel more? Sure, he was proud, but even that was fleeting.

"Okay, now, sit your ass down, McBride, and tell me what the hell is wrong."

The next morning, after his shift, Liam went straight to the white, Cape Cod–style home where he'd grown up and his dad still lived with Doris. He always had mixed feelings returning here. In the beginning, it was comforting because he felt his ma's presence. But that had faded and this was now as much Doris's home as it had been Bridget McBride's.

He rang the bell and waited. The rhododendrons his ma had loved so much needed trimming, but it was too late in the season to do it now. She had taught him they needed pruning immediately after they finished blossoming or you'd be cutting off next year's flower buds. Helping her trim them one day had actually been punishment for a transgression he no longer remembered. He rubbed his chest, recalling how, that same day, she'd bought him a treat from the ice-cream truck and let him eat it before supper. She'd winked and laughed as they sat on the front steps eating their ice cream.

Doris answered the door, surprise and pleasure evident in her expression. "Liam, it's good to see you. C'mon in."

"Hi, Doris, is my dad here?" He gave Doris a quick hug and she kissed his cheek.

"Yeah, he's out back if you want to go on through the house." She stepped aside. "Can I get you anything? We've already had breakfast but I can get you coffee or a muffin."

"I'm good. Thanks. I can't stay long."

"How's Ellie doing?" Doris asked as they went through the kitchen to the back deck.

"She's doing good." Other than a cancer scare and being left to face it alone, but he wasn't about to get into all that right now. "She's looking forward to the second trimester which is supposedly much easier."

"Normally, yes, it is but I've never been pregnant with twins."

"That makes two of us."

She laughed and opened the door. "Tim? Liam's here to see you."

His dad paused in the middle of raking leaves and waved. Liam went across the deck and down the steps.

"So glad you're here. I wanted to congratulate you myself, Captain." His dad stuck out his hand and pulled him in for an awkward shoulder hug.

"You knew?" Liam asked when they pulled apart.

"I may have heard something." Mac said and grinned.

"I haven't been gone from the department for that long. I still know a few people."

"Thanks." Liam cleared his throat.

Mac frowned. "What's wrong? You don't look like a man who has just gotten what he's been working toward for years."

Liam swallowed. How was he supposed to explain how hollow he felt? Sure, he was proud of making captain but after running out on Ellie the way he had, all he could think about was how much he'd hurt her. *Selfish much, McBride?* Why was he thinking about his own pain? He should be there comforting Ellie, helping her deal with her pain. Had he thought that, if he wasn't there, he'd be able to better handle the fear?

"What's on your mind, son?" His dad leaned against the rake.

Liam explained what had happened. He hated admitting his cowardice but he couldn't hide from it any longer. "Ellie found a lump and I shut down. I'm not sure I have the kind of courage you had to open myself again to love someone I might lose."

"It's not courage." Mac shook his head.

"Then what is it?"

"It's finding something that's more important to you than your fear." Mac met Liam's gaze. "Is Ellie that important thing for you, son?"

Ellie retrieved her jacket and closed her locker with a sigh. Liam had barely been gone twenty-four hours and the pain of missing him still throbbed, an ache that wouldn't go away. He'd texted earlier in the day but had been vague when she'd asked if he was coming back today, saying he would try but had some business to take care of first.

Had she pushed him too hard? Demanded too much? She pulled the jacket on and grabbed her purse. Maybe she wanted more than Liam could give. That wasn't his fault, nor was it hers. It was just…sad.

She stretched her neck, trying to muster up some energy as she dug around in her purse for her keys. Trudging out to her car, she glanced up and stopped in her tracks. Liam was leaning against her car, arms crossed, head bowed.

"Liam?" She continued walking toward him.

His head snapped up and he blinked, searching her face. "Hey."

She stopped when she was right in front of him. "Is everything okay?"

He reached out and rested his hands on her shoulders, gently massaging them. "It is now. Have you had any news yet?"

She shook her head, not trusting her voice. The look shining in his eyes was making something inside her spring to life, something that resembled hope. Hope was dangerous. Hope made you do things, say things. Hope could be devastating, even if you were careful.

He squeezed her shoulders. "We need to talk."

Talk. Yeah, they needed to talk, but for the moment she was relieved to see him. She did her best to tamp down the hope clamoring for freedom. He might want to talk about logistics or shared custody once the babies were born.

He was peering at her expectantly. Right. She hadn't answered him. "Okay. Come back to my place?"

"I have something I want to show you first, if that's okay."

She nodded, still trying to figure out his mood.

He took her hand in his. "Let's take my truck. We can come back for your car."

"W-what did you want to show me?"

"Our future," he said as he opened the passenger door.

Her mouth dropped open and she stared at him. He put his thumb under her chin and closed her mouth before giving her a chaste kiss.

"Liam, what in the world is this all about?" She still couldn't figure out his mood. He seemed a combination of excited and apprehensive. Or maybe she was crazy. Pregnancy hormones—times two!—were making her giddy.

"I need your opinion on something." He slipped behind the wheel but turned toward her instead of starting the engine. "I need to apologize for taking off on you. I shouldn't have done that."

"And I shouldn't have accused you of abandoning me." She sucked in a breath. "I may have overreacted."

He took her hand and brought it to his lips. "I should have explained myself better. I regret how I handled things with my mom, and yet I was doing the same thing with you."

"I know of a good support group for grieving families, if you're interested." She squeezed his hand. "Maybe we could both benefit from it, but first, I have to see what you want to show me."

He dropped her hand and started the truck. Although he didn't say anything else, he glanced at her several times as he drove across town. Clearing his throat, he made the turn into the Coopers' long driveway.

"Why are you taking me to your sister's house?"

"Meg's isn't the only house here." Liam pulled his truck up to the cottage-style home across the yard from his sister's house. Putting his truck in Park, he shut off the engine. Jumping out of the pickup, he hustled around to her side.

"Careful," he said as he helped her out. "This would have been better in the daylight but I couldn't wait until tomorrow."

She stared up at him, puzzled. "I don't understand what we're doing here."

He ran his finger under the collar of his jacket. "Like I said… I was picturing our future."

Her heart stuttered, then pounded so hard she was surprised it didn't jump out of her chest. She glanced down, expecting to see it flopping like a fish on the ground.

He made a sweeping motion with his hand to encompass the large, open yard between this house and his sister's. "I see kids—our kids and their cousins—running around this yard. Maybe even a dog of our own chasing after them. Baseball games, touch football, along with some hot dogs and burgers on the grill in the summer."

He turned so he was standing in front of her and took both her hands in his and cleared his throat. "I love you, Ellie Harding. No matter what. Now and forever. In sickness and in health. Will you marry me and live here with me?"

Her mouth opened and closed like that fish she'd been imagining a few moments ago. "But…but what about your job? Your house in Boston?"

"When Chief Harris called me in to tell me I'd made captain, we—"

"Wait…what?" She took her hand out of his and jabbed him in the shoulder. "You made captain and are just now telling me?"

He shrugged. "It wasn't important."

"How can you say that? Of course that's important."

"Not as important to me as you and our babies. This right here, with you, is what I want. Chief Harris is always asking me when I was going to sell him my three-decker and yesterday I told him to make me an offer. I tracked down the owner of this one and he's willing to sell. So whaddaya say, should we make an offer on this place?"

Overcome with emotion that her dreams were coming true, all she could do was shake her head and choke back a sob. All the color drained from Liam's face and she realized he'd misunderstood. She threw herself at him and began blubbering incoherently.

He held her and rubbed her back. Finally she raised her head. "I love you, too," she choked out.

He grinned, his eyes suspiciously shiny. "So, that's a yes?"

She nodded vigorously.

"Wait…" He set her away from him. "I was supposed to do this first."

He reached into his pocket and pulled out a ring. "It was my mother's. My dad gave it to me today. Will you marry me?"

"Yes."

He slipped the ring on her finger and kissed her. She pulled away first.

"I haven't gotten the all clear yet on the biopsy," she warned.

"And I don't have another job yet," He brushed the hair back from her face and dried her damp cheeks. "We'll work out all the details."

"McBride, are you telling me I just accepted a proposal of marriage from someone who is unemployed?"

"You're not going to let a little thing like that stop you, are you?" He frowned, then laughed. "I'm still employed and will have to divide my time for now. While I was waiting for you to get off work, my dad called to let me know the state fire investigator's office here in Vermont was looking for someone."

"Would that kind of work make you happy?"

He pressed his hand against her stomach. "I have all I need right here with you and these guys to make me happy."

"What if I don't get good news from the biopsy?"

"Then we'd deal with it together. I'm not going anywhere. Ellie. You've got the entire McBride clan with you, for whatever comes along."

Epilogue

Six months later

"Hey, bud, you didn't have to make this a competition to see if you could get here before your sister or your cousin," Liam whispered to his newborn son, Sean, who was staring up at him. He turned to the similar bundle cradled close on his other side. "And you, Miss Bridget, you'll be keeping all the boys in line, won't you?"

His newborn daughter twitched in her sleep and Liam leaned down to press a kiss to the top of her head. He glanced up at Ellie, his precious wife, who, despite the mad dash to the hospital several weeks early, lay smiling at him.

"You done good, Harding," he said, blinking back a sudden burning in the back of his eyes. "Or should I say 'McBride'? You're one of us now, Ellie."

"You didn't do so bad yourself, McBride," she whispered and sniffled, her lips quivering.

He swallowed and his smile faltered as he adjusted his precious bundles in his arms. "I hope both of you heard that, because it might be the last time she says something like that."

Ellie wiggled her feet under the covers. "Meg is going to be so jealous I can finally see my feet."

Liam shook his head and glanced down at his son. "Looks like the women in this family are just as competitive."

"At least now I can put on my own shoes." Ellie yawned and lay back against the covers. "Good thing you and Riley finished the nursery."

Liam nodded in agreement. The last few months had been hectic, what with a wedding, selling one house and buying another, and starting his new job as a state fire investigator. But he wouldn't have traded one minute of it for anything. Even having to wait for Ellie's biopsy results had been worth the nerves. And the celebration when the all clear came back had been—he grinned at the babies in his arms—best kept private.

"What are you grinning about over there?"

He shifted the babies and stood up. "I was thinking how lucky I am and how I can't wait to start this phase of our lives."

She lifted an eyebrow. "This phase?"

Coming to stand next to the bed, he gently lowered their son into Ellie's waiting arms. "Changing diapers, chasing rug rats around the yard, drying tears and retrieving Barbies from toilets."

Ellie yawned again as she cuddled her son. "I guess I better rest up. Sounds like I'm going to be busy."

Liam leaned over and kissed his wife. "I was talking about us. Ellie, we're in this together. For today and always. No matter what the future brings it's you and me together, sharing everything. Partners."

"Intimate partners," she said and laughed.

As always, her laughter drew him close and filled his heart and world with love.

* * * * *

Melissa Senate has written many novels for Harlequin and other publishers, including her debut, *See Jane Date*, which was made into a TV movie. She also wrote seven books for Harlequin's Special Edition line under the pen name Meg Maxwell. Her novels have been published in over twenty-five countries. Melissa lives on the coast of Maine with her teenage son; their rescue shepherd mix, Flash; and a lap cat named Cleo. For more information, please visit her website, melissasenate.com.

Books by Melissa Senate

Harlequin Special Edition

Dawson Family Ranch

For the Twins' Sake

The Wyoming Multiples

The Baby Switch!
Detective Barelli's Legendary Triplets
Wyoming Christmas Surprise
To Keep Her Baby
A Promise for the Twins

Furever Yours

A New Leash on Love

Visit the Author Profile page at Harlequin.com for more titles.

Detective Barelli's Legendary Triplets

MELISSA SENATE

Dedicated to my darling Max.

Chapter 1

The first thing Norah Ingalls noticed when she woke up Sunday morning was the gold wedding band on her left hand.

Norah was not married. Had never been married. She was as single as single got. With seven-month-old triplets.

The second thing was the foggy headache pressing at her temples.

The third thing was the very good-looking stranger lying next to her.

A memory poked at her before panic could even bother setting in. Norah lay very still, her heart just beginning to pound, and looked over at him. He had short, thick, dark hair and a hint of five-o'clock shadow along his jawline. A scar above his left eyebrow. He was on his back, her blue-and-white quilt half covering him down by his belly button. An innie. He had an impressive six-pack. Very little chest hair. His biceps and triceps were something to behold. The man clearly worked out. Or was a rancher.

Norah bolted upright. Oh God. Oh God. Oh God. He wasn't a rancher. He was a secret service agent! She remembered now. Yes. They'd met at the Wedlock Creek Founder's Day carnival last night and—

And had said no real names, no real stories, no real anything. A fantasy for the night. That had been her idea. She'd insisted, actually.

The man in her bed was not a secret service agent. She had no idea who or what he was.

She swallowed against the lump in her parched throat.

She squeezed her eyes shut. What happened? *Think, Norah!*

There'd been lots of orange punch. And giggling, when Norah was not a giggler. The man had said something about how the punch must be spiked.

Norah bit her lower lip hard and looked for the man's left hand. It was under the quilt. Her grandmother's hand-me-down quilt.

She sucked in a breath and peeled back the quilt enough to reveal his hand. The same gold band glinted on his ring finger.

As flashes of memories from the night before started shoving into her aching head, Norah eased back down, lay very still and hoped the man wouldn't wake before she remembered how she'd ended up married to a total stranger. The fireworks display had started behind the Wedlock Creek chapel and everything between her and the man had exploded, too. Norah closed her eyes and let it all come flooding back.

A silent tester burst of the fireworks display, red and white just visible through the treetops, started when she and Fabio were on their tenth cup of punch at the carnival. The big silver punch bowl had been on an unmanned table near the food booths. Next to the stack of plastic cups was a lockbox with a slot and a sign atop it: Two Dollars A Cup/Honor System. Fabio had put a hundred-dollar bill in the box and taken the bowl and their cups under a maple tree, where they'd been sitting for the past half hour, enjoying their punch and talking utter nonsense.

Not an hour earlier Norah's mother and aunt Cheyenne had insisted she go enjoy the carnival and that they'd babysit the triplets. She'd had a corn dog, won a little stuffed dolphin in a balloon-dart game, which she'd promptly lost somewhere, and then had met the very handsome newcomer to town at the punch table.

"Punch?" he'd said, handing her a cup and putting a five-dollar bill in the box. He'd then ladled himself a cup.

She drank it down. Delicious. She put five dollars in herself and ladled them both two more cups.

"Never seen you before," she said, daring a glance up and down his six-foot-plus frame. Muscular and lanky at the same time. Navy Henley and worn jeans and cowboy boots. Silky, dark hair and dark eyes. She could look, but she'd never touch. No sirree.

He extended his hand. "I'm—"

She held up her own, palm facing him. "Nope. No real names. No real stories." She was on her own tonight, rarely had a moment to herself, and if she was going to talk to a man, a handsome, sexy, no-ring-on-his-finger man—something she'd avoided since becoming a mother—a little fantasy was in order. Norah didn't date and had zero interest in romance. Her mother, aunt and sister always shook their heads at that and tried to remind her that her faith in love, and maybe herself, had been shaken, that was all, and she'd come around. That was all? Ha. She was done with men with a capital *D*.

He smiled, his dark brown eyes crinkling at the corners. Early thirties, she thought. And handsome as sin. "In that case, I'm… Fabio. A…secret service agent. That's right. Fabio the secret service agent. Protecting the fresh air here in Wedlock Creek."

She giggled for way too long at that one. Jeez, was there something in the punch? Had to be. When was the last time she'd giggled? "Kind of casually dressed for a Fed," she pointed out, admiring his scuffed brown boots.

"Gotta blend," he said, waving his arm at the throngs of people out enjoying the carnival.

"Ah, that makes sense. Well, I'm Angelina, international flight attendant." Where had *that* come from? Angelina had a sexy ring to it, she thought. She picked up a limp fry from the plate he'd gotten from the burger booth across the field. She dabbed it in the ketchup on the side and dangled it in her mouth.

"You manage to make that sexy," he said with a grin.

Norah Ingalls, single mother of drooling, teething triplets, sexy? LOL. Ha. That was a scream. She giggled again and he tipped up her face and looked into her eyes.

Kiss me, you fool, she thought. *You Fabio. You secret*

service agent. But his gaze was soft on her, not full of lascivious intent. Darn.

That was when he suggested they sit, gestured at the maple tree, then put the hundred in the lockbox and took the bowl over to their spot. She carried their cups.

"Have more punch," she said, ladling him a cup. And another. And another. He told her stories from his childhood, mostly about an old falling-down ranch on a hundred acres, but she wasn't sure what was true and what wasn't. She told him about her dad, who'd been her biggest champion. She told him the secret recipe for her mother's chicken pot pie, which was so renowned in Wedlock Creek and surrounding towns that the *Gazette* had done an article on her family's pie diner. She told him everything but the most vital truth about herself.

Tonight, Norah was a woman out having fun at the annual carnival, allowing herself for just pumpkin-hours to bask in the attention of a good-looking, sexy man who was sweet and smart and funny as hell. At midnight—well, 11:00 p.m. when the carnival closed— she'd turn back into herself. A woman who didn't talk to hot, single men.

"What do you think the punch is spiked with?" she asked as he fed her a cold french fry and poured her another cup.

He ran two fingers gently down the side of her cheek. "I don't know, but it sure is nice to forget myself, just for a night when I'm not on duty."

Duty? *Oh, right*, she thought. He was a secret service agent. She giggled, then sobered for a second, a poke of real life jabbing at her from somewhere.

Now the first booms of the fireworks were coming

fast and there were cheers and claps in the distance, but they couldn't see the show from their spot.

"Let's go see!" she said, taking his hand to pull him up.

But Fabio's expression had changed. He seemed lost in thought, far away.

"Fabio?" she asked, trying to think through the haze. "You okay?"

He downed another cup of punch. "Those were fireworks," he said, color coming back into his face. "Not gunfire."

She laughed. "Gunfire? In Wedlock Creek? There's no hunting within town limits because of the tourism and there hasn't been a murder in over seventy years. Plus, if you crane your neck, you can see a bit of the fireworks past the trees."

He craned that beautiful neck, his shoulder leaning against hers. "Okay. Let's go see."

They walked hand in hand to the chapel, but by the time they got there—a few missed turns on the path due to their tipsiness—the fireworks display was over. The small group setting them off had already left the dock, folks clearing away back to the festival.

The Wedlock Creek chapel was all lit up, the river behind it illuminated by the glow of the almost full moon.

"I always dreamed of getting married here," she said, gazing up at the beautiful white-clapboard building, which looked a bit like a wedding cake. It had a vintage Victorian look with scallops on the upper tiers and a bell at the top that almost looked like a heart. According to town legend, those who married here would—whether through marriage, adoption, luck, science or happenstance—be blessed with multiples: twins or triplets or even quadruplets. So far, no quintuplets. The town and county was packed with multiples of those who'd gotten married at the chapel, proof the legend was true.

For some people, like Norah, you could have triplets and not have stepped foot in the chapel. Back when she'd first found out she was pregnant, before she'd told the baby's father, she'd fantasized about getting married at the chapel, that maybe they'd get lucky and have multiples even if it was "after the fact." One baby would be blessing enough. Two, three, even four—Norah loved babies and had always wanted a houseful. But the guy who'd gotten her pregnant, in town on the rodeo circuit, had said, "Sorry, I didn't sign up for that," and left town before his next event. She'd never seen him again.

She stared at the chapel, so pretty in the moonlight, real life jabbing her in the heart again. *Where is that punch bowl?* she wondered.

"You always wanted to marry here? Then let's get married," Fabio said, scooping her up and carrying her into the chapel.

Her laughter floated on the summer evening breeze. "But we're three sheets to the wind, as my daddy used to say."

"That's the only way I'd get hitched," he said, slurring the words.

"Lead the way, cowboy." She let her head drop back.

Annie Potterowski, the elderly chapel caretaker, local lore lecturer and wedding officiant, poked her head out of the back room. She stared at Norah for a moment, then her gaze moved up to Fabio's handsome face. "Ah, Detective Barelli! Nice to see you again."

"You know Fabio?" Norah asked, confused. Or was his first name really Detective?

"I ran into the chief when he was showing Detective Barelli around town," Annie said. "The chief's my second cousin on my mother's side."

Say that five times fast, Norah thought, her head beginning to spin.

And Annie knew her fantasy man. Her fantasy groom! *Isn't that something*, Norah thought, her mind going in ten directions. Suddenly the faces of her triplets pushed into the forefront of her brain and she frowned. Her babies! She should be getting home. Except she felt so good in his arms, being carried like she was someone's love, someone's bride-to-be.

Annie's husband, Abe, came out, his blue bow tie a bit crooked. He straightened it. "We've married sixteen couples tonight. One pair came as far as Texas to get hitched here."

"We're here to be the seventeenth," Fabio said, his arm heavy around Norah's.

"Aren't you a saint!" Annie said, beaming at him. "Oh, Norah, I'm so happy for you."

Saint Fabio, Norah thought and burst into laughter. "Want to know a secret?" Norah whispered into her impending husband's ear as he set her on the red velvet carpet that created an aisle to the altar.

"Yes," he said.

"My name isn't really Angelina. It's Norah. With an *h*."

He smiled. "Mine's not Fabio. It's Reed. Two *e*'s." He staggered a bit.

The man was as tipsy as she was.

"I never thought I'd marry a secret service agent,"

she said as they headed down the aisle to the "Wedding March."

"And we could use all your frequent flyer miles for our honeymoon," Reed added, and they burst into laughter.

"Sign here, folks," Annie said as they stood at the altar. The woman pointed to the marriage license. Norah signed, then Reed, and Annie folded it up and put it in an addressed, stamped envelope.

I'm getting married! Norah thought, gazing into Reed's dark eyes as he stood across from her, holding her hands. She glanced down at herself, confused by her shorts and blue-and-white T-shirt. Where was her strapless, lace, princess gown with the beading and sweetheart neckline she'd fantasized about from watching *Say Yes to the Dress*? And should she be getting married in her beat-up slip-on sneakers? They were hardly white anymore.

But there was no time to change. Nope. Annie was already asking Reed to repeat his vows and she wanted to pay attention.

"Do you, Reed Barelli, take this woman, Norah Ingalls, to be your lawfully wedded wife, for richer and for poorer, in sickness and in health, till death do you part?"

"I most certainly do," he said, then hooted in laughter.

Norah cracked up, too. Reed had the most marvelous laugh.

Annie turned to Norah. She repeated her vows. Yes, God, yes, she took this man to be her lawfully wedded husband.

"By the power vested in me by the State of Wyoming, I now pronounce you husband and wife! You may kiss your bride."

Reed stared at Norah for a moment, then put his hands on either side of her face and kissed her, so tenderly, yet passionately, that for a second, Norah's mind cleared completely and all she felt was his love. Her new husband of five seconds, whom she'd known for about two hours, truly loved her!

Warmth flooded her, and when rice, which she realized Abe was throwing, rained down on them, she giggled, drunk as a skunk.

Reed Barelli registered his headache before he opened his eyes, the morning sun shining through the sheer white curtains at the window. Were those embroidered flowers? he wondered as he rubbed his aching temples. Reed had bought a bunch of stuff for his new house yesterday afternoon—everything from down pillows to coffee mugs to a coffee maker itself, but he couldn't remember those frilly curtains. They weren't something he'd buy for his place.

He fully opened his eyes, his gaze landing on a stack of books on the bedside table. A mystery. A travel guide to Wyoming. And *Your Baby's First Year.*

Your Baby's First Year? Huh?

Wait a minute. He bolted up. Where the hell was he? This wasn't the house he'd rented.

He heard a soft sigh come from beside him and turned to the left, eyes widening.

Holy hell. There was a woman sleeping in his bed.

More like he was in *her* bed, from the looks of the place. He moved her long reddish-brown hair out of her face and closed his eyes. Oh Lord. Oh no. It was her—

Angelina slash Norah. Last night he'd given in to her game of fantasy, glad for a night to eradicate his years as a Cheyenne cop.

He blinked twice to clear his head. He wasn't a Cheyenne cop anymore. His last case had done him in and, after a three-week leave, he'd made up his mind and gotten himself a job as a detective in Wedlock Creek, the idyllic town where he'd spent several summers as a kid with his maternal grandmother. A town where it seemed nothing could go wrong. A town that hadn't seen a murder in over seventy years. Hadn't Norah mentioned that last night?

Norah. Last night.

He lifted his hand to scrub over his face and that was when he saw it—the gold ring on his left hand. Ring finger. A ring that hadn't been there before he'd gone to the carnival.

What the…?

Slowly, bits and pieces of the evening came back to him. The festival. A punch bowl he'd commandeered into the clearing under a big tree so he and Norah could have the rest of it all to themselves. A clearly heavily *spiked* punch bowl. A hundred-dollar bill in the till, not to mention at least sixty in cash. Norah, taking his hand and leading him to the chapel.

She'd always dreamed of getting married, she'd said.

And he'd said, "Then let's get married."

He'd said that! Reed Barelli had uttered those words!

He held his breath and gently peeled the blue-and-white quilt from her shoulder to look at her left hand—which she used to yank the quilt back up, wrinkling her cute nose and turning over.

There was a gold band on her finger, too.

Holy moly. They'd really done it. They'd gotten married?

No. Couldn't be. The officiant of the chapel had called him by name. Yes, the elderly woman had known him, said she'd seen the chief showing him around town yesterday when he'd arrived. And she'd seemed familiar with Norah, too. She knew both of them. She wouldn't let them drunk-marry! That was the height of irresponsible. And as a man of the law, he would demand she explain herself and simply undo whatever it was they'd signed. Dimly, he recalled the marriage license, scrawling his name with a blue pen.

Norah stirred. She was still asleep. For a second he couldn't help but stare at her pretty face. She had a pale complexion, delicate features and hazel eyes, if he remembered correctly.

If they'd made love, *that* he couldn't remember. And he would remember, drunk to high heaven or not. What had been in that punch?

Maybe they'd come back to her place and passed out in bed?

He closed his eyes again and slowly opened them. *Deep breaths, Barelli.* He looked around the bedroom to orient himself, ground himself.

And that was when he saw the framed photograph on the end table on Norah's side. Norah in a hospital bed, in one of those thin blue gowns, holding three newborns against her chest.

Ooh boy.

Chapter 2

"I'm sure we're not really married!" Norah said on a high-pitched squeak, the top sheet wrapped around her as she stood—completely freaked out—against the wall of her bedroom, staring at the strange man in her bed.

A man who, according to the wedding ring on her left hand—and the one on his—*was* her husband.

She'd pretended to be asleep when he'd first started stirring. He'd bolted upright and she could feel him staring at her. She couldn't just lie there and pretend to be asleep any longer, even if she was afraid to open her eyes and face the music.

But a thought burst into her brain and she'd sat up, too: she'd forgotten to pick up the triplets. As her aunt's words had come back to her, that Cheyenne didn't expect her to pick up the babies last night, that she'd take them to the diner this morning, Norah had calmed down. And slowly had opened her eyes. The sight of the stranger awake and staring at her had her leaping out of bed, taking the sheet with her. She was in a camisole and underwear.

Oh God, had they…?

She stared at Reed. In her bed. "Did we?" she croaked out.

He half shrugged. "I don't know. Sorry. I don't think so, though."

"The punch was spiked?"

"Someone's idea of a joke, maybe."

"And now we're married," she said. "Ha ha."

His gaze went to the band of gold on his finger, then back at her. "I'm sure we can undo that. The couple who married us—they seemed to know both of us. Why would they have let us get married when we were so drunk?"

Now it was her turn to shrug. She'd known Annie since she was born. The woman had waitressed on and off at her family's pie diner for years to make extra cash. How could she have let Norah do such a thing? Why hadn't Annie called her mother or aunt or sister and said, *Come get Norah, she's drunk off her butt and trying to marry a total stranger*? It made no sense that Annie hadn't done just that!

"She seemed to know you, too," Norah said, wishing she had a cup of coffee. And two Tylenol.

"I spent summers in Wedlock Creek with my grandmother when I was a kid," he said. "Annie may have known my grandmother. Do the Potterowskis live near the chapel? Maybe we can head over now and get this straightened out. I'm sure Annie hasn't sent in the marriage license yet."

"Right!" Norah said, brightening, tightening the sheet around her. "We can undo this! Let's go!"

He glanced at his pile of clothes on the floor beside the bed. "I'll go into the bathroom and get dressed." He stood, wearing nothing but incredibly sexy black boxer briefs. He picked up the pile and booked into the bathroom, shutting the door.

She heard the water run, then shut off. A few minutes later the door opened and there he was, dressed like Fabio from last night.

She rushed over to her dresser, grabbed jeans and a T-shirt and fresh underwear, then sped past him into the bathroom, her heart beating like a bullet train. She quickly washed her face and brushed her teeth, got dressed and stepped back outside.

Reed was sitting in the chair in the corner, his elbows on his knees, his head in his hands. How could he look so handsome when he was so rumpled, his hair all mussed? He was slowly shaking his head as if trying to make sense of this.

"So you always wanted to be a secret service agent?" she asked to break the awkward silence.

He sat up and offered something of a smile. "I have no idea why I said that. I've always wanted to be a cop. I start at the Wedlock Creek PD on Monday. Guess you're not a flight attendant," he added.

"I've never been out of Wyoming," she said. "I bake for my family's pie diner." That was all she'd ever wanted to do. Work for the family business and perfect her savory pies, her specialty.

The diner had her thinking of real life again, Bella's, Bea's and Brody's beautiful little faces coming to mind. She missed them and needed to see them, needed to hold them. And she had to get to the diner and let her family know she was all right. She hadn't called once to check in on the triplets last night. Her mom and aunt had probably mentioned that every hour on the hour. *No call from Norah? Huh. Must be having a good time.* Then looking at each other and saying *Not* in unison, bursting into laughter and sobering up fast, wondering what could have happened to her to prevent her from calling every other minute to make sure all was well with the babies.

Her phone hadn't rung last night, so maybe they'd just thought she'd met up with old friends and was having fun. She glanced at her alarm clock on the bedside table. It was barely six o'clock. She wouldn't be expected at the diner until seven.

Reed was looking at the photo next to the clock. The one of her and her triplets taken moments after they were born. He didn't say a word, but she knew what he was thinking. Anyone would. *Help me. Get me out of this. What the hell have I done? Triplets? Ahhhhh!* She was surprised he didn't have his hands on his screaming face like the kid from the movie *Home Alone.*

Well, one thing Norah Ingalls was good at? Taking care of business. "Let's go see Annie and Abe," she said. "They wake up at the crack of dawn, so I'm sure they'll be up."

His gaze snapped back to hers. "Good idea. We can catch them before they send the marriage license into the state bureau for processing."

"Right. It's not like we're really married. I mean, it's not *legal.*"

He nodded. "We could undo this before 7:00 a.m. and get back to our lives," he said.

This was definitely not her life.

* * *

Norah poked her head out the front door of her house, which, thank heavens, was blocked on both sides by big leafy trees. The last thing she needed was for all of Wedlock Creek to know a man had been spotted leaving her house at six in the morning. Norah lived around the corner from Main Street and just a few minutes' walk to the diner, but the chapel was a good half mile in the other direction.

"Let's take the parallel road so no one sees us," she said. "I'm sure you don't want to be the center of gossip before you even start your first day at the police station."

"I definitely don't," he said.

They ducked down a side street with backyards to the left and the woods and river to the right. At this early hour, no one was out yet. The Potterowskis lived in the caretaker's cottage to the right of the chapel. Norah dashed up the steps to the side door and could see eighty-one-year-old Annie in a long, pink chenille bathrobe, sitting down with tea and toast. She rang the bell.

Annie came to the door and beamed at the newlyweds. "Norah! Didn't expect to see you out and about so early. Shouldn't you be on your honeymoon?" Annie peered behind Norah and spied Reed. "Ah, there you are, handsome devil. Come on in, you two. I just made a pot of coffee."

How could the woman be so calm? Or act like their getting married was no big deal?

Norah and Reed came in but didn't sit. "Annie," Norah said, "the two of us were the victims of spiked punch at the festival last night! We were drunk out of our minds. You had to know that!"

Annie tilted her head, her short, wiry, silver curls bouncing. "Drunk? Why, I don't recall seeing you two acting all nutty and, trust me, we get our share of drunk couples and turn them away."

Norah narrowed her eyes. There was no way Annie hadn't known she was drunk out of her mind! "Annie, why would I up and marry a total stranger out of the blue? Didn't that seem weird?"

"But Reed isn't a stranger," Annie said, sipping her coffee. "I heard he was back in town to work at the PD." She turned to him. "I remember you when you were a boy. I knew your grandmother Lydia Barelli. We were dear friends from way back. Oh, how I remember her hoping you'd come live in Wedlock Creek. I suppose now you'll move to the ranch like she always dreamed."

Reed raised an eyebrow. "I've rented a house right in town. I loved my grandmother dearly, but she was trying to bribe me into getting married and starting a family. I had her number, all right." He smiled at Annie, but his chin was lifted. The detective was clearly assessing the situation.

Annie waved her hand dismissively. "Well, bribe or not, you're married. Your dear grandmother's last will and testament leaves you the ranch when you marry. So now you can take your rightful inheritance."

Norah glanced from Annie to Reed. What was all this about a ranch and an inheritance? If Reed had intended to find some drunk fool to marry to satisfy the terms and get his ranch, why would he have rented a house his first day in town?

The detective crossed his arms over his chest. "I have no intention of moving to the ranch, Annie."

"Oh, hogwash!" Annie said, waving her piece of

toast. "You're married and that's it. You should move to the ranch like your grandmamma intended, and poor Norah here will have a father for the triplets."

Good golly. Watch out for little old ladies with secret agendas. Annie Potterowski had hoodwinked them both!

Norah watched Reed swallow. And felt her cheeks burn.

"Annie," Norah said, hands on hips. "You did know we were drunk! You let us marry anyway!"

"For your own good," Annie said. "Both of you. But I didn't lure you two here. I didn't spike the punch. You came in here of your own free will. I just didn't stop you."

"Can't you arrest her for this?" Norah said to Reed, narrowing her eyes at Annie again.

Annie's eyes widened. "I hope you get a chance to leave town and go somewhere exotic for your honeymoon," she said, clearly trying to change the subject from her subterfuge. "New York City maybe. Or how about Paris? It's so romantic."

Norah threw up her hands. "She actually thinks this is reasonable!"

"Annie, come on," Reed said. "We're not *really* married. A little too much spiked punch, a wedding chapel right in our path, no waiting period required—a recipe for disaster and we walked right into it. We're here to get back the marriage license. Surely you haven't sent it in."

"We'll just rip it up and be on our way," Norah said, glancing at her watch.

"Oh dear. I'm sorry, but that's impossible," Annie said. "I sent Abe to the county courthouse in Brewer about twenty minutes ago. I'm afraid your marriage license—and the sixteen others from yesterday—are well on their way to being deposited. There's a mail slot right in front of the building. Of course, it's Sunday and they're closed, so I reckon you won't be able to drive over to try to get it back."

Reed was staring at Annie with total confusion on his face. "Well, we'll have to do something at some point."

"Yeah," Norah agreed, her head spinning. Between all the spiked punch and the surprise this morning of the wedding rings, and now what appeared to be this crazy scheme of Annie's to not undo what she'd allowed to happen...

"I need coffee," Reed said, shaking his head. "A vat of coffee."

Norah nodded. "Me, too."

"Help yourself," Annie said, gesturing at the coffeepot on the counter as she took a bite of her toast.

Reed sighed and turned to Norah. "Let's go back to your house and talk this through. We need to make a plan for how to undo this."

Norah nodded. "See you, Annie," she said as she headed to the door, despite how completely furious she was with the woman. She'd known Annie all her life and the woman had been nothing but kind to her. Annie had even brought each triplet an adorable stuffed basset hound, her favorite dog, when they'd been born, and had showered them with little gifts ever since.

"Oh, Norah? Reed?" Annie called as they opened the door and stepped onto the porch.

Norah turned back around.

"Congratulations," the elderly officiant said with a sheepish smile and absolute mirth glowing in her eyes.

* * *

Reed had been so fired up when he'd left Norah's house for the chapel that he hadn't realized how chilly it was this morning, barely fifty-five degrees. He glanced over at Norah; all she wore was a T-shirt and her hands were jammed in her pockets as she hunched over a bit. She was cold. He took off his jacket and slipped it around Norah's shoulders.

She started and stared down at the jacket. "Thank you," she said, slipping her arms into it and zipping it up. "I was so out of my mind before, I forgot to grab a sweater." She turned to stare at him. "Of course, now you'll be cold."

"My aching head will keep me warm," he said. "And I deserve the headache—the literal and figurative one."

"We both do," she said gently.

The breeze moved a swath of her hair in her face, the sun illuminating the red and gold highlights, and he had the urge to sweep it back, but she quickly tucked it behind her ear. "I'm a cop. It's my job to serve and protect. I had no business getting drunk, particularly at a town event."

"Well, the punch was spiked with something very strong. And you weren't on duty," she pointed out. "You're not even on the force till tomorrow."

"Still, a cop is always a cop. Unfortunately, by the time I realized the punch had to be spiked, I was too affected by it to care." He wouldn't put himself in a position like that again. Leaving Cheyenne, saying yes to Wedlock Creek—even though it meant he couldn't live in his grandmother's ranch—trying to switch off the city cop he'd been… He'd let down his guard and he'd paid for it with this crazy nonsense. So had Norah.

Damn. Back in Cheyenne, his guard had been so up he'd practically gotten himself killed during a botched stakeout. Where the hell was the happy medium? Maybe he'd never get a handle on *just right*.

"And you said you were glad to forget? Or something like that?" she asked, darting a glance at him.

He looked out over a stand of heavy trees along the side of the road. *Let it go*, he reminded himself. No rehashing, no what-ifs. "I'm here for a fresh start. Now I need a fresh start to my fresh start." He stopped and shook his head. What a mess. "Sixteen couples besides us?" he said, resuming walking. "It's a little too easy to get married in the state of Wyoming."

"Someone should change the law," Norah said. "There should be a waiting period. Blood tests required. Something, anything, so you can't get insta-married."

That was for sure. "It's like a mini Las Vegas. I wonder how many of those couples meant to get married."

"Oh, I'm sure all of them. The Wedlock Creek Wedding Chapel is famous. People come here because of the legend."

He glanced at her. "What legend?"

"Just about everyone who marries at the chapel becomes the parent of multiples in some way, shape or form. According to legend, the chapel has a special blessing on it. A barren witch cast the spell the year the chapel was built in 1895."

Reed raised an eyebrow. "A barren witch? Was she trying to be nice or up to no good?"

"No one's sure," she said with a smile. "But as the mother of triplets, I'm glad I have them."

Reed stopped walking.

She'd said it. It was absolutely true. She was the

mother of *triplets*. No wonder Annie Potterowski had called him a saint last night. The elderly woman had thought he was knowingly marrying a single mother of three babies! "So you got married at the chapel?" He supposed she was divorced, though that must have been one quick marriage.

She glanced down. "No. I never did get married. The babies' father ran for the hills about an hour after I told him the news. We'd been dating for only about three months at that point. I thought we had something special, but I sure was wrong."

Her voice hitched on the word *wrong* and he took her hand. "I'm sorry." The jerk had abandoned her? She was raising baby triplets on her own? One baby seemed like a handful. Norah had three. He couldn't even imagine how hard that had to be.

She bit her lip and forced a half smile, slipping her hand away and into her pocket. "Oh, that's all right. I have my children, who I love to pieces. I have a great family, work I love. My life is good. No complaints."

"Still, your life can't be easy."

She raised an eyebrow. "Whose is? Yours?"

He laughed. "Touché. And I don't even have a pet. Or a plant for that matter."

She smiled and he was glad to see the shadow leave her eyes. "So, what's our plan for getting back our marriage license? I guess we can just drive out to Brewer first thing in the morning and ask for it back. If we get to the courthouse early and spring on them the minute they open, I'm sure we'll get the license back before it's processed."

"Sounds good," he said.

"And if we can't get it back for whatever reason, we'll just have the marriage annulled."

"Like it never happened," he said.

"Exactly," she said with a nod and smile.

Except it had happened and Reed had a feeling he wouldn't shake it off so easily, even with an annulment and the passage of time. The pair of them had gotten themselves into a real pickle as his grandmother used to say.

"So I guess this means you really didn't secretly marry me to get your hands on your grandmother's ranch," Norah said. "Between renting a house the minute you moved here yesterday and talking about annulments, that's crystal clear."

He thought about telling her why he didn't believe in marriage but just nodded instead. Last night, as he'd picked her up and carried her into that chapel, he'd been a man—Fabio the secret service agent—who *did* believe in marriage, who wanted a wife and a house full of kids. He'd liked being that guy. Of course, with the light of day and the headache and stone-cold reality, he was back to Reed Barelli, who'd seen close up that marriage wasn't for him.

Reed envisioned living alone forever, a couple of dogs to keep him company, short-term relationships with women who understood from the get-go that he wasn't looking for commitment. He'd thought the last woman he'd dated—a funny, pretty woman named Valerie was on the same page, but a few weeks into their relationship, she'd wanted more and he hadn't, and it was a mess. Crying, accusations and him saying over and over *But I told you on the first date how I felt*. That was six months ago and he hadn't dated since. He missed sex like crazy, but he wasn't interested in hurting anyone.

They walked in silence, Norah gesturing that they should cross Main Street. As they headed down Norah's street, Sycamore, he realized they'd made their plan and there was really no need for that coffee, after all. He'd walk her home and then—

"Norah! You're alive!"

Reed glanced in the direction of the voice. A young blond woman stood in front of Norah's small, white Cape Cod house, one hand waving at them and one on a stroller with three little faces peering out.

Three. Little. Faces.

Had a two-by-four come out of nowhere and whammed him upside the head?

Just about everyone who marries at the chapel becomes the parent of multiples in some way, shape or form.

Because he'd just realized that the legend of the Wedlock Creek chapel had come true for him.

Chapter 3

Norah was so relieved to see the babies that she rushed over to the porch—forgetting to shove her hand into her pocket and hide the ring that hadn't been on her finger yesterday.

And her sister, Shelby, wasn't one to miss a thing. Shelby's gaze shifted from the ring on Norah's hand to Reed and his own adorned left hand, then back to Norah. "I dropped by the diner this morning with a Greek quiche I developed last night, and Aunt Cheyenne and Mom said they hadn't heard from you. So I figured I'd walk the triplets over and make sure you were all right." She'd said it all so casually, but her gaze darted hard from the ring on Norah's hand to Norah, then back again. And again. Her sister was dying for info. That was clear.

"I'm all right," Norah said. "Everything is a little

topsy-turvy, but I'm fine." She bent over and faced the stroller. "I missed you little darlings." She hadn't spent a night away from her children since they were born.

Shelby gave her throat a little faux clear. "I notice you and this gentleman are wearing matching gold wedding bands and taking walks at 6:30 a.m." Shelby slid her gaze over to Reed and then stared at Norah with her "tell me everything this instant" expression.

Norah straightened and sucked in a deep breath. Thank God her sister was here, actually. Shelby was practical and smart and would have words of wisdom.

"Reed Barelli," Norah said, "this is my sister, Shelby Mercer. Shelby, be the first to meet my accidental husband, Detective Reed Barelli of the Wedlock Creek PD...well, starting tomorrow."

Shelby's green eyes went even wider. She mouthed *What?* to Norah and then said, "Detective, would you mind keeping an eye on the triplets while my sister and I have a little chat?"

Reed eyed the stroller. "Not at all," he said, approaching warily.

Norah opened the door and Shelby pulled her inside. The moment the door closed, Shelby screeched, *"What?"*

Norah covered her face with her hands for a second, shook her head, then launched into the story. "I went to the carnival on Mom and Aunt Cheyenne's orders. The last thing I remember clearly is having a corn dog and winning a stuffed dolphin, which I lost. Then it's just flashes of the night. Reed and I drinking spiked punch—the entire bowl—and going to the chapel and getting married."

"Oh, phew," Shelby said, relief crossing her face.

"I thought maybe you flew to Las Vegas or something crazy. There's no way Annie or Abe would have let you get drunk-married to some stranger. I'm sure you just *think* you got married."

"Yeah, we'd figured that, too," Norah said. "We just got back from Annie's house. Turns out she knows Reed from when he spent summers here as a kid. Apparently she was friends with his late grandmother. She called him a saint last night. Annie married us with her blessing! And our marriage license—along with sixteen others—is already at the county courthouse."

"Waaah! Waah!" came a little voice from outside.

"That sounds like Bea," Norah said. "I'd better go help—"

Shelby stuck her arm out in front of the door. "Oh no, you don't, Norah Ingalls. The man is a police officer. The babies are safe with him for a few minutes." She bit her lip. "What are you two going to do?"

Norah shrugged. "I guess if we can't get back the license before it's processed, we'll have to get an annulment."

"The whole thing is nuts," Shelby said. "Jeez, I thought my life was crazy."

Norah wouldn't have thought anything could top what Shelby had been through right before Norah had gotten pregnant. Her sister had discovered her baby and a total stranger's baby had been switched at birth six months after bringing their boys home from the Wedlock Creek Clinic. Shelby and Liam Mercer had gotten married so that they could each have both boys—and along the way they'd fallen madly in love. Now the four of them were a very happy family.

"You know what else is crazy?" Norah said, her

voice going shaky. "How special it was. The ceremony, I mean. Me—even in my T-shirt and shorts and grubby slip-on sneakers—saying my vows. Hearing them said back to me. In that moment, Shel, I felt so…safe. For the first time in a year and a half, I felt safe." Tears pricked her eyes and she blinked hard.

She was the woman who didn't want love and romance. Who didn't believe in happily-ever-after anymore. So why had getting married—even to a total stranger—felt so wonderful? And yes, so safe?

"Oh, Norah," her sister said and pulled her into a hug. "I know what you mean."

Norah blew out a breath to get ahold of herself. "I know it wasn't real. But in that moment, when Annie pronounced us husband and wife, the way Reed looked at me and kissed me, being in that famed chapel…it was an old dream come true. Back to reality, though. That's just how life is."

Shelby squeezed her hand. "So, last night, did the new Mr. and Mrs. Barelli…?"

Norah felt her cheeks burn. "I don't know. But if we did, it must have been amazing. You saw the man."

Shelby smiled. "Maybe you can keep him."

Norah shook her head. Twice. "I'm done with men, remember? *Done.*"

Shelby let loose her evil smile. "Yes, for all other men, sure. Since you're married now."

Norah swallowed. But then she remembered this wasn't real and would be rectified. Brody let out a wail and once again she snapped back to reality. She was no one's bride, no one's wife. There was a big difference between old dreams and the way things really were.

"I'd better go save the detective from the three little screechers."

Norah opened the door and almost gasped at the sight on the doorstep. Brody was in Reed's strong arms, the sleeves of his navy shirt rolled up. He lifted the baby high in the air, then turned to Bea and Bella in the stroller and made a funny face at them before lifting Brody again. "Upsie downsie," Reed said. "Downsie upsie," he added as he lifted Brody again.

Baby laughter exploded on the porch.

Norah stared at Reed and then glanced over at Shelby, who was looking at Reed Barelli in amazement.

"My first partner back in Cheyenne had a baby, and whenever he started fussing, I'd do that and he'd giggle," Reed explained, lifting Brody one more time for a chorus of more triplet giggles.

Bea lifted her arms. Reed put Brody back and did two upsie-downsies with Bea, then her sister.

"I'll let Mom and Aunt Cheyenne know you might not be in today," Shelby said very slowly. She glanced at Reed, positively beaming, much like Annie had done earlier. "I'll be perfectly honest and report you have a headache from the sweet punch."

"Thanks," Norah said. "I'm not quite ready to explain everything just yet."

As her sister said goodbye and walked off in the direction of the diner, Norah appreciated that Shelby hadn't added a "Welcome to the family." She turned back to Reed. He was twisting his wedding ring on his finger.

"So you were supposed to work today?" he asked.

"Yes—and Sundays are one of the busiest at the Pie Diner—but I don't think I'll be able to concentrate. My mom and aunt will be all over me with questions. And now that I think about it, with the festival and carnival continuing today, business should be slow. I'll just make my pot pies here and take them over later, once we're settled on what to say if word gets out."

"Word will get out?" he said. "Oh no—don't tell me Annie and Abe are gossips."

"They're *strategic*," Norah said. "Which is exactly how we ended up married and not sent away last night."

"Meaning they'll tell just enough people, or the right people, to make it hard for us to undo the marriage so easily."

"She probably has a third cousin at the courthouse!" Norah said, throwing up her hands. But town gossip was the least of her problems right now, and boy did she have problems, particularly the one standing across from her looking so damned hot.

She turned from the glorious sight of him and racked her brain, trying to think who she could ask to babysit this morning for a couple hours on such short notice so she could get her pies done and her equilibrium back.

Her family was out of the question, of course. Her sister was busy enough with her own two kids and her secondhand shop to run, plus she often helped out at the diner. There was Geraldina next door, who might be able to take the triplets for a couple of hours, but her neighbor was another huge gossip and maybe she'd seen the two of them return home last night in God knew what state. For all Norah knew, Reed Barelli had carried her down the street like in *An Officer and a Gentleman* and swept her over the threshold of her house.

Huh. Had he?

"You okay?" he asked, peering at her.

Her shoulders slumped. "Just trying to figure out a sitter for the triplets while I make six pot pies. The usual suspects aren't going to work out this morning."

"Consider me at your service, then," he said.

"What?" she said, shaking her head. "I couldn't ask that."

"Least I can do, Norah. I got you into this mess. If I remember correctly, last night you said you'd always wanted to get married at that chapel and I picked you up and said 'Then let's get married.'" He let out a breath. "I still can't quite get over that I did that."

"I like being able to blame it all on you. Thanks." She smiled, grateful that he was so…nice.

"Besides, and obviously, I like babies," he said, "and all I had on my agenda today was re-familiarizing myself with Wedlock Creek."

"Okay, but don't say I didn't try to let you off the hook. Triplet seven-month-olds who are just starting to crawl are pretty wily creatures."

"I've dealt with plenty of wily creatures in my eight-year career as a cop. I've got this."

She raised an eyebrow and opened the door, surprised when Reed took hold of the enormous stroller and wheeled in the babies. She wasn't much used to someone else…being there. "Didn't I hear you tell Annie that you had no intention of ever getting married? I would think that meant you had no intention of having children, either."

"Right on both counts. But I like other people's kids. And babies are irresistible. Besides, yours already adore me."

Brody was sticking up his skinny little arms, smiling at Reed, three little teeth coming up in his gummy mouth.

"See?" he said.

Norah smiled. "Point proven. I'd appreciate the help. So thank you."

Norah closed the door behind Reed. It was the strangest feeling, walking into her home with her three babies—and her brand-new husband.

She glanced at her wedding ring. Then at his.

Talk about crazy. For a man who didn't intend to marry or have kids, he now had one huge family, even if that family would dissolve tomorrow at the courthouse.

As they'd first approached Norah's house on the way back from Annie and Abe's, Reed had been all set to suggest they get in his SUV, babies and all, and find someone, anyone, to open the courthouse. They could root through the mail that had been dumped through the slot, find their license application and just tear it up. Kaput! No more marriage!

But he'd been standing right in front of Norah's door, cute little Brody in his arms, the small, baby-shampoo-smelling weight of him, when he'd heard what Norah had said. Heard it loud and clear. And something inside him had shifted.

You know what else is crazy, how special it was. The ceremony, I mean. Me—even in my T-shirt and shorts and grubby slip-on sneakers—saying my vows. Hearing them said back to me. In that moment, Shel, I felt so... safe. For the first time in a year and a half, I felt safe.

He'd looked at the baby in his arms. The two little girls in the stroller. Then he'd heard Norah say something about a dream come true and back to reality.

His heart had constricted in his chest when she'd said she'd felt safe for the first time since the triplets were born. He'd once overheard his mother say that the only time she felt safe was when Reed was away in Wedlock Creek with his paternal grandmother, knowing her boy was being fed well and looked after.

Reed's frail mother had been alone otherwise, abandoned by Reed's dad during the pregnancy, no child support, no nothing. She'd married again, more for security than love, but that had been short-lived. Not even a year. Turned out the louse couldn't stand kids. His mother had worked two jobs to make ends meet, but times had been tough and Reed had often been alone and on his own.

He hated the thought of Norah feeling that way— unsteady, unsure, alone. This beautiful woman with so much on her shoulders. Three little ones her sole responsibility. And for a moment in the chapel, wed to him, she'd felt safe.

He wanted to help her somehow. Ease her burden. Do what he could. And if that was babysitting for a couple hours while she worked, he'd be more than happy to.

She picked up two babies from the stroller, a pro at balancing them in each arm. "Will you take Bea?" she asked.

He scooped up the baby girl, who immediately grabbed his cheek and stared at him with her huge gray-blue eyes, and followed Norah into the kitchen. A playpen was wedged in a nook. She put the two babies inside and Reed put Bea beside them. They all immediately reached for the little toys.

Norah took an apron from a hook by the refrigerator. "If I were at the diner, I'd be making twelve pot pies—

five chicken and three turkey, two beef, and two veg-gie—but I only have enough ingredients at home to do six—three chicken and three beef. I'll just make them all here and drop them off for baking. The oven in this house can't even cook a frozen pizza reliably."

Reed glanced around the run-down kitchen. It was clean and clearly had been baby-proofed, given the cov-ered electrical outlets. But the refrigerator was strangely loud, the floor sloped and the house just seemed...old. And, he hated to say it, kind of depressing. "Have you lived here long?"

"I moved in a few months after finding out I was pregnant. I'd lived with my mom before then and she wanted me to continue living there, but I needed to grow up. I was going to be a mother—of three—and it was time to make a home. Not turn my mother into a live-in babysitter or take advantage of her generosity. This place was all I could afford. It's small and dated but clean and functional."

"So a kitchen, living room and bathroom down-stairs," he said, glancing into the small living room with the gold-colored couch. Baby stuff was every-where, from colorful foam mats to building blocks and rattling toys. There wasn't a dining room, as far as he could see. A square table was wedged in front of a win-dow with one chair and three high chairs. "How many bedrooms upstairs?"

"Only two. But that works for now. One for me and one for the triplets." She bit her lip. "It's not a palace. It's hardly my dream home. But you do what you have to. I'm their mother and it's up to me to support us."

Everything looked rumpled, secondhand, and it prob-ably was. The place reminded him of his apartment as a kid. His mother hadn't even had her own room. She'd slept on a pull-out couch in the living room and folded it up every morning. She'd wanted so much more for the two of them, but her paycheck had stretched only so far. When he was eighteen, he'd enrolled in the police academy and started college at night, planning to give his mother a better standard of living. But she'd passed away before he could make any of her dreams come true.

A squeal came from the playpen and he glanced over at the triplets. The little guy was chewing on a cloth book, one of the girls was pressing little "piano" keys and the other was babbling and shaking keys.

"Bea's the rabble-rouser," Norah said as she began to sauté chicken breasts in one pan, chunks of beef in another, and then set a bunch of carrots and onions on the counter. "Bella loves anything musical, and Brody is the quietest. He loves to be read to, whereas Bea will start clawing at the pages."

"Really can't be easy raising three babies. Especially on your own," he said.

"It's not. But I'll tell you, I now know what love is. I mean, I love my family. I thought I loved their father. But the way I feel about those three? Nothing I've ever experienced. I'd sacrifice anything for them."

"You're a mother," he said, admiring her more than she could know.

She nodded. "First and foremost. My family keeps trying to set me up on dates. Like any guy would say yes to a woman with seven-month-old triplets." She glanced at Reed, then began cutting up the carrots. "I sure trapped you."

He smiled. "Angelina, international flight attendant,

wasn't a mother of three, remember? She was just a woman out having a good time at a small-town carnival."

She set down the knife and looked at him. "You're not angry that I didn't say anything? That I actually let you marry me without you knowing what you were walking into?"

He moved to the counter and stood across from her. "We were both bombed out of our minds."

She smiled and resumed chopping. "Well, when we get this little matter of our marriage license ripped up before it can be processed, I'll go back to telling my family to stop trying to fix me up and you'll be solving crime all over Wedlock Creek."

"You're not looking for a father for the triplets?" he asked.

"Maybe I should be," she said. "To be fair to them. But right now? No. I have zero interest in romance and love and honestly no longer believe in happily-ever-after. I've got my hands full, anyway."

Huh. She felt the same way he did. Well, to a point. Marriage made her feel safe, but love didn't. Interesting, he thought, trying not to stare at her.

As she pulled open a cabinet, the hinge broke and it almost hit her on the head. Reed rushed over and caught it before it could.

"This place is falling down," he said, shaking his head. "You could have been really hurt. And you could have been holding one of the triplets."

She frowned. "I've fixed that three times. I'll call my landlord. She'll have it taken care of."

"Or I could take care of it right now," he said, surveying the hinge. "Still usable. Have a power drill?"

"In that drawer," she said, pointing. "I keep all the tools in there."

He found the drill and fixed the hinge, making sure it was on tight. "That should do it," he said. "Anything else need fixing?"

"Wow, he babysits *and* is handy?" She smiled at him. "I don't think there's anything else needing work," she said, adding the vegetables into a pot bubbling on the stove. "And thank you."

When the triplets started fussing, he announced it was babysitting time. He scooped up two babies and put them in Exersaucers in the living room, then raced back for the third and set Brody in one, too. The three of them happily played with the brightly colored attachments, babbling and squealing. He pulled Bea out—he knew she was Bea by her yellow shirt, whereas Bella's was orange—and did two upsie-downsies, much to the joy of the other two, who laughed and held up their arms.

"Your turn!" he said to Bella, lifting her high to the squeals of her siblings. "Now you, Brody," he added, putting Bella back and giving her brother his turn.

They sure were beautiful. All three had the same big cheeks and big, blue-gray eyes, wisps of light brown hair. They were happy, gurgling, babbling, laughing seven-month-olds.

Something squeezed in his chest again, this time a strange sensation of longing. With the way he'd always felt about marriage, he'd never have this—babies, a wife making pot pies, a family. And even in this tired old little house, playing at family felt...nicer than he expected.

Brody rubbed his eyes, which Reed recalled meant he was getting tired. Maybe it was nap time? It was barely seven-thirty in the morning, but they'd probably woken before the crack of dawn.

"How about a story?" he asked, sitting on the braided rug and grabbing a book from the coffee table. *"Lulu Goes to the Fair."* A white chicken wearing a baseball cap was on the cover. "Your mother and I went to the fair last night," he told them. "So this book will be perfect." He read them the story of Lulu wanting to ride the Ferris wheel but not being able to reach the step until two other chickens from her school helped her. Then they rode the Ferris wheel together. The end. Bella and Brody weren't much interested in Lulu and her day at the fair, but Bea was rapt. Then they all started rubbing their eyes and fussing.

It was now eight o'clock. Maybe he'd put the babies back in the playpen to see if he could help Norah. Not that he could cook, but he could fetch.

He picked up the two girls and headed back into the kitchen, smiled at Norah, deposited the babies in the playpen and then went to get Brody.

"Thank you for watching them," she said. "And reading to them."

"Anytime," he said. Which felt strange. Did he mean that?

"You're sure you didn't win Uncle of the Year or something? How'd you get so good with babies?"

"Told you. I like babies. Who doesn't? I picked up a few lessons on the job, I guess."

Why had he said "anytime" though? That was kind of loaded.

With the babies set for the moment, he shook the thought from his scrambled head and watched Norah cook, impressed with her multitasking. She had six tins covered in pie crust. The aromas of the onions and chicken and beef bubbling in two big pots filled the kitchen. His stomach growled. Had they eaten breakfast? He suddenly realized they hadn't.

"I made coffee and toasted a couple of bagels," she said as if she could read his mind. She was so multitalented, he wouldn't be surprised if she could. "I have cream cheese and butter."

"You're doing enough," he said. "I'll get it. What do you want on yours?"

"Cream cheese. And thanks."

He poured the coffee into mugs and took care of the bagels, once again so aware of her closeness, the physicality of her. He couldn't help but notice how incredibly sexy she was, standing there in her jeans and maroon T-shirt, the way both hugged her body. There wasn't anywhere to sit in the kitchen, so he stood by the counter, drinking the coffee he so desperately needed.

"The chief mentioned the Pie Diner is the place for lunch in Wedlock Creek. I'm sure I'll be eating one of those pies tomorrow."

She smiled. "Oh, good. I'll have to thank him for that. We need to attract the newcomers to town before the burger place gets 'em." She took a long sip of her coffee. "Ah, I needed that." She took another sip, then a bite of her bagel. She glanced at him as if she wanted to ask something, then resumed adding the pot pie mixtures into the tins. "You moved here for a fresh start, you said?"

He'd avoided that question earlier. He supposed he could answer without going into every detail of his life.

He sipped his coffee and nodded. "I came up for my grandmother's funeral a few months ago. She was the last of my father's family. When she passed, I suddenly wanted to be here, in Wedlock Creek, where I'd spent those good summers. After a bad stakeout a few weeks ago that almost got me killed and did get my partner injured, I'd had it. I quit the force and applied for a job in Wedlock Creek. It turns out a detective had retired just a few weeks prior."

"Sorry about your grandmother. Sounds like she was very special to you."

"She was. My father had taken off completely when I was just a month old, but my grandmother refused to lose contact with me. She sent cards and gifts and called every week and drove out to pick me up every summer for three weeks. It's a three-hour drive each way." He'd never forget being seven, ten, eleven and staring out the window of his apartment, waiting to see that old green car slowly turn up the street. And when it did, emotion would flood him to the point that it would take him a minute to rush out with his bag.

"I'm so glad you had her in your life. You never saw your dad again?"

"He sent the occasional postcard from all over the west. Last one I ever got was from somewhere in Alaska. Word came that he died and had left instructions for a sea burial. I last saw him when I was ten, when he came back for his dad's funeral—my grandfather."

"And your mom?"

"It was hard on her raising a kid alone without much money or prospects. And it was just me. She remarried, but that didn't work out well, either, for either of us." He took a long slug of the coffee. He needed to change the subject. "How do you manage three babies with two hands?"

She smiled and lay pie crust over the tins, making some kind of decoration in the center. "Same way you did bringing the triplets from the kitchen to the living room. You just have to move fast and be constantly on guard. I do what I have to. That's just the way it is."

An angry wail came from the playpen. Then another. The three Ingalls triplets began rubbing their eyes again, this time with very upset little faces.

"Perfect timing," she said. "The pies are assembled." She hurried to the sink to wash her hands, then hurried over to the playpen. "Nap time for you cuties."

"I'll help," Reed said, putting down his mug.

Brody was holding up his arms and staring at Reed. Reed smiled and picked him up, the little weight sweet in his arms. Brody reached up and grabbed Reed's cheek, like his sister had, not that there was much to grab. Norah scooped up Bea and Bella. They headed upstairs, the unlined wood steps creaky and definitely not baby-friendly when they would start to crawl, which would probably be soon.

The nursery was spare but had the basics. Three cribs, a dresser and changing table. The room was painted a pale yellow with white stars and moons stenciled all over.

"Ever changed a diaper?" she asked as she put both babies in a crib, taking off their onesies.

"Cops have done just about everything," he said. "I've changed my share of diapers." He laid the baby on the changing table. "Phew. Just wet." He made quick work of the task, sprinkling on some cornstarch powder and fastening a fresh diaper.

"His jammies are in the top drawer. Any footsie ones."

Reed picked up the baby and carried him over to the dresser, using one hand to open the drawer. The little baby clothes were very neatly folded. He pulled out the top footed onesie, blue cotton with dinosaurs. He set Brody down, then gently put his little arms and legs into the right holes, and there Brody was, all ready for bed. He held the baby against his chest, Brody's impossibly little eyes drooping, his mouth quirking.

He tried to imagine his own father holding him like this, his own flesh and blood, and just walking away. No look back. No nothing. How was it possible? Reed couldn't fathom it.

"His crib is on the right," Norah said, pointing as she took one baby girl out of the crib and changed her, then laid her down in the empty crib. She scooped up the other baby, changed her and laid her back in the crib.

He set Brody down and gave his little cheek a caress. Brody grabbed his thumb and held on.

"He sure does like you," Norah whispered.

Reed swallowed against the gushy feeling in the region of his chest. As Brody's eyes drifted closed, the tiny fist released and Reed stepped back.

Norah shut off the light and turned on a very low lullaby player. After half a second of fussing, all three babies closed their eyes, quirking their tiny mouths and stretching their arms over their heads.

"Have a good nap, my loves," Norah said, tiptoeing toward the door.

Reed followed her, his gold band glinting in the dim light of the room. He stared at the ring, then at his surroundings. He was in a nursery. With the woman he'd accidentally married. And with her triplets, whom he'd just babysat, read to and helped get to nap time.

What the hell had happened to his life? A day ago he'd been about to embark on a new beginning here in Wedlock Creek, where life had once seemed so idyllic out in the country where his grandmother had lived alone after she'd been widowed. Instead of focusing on reading the WCPD manuals and getting up to speed on open cases, he was getting his heart squeezed by three eighteen-pound tiny humans.

And their beautiful mother.

As he stepped into the hallway, the light cleared his brain. "Well, I guess I'd better get going. Pick you up at eight thirty tomorrow for the trip to Brewer? The courthouse opens at nine. Luckily, I don't report for duty until noon."

"Sounds good," she said, leading the way downstairs. "Thanks for helping. You put Brody down for his nap like a champ."

But instead of heading toward the door, he found himself just standing there. He didn't want to leave the four Ingalls alone. On their own. In this falling-down house.

He felt…responsible for them, he realized.

But he also needed to take a giant step backward and catch his breath.

So why was it so hard to walk out the door?

Chapter 4

At exactly eight thirty on Monday morning, Norah saw Reed pull up in front of her house. He must be as ready to get this marriage business taken care of as she was. Yesterday, after he'd left, she'd taken a long, hot bubble bath upstairs, ears peeled for the triplets, but they'd napped for a good hour and a half. In that time, a zillion thoughts had raced through her head, from the bits and pieces she remembered of her evening with Fabio to the wedding to waking up to find Detective Reed Barelli in her bed to how he played upsie-downsie with the triplets and read them a story. And fixed her bagel. And the cabinet.

She couldn't stop thinking about him, how kind he'd been, how good-natured about the whole mess. It had been the man's first day in town. And he'd found himself married to a mother of three. She also couldn't stop thinking about how he'd looked in those black boxer briefs, how tall and muscular he was. The way his dark eyes crinkled at the corners.

After the triplets had woken up, she'd gotten them into the stroller and moseyed on down to the Pie Diner with her six contributions. She'd been unable to keep her secret and had told her mother and aunt everything, trying to not be overheard by their part-time cook and the two waitresses coming in and out. She'd explained it all and she could see on her sister's face how relieved Shelby was at not having to keep her super-juicy family secret anymore.

"That Annie!" Aunt Cheyenne had said with a wink. "Always looking out for us."

Arlena Ingalls had had the same evil smile. "Handsome?"

"Mom!" Norah had said. "He's a stranger!"

"He's hardly that now," her mother had pointed out, glancing at an order ticket and placing two big slices of quiche Lorraine on a waitress's tray.

Aunt Cheyenne had laughed. "I have to hand it to you. We send you to the carnival for your first night out in seven months and you come home married. And to the town's new detective. I, for one, am very impressed."

After talk had turned to who had possibly spiked the punch, Norah, exasperated, had left. Her mother had offered to watch the triplets this morning so that Norah could get her life straightened out and back together. "If you absolutely have to," her mother had added.

Humph, Norah thought now, watching Reed get out of his dark blue SUV. As if marriage was the be-all and end-all. As if a good man was a savior. They didn't even know if Reed was a good man.

But she did, dammit. That had been obvious from the get-go, from the moment he'd stuffed that hundred in the till box to pay what he'd thought was fair for swiping all the punch to picking her up and taking her into the chapel to fulfill her dream of getting married there. He was a good man when bombed out of his ever-loving mind. He was a good man stone-cold sober, who played upsie-downsie with babies, making sure each got their turn. He'd fixed her broken cabinet.

And damn, he really was something to look at. His thick, dark hair shone in the morning sun. He wore charcoal-colored pants, a gray button-down shirt and black shoes. He looked like a city detective.

In the bathtub, as she'd lain there soaking, and all last night in bed, in between trips to the nursery to see why one triplet or another was crying or shrieking, she'd thought about Reed Barelli and how he'd looked in those boxer briefs. She was pretty sure they hadn't had sex. She would remember, wouldn't she? Tidbits of the experience, at least. There was no way that man, so good-looking and sexy, had run his hands and mouth all over her and she hadn't remembered a whit of it.

Anyway, their union would be no more in about a half hour. It was fun to fantasize about what they might have done Saturday night, but only because it was just that—fantasy. And Reed would be out of her life very soon, just someone she'd say hi to in the coffee shop or grocery store. Maybe they'd even chuckle at the crazy time they'd up and gotten married by accident.

She waited for the doorbell to ring, but it didn't. Reed wouldn't be one to wait in the car and honk, so she peered out the window. He stood on the doorstep, typing something into his phone. Girlfriend, maybe.

The man had to be involved with someone. He'd probably been explaining himself from the moment he'd left Norah's house this morning. Poor guy.

Her mom had already come to pick up the babies, so she was ready to go. She wore a casual cotton skirt and top for the occasion of getting back their marriage license, but in the back of her mind she was well aware she'd dolled up a little for the handsome cop. A little mascara, a slick of lip gloss, a tiny dab of subtle perfume behind her ears.

Which was all ridiculous, considering she was spending her morning undoing her ties to the man!

A text buzzed on her phone.

Not sure if the cutes are sleeping, so didn't want to ring the doorbell.

Huh. He hadn't been texting a girlfriend; he'd been texting *her*. Maybe there was no girlfriend.

She glanced at the text again. The warmth that spread across her heart, her midsection, made her smile. The cutes. An un-rung doorbell so as not to disturb the triplets. If she needed more proof that Reed Barelli was top-notch, she'd gotten it.

She took a breath and opened the door. Why did he have to be so good-looking? She could barely peel her eyes off him. "Morning," she said. "My mom has the triplets, so we're good to go."

"I got us coffee and muffins," he said, holding up a bag from Java Joe's. "Light, no sugar, right? That's how you took your coffee yesterday."

She smiled. "You don't miss much, I've been noticing."

"Plight of the detective. Once we see it, it's imprinted."

"What kind of muffins?" she asked, trying not to stare at his face.

"I took you for a cranberry-and-orange type," he said, opening the passenger door for her.

She smiled. "Sounds good." She slid inside his SUV. Clean as could be. Two coffees sat in the center console, one marked *R*, along with a smattering of change and some pens in one of the compartments.

"And I also got four other kinds of muffins in case you hate cranberry and orange," he said, handing her the cup that wasn't marked regular.

Of course he had, she thought, her heart pinging. She kept her eyes straight ahead as he rounded the hood and got inside. When he closed his door, she was ridiculously aware of how close he was.

"Thanks," she said, touched by his thoughtfulness.

"So, it's a half hour to the courthouse, we'll get back our license and that's that." He started the SUV and glanced at her.

She held his gaze for a moment before sipping her coffee to have something to do that didn't involve looking at him.

Would be nice to keep the fantasy going a little longer, she thought. *That we're married, a family, my mom is babysitting while we go off to the county seat to... admire the architecture, have brunch in a fancy place.* Once upon a time, this was all she'd wanted. To find her life's partner, to build a life with a great guy, have children, have a family. But everything had gotten turned on its head. Now she barely trusted herself, let alone anyone she wasn't related to.

Ha, maybe that was why she seemed to trust Reed. He was related to her. For the next half hour, anyway.

By the time they arrived at the courthouse, a beautiful white historic building, she'd finished her coffee and had half a cranberry-and-orange muffin and a few bites of the cinnamon chip. Reed was around to open her door for her before she could even reach for the handle. "Well, this is it—literally and figuratively."

"This is it," she repeated, glancing at him. He held her gaze for a moment and she knew he had to be thinking, *Thank God. We're finally here. Let's get this marriage license ripped up!*

They headed inside. The bronze mail slot on the side of the door loomed large. She could just imagine sneaky, old Abe Potterowski racing over and shoving all the licenses in. As they entered through the revolving door, Norah glanced at the area under the mail slot. Just an empty mail bucket was there.

Empty. Of course it was. Every step of this crazy process was going to be difficult.

After getting directions to the office that handled marriage licenses, they took the elevator to the third floor.

Maura Hotchner, County Clerk was imprinted on a plaque to the left of the doorway to Office 310. They went in and Norah smiled at the woman behind the desk.

"Ms. Hotchner, my name is Norah—"

"Good morning!" the woman said with a warm smile. "Ms. Hotchner began her maternity leave today. I'm Ellen Wheeler, temporary county clerk and Ms. Hotchner's assistant. How may I help you?"

Norah explained that she was looking for her marriage license and wanted it back before it could be processed.

"Oh dear," Ellen Wheeler said. "Being my first day and all taking over this job, I got here extra early and processed all the marriage licenses deposited into the mail slot over the weekend. Do you believe there were seventeen from Wedlock Creek alone? I've already put the official decrees for all those in the mail."

Norah's heart started racing. "Do you mean to tell me that my marriage to this man is legally binding?"

The county clerk looked from Norah to Reed, gave him a "my, you're a handsome one" smile, then looked back at Norah. "Yes, ma'am. It's on the books now. You're legally wed."

Oh God. Oh God. Oh God. This can't be happening.

She glanced at Reed, whose face had paled. "Can't you just erase everything and find our decree and rip it up? Can you just undo it all? I mean, you just processed it—what?—fifteen minutes ago, right? That's what the delete key is for!"

The woman seemed horrified by the suggestion. "Ma'am, I'm sorry, but I most certainly cannot just 'erase' what is legally binding. The paperwork has been processed. You're officially married."

Facepalm. "Is this the correct office to get annulment forms?" Norah asked. At least she wouldn't walk out of there empty-handed. She would get the ball rolling to undo this…crazy mistake.

Ellen's face went blank as she stared from Norah to Reed to their wedding rings and then back at Norah. "I have them right here."

Norah clutched the papers and hurried away. She

could barely get to the bench by the elevators without collapsing.

Reed put his hand on her shoulder. "Are you all right? Can I get you some water?"

"I'm fine," she said. "No, I'll be fine. I just can't believe this. We're married!"

"So we are," he said, sitting beside her. "We'll fill out the annulment paperwork and I'm sure it won't take long to resolve this."

She glanced at the instruction form attached to the form. "Grounds for annulment include insanity. That's us, all right."

He laughed and held her gaze for a moment, then shoved his hands into his pockets and looked away.

"I guess I'll fill this out and then give it to you to sign?" she said, flipping through the few pages. She hated important forms with their tiny boxes. She let out a sigh.

He nodded and reached out his hand. "Come on. Let's go home."

For a split second she was back in her fantasy of him being her husband and having an actual home to go to that wasn't falling down around her with sloping floors and a haunted refrigerator. She took his hand and never wanted to let go.

She really was insane. She had to be. What the hell was going on with her? It's like she had a wild crush on this man.

Her husband!

As Reed turned onto the road for Wedlock Creek, he could just make out the old black weather vane on top of his grandmother's barn in the distance. The house wasn't in view; it was a few miles out from here, but that weather vane, with its arrows and mother and baby buffalo, had always been a landmark when that old green car would get to this point for his stay at his grandmother's.

"See that weather vane?" he said, pointing.

Norah bent over a bit. "Oh yes, I do see it now."

"That's my grandmother's barn. When I was a kid heading up here from our house, I'd see that weather vane and all would be right in the world."

"I'd love to see the property," she said. "Can we stop?"

He'd driven over twice Saturday morning, right after he'd arrived in Wedlock Creek, but he'd stayed in the car. He loved the old ranch house and the land, and he'd keep it up, but it was never going to be his, so he hadn't wanted to rub the place in his own face. Though, technically, until his marriage was annulled, it *was* his. His grandmother must be mighty happy right now at his situation. He could see her thinking he'd finally settle down just to be able to have the ranch, then magically fall madly in love with his wife and be happy forever. Right.

He pulled onto the gravel road leading to the ranch and, as always, as the two-story, white farmhouse came into view, his heart lurched. Home.

God, he loved this place. For some of his childhood, when his grandfather had been alive, he'd stayed only a week, which was as long as the grouchy old coot could bear to have him around. But when he'd passed, his grandmother had him stay eight weeks, almost the whole summer. A bunch of times his grandmother had told his mother she and Reed could move in, but his mother had been proud and living with her former mother-in-law had never felt right.

Norah gasped. "What a beautiful house. I love these farmhouses. So much character. And that gorgeous red door and the black shutters…"

He watched her take in the red barn just to the left of the house, which was more like a garage than a place for horses or livestock. Then her gaze moved to the acreage, fields of pasture with shade trees and open land. A person could think out here, dream out here, *be* out here.

"I'd love to see inside," she said.

He supposed it was all right. He did have a key, after all. Always had. And he was married, so the property was out of its three-month limbo, since he'd fulfilled the terms of the will.

He led the way three steps up to the wide porch that wrapped around the side of the house. How many chocolate milks had he drunk, how many stories had his grandmother told him on this porch, on those two rocking chairs with the faded blue cushions?

The moment he stepped inside, a certain peace came over him. Home. Where he belonged. Where he wanted to be.

The opposite of how he'd felt about the small house he'd rented near the police department. Sterile. Meh. Then again, he'd had the place only two days and hadn't even slept there Saturday night. His furniture from his condo in Cheyenne fit awkwardly, nothing quite looking right no matter where he moved the sofa or the big-screen TV.

"Oh, Reed, this place is fantastic," Norah said, looking all around. She headed into the big living room with its huge stone fireplace, the wall of windows facing the fields and huge trees and woods beyond.

His grandmother had had classic taste, so even the furniture felt right to him. Brown leather sofas, club chairs, big Persian rugs. She'd liked to paint and her work was hung around the house, including ones of him as a boy and a teenager.

"You sure were a cute kid," Norah said, looking at the one of him as a nine-year-old. "And I'm surprised I never ran into you during your summers here. I would have had the biggest crush on that guy," she added, pointing at the watercolor of him at sixteen.

He smiled. "My grandmother didn't love town or people all that much. When I visited, she'd make a ton of food and we'd explore the woods and go fishing in the river just off her land."

The big, country kitchen with its white cabinets and bay window with the breakfast nook was visible, so she walked inside and he followed. He could tell she loved the house and he couldn't contain his pride as he showed her the family room with the sliders out to a deck facing a big backyard, then the four bedrooms upstairs. The master suite was a bit feminine for his taste with its flowered rose quilt, but the bathroom was something—spa tub with jets, huge shower, the works. Over the years he'd updated the house as presents for his grandmother, happy to see her so delighted.

"I can see how much this place means to you," Norah said as they headed back downstairs into the living room. "Did it bother you that your grandmother wrote her will the way she did? That you had to marry to inherit it?"

"I didn't like it, but I understood what she was trying

to do. On her deathbed, she told me she knew me better than I knew myself, that I did need a wife and children and this lone-wolf-cop nonsense wouldn't make me happy."

Maybe your heart will get broken again, but loss is part of life, Lydia Barelli had added. *You don't risk, you don't get.*

Broken again. Why had he ever told his grandmother that he'd tried and where had it gotten him? Those final days of his grandmother's life, he hadn't been in the mood to talk any more about the one woman he'd actually tried to be serious about. He'd been thinking about proposing, trying to force himself out of his old, negative feelings, when the woman he'd been seeing for almost a year told him she'd fallen for a rich lawyer—sorry. He hadn't let himself fall for anyone since, and that was over five years ago. Between that and what he'd witnessed about marriage growing up? Count him out.

Reed hadn't wanted to disappoint his beloved grandmother and had told her, "Who knows what the future holds?" He couldn't outright lie and say he was sure he'd change his mind about marriage. But he wouldn't let his grandmother go on thinking no one on this earth would ever love him. She wouldn't have been able to abide that.

"*Have* you been happy?" Norah asked, glancing at him, then away as if to give him some privacy.

He shrugged. "Happy enough. My work was my life and it sustained me a long time. But when I lost the only family I had, someone very special to me, I'll tell you, I *felt* it."

"It?" she repeated.

"Loss of…connection, I guess."

She nodded. "I felt that way when my dad died, and

I had my mother, aunt and sister crying with me. I can't imagine how alone you must have felt."

He turned away, looking out the window. "Well, we should get going. I have to report to the department for my orientation at noon. Then it's full-time tomorrow."

"Thanks for showing me the house. I almost don't want to leave. It's so…welcoming."

He glanced around and breathed in the place. They had to leave. *He* had to leave. Because this house was never going to be his. And being there hurt like hell.

Chapter 5

Reed sat in his office in the Wedlock Creek Police Department, appreciating the fact that he had an office, even if it was small, with a window facing Main Street, so he could see the hustle and bustle of downtown. The two-mile-long street was full of shops and restaurants and businesses. The Pie Diner was just visible across the street if he craned his neck, which he found himself doing every now and again for a possible sighting of Norah.

His wife for the time being.

He hadn't seen her around today since dropping her off. But looking out the window had given him ideas for leads and follow-ups on a few of the open cases he'd inherited from his retired predecessor. Wedlock Creek might not have had a murder in over seventy years—knock on wood—but there was the usual crime, ranging from the petty to the more serious. The most pressing involved a missing person's case that would be his focus. A thirty-year-old man, an ambulance-chasing attorney named David Dirk who was supposed to get married this coming Saturday, had gone missing three days ago. No one had heard from him and none of his credit cards had been used, yet there was no sign of foul play.

David Dirk. Thirty. Had to be the same guy. When Reed was a kid, a David Dirk was his nearest neighbor and they'd explore their land for hours during the summers Reed had spent at his grandmother's. David had been a smart, inquisitive kid who'd also had a father who'd taken off. He and Reed would talk about what jerks their dads were, then laud them as maybe away on secret government business, unable to tell their wives or children that they were really saving the world. That was how much both had needed to believe, as kids, that their fathers were good, that their fathers did love them, after all. David's family had moved and they'd lost touch as teenagers and then time had dissolved the old ties.

Reed glanced at the accompanying photo stapled to the left side of the physical file. He could see his old friend in the adult's face. The same intense blue eyes behind black-framed eyeglasses, the straight, light brown hair. Reed spent the next hour reading through the case file and notes about David's disappearance.

The man's fiancée, Eden Pearlman, an extensions specialist at Hair Palace on Main Street, was adamant that something terrible had happened to her "Davy Darling" or otherwise he would have contacted her. According to Eden, Davy must be lying gravely injured in a ditch somewhere or a disgruntled associate had hurt him, because marrying her was the highlight of his life. Reed sure hoped neither was the case. He would interview Ms. Pearlman tomorrow and get going on the investigation.

In the meantime, though, he called every clinic and hospital within two hours to check if there were any John Does brought in unconscious. Each one said no. Then Reed read through the notes about David's last case, which he'd won big for his client a few days prior to his disappearance. A real-estate deal that had turned ugly. Reed researched the disgruntled plaintiff, who'd apparently spent the entire day that David was last seen at a family reunion an hour away. Per the notes, the plaintiff was appealing and had stated he couldn't wait to see his opponent and his rat of a lawyer in court again, where he'd prevail this time. Getting rid of David in some nefarious way certainly wouldn't get rid of the case; Reed had his doubts the man had had anything to do with David's disappearance.

So where are you, David? What the heck happened to you?

Frustrated by the notes and his subsequent follow-up calls getting him nowhere, Reed packed up his files at six. Tomorrow would be his first full day on the force and he planned to find David Dirk by that day's end. Something wasn't sitting right in his gut about the case, but he couldn't put his finger on it. He'd need to talk to the fiancée and a few other people.

As he left the station, he noticed Norah coming out of a brick office building, wheeling the huge triple stroller. He eyed the plaque on the door: Dr. Laurel McCray, Pediatrician. Brody in the front was screaming his head off. Bella was letting out shrieks. Or was that Bea? All he knew for sure was that one of the girls, seated in the middle, was quiet, picking up Cheerios from the narrow little tray in front of her and eating them.

He crossed the street and hurried up to her. "Norah? Everything okay?"

She looked as miserable as the two little ones. "I just came from their pediatrician's office. Brody was tugging at his ear all afternoon and crying. Full-out ear infection. He's had his first dose of antibiotics, but they haven't kicked in yet."

"Poor guy," Reed said, kneeling and running a finger along Brody's hot, tearstained cheek. Brody stopped crying for a moment, so Reed did it again. When he stood, Brody let out the wail of all wails.

"He really does like you," Norah said, looking a bit mystified for a moment before a mix of mom weariness came over her. "Even Bella has stopped crying, so double thank you."

As if on cue, Bella started shrieking again and, from the smell of things, Reed had a feeling she wasn't suffering from the same issue as her brother. People walking up and down the street stared, of course, giving concerned smiles but being nosey parkers.

Norah's shoulders slumped. "I'd better get them home."

"Need some help?" he asked. "Actually, I meant that rhetorically, so don't answer. You do need help and I'm going home with you."

"Reed, I can't keep taking advantage of how good you are with babies."

"Yes, you can. I mean, what are husbands for if not for helping around the house?"

She laughed. "I can't believe you actually made me laugh when I feel like crying."

"Husbands are good for that, too," he said before he could catch himself. He was kidding, trying to lighten her load, but he actually *was* her husband. And there was nothing funny about it.

"Well, you'll be off the hook in a few days," she said. "I filled out the annulment form and all you have to do is sign it and I'll send it in. It's on my coffee table."

She hadn't wasted any time. Or Norah Ingalls was just very efficient, despite having triplet babies to care for on her own. He nodded. "Well, then, I'm headed to the right place."

Within fifteen minutes they were in Norah's cramped, sloping little house. He held poor Brody while Norah changed Bella, who'd stopped shrieking, but all three babies were hungry and it was a bit past dinner-time.

Reed was in charge of Brody, who was unusually responsive to him, especially when his little ears were hurting, so he sat in front of Brody's high chair, feeding him his favorite baby food, cereal with pears. Norah was on a chair next to him, feeding both girls. Bella was in a much better mood now that her Cheerios had been replenished and she was having pureed sweet potatoes. Bea was dining on a jar of pureed green beans.

Reed got up to fill Brody's sippy cup with water when he stopped in his tracks.

On the refrigerator, half underneath a Mickey Mouse magnet, was a wedding invitation.

Reed stared at it, barely able to believe what he was seeing.

Join Us For
The Special Occasion of Our Wedding
Eden Pearlman and David Dirk...

Norah was invited to the wedding? He pulled the invitation off the fridge. "Bride or groom?" he asked, holding up the invitation.

Norah glanced up, spoon full of green bean mush midway to Bea's open mouth. "Groom, actually. I'm surprised he invited me. I dated David Dirk for two weeks a couple years ago. He ditched me for the woman he said was the love of his life. She must be, because I got that invitation about six weeks ago."

"You only dated for two weeks?" Reed asked.

She nodded. "We met at the Pie Diner. He kept coming in and ordering the pot pie of the day. I thought it was about the heavenly pot pies, but apparently it was me he liked. He asked me out. We had absolutely nothing in common and nothing much to talk about over coffee and dinner. But I'll tell ya, when my sister, Shelby, needed an attorney concerning something to do with her son Shane, I recommended David based on his reputation. He represented her in a complicated case and she told me he did a great job."

He tucked that information away. "No one has seen or heard from him in three days. According to the case notes, his fiancée thinks there was foul play, but my predecessor found no hint of that."

"Hmm. David was a real ambulance chaser. He had a few enemies. Twice someone said to me, 'How could you date that scum?'"

His eyebrow shot up. "Really? Recall who?"

"I'll write down their names for you. Gosh, I hope

David's okay. I mean, he was a shark, but, like I said, when Shelby *needed* a shark, he did well by her. I didn't get to know him all that well, but he was always a gentleman, always a nice guy. We just had nothing much to say to each other. Zero chemistry."

He was about to put the invitation back on the fridge. "Mind if I keep this?" he asked.

She shook her head. "Go right ahead." She turned back to her jars of baby food and feeding the girls. "Brody seems calmer. The medicine must have kicked in." She leaned over and gave his cheek a gentle stroke. "Little better now, sweet pea?"

Brody banged on his tray and smiled.

"Does that mean you want some Cheerios?" Reed asked, sitting back down. He handed one to Brody, who took it and examined it, then popped it in his mouth, giving Reed a great gummy smile, three little jagged teeth making their way up.

Bea grabbed her spoon just as Norah was inching it toward her mouth and it ended up half in Bea's hair, half in Norah's.

"Oh, thanks," Norah said with a grin. "Just what I wanted in my hair." She tickled Bea's belly. "And now the three of you need a bath." She laughed and shook her head.

By eight o'clock, Norah had rinsed the baby food from her hair, all three babies had been fed, bathed, read to and it was time for bed. Reed stood by the door as Norah sang a lullaby in her lovely whispered voice. He almost nodded off himself.

"Well, they're asleep," she said, walking out of the nursery and keeping the door ajar. "I can't thank you enough for your help tonight, Reed."

"It was no trouble."

For a moment, as he looked into her hazel eyes, the scent of pears clinging to her shirt, he wanted to kiss her so badly that he almost leaned forward. He caught himself at the last second. What the hell? He couldn't kiss Norah. They weren't a couple. They weren't even dating.

Good Lord, they were married.

And he wanted to kiss her, passionately, kiss her over to that lumpy-looking gold couch and explore every inch of her pear-smelling body. But he couldn't, not with everything so weird between them. And things were definitely weird.

He was supposed to sign annulment papers. But those papers on the coffee table had been in his line of vision for the past two hours and he'd ignored them. Even after Norah had mentioned them when they'd first arrived tonight. "There are the papers," she'd said, gesturing with her chin. Quite casually.

But he'd bypassed the forms and fed Brody instead. Rocked the little guy in his arms while Norah gave his sisters a bath. Changed Brody into pajamas and sang his own little off-key lullaby about where the buffalos roamed.

And all he could think was *How can I walk away from this woman, these babies? How can I just leave them?*

He couldn't. Signing those annulment papers would mean the marriage never happened. They'd both walk away.

He didn't want to. Or he couldn't. One or the other. He might not want love or a real marriage, but that didn't mean he couldn't step up for Norah.

And then the thought he'd squelched all day came right up in Technicolor.

And if you stay married to Norah, if you step up for her, you can have your grandmother's ranch. You can live there. You can go home. You can all go home, far away from this crummy little falling-down house.

Huh. Maybe he and his new bride could make a deal.

They could *stay* married. She'd feel safe every day.

And he could have the Barelli ranch fair and square.

She'd said she was done with romance, done with love. So was he.

He wondered what she'd think of the proposition. She might be offended and smack him. Or simply tell him the idea was ludicrous. Or she might say, "You know what, you've got yourself a deal" and shake on it. Instead of kiss. Because it would be an arrangement, not anything to do with romance or feelings.

He'd take these thoughts, this idea, back to the sterile rental and let it percolate. A man didn't propose a romance-less marriage without giving it intense consideration from all angles.

But only one thought pushed to the forefront of his head: that he wasn't walking away from Norah and the triplets. No way, no how. Like father, *not* like son.

Norah was working on a new recipe for a barbecue pot pie when the doorbell rang. Which meant it wasn't Reed. He'd just left ten minutes ago and wouldn't ring the bell knowing the triplets were asleep. Neither would her sister, mother or aunt.

Please don't be someone selling something, she thought as she headed to the front door.

Amy Ackerman, who lived at the far end of the

street, stood at the door, holding a stack of files and looking exasperated. "Oh, thank God, you're here, Norah. I have to ask the biggest favor."

Norah tried to think of the last time someone had asked a favor of her. Early in her pregnancy, maybe. Before she started showing for sure. People weren't about to ask favors from a single mother of triplets.

"Louisa can't teach the zero-to-six-month multiples class and it starts Wednesday!" Amy shrieked, balancing her files in her hands. "Sixteen people have signed up for the class, including eight pregnant mothers expecting multiples. I can't let them down."

Amy was the director of the Wedlock Creek Community Services Center, which offered all kinds of classes and programming for children and adults. The multiples classes were very popular—the center offered classes in preparing for and raising multiples of all ages. How to feed three-week-old twins at once. How to change triplets' diapers when they were all soaked. How to survive the terrible twos with two the same age. Or three. Or four, in several cases.

During her pregnancy, Norah had taken the prep class and then the zero-to-six-month class twice herself. At the time, she'd been so stressed out about what to expect that she'd barely retained anything she'd learned, but she remembered being comforted by just being there. She'd been the only one without a significant other or husband, too. She'd gotten quite a few looks of pity throughout and, during any partner activities, she'd had to pair up with the instructor, Louisa.

"Given that you just graduated from the real-life course now that the babes are seven months," Amy said, "will you teach it? You'll get the regular fee plus an emergency bonus. The class meets once a week for the next six weeks."

Norah stared at Amy, completely confused. "Me? Teach a class?"

"Yes, you. Who better? Not only do you have triplets, but you're a single mom. You're on your own. And every time I see you with those three little dumplings, I think, 'There goes a champ.'"

Huh. Norah, champ. She kind of liked it.

She also knew she was being buttered up big-time. But still, there was sincerity in Amy's eyes and the woman had always been kind to her. In fact, the first time Norah had signed up for the zero-to-six-month class, Amy had waived the course fee for her, and it wasn't cheap.

But how could she teach a class in anything? She was hardly a pro at being the mother of triplets. Last week Norah had made the rookie mistake of guiding her shopping cart in the grocery store a little too close to the shelves. Bella had managed to knock over an entire display of instant ramen noodles and either Bea or Brody had sent a glass jar of pickles crashing to the floor, blocking the path of a snooty woman who'd given Norah a "control your spawn" dirty look.

Then there was the time Norah had been waiting for a phone call from the pediatrician with test results, couldn't find her phone in her huge tote bag with its gobs of baby paraphernalia and had let go of the stroller for a second to dig in with both hands. The stroller had rolled away, Norah chasing after it. She'd caught someone shaking his head at her. Then there were all the times Norah had been told her babies should be wearing hats, shouldn't have pacifiers and "Excuse me, but are you really feeding your child nonorganic baby food? Do you know what's in that?"

Not to mention all the secret shame. How Brody had almost fallen off the changing table when she'd raced to stop Bea from picking up the plastic eye from a stuffed animal that had somehow come off in her crib. Norah could go on and on and on. She was no Super Mom of Multiples, ages zero to six months.

Thinking of all that deflated her, despite the fact that a minute ago, just being asked to teach the course had made her feel almost special, as though she had something to share with people who could use her help.

"Amy, I'm sorry, but I don't think—" Norah began.

Amy held up a hand. "If anyone is qualified to teach this class, it's you, Norah. And I promise you, I'm not just saying that because I'm desperate. Though I am desperate to find the right instructor. And that's you."

Norah frowned. "I make so many mistakes. All the time."

"Oh. You mean you're human? It's *not* easy taking care of baby triplets? Really?"

Norah found herself smiling. "Well, when you put it like that."

"There's no other way to put it."

"You know what, Amy? Sign me up. I will teach the class." Yeah, she would. Why not? She most certainly *had* been taking care of triplet babies—on her own— for seven months.

But she would have to hire a sitter or ask her mom or aunt to watch the triplets while she taught.

The fee for teaching was pretty good; paying a sitter every week would still leave a nice little chunk left over, and now she'd be able to afford to buy a wall-unit

air conditioner for the downstairs. Norah had a feeling
her mom and aunt would insist on watching the babies,
though; both women had taken the class when Norah
was in her ninth month. And even Shelby had signed
up when she'd found herself the mother of not one but
two six-month-old babies and needed to learn how to
multitask on the quick.

The relief that washed over Amy's face made Norah
smile. "You've saved me! Here's Louisa's syllabus and
notes. You don't have to use her curriculum, though.
You may have different ideas. It's your class now, so
you make it your own."

That sounded good. "I'm looking forward to it," she
said. "And thanks for asking me."

As Amy left, Norah carried the folder into the kitchen
and set it down beside the bowl containing her special
barbecue sauce, which wasn't quite there yet. Norah's
regular barbecue sauce was pretty darn good, but she
liked creating specials for the pot pies and wanted something with more of a Louisiana bite. She'd try a new
batch, this time with a drop more cayenne pepper and
a smidge less molasses. She'd just have to keep trying
bits and dashes until she got it just right, which, now
that she thought about it, was sometimes how parenting went. Yeah, there were basics to learn, but sometimes you had to be there, doing it, to know what to do.

As she headed to the coffeepot for a caffeine boost,
she noticed the manila envelope on the counter. The
annulment papers were inside. A yellow Post-it with
Reed's name on the outside. Tomorrow she'd drop it off
at the station and he'd sign them and she'd send them in
or he would. And that would be the end of that.

No more Reed to the rescue, which had been very nice today.

No more fantasy husband and fantasy father.

No more sexy man in her kitchen and living room.

More than all that, she liked the way Reed made her feel. Despite his offers to help, he never looked at her as though she was falling apart or unable to handle all she had on her plate. He made her feel like she could simply use another hand…a partner.

Could the annulment papers accidentally fall behind the counter and disappear? She smiled. She liked this new and improved Norah. Kicking butt and teaching a class. Suddenly wanting her accidental husband to stick around.

Maybe because she knew he wouldn't?

Anyway, one out of two wasn't bad, though. At least she had the class.

Tomorrow she'd be out a husband.

Chapter 6

Norah had filled her tenth pulled pork pot pie of the morning when she noticed Reed Barelli pacing the sidewalk that faced the back windows of the Pie Diner's kitchen. He seemed to be deep in thought. She was dying to know about what. His missing person's case? Or maybe even…her? The annulment papers he'd forgotten to sign last night on his way out?

It's not like I reminded him, she thought. The way he'd come to her rescue last night like some Super Husband had brought back all those old fantasies and dreams. Of someone having her back. Someone to lean on, literally and figuratively. And, oh, how she would love to lean on that very long, sexy form of his, feel those muscular arms wrapped around her.

Focus on your work, she admonished herself. She topped the pot pie with crust and made a design in the center, then set the pie on the tray awaiting the oven for the first of the lunch rush.

"Norah?" a waitress named Evie called out. "There's someone here to see you."

Had to be Reed. He was no longer out back. She quickly washed her hands and took off her apron, then left the kitchen. Reed sat at the far end of the counter. Since it was eleven, late for breakfast and early for lunch, the Pie Diner had very few customers. He was alone at the counter except for their regular, Old Sam, who sat at the first spot just about all day, paying for one slice of pie and coffee and getting endless refills and free pot pie for lunch, which had been the case for over a decade. Norah's mom had a soft spot for the elderly widower who reminded her of her late dad, apparently.

Reed looked...serious. Her heart sank. He must be there to sign the papers.

"I have the papers in my bag," she said. "Guess we both forgot last night. Follow me to the back office and you can sign them there if you want."

He glanced around, then stood and trailed her into the kitchen. The large office doubled as a kiddie nook and the triplets were napping in their baby swings.

She grabbed her tote bag from where it hung on the back of the desk chair and pulled out the annulment papers from the manila envelope.

But Reed wasn't taking the papers. He was looking at the babies.

"I'm glad they're here," he said. "Because I came to say something kind of crazy and seeing the triplets re-inforces that it's actually not crazy. That *I'm* not crazy."

She stared at him, no idea what he could be talk-ing about.

He took the papers from her and set them down on the desk. "Instead of signing those, I have a proposition for you."

Norah tilted her head and caught her mother and aunt and sister all staring at them. She could close the door and give them some privacy, but then she'd only have to repeat what he'd said to her family, so they might as well get the earful straight from him. Besides, they'd never forgive her if she shut them out of this juicy part.

"A proposition?" she repeated.

Out of the corner of her eye, she could see her mother, sister and aunt all shuffle a step closer to the office.

He nodded. "If I sign those papers and you return them to the county clerk, poof, in a week, we're not married anymore. Never happened. Drunken mistake. Whoops. Except it *did* happen. And the intensive couple of days I've been a part of your life makes me unable to just walk away from you and Bella, Bea and Brody. I can't. A man doesn't do that, Norah."

Did she hear a gasp or two or three coming from the kitchen?

She stared at him. "Reed. We got married by accident. By drunken mistake, as you perfectly put it."

"Maybe so. But we also got married. We both stood up there and said our vows. Drunk off our tushes or not, Norah, we got married."

She gaped at him. "So you feel you have to stand by vows you made under total insanity and drunken duress? Why do you think both of those are grounds for annulment?"

"I stand by you and the triplets. And if we're married, if we stay married, I also get to have the Barelli ranch fair and square. I was never planning on getting married. You said you weren't, either. We're both done with love and all that nonsense about happily-ever-after. So why not partner up, since we're already legally bound, and get what we both need?"

"What do I need exactly?" she asked, narrowing her eyes on him.

"You need a safe home, for one. A place big enough for three children growing every single day. You need financial stability and security. You need someone there for you 24/7, having your back, helping, sharing the enormous responsibility of raising triplets. That's what you need."

No kidding. She did need that. She *wanted* that more than she could bear to admit to herself. She also wanted to take responsibility for her own life, her own children, and do it on her own. And it was harder than she even imagined it would be, than her mother had warned her it would be when she'd been so set on moving out and going it alone.

She couldn't be stubborn at the triplets' expense. She would focus on that instead of on how crazy Reed's proposal was. Because when it came right down to it, he was absolutely right about what she needed.

And what *he* needed was his grandmother's ranch. She'd witnessed just how great that need was when they'd been together at the house. The ranch meant so much to him. It was home. It was connection to his family. It was his future. And his being able to call the ranch home came down to her saying yes to his proposition.

Hmm. That proposition was a business deal of sorts. She thought, at least. "I get stability and security and you get the Barelli ranch."

He eyed her and she could tell he was trying to read

her. She made sure she had on her most neutral expression. She had no idea what she thought of his proposal. Stay legally married to a man she'd known for days? For mutual benefit?

"Right," he said. "I need it more than I ever realized. It's home. The only place that's ever felt like home. You could move out of that falling-down, depressing little place and move to the ranch with room and wide-open spaces for everyone."

Her house *was* falling down and depressing. She hated those steep, slippery wooden stairs. And the lease was month to month. It would be a snap to get out of.

But the man was talking about serious legal stuff. Binding. He was talking about keeping their marriage on the books.

She looked up at him. "So we just rip up the papers and, voilà, we're married?"

"We are truly married, Norah. Yeah, we can go through with the annulment. Or we can strike a bargain that serves us both. Neither of us is interested in a real marriage about love and all that jazz. We've both been burned and we're on the same page. Our marriage would be a true partnership based on what we need. I think we'll be quite happy."

Quite happy? She wasn't so sure she'd be even close to happy. Comfortable, maybe. Not afraid, like she was almost all the time.

And what would it be like to feel the way she had during the ceremony? Safe. Secure. Cherished. Sure, the man "promising" those things had been drunk off his behind, but here he was, sober as a hurricane, promising those things all over again.

Maybe not to cherish her. But to stand at her side.

God, she wanted that. Someone trustworthy at her side, having her back, being there.

But what did Reed Barelli, bachelor, know about living 24/7 with babies? What if she let herself say yes to this crazy idea, moved to that beautiful homestead and breathed for the first time in over seven months, and he couldn't handle life with triplets after a week? He had no idea what he was in for.

She raised an eyebrow. "What makes you think you want to live with three seven-month-old, teething babies? Are you nuts?"

He smiled. "Insane, remember?"

He had to be. She had to be. But what did she have to lose? If the partnership didn't work out, he would sign the papers and that would be that.

She could give this a whirl. After all, they were already married. She didn't have to do anything except move into a beautiful ranch house with floors that didn't creak or slope and with an oven that worked all the time. Of course, she would be living with Reed Barelli. Man. Gorgeous man. What would *that* be like?

"Let's try," he whispered.

She looked up at him again, trying to read him. If she said, "Yes, let's try this wild idea of yours," he'd get his ranch. If she said no, he'd never have the only place that had ever felt like home. Reed wouldn't marry just to get the ranch; she truly believed that. But because of a big bowl of spiked punch, he had his one chance. He'd been so kind to her, so good to the triplets.

Brody let out a sigh and Norah glanced over at her son. His little bow-shaped mouth was quirking and a hand moved up along his cheek. The partnership would benefit the triplets and that was all she needed to know.

"I was about to say 'Where do I sign?' but I guess I'm not signing, after all." She picked up the papers and put them back in her tote bag.

The relief that crossed Reed's face didn't go unnoticed. Keeping that ranch meant everything to him. Even if it meant being awakened at 2:00 a.m. by one, two or three crying babies. And again at 3:00 a.m.

Out of the corner of her eye, Norah caught her mother hurrying back over to her station, pretending to be very busy whisking eggs. She poked her head out of the office. "Did y'all hear this crazy plan of his?"

"What? No, we weren't eavesdropping," her mother said. "Okay, we were. And I for one think his crazy plan isn't all that crazy."

"Me, too," Cheyenne said from in front of the oven. "You each get what you need."

Even if it's not what we really want, Norah thought. Reed didn't want to be married. Just as she didn't. Sure, it felt good and safe. But even a good man like Reed couldn't be trusted with her stomped-on heart. No one could. It wasn't up for grabs, hadn't been since the day after she'd found out she was pregnant and had been kicked to the curb.

Shelby sidled over and took Norah's hand. "You don't mind if I borrow your wife, do you?" she asked Reed.

What also didn't go unnoticed? How Reed swallowed, uncomfortably, at the word *wife.*

Wife. Norah was someone's wife. Not just someone's—this man's. This handsome, kind, stand-up man.

"Of course," he said. "I'll keep an eye on the triplets."

Shelby gave him a quick smile, then led Norah by the hand to the opposite end of the kitchen. "Don't forget to figure out the rules."

"The rules?" Norah repeated.

"Just what kind of marriage will this be?" her sister asked. "He used the word *partnership*, but you're also husband and wife. So are you sharing a bedroom?"

Norah felt her face burn. She was hardly a prude, but the thought of having sex with Reed Barelli seemed... sinful in a very good way. They'd hardly worked up to the level of sex. Even if they were married. They weren't even at the first-kiss stage yet.

Norah pictured Reed in his black boxer briefs. "I guess we'll need to have a conversation about that."

"Yeah, you will," Shelby said. "Been there, done that with my own husband back when we first got together. Remember, Liam and I only got married so we could each have both our babies—the ones we'd raised for six months and the ones who were biologically ours."

Norah would never forget that time in Shelby's life. And the fact that all had turned out very well for her sister was a bonus. It wasn't as if Norah and Reed Barelli were going to fall in love. She had zero interest in romance. Yes, Reed was as hot as a man got, but nice to look at was different than feeling her heart flutter when she was around him. That wasn't going to happen. Not to a woman who'd been burned. Not to a busy mother of baby triplets. And it certainly wouldn't happen to Reed. He was even more closed to the concept of love and romance than she was. And as if he'd fall for a woman who'd lost all sex appeal. She smelled like strained apricots and spit-up and baby powder when she wasn't smelling like chicken pot pie. She wasn't exactly hot stuff these days.

"No matter what you're thinking, Norah, don't forget one thing," Shelby said.

Norah tilted her head. "What's that?"

Shelby leaned in and whispered, "He's a man."

"Meaning?"

"What's the statistic about how many times per second men think about sex?" Shelby asked.

Norah let out a snort-laugh and waved a hand down the length of herself. "Oh yeah, I am irresistible." She was half covered in flour. Her hair was up in a messy bun. She wore faded overalls and yellow Crocs.

"Trust me," Shelby said. "The issue will arise." She let out a snort herself. "Get it? *Arise*." She covered her mouth with her hand, a cackle still escaping.

"You're cracking jokes at a time like this?" Norah said, unable to help the smile.

"I'm just saying. You need to be prepared, Norah. Your life is about to change. And I'm not just talking about a change in address."

That was for sure. She'd be living with a man. Living with Reed Barelli. "Your words of wisdom?" she asked her sister.

"Let what happens happen. Don't fight it."

Norah narrowed her eyes. "What's gonna happen?"

"Let's see. Newlyweds move in together..."

Norah shook her head. "You can stop right there, sistah. We may be newlyweds, but like Reed said, this is a partnership. No hanky-panky. This isn't about romance or love. Nothing is *arising*."

"We'll see. But just know this, Norah. It's nice to be happy. Trust me on that."

Norah loved that her sister was happy. But the pursuit of happiness wasn't why Norah was saying yes to Reed's proposition.

"I'm finally at a good place, Shel," Norah said. "It

took me a long time to bounce back from being abandoned the way I was. Lied to. Made a fool of. I might not be skipping all over town, but I'm not *un*happy. And I'm not throwing away my equilibrium when my first and foremost job is to be a good mother. I will not, under any circumstances, fall for a guy who's made it crystal clear he feels the same way I do—that love is for other people."

Shelby squeezed her hand. "Well, just know that anytime you need a sitter for an evening out with your husband, I'm available."

"I no longer need sitters because I'll have a live-in sitter."

"Answer for everything, don't you?" Shelby said with a nudge in Norah's midsection. She threw her arms around her and squeezed. "Everything's going to be fine. You'll see."

Norah went back into the office and stared hard at her sleeping babies, then at Reed, who leaned against the desk looking a bit…amused, was it?

"Your sister is right," he said. "Everything *is* going to be fine."

Norah wasn't so sure of that.

And had he heard *everything* they'd said?

Chapter 7

Thanks to the Wedlock Creek PD going digital, copies of all the case files were now a click away and on Reed's smartphone. He was almost glad to have a confounding case to focus on for the next couple of hours while Norah packed for herself and the triplets.

For a while there he'd thought she might say no. The idea *was* crazy. To stay married? As a business partnership? Nuts. Who did that?

People like him whose wily grandmother had him over a barrel.

People like her who could use a solid place to land.

When he'd left the Pie Diner, the annulment papers back in the envelope, unsigned, the ranch rightfully his after a visit to his grandmother's attorney, an unfamiliar shot of joy burst inside him to the point he could have been drunk on spiked punch. The ranch was home for real. He'd wake up there every day. Walk the land he'd explored as a child and teenager. Finally adopt a dog or two or three and a couple of black cats that he'd always been partial to. He was going home.

But right now he was going to find David Dirk, who hadn't been seen or heard from in days. Reed sat in his SUV and read through the notes on his phone. Dirk's fiancée, Eden Pearlman, twenty-five, hair stylist, never before married, no skeletons in the closet, per his predecessor's notes, had agreed to meet with him at her condo at the far end of Main Street.

He stood in front of the building and took it in: five-story, brick, with a red canopy to the curb and a part-time doorman who had seen David Dirk leave for his office four days ago at 8:45 a.m., as usual, briefcase in one hand, travel mug of coffee in the other. He'd been wearing a charcoal-gray suit, red-striped tie. According to his predecessor's notes, David had had a full day's appointments, meetings with two clients, one prospective client, but had mostly taken care of paperwork and briefs. His part-time administrative assistant had worked until three that day and noted that David had seemed his usual revved-up self. Except then he vanished into thin air instead of returning home to the condo he shared with his fiancée of eight months.

Looking worried, sad and hopeful, Eden closed the door behind Reed and sat on a chair.

Reed sat across from her. "Can you tell me about the morning you last saw Mr. Dirk?"

Eden pushed her light blond hair behind her shoulders and took a breath. "It was just a regular morning. We woke up, had breakfast—I made him a bacon-and-cheese omelet and toast—and then David left for his office. He texted me a Thinking about you, beautiful at around eleven. That's the last time I heard from him. Which makes me think whatever went wrong happened soon after because he would have normally texted a cute little something a couple hours later and he didn't. He always texted a few times a day while at work. I just know something terrible happened! But I don't want that to be true!" She started crying, brown streaks under her eyes.

Reed reached for the box of tissues on the end table and handed it to her. She took it and dabbed at her eyes. "I know this isn't easy, Ms. Pearlman. I appreciate that you're talking to me. I'm going to do everything I can to find your fiancé. I knew David when I was a kid. We used to explore the woods together when I'd come up summers to stay with my grandmother. I have great memories of our friendship."

She sniffled and looked up at him. "So it's personal for you. That's good. You'll work hard to find my Davy Doo."

He wondered if any old girlfriend of his had ever referred to him as Reedy Roo or whatever. He hoped not. "What did you talk about over breakfast?" he asked.

"The wedding mostly. He was even trying to convince me to elope to Las Vegas—he said he wanted me to be his wife already and that we could even fly out that night. He's so romantic."

Hmm, making a case for eloping? Had Dirk wanted to get out of town fast? Was there a reason he'd wanted to go to Las Vegas in particular? Or was there a reason he'd wanted to marry Eden even faster than the weekend? "Did you want to elope?"

She shook her head. "My mother would have my

head! Plus, all the invitations were out. The wedding is this Saturday!"

"Where?" he asked, trying to recall the venue on the invitation.

"The Wedlock Creek chapel—this Saturday night," she said, sniffling again. "What if he's not back by then?"

"I'm going to go out there and do my job," he said. "I'll be in touch as soon as I have news."

She stood and shook his hand. "Thanks, Detective. I feel better knowing an old friend of David's is on the case."

Back in his SUV, Reed checked David Dirk's financials again. None of his credit cards had been used in the past twenty-four hours. Reed's predecessor had talked to five potential enemies of David's from opposing cases, but none of the five had struck the retired detective as holding a grudge. Reed flipped a few more pages in the man's notes. Ah, there it was. "According to friends and family, however, David wouldn't have just walked out on Eden. He loved her very much."

So what did happen to you, David Dirk? Reed wondered.

Reed had sent a small moving truck with two brawny guys to bring anything Norah wanted from the house to the ranch, but since the little rental had come furnished, she didn't have much to move. Her sister had given her way too many housewarming gifts from her secondhand shop, Treasures, so Norah had packed up those items and her kitchen stuff and everything fit into a small corner of the moving truck. It was easier to focus on wrapping up her picture frames than on actually setting them on surfaces in Reed's home.

She was moving in with him? She was. She'd made a deal.

Norah had never lived with a man. She'd lived on her own very briefly in this little dump, just under a year, and while she liked having her own place and making her way, she'd missed hearing her mom in the kitchen or singing in the shower. Did Reed sing in the shower? Probably not. Or maybe he did. She knew so little about him.

She gave the living room a final sweep. This morning she'd done a thorough cleaning, even the baseboards because she'd been so wired, a bundle of nervous energy about what today and tomorrow and the future would be like. She was taking a big leap into the unknown.

"We're all set, miss," the big mover in the baseball cap said, and Norah snapped out of her thoughts.

She was about to transfer the triplets from their playpen to their car seats, then remembered her mom had them for the day to allow Norah a chance to settle in at Reed's. She stood in the doorway of her house, gave it a last once-over and then got in her car. She pulled out, the truck following her.

In fifteen minutes they were at the farmhouse. Reed told the movers to place all the items from the truck in the family room and that Norah would sort it all later. Once the movers were gone and it was just Norah and Reed in the house, which suddenly seemed so big and quiet, it hit her all at once that this was now her home. She *lived* here.

"I want you to feel comfortable," he said. "So change anything you want."

"Did we talk about sleeping arrangements?" she asked, turning away and trying to focus on an oil painting of two pineapples. They hadn't, she knew that full well.

"I'll leave that to you," he said.

"As if there's more than one option?"

He smiled. "Why don't you take the master bedroom? It's so feminine, anyway." He started for the stairs. "Come, I'll give you more of a tour."

She followed him to the second level. The first door on the left was open to the big room with its cool white walls and huge Oriental rug and double wood dresser and big round mirror. A collection of old perfume dispensers was on a tray. A queen-size four-poster was near the windows overlooking the red barn, the cabbage-rose quilt and pillows looking very inviting. Norah could see herself falling asleep a bit easier in this cozy room. But still. "I feel like you should have the master suite. It's your house, Reed."

"I'd really rather have the room I had as a kid. It's big and has a great view of the weeping willow I used to read under. My grandmother kept it the same for when I'd come visit through the years. I'm nostalgic about it. So you take the master."

"Well, if you insist that I take the biggest room with the en suite bath, who am I to say no?" She grinned and he grinned back. She walked inside the room and sat on the bed, giving it a test. "Baby-bear perfect. I'll take it." She flopped back and spread out her arms, giving in to this being home.

"Good, it's settled."

A vision of Reed Barelli in his black boxer briefs and nothing else floated into her mind again, the way he'd looked lying next to her, all hard planes and five-o'clock shadow, long, dark eyelashes against his cheeks. She had a crazy thought of the two of them in bed.

And crazy it was, because their marriage was platonic. Sexless.

Focus, Norah. Stop fantasizing, which is bad for your health, anyway. Men can't be trusted with any part of your anatomy. That little reminder got her sitting up. "My sister says we need to talk about how this is going to work."

"Your sister is right. I made a pot of coffee before you came. Let's go talk."

She followed him downstairs and into the kitchen. On the refrigerator was a magnet holding a list of emergency numbers, everything from 9-1-1 to poison control to the clinic and closest hospital. His work and cell numbers were also posted, which meant he'd put up this sheet for her.

He poured coffee and fixed hers the way she liked, set them both on the round table in front of the window and sat down. "I have a feeling we'll just have to deal with things as they come up."

She sat across from him, her attention caught by the way the light shone on the side of his face, illuminating his dark hair. He was too handsome, his body too muscular and strong, his presence too...overwhelming.

"But I suppose the most important thing is that you feel comfortable here. This is now your home. Yours and the triplets. You and they have the run of the place. The crawl of the place."

She smiled. "I guess that'll take some getting used to." She glanced out the window at the fields she could imagine Bella, Bea and Brody running like the wind in just several months from now.

"No rush, right?" he said.

I could do this forever, she finished for him and realized that really was probably the case for him. He seemed to be at ease with the situation, suddenly living with a woman he'd accidentally slash drunk-married, appointing himself responsible for her and her three children. Because he wasn't attracted to her physically, most likely. Or emotionally. Men who weren't interested in marriage generally went for good-time girls who were equally not interested in commitment. Norah Ingalls was anything but a good-time girl. Unless you counted their wedding night. And you couldn't because neither of them could remember it.

Detective Reed Barelli's job was to serve and protect and that was what he was doing with his accidental wife. That was really what she had to remember here—and not let her daydreams get a hold on her. The woman he'd thought he was getting was Angelina, international flight attendant. Not Norah.

There was no need to bring up her sister Shelby's bedroom questions again or exactly what kind of marriage this was. That was clear. They were platonic. Roommates. Sharing a home but not a bed. Helping each other out. Now that she had that square in her mind, she felt more comfortable. There were boundaries, which was always good. She could ogle her housemate, stare at his hotness, but she'd never touch, never kiss and never get her heart and trust broken again.

"Anything else we should cover?" he asked.

She bit her lip. "I think you're right. We'll deal with

whatever comes up. Right now we don't know what those things might be."

"For instance, you might snore really loud and keep me awake all night and I'll have to remember to shut my door every night to block out the freight train sounds."

She smiled. "I don't snore."

"Not an issue, then," he said, and she realized that, again, he was trying to break the ice, make her feel more comfortable.

She picked up her mug. "You know who might keep you awake, though? The three teething seven-month-olds you invited to live here with you."

"They're supposed to do that, so it's all good."

"Does anything rattle you?" she asked, wondering if anything did.

"Yes, actually. A few things. The first being the fact that we're married. Legally married."

Before she could even think how to respond to that, he changed the subject.

"So what's on your agenda for today?" he asked.

"I figure I'll spend the next couple of hours unpacking, then I'll be working this afternoon. It's Grandma's Pot Pie Day, so I'll be making about fifty classics—chicken, beef, vegetable—from my grandmother's recipes. Oh—and I'll be writing up a class syllabus, too."

He took a sip of his coffee and tilted his head. "A class syllabus?"

She explained about the director of the community services center asking her to teach the multiples class for parents and caregivers of zero-to-six-month-olds. "I tried to get out of it—I mean, I'm hardly an expert—but she begged."

"You *are* an expert. You're a month out of the age

group. Been there, done that and lived to tell the tale. And to teach the newbies what to do."

She laughed. "I guess so!"

Norah always thought of herself as barely hanging on, a triplet's lovie falling out of the stroller, a trail of Cheerios behind them on the sidewalk, a runny nose, a wet diaper. Well-meaning folks often said, "I don't know how you do it," when they stopped Norah on the street to look at the triplets. Most of the time she didn't even feel like she *was* doing it. But all three babies were alive and well and healthy and happy, so she must be. She could do this and she would. She *did* have something to offer the newbie multiples moms of Wedlock Creek.

She sat a little straighter. She had graduated from the zero-to-six-month age range, hadn't she? And come through just fine. She was a veteran of those first scary six months. And yeah, you bet your bippy she'd done it alone. With help from her wonderful family, yes. But alone. She could teach that class blindfolded.

He covered her hand with his own for a moment and she felt the two-second casual touch down to her toes.

"Well, I'd better start unpacking," she said, feeling like a sixteen-year-old overwhelmed by her own feelings.

"If you need help, just say the word."

He was too good. Too kind. Too helpful. And too damned hot.

She slurped some more coffee, then stood and carried the mug into the family room, where the movers had put her boxes. But she wanted to be back in the kitchen, sitting with...her husband and just talking.

Her husband. She had a husband. For real. Well, sort of for real.

She didn't expect it to feel so good. She'd just had an "I'm doing all right on my own" moment. But it was nice to share the load. Really, really nice.

After walking Norah to the Pie Diner and taking a slice of Grandma's Classic Beef Pot Pie to go, Reed was glad the diner was so busy, because he kept seeing Norah's mom and aunt casting him glances, trying to sneak over to him for news and information about how Norah's move-in had gone. Luckily, they'd kept getting waylaid by customers wanting more iced tea and "could they have sausage instead of bacon in their quiche Lorraine?" and "were the gluten-free options really gluten free?"

Move-in had gone just fine. He was comfortable around Norah for some reason he couldn't figure out. He'd never lived with a woman, despite a girlfriend or two dumping him over his refusal for even that, let alone an engagement ring.

As far as tonight went, he'd simply look at his new living arrangement the way he would with any roommate. They were sharing a home. Plain and simple. The snippets he'd overheard from Norah's conversation with her sister wouldn't apply. There would be no sex. No kissing. No romance. As long as he kept his mind off how pretty and sexy she was and remembered why they were staying married, he'd be fine.

That settled in his head, he hightailed it out of the Pie Diner with his to-go bag and took a seat at a picnic table edging the town green, waving at passersby, chatting with Helen Minnerman, who had a question about whether it was against the law for her neighbor's Chihuahua to bark for more than a minute when outside—no, it was not—and helping a kid around ten or eleven up from under his bike when he slid from taking a turn too fast.

Life in Wedlock Creek was like this. Reed could get used to this slower pace. A man could think out here in all this open space and fresh air, which was exactly what he was doing, he realized. Too much thinking. About his new wife and what it would be like to wake up every morning knowing she was in bed down the hall. In the shower, naked under a spray of steamy water and soap. Making waffles in his kitchen. Their kitchen. Caring for babies who had him wrapped around their tiny fingers after just a few days of knowing them.

But all his thinking hadn't gotten him closer to finding David Dirk. In fifteen minutes he was meeting Dirk's closest friend, a former law associate, so hopefully the man would be able to shed some light.

Reed finished the last bite of the amazing beef pot pie, then headed for Kyle Kirby's office in a small, brick office building next to the library.

Kirby, a tall, lanky man with black eyeglasses, stood when Reed entered, then gestured for him to sit. "Any luck finding David?"

Reed sat. "Not yet. And to be honest, not much is making sense. I've looked into all the possibilities and I'm at a loss."

Kirby was chewing the inside of his lip—as if he knew more than he wanted to say. He was looking everywhere but at Reed.

Reed stared at him. "Mr. Kirby, if you know where David is or if he's okay or not, tell me now."

Was that sweat forming on the guy's forehead despite the icy air-conditioning?

"I wish I could help. I really do." He stood. "Now, if those are all your questions, I need to get back to work."

Reed eyed him and stood. This was strange. Reed had done his homework on Kyle Kirby's relationship with David and the two were very close friends, had been since David had moved back to Wedlock Creek to settle down after graduating from law school. Kirby had no skeletons in his closet and there was no bad blood between him and David. So what was the guy hiding?

Frustrated, Reed put in a couple more hours at the station, working on another case—a break-in at the drugstore. A promising lead led to a suspect, and another hour later, Reed had the man in custody. The solid police work did nothing to help his mood over his inability to figure out what had happened to David. It was as if he had just vanished into thin air.

One staff meeting and the receptionist's birthday cake celebration later, Reed headed home. He almost drove to the house he'd rented and would need to find a new tenant for. It still hadn't sunk in that the Barelli ranch was his, was home, and that when he arrived, he wouldn't walk into an empty house. Norah would be there. Bella, Bea and Brody would be there. And tonight he was grateful for the company. Company that wouldn't be leaving. *That* would definitely take some getting used to.

He pulled up at the ranch, glad to see Norah's car. Inside he found her in the kitchen, the triplets in their big playpen near the window. Bella was chewing on a cloth book, Brody was banging on a soft toy piano and

Bea was shaking a rattling puppy teether. The three looked quite happy and occupied.

"Something sure smells good," he said, coming up behind Norah and peeking into the big pot on the stove. "Pot pies for the diner?"

"Meatballs and spaghetti for us," she said. "I remember you mentioned you loved meatballs and spaghetti the night we met, so I figured it would be a good first dinner for us as—"

He smiled. "Official husband and wife."

"Official husband and wife," she repeated. She turned back to the pot, using a ladle to scoop out the meatballs and fragrant sauce into a big bowl. Was it Reed's imagination or did she look a little sad?

"You okay?" he asked.

She didn't answer. She picked up the pot of spaghetti and drained it into a colander over the sink, then added it to the bowl of meatballs and stirred it. Before he could say another word, the oven timer dinged and she took out heavenly smelling garlic bread.

"Well, can I at least help with anything?" he asked.

"Nope. The babies have eaten. Dinner is ready. The table is set. So let's eat."

She'd poured wine. There was ice water. A cloth napkin. He hadn't been treated to this kind of dinner at home in a long, long time, maybe not since he'd last visited his grandmother just weeks before she'd died.

"This is nice. I could get used to this," he said. "Thank you."

"You will get used to it because I love to cook and, given everything you're doing for me and the triplets, making dinner is the least I can do."

But as they chatted about their days and the triplets and she filled him in on some upcoming events in town, Norah seemed to get sadder. And sadder. Something was wrong.

"Norah. This marriage is meant to be a true partnership. So if something is bothering you, and something clearly is, tell me. Let's talk about it."

She poked at her piece of garlic bread. "It's silly."

"I'm sure it's not."

"It's just that, there I was, cooking at the stove in this beautiful country kitchen, my dream kitchen, the triplets happily occupied in the playpen, and my husband comes home, except he's not really my husband in the way I always thought it would go. I'm not complaining, Reed. I'm just saying this is weird. I always wanted something very different. Love, forever, growing old together on the porch. The works."

"It's not quite what I expected for myself, either," he said, swirling a bite of spaghetti. "It'll take some getting used to. But we'll get to know each other and soon enough we'll seem like any other old married couple."

"Kind of backward to have to get to know your spouse." She gave him a wistful smile and took a sip of wine.

"The triplets' father—you wanted to marry him?"

Norah put down her fork as though the mention of him cost her her appetite. "I just don't understand how someone could seem one way and truly be another way. I got him so wrong. I thought he was crazy about me. He was always talking about us and the future. But then the future presented itself in the form of my pregnancy and everything changed. I'll never forget the look on his face when I told him I was pregnant. A combo of freaked out and horrified."

"Sorry."

"And now everything I wanted—the loving husband, the babies, a home for us—is right here and it's all…"

He touched her hand. "Not like the old dreams."

She lifted her chin and dug her fork into a meatball with gusto. "I'm being ridiculous. I'm sitting here moping over what isn't and what wasn't. My life is my life. Our deal is a good one. For both of us. And for those three over there," she added, gesturing at the playpen. She focused on them for a moment and then turned back to him. "Okay, full speed ahead on the marriage partnership. My head is back in the game."

The meatball fell off her fork and plopped back onto her plate, sending a splatter of sauce onto both of them—her cheek and his arm. They both laughed and then he reached out and dabbed away the sauce from her cheek as she did the same to his arm.

"Anytime you need to talk this through, just tell me," he said. "And we'll work it out."

"You, too, you know."

He nodded. "Me, too."

As she pushed around spaghetti and twirled it but never quite ate any more, he realized she had the same funny pit in the middle of her stomach that he had in his, just maybe caused by a different emotion. She'd wanted something so much more—big passion, real romance, everlasting love—and had to settle for plain ole practical for a good reason. He'd planned on going it alone, never committing, but he had committed in a huge way, even if his heart wasn't involved. He was responsible for this family of four. Family of five now, including him.

He wouldn't let Norah down. Ever. But he knew he'd never be able to give her what she wanted in the deepest recesses of her heart.

Chapter 8

There was no way Reed was getting any sleep tonight. Not with Norah down the hall, sleeping in who knew what. Maybe she slept naked, though he doubted she'd choose her birthday suit for her first night in her new home with her new partnership-husband. Twice he'd heard her get out of bed—the floor creaked a bit in that room—and go into the nursery. One of the babies had been fussing a bit and she sang a lullaby that almost had him drifting off. Almost. Norah had a beautiful voice.

He glanced at the clock: 2:12 a.m. He heard a faint cry. Then it grew louder. If he wasn't mistaken, that was Brody. He waited a heartbeat for the telltale creak of the master bedroom floor, but it didn't come. Only another cry did.

Reed got out of bed, making sure he was in more than his underwear. Check. A T-shirt and sweats. He headed to the nursery and gently pushed the door open wider. One frustrated, red-faced little one was sitting up in his crib, one fist around the bar.

"Hey there, little guy," Reed said in his lowest voice to make sure he wouldn't wake Brody's sisters. "What's going on? What's with the racket?"

Brody scrunched up his face in fury that Reed wasn't picking him up fast enough. His mouth opened to let loose a wail, but Reed snatched him up and, as always, the sturdy little weight of him felt like pure joy in his arms. Brody wore light cotton footie pajamas and one sniff told Reed he was in the all clear for a middle-of-the-night, heavy-duty diaper change. He brought the baby over to the changing table and took off the wet diaper, gave Brody a sprinkle of cornstarch, then put on a new diaper like a pro. All the while, Brody looked at him with those huge slate-blue eyes.

Reed picked him up and held him against his chest, walking around the nursery while slightly rocking the little guy. Brody's eyes would flutter closed, then slowly open as if making sure Reed hadn't slipped him inside his crib and left. This went on four more times, so Reed sat in the rocker and Brody let out the sigh of all sighs and closed his eyes, his lips quirking and then settling.

"Guess that means you're comfortable, then," Reed whispered. He waited a few seconds, then stood, but the baby opened his eyes. Reed almost laughed. "Busted. You caught me." Reed sat back down, figuring he might be there awhile. Maybe all night. "Want to hear a story?"

Brody didn't make a peep in response, but Reed took that for a yes anyway.

"Once upon a time, there was a little boy named Beed Rabelli. That's not me, by the way."

Did Brody believe him? Probably not. But it made the story easier to tell.

"Well, this little kid, Beed, did everything to try to win his father's approval. His father's interest. But no matter what Beed did, pretending to be interested in things he really didn't even like, his father barely paid attention to him. He only came around every now and then as it was. But one day, Beed's dad never came around again and Beed started getting postcards from far-off places."

Brody moved his arm up higher by his ear and Reed smiled at how impossibly adorable the baby was. And what a good listener.

"So one day, Beed and his friend David Dirk were riding bikes and exploring the woods and they got to talking about how even though they pretty much had the same type of not-there dad, it didn't mean their dads didn't love them or care about them. Their dads were just…free spirits who had to follow the road in their souls. Or something like that. Anyway, Brody, I just want you to know that your father is like that and that's why he's not here. I don't want you to spend one minute wondering why he doesn't care about you, because I'm sure he does. He's just following that road that took him far away from here and—"

Reed stopped talking. Where the hell was this coming from? Why was he saying anything of this to Brody?

Because he cared about this little dude, that was why. And it was important to know because at some level it was very likely true.

He heard a sniffle and glanced toward Bea's and

Bella's cribs. They were both fast asleep. He heard the sound again and realized it was coming from outside. Reed put Brody gently back inside his crib, and *booyah*—the baby did not open those eyes again. Either Reed had bored him to sleep or a story worked like it always had since time began.

He tiptoed out to investigate the sound of the sniffle. Was Norah so upset about her lost dreams that she was crying in the middle of the night?

He froze at the sight of her standing to the left of the nursery door, tears in her eyes.

"Norah? What's wrong?"

She grabbed him, her hands on the sides of his face, and pulled him close, laying one hell of a kiss on him. Damn, she smelled so good and her skin was so soft. Everything inside him was on fire. He backed her up against the wall and pressed against her, deepening the kiss, his hands roaming her neck, into her hair, down along her waist. He wanted to touch her everywhere.

"So you're not upset," he whispered against her ear, then trailed kisses along her beautiful neck.

"I was touched enough that you'd gotten up at a baby crying," she said. "And then as I was about to walk in, I heard you talking to Brody and couldn't help eavesdropping. I can't tell you how anxious I've been about the questions that would be coming my way someday, maybe at age three or four. 'Where's my father? Why doesn't Daddy live with us? Why doesn't Daddy ever see us? Doesn't he care about us?'"

Norah wiped under her eyes and leaned the front of her luscious body against Reed's. "I had no idea what I would say, how I could possibly make it okay for them. And one 2:00 a.m. diaper change later, you've settled it."

"Eh, I didn't say anything I hadn't worked out over the past twenty-nine years."

She smiled and touched his face, and he leaned his cheek against it. Then he moved in for another kiss, hoping reality and the night-light in the hallway wouldn't ruin the moment and make her run for her room.

She didn't. She kissed him back, her hands on his chest, around his neck, in his hair. He angled them down the hall toward his room and they fell backward onto his bed, the feel of her underneath him, every part of her against him, almost too much to bear.

He slid his hands under her T-shirt and pulled it over her head, then tugged off his own shirt and flung it behind him. He lay on top of her, kissing her neck, her shoulder, between her luscious breasts.

And then he felt her shift. Just slightly. The equivalent of a bitten lower lip. A hesitation.

He pulled back and looked at her. "Too fast?"

"Way too fast," she said. "Not that I'm not enjoying it. Not that I didn't start it."

He laughed. "That was hot. Trust me."

Her smile faded. "You've made it very clear what this marriage is, Reed. 'Friends with benefits' when we're married is too weird. Even for us. I think we need to keep some very clear boundaries."

She turned away from him and quickly put her T-shirt back on. He did the same.

"An emotional moment, the middle of the night, then there's me, still probably highly hormonal. Of course I jumped your bones."

She's trying to save face. Let her. "Believe me, if you hadn't kissed me, I would have kissed you first."

"Oh," she said, a bit of a smile back on her pretty

face. "I guess we know where we stand, then. We're foolishly attracted to each other on a purely physical level, and we went with the moment, then wised up. We'll just keep our hands to ourselves from now on. So that this partnership has a fighting chance."

She was right. If they screwed this up with great sex, that could lead to who knew what, like other expectations, and suddenly she would be throwing annulment papers at him, all his plans to stand by her and the triplets would fall to pot. And so would this ranch—home.

He nodded. Twice to convince himself of just how right she was. "We both know where romance leads. Trouble. Heartache. Ruin."

"Well, at least the mystery is gone. You've seen my boobs."

He had to laugh. But he sobered up real fast when he realized the mystery was hardly gone. He had yet to truly touch her.

"So if I let what happens happen and then we realize it's a bad idea, what does that mean?" Norah asked Shelby the next morning as they sat at a corner table for two in Coffee Talk, their favorite place to catch up in Wedlock Creek. Their huge strollers against the wall behind them, triplets asleep and Shelby's toddler sons drifting off after a morning running around the playground, the sisters shared a huge slice of delicious crumbly coffee cake. Of course they'd never have pie anywhere but at their own family restaurant.

"Ooh, so something happened?" Shelby asked, sipping her iced mocha.

"In the middle of the night last night, I thought I heard one of the babies crying, but when I went to the nursery, Reed was sitting in the rocker with Brody in his arms, telling him a story about himself and relating it to Brody. I stood there in tears, Shel. This is going to sound crazy, but in that moment, my heart cracked open."

Shelby's mouth dropped open. "You're falling in love!"

"Oh God, I think I am. I was so touched and so hormonal that I threw myself at him. But then I realized what an idiot I was being and put the kibosh on that."

"What? Why?"

"Shelby, he's made it crystal clear he married me for his ranch. And because he feels some kind of chivalrous duty toward me, as if annulling our marriage means he's walking away from his responsibilities. He's not responsible for us!"

"He feels he is," Shelby said. "The man's a police officer. Serve and protect. It's what he does."

Maybe that was a good reminder that Reed was operating on a different level—the cop level, the responsibility level. His father had walked away from him and his mother, the triplets' father had walked away from them and Norah, and Reed couldn't abide that, couldn't stand it. So he was stepping in. Attracted to her physically or not, Reed's feelings where she was concerned weren't of the romantic variety. He was trying to right wrongs.

"Um, excuse me?" a woman asked as she approached the table.

"Hi," Norah said. "Can we help you?"

"I noticed your triplets," she said, looking at Bella, Bea and Brody, who were all conked out in their stroller wedged up against the wall. "So it's true? If you get married at the Wedlock Creek chapel, you'll have multiples?"

"I didn't get married at the chapel and still had triplets," Norah said.

"And I did get married at the chapel and had one baby," Shelby said, "but ended up with twins, sort of." At the woman's puzzled expression, she added, "It's a long story."

Norah took a sip of her iced coffee. "Well, the legend does say if you marry at the chapel you'll have multiples in some way, shape or form. Are you hoping for a houseful of babies all at the same time?" she asked the woman.

"My fiancé is a twin and so we have a good chance of having twins ourselves, but he wants to increase our luck. I just figure the legend is just that—a silly rumor."

"No way," Shelby said. "Last year alone, there were five multiple births—two sets of triplets and three twins. The year before, four sets of twins and one set of triplets. The year before that, one set of quadruplets and two sets of twins. And that's just in Wedlock Creek."

The woman paled. She truly seemed to lose color. "Oh. So the legend is actually true?"

"Well, as true as a legend can be," Shelby said. "But this town is full of multiples. We can both personally attest to that."

"Um, is that a bad thing?" Norah asked gently.

"Well, twins just seem like a lot," the woman said. "One seems like a lot. I want to be a mother, but two at once? I don't know. I don't think I want to help our chances, you know?"

Norah smiled. "Then you definitely don't want to marry at the Wedlock Creek chapel." She upped her chin out the window. "See that woman? Pregnant with triplets. All boys!"

The woman swallowed. "I think we'll marry at the Brewer Hotel. Thanks!" she said and practically ran out.

Shelby laughed. "One baby *is* a lot of work. She's not wrong."

"But the more the merrier," Norah said, lifting her iced coffee for a toast.

"Got that right," Shelby said and tapped her cup. "Of course, you know what this means."

"What what means?"

"You and Reed got married at the chapel. You're going to have more multiples. Omigod, Norah, you're going to have, like, ten children."

She imagined three babies that looked like Reed Barelli. The thought made her smile.

"Jeez, you are far gone," Shelby said.

"Heaven help me. But I am."

She was falling in love with her business partner of a husband. She had to put the brakes on her feelings. But how did you do that when the floodgates just opened again?

Chapter 9

That night, Norah arrived at the Wedlock Creek Community Services Center with her stack of handouts, her laptop, for her slideshow on her favorite baby products, and a case of the jitters. As she stood at the front of the room, greeting students as they entered, she took a fortifying gulp of the coffee she'd brought in a thermos. As she'd left the ranch, she was surprised by how much she wished Reed had been there to see her off and give her a "you've got this" fist bump or something. She was beginning to need him a little too much for comfort. But he was working late, following up on a promising lead about David Dirk, who was still missing.

A woman's belly entered the room before she did. "If my water breaks while I'm sitting down, here's my husband's cell number," she said to Norah with a smile. "I'm not due for another month, but you never know."

You never know. No truer words ever spoken.

Norah smiled and took the card with the woman's husband's information. "I'm glad you're here. And if your water does break, I've got my cell phone at the ready and a list of emergency medical numbers."

"Pray I don't give birth until after the last class!" the woman said on a laugh. "I need to learn everything!" she added and slowly made her way over to the padded, backed benches that had been brought in specifically for women in her condition.

There were several pregnant women with their husbands, mothers, mothers-in-law and various other relatives all wanting to learn the basics of caring for newborn multiples. Several women had infant multiples already. Norah glanced around the room, seeing excitement and nerves on the faces. That was exactly how she'd felt when she'd shown up for the first class.

She was about to welcome her students when the door opened and Reed walked in. "Sorry I'm a minute late," he said, handing her a printout of his online registration form. He took an empty seat next to one of the husbands, giving the man a friendly nod.

Reed was taking her class?

Of course he was.

Norah smiled at him and the smile he gave her back almost undid her. *Don't think about what happened in the hallway last night*, she ordered herself. *Stop thinking about his hands on your bare skin. You're standing in front of a room full of people!*

She sucked in a breath, turned her attention away from Reed and welcomed her students. "Eight months ago, I was all of you," she said. "I was nine months' pregnant with BGG triplets—that's boy, girl, girl—and

I was a nervous wreck. Not only was I about to give birth to three helpless infants who would depend on me for everything, but I was a single mother. I will tell you right now that the most important thing I have learned about being the mother of triplets, particularly in my position, is to ask for help."

Norah looked around the room. All eyes were on her, interested, hanging on her every word, and some were actually taking notes.

So far, so good, she thought. "Ladies, don't expect your husbands to read your minds—if you want him to change Ethan while you change Emelia, ask him! No passive-aggressive stewing at the changing table while he's watching a baseball game. Speak up. Ask for what you need!"

"She's talking to you, Abby," the man next to Reed said and got a playful sock in the arm from his wife.

The students laughed. This was actually going well! She was standing there giving advice. People were responding! "And men, while you have infant twins or triplets or quadruplets, you're not going to be watching the game unless you have a baby or two propped in your arms, one hand on a bottle, the other burping another's little back."

A guy got up and headed for the door. "Just kidding," he said with a grin. More laughter.

Norah smiled. "And you grandmothers-to-be…what I learned from my mother? You're the rock. You're going to be everything to the mother and father of newborn multiples. Not only do you have experience, even if it's not with multiples yourselves, but you've been there, done that in the parenting department. You love those little multiples and you're there to help. Sometimes your brand-new mother of a daughter or daughter-in-law may screech at you that she's doing it her way. Let her. Maybe it'll work, maybe it won't. But what matters is that you're supporting one another. You're there."

She thought of her mother and her aunt Cheyenne and her sister. Her rocks. She couldn't have done it without them—their love and support and good cheer.

"So that's my number one most valuable piece of information I can offer you. Ask for help when you need it. When you think you'll need it. Because you will need it. If some of you don't have a built-in support system, perhaps you can create one when you go home tonight. Friends. Caring neighbors. Folks from your house of worship. Think about the people you can turn to."

From there, Norah started up her slideshow of products she'd found indispensable. She talked about cribs and bassinets. Feeding schedules and sleep schedules. How laundry would take over entire evenings.

"You did all that on your own?" a woman asked.

"I lived on my own, but I have a fabulous mother, fabulous aunt and fabulous sister who were constantly over, taking shifts to helping me out, particularly that first crazy month. So when I tell you help is everything, I mean it. Just don't forget that thank-yous, hugs and homemade pies go a long way in showing appreciation for their support."

Fifty-five minutes later the class was winding down. Norah let them know that in two weeks she'd be bringing in her triplets for show-and-tell with her mom as a volunteer assistant, demonstrating how to perform necessary tasks with three babies. After a question-and-answer session, Norah dismissed the students.

Huh. She'd really done it. She'd taught a class! And she was pretty darn good at it.

One of the last to pack her notebook and get up was a woman who'd come to the class alone. Early thirties with strawberry blond hair, she looked tired and defeated and hadn't spoken much during the period. She walked up to Norah with tears in her eyes.

Oh no. This woman had the look of multiple-itis.

"I have twin six-week-olds," the woman said. "My mother is with them now, thank God. They're colicky and I'm going to lose my mind. My husband and I argue all the time. And I only have twins—the bare minimum to even have multiples—and I'm a falling-apart wreck!"

Norah put her hand on the woman's arm. "I totally hear you." She offered the woman a commiserating smile. "What's your name?"

"Sara Dirk."

Norah noticed Reed's eyebrows shoot up at the name Dirk.

"Welcome, Sara. I'm really glad you're here. I haven't personally dealt with colic, but I've known colicky babies, and let me tell you, you might as well have sextuplets."

Sara finally smiled. "They don't stop crying. Except to breathe. I don't know how my mother does it—the screeching doesn't even seem to bother her. She just walks up and down with one baby while she watches the other in the vibrating baby swing, then switches them. I hear those cries that go on forever and I just want to run away."

Reed walked over and sat in the chair at the side of the desk, collecting Norah's handouts. She knew he was intently listening.

"That's wonderful that your mom is so supportive, Sara. I tell you what. Stop by the Pie Diner tomorrow and let anyone there know that Norah said they're to give you two of your and your mom's favorite kinds of pies on the house."

"I love the Pie Diner's chocolate peanut butter pie. It always cheers me up for a good ten minutes."

Norah smiled. "Me, too. And I'll research some tips for dealing with colic," she said. "I'm sure you have already, but I'll talk to the mothers I know who've dealt with it and survived. I'll email you the links."

"Thanks," she said. "I really appreciate it."

Reed stood with Norah's folders and laptop. He extended his hand to Sara. "Did I hear you say your last name is Dirk?"

Sara nodded.

"Are you related to David Dirk?" he asked.

Sara nodded. "My husband's first cousin."

"I'm Reed Barelli, a detective with the Wedlock Creek Police Department. I also knew David when I was a kid. I'm trying to find him."

"I sure hope he's okay," Sara said. "We just can't figure out what could have happened. The night before he went missing, he stopped by for a few minutes to drop off a drill he'd borrowed from my husband and he seemed so happy."

"Any particular reason why—besides the upcoming wedding, I mean?" Reed asked.

"He said something had been bothering him but that he'd figured out a solution. And then the twins started screaming their heads off, as usual, and there went the conversation. He left and that was the last time I saw him."

"Do you know what was bothering him?" Reed asked.

"No idea. I know he's madly in love with Eden. Things are going well at work, as far as I know."

"When did you see him before that last time?" Reed asked.

"Hmm, maybe a couple nights before. We—my husband and I—needed a sitter for an hour and my mother couldn't do it, so we begged David. He and Eden watched the twins. Do you believe that after babysitting our little screechers, that woman is hoping for triplets or even quadruplets? Craziest thing. She loves the idea."

"More power to her," Norah said.

"Well, I'd better get back and give my mother a break. See you next week, Norah. Oh, and, Detective Barelli, I do hope you find David. Eden must be out of her mind with worry."

Norah watched Reed wait until Sara had left, then hurried to the door and closed it.

"Are you thinking what I'm thinking?" he asked.

"I have so many thoughts running through my head that it could be any number of them."

"About David Dirk. And why he suddenly went missing."

Norah tilted her head and stared at Reed. "What do you mean?"

"Well, let's recount the facts and evidence. David Dirk has a cousin with colicky twins. David Dirk and his fiancée babysit said colicky twins. Despite the screeching in their ears for over an hour, Eden is hoping for multiples."

Norah wasn't sure where he was going with this.

"Okay," she said. "What does that have to do with his disappearance?"

"Well," he continued, "she and David are to be married at the Wedlock Creek chapel, where legend says those who marry will be blessed with multiples. The night before he went missing, David told Sara something was bothering him but he'd figured out a solution. Cut to David's fiancée telling me that on the morning he disappeared, he'd asked her to elope. But she reminded him how badly she wanted to marry at the chapel."

Ah. Now she was getting it. "Oh boy."

"Exactly. Because why would David want to elope instead of marrying at the Wedlock Creek chapel?

"The only reason folks in this town don't get married there is because they don't want multiples." But was David really so freaked out by his cousin's colicky babies and his fiancée wanting sextuplets that he ran away? No way. Who would do that? She herself had dated him, and he'd seemed like a stand-up guy, even if they'd had zero to talk about other than the weather and which restaurants they liked in town.

She remembered the woman who'd approached her and Shelby in the coffee shop yesterday. She'd wanted to avoid that legend like the ole plague. So maybe it was true. David had run!

"I'm thinking so," Reed said. "It's the only thing that makes sense. Yesterday I spoke with a friend of his who seemed nervous, like he was hiding something. Maybe he knew the truth—that David took off on his own—and had been sworn to secrecy."

"What a baby David is," Norah said.

"Pun intended?"

Norah laughed. "Nope. He's just really a baby. Why

not tell Eden how he felt? He has family and friends scared that something terrible happened to him. He had a friend lie to a police officer."

"Based on everything I've heard, I'm ninety-nine percent sure he took off on his own. I just have to find him. Maybe the friend can shed some light. I doubt he'll tell me anything, though."

"So how will you find David, then?"

"The right questions," Reed said. "And maybe my own memories of where David would go when his world felt like it was crashing down. I might know where he is without even realizing it. I need to do some thinking."

She nodded. "So let's go home, then."

"Home to the ranch. I like the sound of that."

Norah smiled and took his hand before she realized they weren't a couple. Why did being a couple feel so natural, then?

"Tell me more about the legend of the Wedlock Creek chapel," Reed said to Norah as they sat in the living room with two craft beers and two slices of the Pie Diner's special fruit pie of the day—Berry Bonanza.

"Well, as far as I know, back in the late 1800s, a woman named Elizabeth Eckard, known for being a bit peculiar, married her true love at the chapel."

"Peculiar how?"

"Some say she was a witch and could cast spells," Norah explained. "It was just rumor, but most shunned her just in case they got on her bad side."

Reed raised an eyebrow. "Apparently her true love wasn't worried."

Norah smiled. "Legend says he was so in love with

Elizabeth, he married her against his parents' wishes, who refused to have anything to do with them."

"Jeez. Harsh."

"Yup. But he loved her and so he married her at the beautiful chapel that she had commissioned to be built. Elizabeth had inherited a bit of money and wanted the new town of Wedlock Creek to have a stately chapel for services of all kinds."

Reed took a bite of the pie. "That must have buttered up the townspeople. Did his family come around?"

"Nope. And the townspeople still shunned her. Some even avoided services at the chapel. But some started noticing that those who attended church seemed luckier than those who didn't. And so everyone started going."

Reed shook his head. "Of course."

"Well, the luck didn't extend to Elizabeth. All she wanted was children—six. Three boys and three girls. But she never did get pregnant. After five years of trying, her husband told her there was no point being married to her if she couldn't give him a family, and he left her."

"That's a terrible story," Reed said, sipping his beer.

Norah nodded. "But Elizabeth loved children and ended up turning her small house into a home for orphans. She had the children she'd always wanted so much, after all. But when her only sister found herself in the same position, not getting pregnant, her sister's husband went to the officiants of the chapel and demanded an annulment. That night, Elizabeth crept out to the chapel at midnight and cast a spell that those who married at the chapel would not only be blessed with children, but multiples."

"Come on," Reed said.

Norah shrugged. "Nine months later, Elizabeth's sister had twin girls. And all the couples who married at the church that year also had multiples. Whispers began that Elizabeth had blessed the church with a baby spell."

"Did she ever marry again? Have her own multiples?"

Norah shook her head. "No, but she took in orphans till her dying day, then hired people to keep the home going. It was going strong until the 1960s, when foster care became more prominent."

"It's crazy that I actually think that David Dirk, reasonable, intelligent, suspicious of everything, believes in this legend to the point that he fled town to avoid marrying at the chapel. It's just an old legend. There's no blessing or spell."

"Then what accounts for all the multiples?" Norah asked.

"A little help from science?" he asked.

"Maybe sometimes," she said. "But I know at least ten women who married at the chapel and had multiples without the help of a fertility doctor."

"Don't forget me," he said.

"You?"

"I married at the chapel and now I have triplets."

She smiled, but the beautiful smile faded. "Are you their father, Reed? I mean, we didn't actually ever talk about that. You said you felt responsible for them and me. You said you would help raise them and help support them and be there for them. But are you saying you want to be their father?"

He flinched and realized she caught it. "I—" He grabbed his beer and took a swig, unsure how to answer. *Did* he want to be the triplets' father? He was their mother's husband—definitely. He was doing all the things Norah said when it came to caring for Bella, Bea and Brody. He was there for them. But was he their *father*?

That word was loaded.

"This is a partnership," she said, her voice formal as she sat straighter. "Of course you're not their *father*." She waved a hand in the air and made a strange snorting noise, then cut a forkful of berry pie. "It was silly of me to even use the term." A forced smile was plastered on her face. "So where do you think David Dirk is?"

Should he let her change the subject? If he were half the person she thought he was, he wouldn't. They'd talk this out. But he had no idea how he felt about this. Their *father*? Was he anyone's father? Could he be? Did he *want* to be?

"Norah, all I know for sure is that I want to take care of the four of you. I'm responsible for you all."

Her lips were tightly pressed. "Because you drunk-married me."

"I'm legally wed to you. It might have been because of spiked punch, but being married serves us both."

"You got your ranch," she said, staring at him. "And I got some security. I just have to keep reminding myself of that. Why we're here. Why we did this. Crazy as it really is."

Was it all that crazy? No. They both got what they needed.

He wasn't anyone's father. Reed Barelli? A father? With his craptastic model of paternity?

"It's good to know, to remember, what we are," she said, her voice higher pitched.

Higher pitched because she was upset? Or because

she was stating a fact? They'd almost had sex, but she'd called a halt and wisely so. She knew messing around with their partnership could have terrible consequences. Anything that could put conflict between them could ruin a good thing. And this marriage was a good thing. For both of them.

He was no one's father. He was Norah's husband and caretaker of her children. Guardian of them all.

None of this sounded right. Or felt right. His shoulders slumped and he slugged down the rest of the beer.

"Maybe I should go pick up the babies," she said. "My mom wants to keep them overnight, but I'm sure she'd rather have a solid night's sleep."

She wanted—needed—a buffer, he realized. And so did he.

"I'll go with you," he said. "Tell you the truth, I miss their little faces."

She bit her lip and lifted her chin, and he also realized he'd better stop saying things like that, despite the fact that it was the truth. His affection for the triplets was also a good thing—the fact that they had his heart meant he'd be a good provider, a good protector.

And that was what he'd vowed to be.

Chapter 10

The next morning, Norah woke very early and made twelve pot pies to deliver to the Pie Diner, the need to keep her eyes and mind on the various pots and timers a help in keeping her mind off Reed. But as she slid the last three pies from the oven, the smell of vegetable pot pie so comforting and tantalizing that she took out a frozen one to heat up for her breakfast, she couldn't stop hearing him say he wasn't the triplets' father.

She knew that. And of course, he didn't say it outright because he was Reed Barelli. But she'd been under the impression that fatherhood was part of the deal. Until she'd heard what had come stumbling out of her own mouth last night. He'd said again that being married, spiked punch or not, served them both. And she'd said something like, "Right, you got your ranch, I got some security."

Security. That was very different than "a father for my children."

Her shoulders slumped. Maybe she hadn't thought this through quite far enough. A father for her kids should have been first on her list, no?

Except you weren't looking for a father for your kids, dummy, she reminded herself. *You weren't looking for anyone. You got yourself in a situation and you didn't undo it so that you and your babies could have that security: a safe house, another caring adult, the financial burden lifted a bit, one more pair of hands. All that in a kind, supportive—and yes, sexy as all get-out—husband.*

No one, certainly not Reed Barelli, had used the word *father*.

Okay. She just had to let it sink in and accept it. Her marriage was platonic. Her husband was not her children's father. She had a good setup. It was good for the both of them.

"Do people eat pot pie for breakfast?" Reed asked as he walked into the kitchen in a T-shirt and navy sweats. Even his bare feet were sexy. His hair was adorably rumpled and as the sunlight illuminated half his face, he looked so beautiful she just stood there and stared at him until he tilted his head.

"Pot pie is appropriate for all meals," she said. "Seven a.m. Three p.m. Six p.m."

"Good, because this kitchen smells so good I'm now craving it."

"You're in luck because I have six frozen in the freezer. Just pop one in the oven for a half hour. It'll be ready when you're out of the shower." She glanced at her watch. "I'm going to drop these off at the Pie Diner and pick up the babies, bring them home and then go to Sara Dirk's with some frozen pot pies. I think she could use a freezer full of easily reheatable meals."

"That's thoughtful of you. Tell you what. Why don't you go to Sara's and I'll deliver the pies and pick up the rug rats and bring them home. I'm not on duty till noon."

"I can pick up the triplets," she said, her stomach twisting. "They're my children and I—"

"Norah," he said, stepping closer. He took both her hands and held them. "That's why I'm here. That's why you're here. I'm now equally responsible for them. So go."

He sure did use the word *responsible* a lot. She had to keep that in mind. *Responsible* was how he'd gotten himself married to her in the first place. He'd heard the plaintive, wistful note in her voice—*I've always dreamed of getting married here*—and instead of running for the hills, he'd felt responsible for her lost dreams and picked her up in his arms and carried her inside the chapel and vowed to love, honor and cherish her for the rest of his days.

She glanced down at their entwined hands. Why did it have to feel so good? Why did she have to yearn for more than the deal they'd struck? "Thank you, then," she managed to say, moving to the freezer to pull out six pot pies for Sara. The icy blast felt good on her hot, Reed-held hands and brought her back to herself a bit. "I'll pop one in the oven for you. Thirty minutes, okay?"

"Got it. See you back at home in a bit."

Back at home. Back at home. As she carried her bag to the door, she looked around and realized this ranch didn't feel like home, that she wasn't quite letting herself feel that it was hers, too. It wasn't. Not really. Just like Reed wasn't the triplets' father.

Because he was holding back just as she was. For self-preservation.

Stop thinking, she ordered herself as she got into her car and turned on the radio, switching the station until she found a catchy song she couldn't resist singing along to. A love song that ended up reminding her of the hot guy taking a shower right now. Grr, why did everything always come back to Reed Barelli?

"So how's married life?" Norah's mother, Arlena, asked as she set a slice of apple pie in front of Reed at the counter of the Pie Diner.

"Things are working out great," Reed said quite honestly.

"It's nice having someone to come home to, isn't it?" Cheyenne said, sidling up with a coffeepot in each hand. She refilled two tables behind them, then poured Reed a fresh cup.

"You two," Shelby chided. "Leave the poor detective alone. We all know theirs isn't a real marriage."

Reed stiffened, glancing at Shelby. Norah's sister was sharp and cautious, a successful business owner, and had held her own against one of the wealthiest and most powerful businessmen in Wedlock Creek, Liam Mercer, whom she'd eventually married. He felt like Shelby was trying to tell him something. Or trying to get across a message. But what?

Their marriage *was* real. They might not be loving and cherishing, but they were honoring each other's deepest wishes and needs.

But still, he couldn't shake what she'd said. *Not a real marriage. Not a real marriage. Not a real marriage.*

If their union wasn't real, then why would he feel such responsibility for her children? And he did. He had from day one when he'd woken up with the wedding ring and seen that photo of Norah and her triplets on the day they were born.

"Well, everyone's happy, including my beloved little grandbabies, so that's what matters," Arlena said, taking away Reed's empty plate.

Cheyenne nodded.

Shelby nodded extra sagely.

Arlena returned with the stroller, parking it beside Reed. "Look who's here to take you home," she cooed to the triplets. She frowned, then looked at him. "What do they call you?"

"Call me?" he repeated.

"Call you," Norah's mother repeated. "Da-da? Papa? Reed? Mama's husband?"

He felt his cheeks sting. Had Norah talked to her mom about their conversation? He doubted there'd been time. "They don't talk yet, so, of course, they don't call me anything."

"They'll be taking any day," she said, clearly uninterested in letting this line of questioning go. He should suggest detective work on the side for Arlena Ingalls.

He swallowed and got up from the bar stool, refusing to take the twenty Cheyenne tried to foist back at him. He put the bill under his empty coffee mug and got out of there fast with the giant stroller. Or as fast as anyone could make their way around tables in a diner while pushing a three-seat stroller with a yellow-and-silver polka-dotted baby bag hanging off the handle.

Anyway, what he'd said in regard to "how married life was" was true: things *were* great. He and Norah had to get used to each other—that was all. Yes, he'd made a mistake in not being clear about the father title, but the subject hadn't come up even though it was really the root and heart of staying married in the first place.

What the hell was wrong with him? How could he be so damned dense sometimes?

And what *were* the triplets going to call him?

He didn't like the idea of them calling him Reed.

Humph.

Frowning again, he settled the babies in their car seats, got the stroller in the trunk of his SUV and drove to the ranch, grateful, as always, that he was making this drive, that he was going home to the ranch. The summer sun lit the pastures through the trees and, as expected, the sight of the homestead relaxed Reed in a way nothing could. He remembered running out to the crazy weeping willow, which always looked haunted, with David Dirk when they were nine, David talking about his uncle who'd just won a quarter million dollars in Vegas and "was so lucky" that their lives were changing. He remembered David saying that if only his mother could win that kind of money, they'd have everything and wouldn't need anything else. As if money alone—

Wait a minute. Reed pulled the car over and stared hard at that weeping willow.

Could David have gone to Las Vegas? To try to win a pot of money to make having multiples more palatable? Or just easier? Or maybe he'd gone there to hide out for a few days before the wedding, to think through what he wanted?

He pulled out his phone and called David's bank. In seconds he was switched over to the manager and reintroduced himself as the detective working on the Dirk disappearance. Reed's predecessor had noted that David hadn't taken out a large sum of cash before he'd gone missing. But David had never been a gambler. He wouldn't risk more than five hundred bucks on slots and tables, even for the chance of a big payday. "Can you tell me if David withdrew around five hundred dollars the week of the tenth?"

"He withdrew two hundred and fifty dollars on the eleventh. Then another hundred on the twelfth."

Well, hardly enough cash for even a cheap flight, a cheap motel and quarters for a few slot machines. But he might have had cash socked away, too.

It was just a hunch. But Reed would bet his ranch that David Dirk was in Vegas, sitting at a slot machine and freaking out about what he was doing—and had done.

Before Norah even got out of her car, she could hear the loud, piercing wails from inside Sara Dirk's house. Screeching babies.

Norah rang the bell and it was a good minute before Sara opened the door, a screaming baby against her chest and frazzled stress etched on her tired face. Behind Sara, Norah could see the other twin crying in the baby swing.

"I thought you could use some easy meals to heat up," Norah said, holding up the bag of pies. "I brought you every kind of pot pie we make at the Pie Diner."

Sara looked on the verge of tears. "That's really nice of you," she managed to say before the baby in her arms let out an ear-splitting wail.

"Could you use a break?" Norah asked, reaching out her arms.

"Oh God, yes," Sara said, handing over the baby girl. "This is Charlotte. And that's Gabrielle," she added, rushing over to the crying one in the swing. She scooped her out and rocked her, and the baby quieted.

Norah held Charlotte against her chest, rubbing the baby's back and murmuring to her.

"A few minutes' reprieve," Sara said. "They like the change, but then they'll start up again."

"Is your husband at work?" Norah asked, giving Charlotte's back little taps to burp her.

Sara nodded. "He works at the county hospital and starts at 5:00 a.m. But the poor guy was up for a couple hours before then. He's such a great dad. He calls and texts as often as he can to check to see if I'm okay, if they're okay."

Norah smiled. "Support is everything."

Sara nodded. "It really is. David's fiancée said she'd come over this morning to help out. I feel so bad for her. Is there still no word on David?"

"Not that I know of."

The doorbell rang and there was Eden, her blond hair in a ponytail. Norah knew Eden from the Pie Diner, like just about everyone in town, so no introductions were necessary. And since David had done his share of dating among the single women in town, Norah's two weeks as David's girlfriend hardly merited a second thought. There wouldn't be any awkwardness in that department with Eden, thank heavens.

Eden burst into tears. "You know what I think?" she asked, taking Gabrielle from Sara and rocking the baby in her arms while sniffling. "I think David up and left.

I think he changed his mind about me and didn't want to break my heart. But—" She let out a wail. "He broke it anyway." She cried, holding the baby close against her, her head gentle against Gabrielle's head.

"That man loves you to death," Sara said. "Everyone knows that."

"Well, he's either dead in a ditch somewhere or he left on his own because he doesn't want to marry me," Eden said, sniffling.

Norah handed her a tissue. It wasn't her place to mention Reed's theory. But maybe she could work in the subject of the chapel to see if Eden brought up whether or not David wanted multiples the way she did.

Before Norah could even think about how to pose a question about marrying at the chapel, Eden's phone rang. Sara took Gabrielle as Eden lunged for her phone in her bag, clearly hoping it was her fiancé.

"It's him!" Eden shrieked. "It's David!"

Norah stared at Eden as she screamed, "Hello, Davy Doo?" into her phone and then realized she should at least pretend to give the woman some privacy.

Eden was listening, her blue eyes narrowing with every passing second, her expression turning murderous. "*What?* I was kidding when I got to your cousin's house today and said I was sure you left on your own because of me! I just said that so everyone would say 'Of course that's not true.' But it is!" she screamed so loudly that both babies startled and stopped fussing entirely.

Whoa boy. So Reed's theory was right.

"Yes, I hear the twins crying again, David. I'm in the same house with them. It's what babies do!" Silence. Eyes narrowing some more. Death expression. And then she said through gritted teeth, "I don't want just *one* baby. I want triplets! Or even quadruplets! Twins at the least!" More listening. More eyes narrowing. "Well, fine! Then I guess we're through!" She stabbed at the End Call button with her finger, threw the phone in her bag, then stormed out. A second later she was back. "I'm sorry you had to hear that. Apparently I was engaged to a weenie twerp! No offense to your husband or his family, Sara," she added, then stormed out again.

Norah stared at Sara, who looked as amazed as Norah felt.

"Omigod," Sara said. "What was that?"

Norah shifted little Charlotte in her arms. "A little miscommunication in expectations before the wedding."

"A little?" Sara shook her head. "And I don't know if I'd classify that as miscommunication. Eden has been talking about getting married at the chapel and having triplets from the first family dinner she was invited to. David knew what she wanted. He probably didn't think too much about it until his cousin had twins—colicky twins—and he realized what he'd be in for. David has witnessed some whopper arguments between me and my husband. He probably just ran scared with the wedding coming so close."

"Well, I'm glad he's okay—that he wasn't hurt or anything like that," Norah said, realizing something had changed. She gasped—Charlotte had fallen asleep in her arms. She glanced at Sara, who was beaming. Sara pointed to the nursery and Norah tiptoed into the room and laid the baby in her crib. The little creature didn't even stir.

"I owe you," Sara said. "Thank you!"

They glanced at Gabrielle, who was rubbing her eyes

and yawning. Easily transferred to the vibrating swing, she, too, was asleep a few seconds later.

"I get to have coffee!" Sara said. "Thank you so much for staying to help."

"Anytime," Norah said. "See you at the next class. Oh, and if your husband hears from David, will you let Reed know?"

"Will do," Sara said.

As Norah headed home, eager to see her own baby multiples, she wondered if she was the one with the problem. She'd picked three men who didn't want to be fathers. She'd dated David, albeit for two weeks. Then her babies' father. Now Reed.

She was chewing that over when she opened the front door to find Reed sitting in the family room with all three babies in their swings, cooing and batting at their little mobiles. He was reading them a story from a brightly colored book with a giraffe on the cover.

Not a father, huh? Sure. The man was father material whether he liked it or not. Knew it or not.

"Have I got news for you," she said and then told him the whole story about Eden and the phone call from David.

Reed shook his head. "At least he's not dead—yet, anyway. Once Eden gets her hands on him…"

"I didn't get the sense he told her where he was or when or if he was coming home."

"I'm ninety-nine percent sure I know where he is— Las Vegas. But it's a big place, and since he's not using his credit cards, he could be at any super-cheap hole-in-the-wall motel. Though now that he's let the cat out of the bag that he's alive and well and afraid of triplets, he might start using his cards and check in somewhere cushy while he lets Eden digest the news."

Not a minute later a call came in from the station. An officer reporting that David Dirk had finally used his MasterCard to check into the fancy Concordia Hotel on the Strip.

"I have to say, Detective. You're good."

"Does that mean you're coming to Vegas with me?" he asked.

Chapter 11

Just like that, Norah found herself on a plane to Las Vegas, a city she'd never been to, with Reed beside her, studying the floor plans of the Concordia Hotel and the streets of Vegas on his iPad.

As she stared out at the clouds below, she knew the answer she should have given was "No. Of course not. I'm not going." But what had come out of her mouth, with barely any hesitation was "Yes." This trip wasn't a honeymoon. Or a vacation. But it wasn't strictly business, either. Or Wedlock Creek police business. David Dirk had every right to disappear; once Reed knew for sure that the man had willingly left town, the case had been closed. But Reed wanted to find David and talk to him old friend to old friend. Bring him home. And Norah wanted some time away from real life with her…husband.

Why, she wasn't quite sure. What would be different in a new environment? They were the same people with the same gulf between them.

Still, the trip was a chance. To experience Reed off duty, away from home, where neither of them had any of their usual responsibilities. To see who they were together in a completely different environment. Maybe there would be nothing between them and Norah could just start to accept that their relationship was exactly what she'd agreed to. A platonic marriage slash business partnership for mutual benefit.

The only problem with that was the fact that just sitting this close to Reed, their sides practically touching, she'd never been so aware of a man and her physical attraction to him in her entire life.

"Of course, I booked us separate rooms," Reed said, turning to glance at her. "Right across the hall from each other."

Too bad the Concordia wasn't completely booked except for one small room with a king-size bed, she thought, mesmerized by the dark hair on his forearms and how the sunlight glinted on his gold wedding band, the one that symbolized their union.

Before she knew it, the plane had landed and they were checking in at the front desk, then being shown to their rooms. Reed had 401. Norah was in 402.

"Meet you in the hallway in twenty minutes?" he asked. "I don't have much of a plan to find David other than to sit in the lobby for a while to see if he passes through. We might get lucky. I tried calling David's friend Kyle Kirby, the one who seemed to be withholding, but he didn't answer his phone or my knock at his door. We're gonna have to do this the boring way."

"It's my chance to see you doing surveillance work," she said. "Not boring at all. See you in twenty," she added and hurried inside her room with her weekend bag.

The room was a bit fancier than she'd expected. King-size bed, wall of windows and a fuzzy white robe hanging on the bathroom door. She called her mom to check on the triplets, who were fine and having their snack, then she freshened up and changed into a casual skirt, silky tank top and strappy sandals.

Twenty minutes later, when she went into the hallway, Reed was standing there and she caught his gaze moving up and down the length of her. He liked strappy, clearly. Good.

He was amazingly handsome, as always. He wore dark pants and a dark buttoned shirt, no tie. He looked like a detective.

They sat in the well-appointed lobby for forty minutes, pretending to be poring over maps of the Strip and brochures and dinner menus. No sign of David. Many people came through the lobby, all shapes and sizes and nationalities. Norah noticed a coffee bar across the lobby and had a hankering for an iced mocha. She definitely needed caffeine.

"Want something?" she asked Reed, who was glancing over the lobby, his gaze shooting to the chrome revolving doors every time they spun.

"Iced coffee, cream and sugar. And thanks."

"Coming right up," she said and sauntered off, wondering if he took his eyes off his surveillance to watch her walk away. She turned back to actually check and almost gasped. He *was* watching her. But then he darted his eyes back to the revolving door. Busted!

This meant that no matter what he had to say about ignoring their attraction to each other, he ignored it only when he had to. There was hope to change things between her and the detective. And she was going for it. What happened in Vegas didn't have to stay in Vegas all the time, right?

Her mood uplifted with her secret plan, Norah stood behind a group of women who had very high-maintenance drink orders—double whip this and no moo that—and studied the board to see if she wanted to try something besides her usual iced mocha when someone said, "Norah?"

She whirled around.

And almost gasped again.

David Dirk himself was staring at her, his mouth agape. "Holy crap, it *is* you," he said, walking over to her. Tall and lanky with light brown hair and round, black glasses, he held an iced coffee in one hand and a small white plate with a crumb cake in the other. "I never took you for a Vegas type."

What did *that* mean? That she couldn't let loose and have fun? Let down the ole hair and have a cocktail or three? Throw away a couple hundred bucks? Okay, maybe fifty at most.

I'm actually here with the detective who's been searching for you for days, she wanted to say. But who knew what David's frame of mind was? He might bolt.

"I'm here with my husband," she said, holding up her left hand and giving it a little wave. She turned and looked toward where Reed was sitting, staring at him hard for a second until she caught his attention. When he looked up and clearly saw David, his eyes practically bugged out of his head.

She turned back to David, who was staring at her ring.

"Oh, wow, congrats!" David said, a genuine smile on his face. "I didn't know you got married. Good for you. And good for your triplets." He bit his lip, looked at the ring again and then promptly burst into tears. He put the drink and the crumb cake down on the counter beside them and slashed each hand under his eyes. "I'm supposed to be getting married tomorrow night. At the chapel," he added, looking stricken.

He sniffled and Norah reached into her bag for her little packet of tissues. He took the whole packet and noisily blew his nose.

"But...?" she prompted, despite knowing exactly what the *but* was.

Tears slipped down his cheeks. Had he always been such a crier? They'd gone to two movies during the two weeks they'd dated, action flicks with very little pathos, so she hadn't had a chance to see him show much emotion.

"I..." He dabbed at his eyes with a wadded-up tissue.

"Whoa, David? David Dirk?" Reed asked with great feigned surprise as he walked up to them.

David stared at Reed, clearly trying to place him. His mouth dropped open, then curved into a grin. "No way. No flipping way! Reed Barelli? Who I last saw when I was thirteen?"

"It's me, man," Reed said, extending his hand.

Instead of taking his hand, David pulled Reed into a hug and sobbed. "You're probably wondering how my life is after all these years. I'll tell you. It sucks. I've ruined everything. Destroyed the best thing that ever happened to me." He pulled a few tissues from the packet and dabbed at his eyes again.

"Why don't we go get a beer?" Reed said, his arm slung around David's shoulders. "We'll catch up." He turned to Norah. "You'll be all right on your own for a couple of hours, honey?"

Honey. It was for show, but it warmed her heart nonetheless.

"Sure," she said. "I'll hit the shops. Maybe get a massage."

"Wait," David said. "*You two* are married? How'd you even meet?" he asked, looking from Reed to Norah.

"Long story," Reed said. "I'll tell you all about it over a cold one. And you can fill me in on what's going on with you."

David nodded, his shoulders slumped. "I let the best thing that ever happened to me get away."

"There's always a second chance if you don't screw it up," Reed said as they headed toward the bar.

Here's hoping so, Norah thought. *For everyone.*

The waiter placed two craft beers and a plate of nachos with the works on the square table in front of Reed and David. David took a chug of his beer, then said, "Okay, you first. How'd you meet Norah?"

He told David the entire story. The truth and nothing but the truth. He and Norah had talked about being generally tight-lipped about their story of origin, but he had a feeling David could use the information and apply it to himself.

Now it was David's eyes that were bugging out of his head.

"Oh man," David said, chugging more beer. "So you'll get it. You got married at the chapel. And now you're the father of triplets."

There was that word again. *Father*.

"What I can't believe is that you actually proposed *staying* married," David said. "The woman handed you annulment papers, man! You were home free."

"I couldn't just walk away from Norah and the babies. How could I?" He knew he didn't need to add, "You of all people should know that." He was sure David had heard it loud and clear. And from his old friend's expression, Reed was certain.

"I don't want to walk away from Eden," David said. "I love her. I know I screwed up by running away. But I had to think. I had to get my head on straight. Spending time with my cousin and those screaming colicky twins of his made me realize I'm not ready for that. I don't want that."

"You don't want *what*, exactly?" Reed asked. "A colicky baby? Twins? Or kids at all?"

David pulled a nacho onto his plate but just stared at it. "I don't know."

How could such a smart guy know so little? "Why not just tell Eden the truth?"

David frowned. "I did when I called her yesterday. She was so angry at me she hung up." Tears glistened in the guy's eyes and he ate the loaded nacho chip in one gulp.

"I think you should call Eden. FaceTime her, actually. And tell her exactly how you feel. Which sounds to me like you love her very much and want to marry her, but you're not ready for children and certainly not ready for multiples."

"That's it, exactly. I want kids someday. Just not now. And not all at once."

"Tell her. You need to have faith in your relationship with her, David. And remember, that showing her you didn't have faith in her, in your relationship, by running, is probably what is stinging her the most."

David seemed to think about that. He nodded, then took a sip of his beer. "So is it as awful as I think?"

Reed took a swig of his beer. "Is what?"

"Living with three screaming babies."

"Actually, I love those little buggers." The minute he said it, he felt his smile fade. He'd do anything for them. Of course he loved them. He had since the day he'd first upsie-downsied Bea on the rickety porch of Norah's old rental house.

"Really?" David asked, eyes wide behind the black-framed glasses.

"Yeah. Huh. I guess being a father can be more instinctive than I thought. There's really nothing to it other than caring and showing up and doing what needs to be done."

David nodded. "Right. I guess I don't want to do any of that—yet."

Reed laughed. "Then you shouldn't. And don't have to. Not everyone is ready for parenthood at the same time." He thought about Norah, who'd had to be ready. And him, too, in a way. But something told Reed he'd been ready for a long time. Waiting to give his heart to little humans in the way his own father hadn't been willing.

So. He *was* their father. Father. Daddy. He laughed, which made David look at him funny.

"Just thinking about something," Reed said.

David got up and polished off his beer, putting a

twenty on the table. "I'm gonna go FaceTime Eden. Wish me luck. I'm gonna need it."

"Go get her," Reed said.

But as he sat there, finishing his beer and helping himself to the pretty good nachos, he realized something that twisted his gut.

Maybe he'd been focusing on the father thing as an excuse not to focus on the marriage thing. Maybe it was only *husband* he had the issue with. *Husband* that he didn't want to be.

Deep down he knew it was true. Of course it was true; it was the whole reason he'd proposed what he'd proposed. A sham of a marriage. So he'd get what he really wanted. His ranch. And a chance to still be the father he'd never had. A chance to do right.

But he also knew deep down that it wasn't what Norah wanted. At all. And she was so independent-minded and used to being on her own that he was pretty sure she wouldn't give up her dreams so soon. She'd tell him the plan wasn't working, that she needed more and she'd hold out for a man who could be a father and a husband.

She deserved that.

Reed sat there long after his beer was gone, his appetite for the nachos ruined. What the hell was going to happen to him and Norah?

If Norah wasn't mistaken, Reed was being…distant.

While Reed had been with David at the bar, she'd gone into the hotel's clothing boutique and bought herself a little black dress she'd have no use for at home. It wasn't cheap and she'd likely wear it every few years, since it was kind of a classic Audrey Hepburn sleeveless with just the right amount of low neckline to make Norah feel a bit more daring than her usual mom-of-three self.

She and Reed had agreed to meet at six thirty for dinner at an Italian restaurant in their hotel that was supposed to have incredible food. But when she came out of her room at six thirty on the nose, all dolled up, including a light dab of perfume in the cleavage, Reed seemed surprised. And kept his eyes on her face. Not even a peek at her in the hotsy-totsy dress.

Instead, he filled her in on what had happened with David, how he'd texted his old buddy an hour ago to ask if he'd spoken to Eden and how things had gone. David hadn't gotten back to him.

Love, marriage, parenthood, life. Why was it so complicated? Why did wanting one thing mean you had to give up another thing? Compromise was everything in life and relationships.

Can I give up wanting what I used to dream about? she asked herself as they walked into Marcello's, so romantic and dimly lit and full of candles and oil paintings of nudes and lovers that Norah figured Reed hadn't known what they were in for. *Can I stay married to a man I'm falling in love with when it's platonic and he wants to keep it that way forever?*

Maybe not forever. Maybe just till the triplets were grown and off starting their lives and he could finally take a breath from the sense of responsibility he felt. Oh, only eighteen years. No biggie.

Face-palm. Could she live this way for eighteen years?

Norah had just noticed a sign on an easel by the long zinc bar that said Closed For Private Event when a woman rushed up to them. The restaurant was closed? Or the bar?

"Oooh," the woman said, ushering them inside the restaurant "You two had better hurry. There's only one table left. Otherwise you'll have to eat standing at the counter along the back."

Huh? She glanced at Reed, who shrugged, and they followed the hostess to a small round table for two. A man and a woman sat a table on a platform in the center of the dining room, a candle between them, wineglasses and a plate of bruschetta.

Hmm, bruschetta, Norah thought. She definitely wanted some of that. "Maybe it's their anniversary," she told Reed. "And they're high rollers or something, so they get a platform."

"You never know in Vegas," he said, his dark eyes flashing in the dimly lit room. He looked so damned hot, this time all in black, again tieless but wearing a jacket and black shoes.

They were seated and Norah couldn't help but notice the fortyish couple at the table beside theirs. The woman sat with her arms crossed over her chest, looking spitting mad. The man was gobbling up Italian bread and slathering it with butter.

"How can you even eat when I'm this upset!" the woman hiss-whispered.

The man didn't quite roll his eyes, but he didn't stop buttering the bread or popping it in his mouth.

"Welcome!" said the woman at the platform table.

Norah turned her attention to her. She and the man beside her stood. They had microphones. Gulp. This was clearly the "special event." Had she and Reed crashed a wedding or something?

Should they get up now and slink out? While all eyes were focused on the couple and it was dead quiet otherwise?

"We'll slip out when she stops talking, when it's less noticeable," Reed whispered.

Norah nodded. *Awk*ward.

"I know it's not easy for you to be here," the woman continued, turning slowly around the room to speak to all tables. "And because you are here, you've taken the first step in your relationship recovery."

Okay, what? Relationship recovery?

Reed raised an eyebrow and looked at Norah; now it was her turn to shrug.

"My name is Allison Lerner," the woman on the platform said. "My husband, Bill, here, and I have been married for thirty-six years. Yes, we got married at eighteen—*badump!* No, seriously, ladies and gents, we have been married for thirty-six years. Some of those years were so bumpy we threatened each other with divorce every other day. Some months were good. Some days were amazing. Do you want to know *why* we didn't divorce despite the arguments, problems, issues, this, that and the other?"

"Yes!" a woman called out.

Allison smiled. "We didn't divorce because—and this is the big secret—we *didn't want* to. Not really. Even when we hated each other. We didn't want to not be married to each other. Not really."

"What the hell kind of special event is this?" Reed whispered. "They're the entertainment?"

"God, I hope not," Norah whispered back.

"All of you taking tonight's Relationship Recovery

seminar are here because you don't want to divorce or separate or go your separate ways, either. So enjoy a glass of wine, folks, order your appetizers and entrées, and once the waiters are off in the kitchen, we'll start the hard work of saving our relationships. Because we want to!"

Norah glanced around. The woman with the arms crossed over her chest had tears in her eyes. Her husband was rubbing her arm—half-heartedly, but hey, at least he was doing something. The entire restaurant must be booked for the seminar.

"I sure got this one restaurant choice wrong," Reed said. "Shall we?" he asked, throwing down his napkin.

"Sir, you can do this," Allison Lerner said from behind them as she put a hand on Reed's arm. She and her husband must have been on the lookout for runners. "You deserve this. You both do. Give yourselves—and your marriage," she added, glancing at their wedding rings, "a chance."

"No, I—" Reed started to say.

"Allison is right," Norah said to Reed. "We need to learn how to fight for our marriage instead of against it."

As Reed gaped at her, she realized how true that was. Reed was fighting against it without even knowing it because he didn't want a real marriage. Norah was fighting against it because she wanted more when she'd agreed to less. Did that even make sense? No wonder she was so confused about her feelings.

"We need to figure out how to make this work, right?" Norah said. "Let's stay."

Reed stared at her, then glanced at Allison's patiently kind face. He sat back down.

"I'm thinking of pasta," Norah said, opening her menu.

He raised his eyebrow at her. Scowled a bit. Then she saw the acquiescence in his eyes and the set of his shoulders. "Okay, okay. I'm in." He opened his menu.

They ordered a delicious-sounding seafood risotto as an appetizer. Norah chose the four-cheese-and-mushroom ravioli for an entrée; Reed went with the stuffed filetto mignon. Norah sure hoped he'd offer her a bite.

"Everyone, take a sip of your beverage—wine, soda, water, what have you," Bill Lerner said from the platform.

Norah and Reed picked up their glasses, clinked and took a sip. The woman next to them frowned. There was no clinking at their table.

"Okay, now put down your drinks," Bill said. "Turn to your partner. Look at your partner and say the first nice thing that comes to you in reference to your partner. Ladies, you begin."

Norah turned to Reed. This was an easy one. "I love how you are with the triplets. I love how you read to them and blow raspberries on Brody's and Bea's arms but not Bella's because you know she doesn't like it. I love that you know which of them likes sweet potatoes and which hates carrots. I feel like I can relax as a parent in my own home…well, *your* home, for the first time since they were born because you're there. Really, really there. It's a good feeling. Better than I even hoped it would be."

Norah felt tears spring to her eyes. She hadn't meant to say all that. But every word was true. Oh hell. That was the entire reason she'd agreed not to rip up the annulment papers—so that exactly what had happened would happen. And she wanted things to change? She wanted more? She was being selfish. Demanding more of Reed than he wanted to give. Putting the triplets' good new fortune in jeopardy. Mommy's love life had to come second. Period.

Reed took her hand and held it. "Thank you. That means a lot to me. Those babies mean a lot to me."

She almost burst into tears but held back the swell of emotion by taking a sip of wine.

"Okay, gentlemen," Allison said from the platform. "Your turn. Say the first true and nice thing you feel about your partner."

Reed took a sip of his wine and then looked at Norah. "I admire you. You've got your act together. You're lovely. You're kind. You're funny. I like seeing you around the house."

Norah laughed. She liked what he'd said. Maybe it wasn't quite as personal as what she'd said, but it came down to him liking her, really liking her, as a person. And liking having her around.

"Okay, gentlemen," Bill said into the mic. "Now look at your partner and tell her how you felt about what she said."

Reed put down his glass of wine, which from his expression, he clearly wanted to gulp. "Maybe I am the triplets' father, after all."

Norah did feel tears sting her eyes this time and she didn't wipe them away. She was also speechless.

"I realized it before you said what you said. I realized it from talking to David Dirk. I love those babies, Norah. They have my heart. I am their father. If they'll have me."

Norah bit her lip. "They'll have you." *I'll have you.*

"Okay, ladies, now tell your partner how the nice thing he said about you made you feel."

Norah took Reed's hand and squeezed it. "You'll never say anything that I'll treasure more than what you just did. The triplets come first. That's just how it is with me."

He tilted his head as if considering something. But he didn't say anything. He just nodded.

"Whew!" Allison said from the platform. "That is quite a bit of work we did all before the entrées were served! Feel free to talk about what we just did or change the subject and enjoy dinner. Once you've had a chance to eat, we'll resume with the next exercise. Of course, after dinner, we'll get into the heavy lifting."

"Luckily we've got plans," Reed whispered. "So we'll have to skip the heavy lifting."

Norah smiled. "Oh?"

"There's something I want to show you. Something more fun than heavy lifting."

"I feel like my head was put back on straight," she said. "So I'd say this Relationship Recovery seminar was a huge success. In just one exercise."

He squeezed her hand but again didn't say anything and cut into his delicious-looking filetto mignon. He cut a bite and instead of lifting the fork to his mouth, reached it out to hers. "Ladies first."

She smiled, feeling her moment-ago resolve to focus on the partnership and not her heart start to waver. How was she supposed to avoid her feelings for Reed Barelli when he was so wonderful?

She took the bite and closed her eyes at how tender and delicious the steak was. "Amazing," she said. "Thank you."

She scooped a ravioli onto his plate. "For you."

And then they ate, drank and didn't talk more about the exercise, which the poor woman at the next table was trying to get her husband to do.

"So you really like my hair this way?" she'd said three times.

The husband shoveled his pasta into his mouth and barely looked up. "Honestly, Kayla, with your hair blonder like that, you look just like you did the day I got the nerve to talk to you after earth science class junior year of high school. Took me a month to get the courage."

The woman gasped and looked like she might faint. Pure joy crossed her face and she reached out her hand and squeezed her husband's. "Oh, Skip."

Sometimes people knew how to say the right things at the right time.

Reed glanced over at the Lerners on the platform. They had their arms linked and were feeding each other fettuccine. Norah's and Reed's plates were practically empty, both of them having just declared they couldn't eat another bite. "I say we slip out now."

Norah smiled. "Let's go."

Reed put a hundred-dollar bill and a fifty on the table, then took her hand and made a point of asking a waiter where the restrooms were, pointing and gesturing for show. They dashed over to the entrance and then quickly ran up the hall. They were free.

"That was unexpected," Norah said on a giggle as they stopped around the corner of the lobby. Her first giggle since her wedding night.

"But worthy," Reed said. "Our marriage feels stronger. We actually did some good work in there."

Norah smiled. "We did. So what did you want to show me?"

"Follow me." He pressed the elevator button. Once they were inside, he pressed the button marked Roof. They rode up forty-two floors and exited into a hallway without any doors except one with a sign that said Roof. Reed pushed open the door and she followed.

It was a roof deck, with couches and chairs and flowers and a bar staffed with a waiter in a tuxedo. Reed took her hand and led her over to the other side of the deck, away from the small groups gathered. She gasped at the view of the Strip, sparkling lights everywhere, all underneath a canopy of stars.

"Something else, huh?" he asked, looking up and then around at the lights.

"Yeah," she said. "Something else. You sure don't see a view like this in Wedlock Creek."

Would she appreciate it even more if Reed were standing a drop closer? With his arm around her? Or behind her, pressed against her, both of his strong arms wrapped around her? Yes, she would. But hadn't she said she wasn't going to be greedy and selfish? She knew what was important. She had to remember that and not want more.

Reed's phone buzzed in his pocket. He pulled it out and read the screen. "It's David Dirk," he whispered. He turned toward the view. "Hey, David." He listened, then smiled. "Great news. And yes, we'd love to. See you in two hours."

Norah's eyebrows shot up. "We'd love to what?"

"Seems we're invited to be David and Eden's witnesses at their wedding at the Luv U Wedding Chapel."

Norah was surprised. "Wait. Eden flew here? She's

giving up the Wedlock Creek chapel and her dream of triplets?"

"I guess she did some soul-searching and decided what she wanted most."

Norah nodded. "That's the key. What you want most. You have to follow that even if it involves some compromise."

And what she wanted most was a good life for her children, the security and safety Reed would provide, the love and kindness, the role model he'd be. She wanted that for her triplets more than she wanted anything. Even if her own heart had to break to get it.

He'd be there, right? Even if he was a million miles away at the same time.

"Wow," Norah said. "She must really love him."

"Well, she's still getting some assurance. Turns out there's a legend associated with the Luv U Wedding Chapel."

"And what would that be?"

"Eden's parents eloped there the summer after high school, scandalizing both sets of parents. Twenty-five years later the Pearlmans are happy as can be. According to Pearlman family legend, if you marry at the Luv U Wedding Chapel in Las Vegas, you're pretty much guaranteed happily-ever-after."

Norah laughed. "That's a really good legend."

Reed nodded. "This has turned out to be a pretty busy day for us. First a marriage counseling seminar over dinner and now we're witnesses at a legend-inspired wedding that almost didn't happen."

"Like ours," she said. "It's pretty crazy that it happened at all."

He looked into her eyes and squeezed her hand. "I'm

glad it did happen, Norah. Our insane wedding changed my life. For the much, much better."

She squeezed his hand back. "Mine, too."

Because I'm in love with my husband. A good thing *and* exactly what wasn't supposed to happen.

I love you, Reed Barelli, she shouted in her head. *I love you!*

She wondered what he was shouting in his head.

Chapter 12

"Well, it's not the Wedlock Creek Wedding Chapel," Eden said, reaching for her "something borrowed," her grandmother's seed-pearl necklace. "But if getting married here blessed my parents with twenty-five so-far happy years and four children, I'll take it."

Norah clasped the pretty necklace for Eden and looked at her reflection in the standing mirror in the bridal room of the Luv U Wedding Chapel. The bride looked absolutely lovely in her princess gown with more lace and beading than Norah had ever seen on one dress. "I love it. Your own family legend."

Eden bit her lip and looked at Norah in the mirror. "Do you really believe in the Wedlock Creek legend? I mean, you had triplets without getting married there."

"Well, actually, I did get married there, just after the fact. So maybe the fates of the universe knew that down the road I'd be getting married at the chapel and so I got my triplets. Just early." She rolled her eyes. "Oh, who the hell knows? I think Reed will tell you the legend is true, though. He got married at the chapel and voilà— father of triplets."

Eden laughed. "Poor guy." Her smile faded as she stared at herself. "Do you think I'm an idiot for forgiving David and marrying him on his terms after what he pulled?"

"I think you know David best and you know what's right and what feels right. No one else can tell you otherwise."

Eden adjusted her long, flowy veil. "I know he loves me. But he did a real bonehead thing just running away. I mean, I *really* thought something happened to him." She frowned. "Maybe he's too immature to get married. I know I'm not about to win Person of the Year or anything, but still."

"Well, he got scared and he didn't know how to deal with it, so he fled. He didn't want to lose you by telling you how he really felt. In the end, though, he did call you and tell you the truth. You two worked it out, because here you are."

Eden's smile lit up her pretty face. "It'll make one hell of a family story, huh? I'll be telling my grandkids about the time Grandpa ran for the hills to avoid having quadruplets."

Norah laughed. "You just might have quadruplets anyway. You never know."

"Mwahaha," Eden said, doing her best evil-laugh impersonation. She turned around to face Norah. "So is this your honeymoon? Is that why you and Reed are here?"

Honeymoons were for real newlyweds. She sighed inwardly. There she went again, wanting more.

Was it wrong to want more when it came to love? If your heart was bursting?

Eden was eyeing her, so she'd better say something reasonable. She had no idea what Reed had told David about the two of them and how they'd ended up married. Probably the truth. She knew Reed Barelli well enough to know that he didn't lie.

"I suppose it's like a mini honeymoon. Reed just started at the police department, so he can't take off any real time." She kind of liked saying that. It was true—in a way. This was like their honeymoon. And since they *were* newlyweds, they should have this time away.

"He must really love you," Eden said, turning back to the mirror to freshen her pink-red lipstick. "He married a single mother of seven-month-old triplets."

Norah felt her heart squeeze. How she wished that were true. Of course, they couldn't go backward and fall in love and then get married. They'd already done the backward thing by getting married first, then actually getting to know each other. She smiled, her heartache easing just a bit. There was hope there, no? If you started out backward, you could only go forward. And forward was love and forever.

Unless your husband was Reed "No Romance" Barelli.

Did a man who didn't believe in romance bring his dry-eyed deal of a wife to see a breathtaking view forty-two flights above the city? Did he do any of the sweet and wonderful things Reed had done? Including offering her the first bite of his incredible filetto mignon?

"He's a great guy," Norah said. He sure was.

Eden smiled and checked that her pearl drop earrings were fastened. "You're so lucky. You have your triplets and your hot new detective husband who's madly in love with you. You have everything."

Oh, if only.

After tearing up a time or two at the wedding and doing her official job as Witness One, Norah watched as David Dirk, looking spiffy in a tuxedo, lifted his bride and carried her out of the Luv U chapel. Reed threw rice and then it was time for the next couple to say their I Do's, so Norah and Reed headed out into the balmy July Las Vegas air.

"Case closed with a happy ending," Reed said. "The best kind of case."

"I think they're going to be just fine," she agreed. "But he'll probably keep doing dumb things."

Reed laughed. "No doubt." He looked over at her. "So should we head back to the hotel? Have a nightcap on the terrace?"

"Sounds good," she said. And too romantic. But there was nothing she'd rather do than continue this night of love and matrimony with her own husband.

They passed a lot of couples holding hands. Brides and grooms with their heads popped out of limo sun-roofs, screaming, "I did!" The happy, drunken energy reminded her of her wedding night.

In ten minutes they were back at the Concordia, taking the elevator to the fourth floor. Reed's room was just like hers. The king-size bed in the center of the room had her attention. Suddenly all she could think about was waking up the morning after her wedding, the shock of seeing Fabio-Reed in her bed, half-naked except for the hot, black boxer briefs, the hard planes of his chest and rippling muscles as he shifted an arm, the way his long eyelashes rested on his cheeks.

"Do you think that on our wedding night we…?" She trailed off, staring at the bed.

"We what?"

"Had sex," she said, turning to face him.

He placed his key card on the dresser, took off his jacket and folded it over the desk chair, then went over to the minibar. "No. In fact, I'm ninety-nine percent sure."

"How?"

He poured two glasses of wine from the little bottles. "Because if I made love to you, Norah, I never would have forgotten it." He held her gaze and she felt her cheeks burn a bit, the warmth spreading down into her chest, to her stomach, to her toes.

She took the wineglass he held out and took a sip, then moved over to the windows, unable to stand so close to him or to look directly at him without spontaneously combusting. Being in his room, the bed, images of him, the very thought of his gorgeous face and incredibly hot body… She wanted him with a fierceness she couldn't remember ever experiencing. She wanted to feel his hands and mouth all over her. She wanted him to be her husband—for real.

Maybe she could show him how it could be, how good it could be between them. That if she of all people could let go of mistrust and walls and actually let herself risk feeling something, then he could, too, dammit. There was no way she could be married to this man, share a home and life with him, and not have him in every sense of the word. And the fact that he was clearly attracted to her gave her the cojones to take a long sip of her wine, put down the glass and sit on the edge of the bed.

He was watching her, but he stayed where he was. On the other side of the bed, practically leaning against the wall.

So now what? Should she throw herself at him? No way was she doing that.

Ugh, this was stupid. Forget it. She wasn't going to beg this man—any man—to want her; all of her, heart, mind, soul, body. Hadn't her smart sister told her to let what would happen just happen? She shouldn't be forcing it.

She sighed a wistful sigh and stood. "Well, I guess I'll head to my room, maybe watch a movie. Something funny." She needed funny. A good laugh.

"Sounds good," he said. "I could go for funny." He grabbed the remote control off the desk and suddenly the guide was on the screen. "Hmm, *Police Academy 3*, *Out of Africa*, *Jerry Maguire* or *Full Metal Jacket*?"

Uh-oh. She hadn't meant they watch together. They were going to lie down on the bed, inches apart, and watch a movie? Really?

"Unless you were hinting that you're sick of me and don't want company," he said with a smile. "I could never get tired of you, so I forget not everyone is dazzled by me 24/7."

She burst out laughing. Hot *and* funny. Who needed the movie? She'd just take him.

"I've seen *Jerry Maguire* at least five times, but you really can't see that enough," she said.

"Really? I've never seen it."

You. Complete. Me, she wanted to scream at him and

then grab him down onto the bed and kiss him every-where on his amazing body.

"Wait, we can't watch a movie without popcorn," he said, picking up the phone. Was the man really order-ing from room service? Yes, he was. He asked for a big bowl of popcorn, freshly popped, two sodas, a bottle of a good white wine and two slices of anything chocolate.

Amazing. "You really know how to watch a movie," she said.

He grinned. "The way I see it, you might as well do everything right."

Yup. That was why he hadn't rushed the annulment papers to the county clerk's too-efficient replacement. Because he did things right. Like stay married to a mother of teething seven-month-old triplets who'd lived in a falling-down dump and made her living by the pot pie.

Twenty minutes later, their little movie feast deliv-ered, they settled on the bed, on top of the blanket, the big bowl of popcorn between them, to watch *Jerry Maguire*.

"Oh, it's the *Mission Impossible* dude," he said, throwing some popcorn into his mouth. They were both barefoot and Norah couldn't stop looking at Reed's sexy feet.

"Don't see many movies, huh?" she asked.

"Never really had much time. Hopefully now in Wedlock Creek, I will. Slower pace of life and all that."

She nodded and they settled down to watch. Reed laughed a lot, particularly at the scenes with Cuba Gooding Jr. By the time Renée Zellweger said Tom Cruise had her at hello, Norah was mush and teary-eyed.

"Softy," Reed said, slinging his arm over so that she could prop up against him. She did.

Great. Now they were cuddling. Sort of. His full attention was on the movie. Norah found it pretty difficult to keep her mind on the TV with her head against Reed's shoulder and him stretched out so close beside her. She ate popcorn and dug into the chocolate cake to take her mind off Reed and sex.

But as the credits rolled, Reed turned onto his side to face her. "Do you believe in that 'you complete me' stuff?"

She turned onto her side, too. "Believe in it? Of course I do."

"So someone else can complete you?" he asked. "You're not finished without a romantic partner?"

"What it *means* is that your romantic partner brings out the best in you, makes you realize and understand the depth of your feelings, makes you feel whole in a way you never did before, that suddenly nothing is missing from your life."

He smiled. "I don't know, Norah. I think it was just a good line."

She shook her head. "Nope. She completes him and he knows it."

He reached out to move a strand of hair that had fallen across her face, but instead of pulling his hand back, he caressed her cheek. "You're a true romantic."

"You are, too. You just don't know it," she said. It was so true. Everything he did was the mark of a romantic. His chivalry. His code of honor. His willingness to watch *Jerry Maguire*. The man had ordered popcorn and chocolate cake from room service, for God's sake. He was a romantic.

The thought made her smile. But now he was staring at her mouth.

His finger touched her lip. "Popcorn crumb," he said.

"Does popcorn have crumbs?"

"Yes," he whispered, his face just inches away. He propped up on his elbow and moved another strand of hair away from her face. There was a combination of tenderness and desire in his eyes, in his expression.

He was *thinking*, she realized, fighting the urge to move his head down and kiss her. *Win out, urge*, she telepathically sent to his brain. *Do it. Kiss her. Kiss. Her.*

And then he did. Softly at first. Passionately a second later.

He moved on top of her, his hands in her hair, his mouth moving from her lips to her neck. She sucked in a breath, her hands roaming his back, his neck, his hair. Thick, silky hair. "Tell me to stop, Norah. This is nuts."

"I don't want you to stop. I want you to make love to me."

He groaned and tore off his shirt, then unzipped her dress. She sat up and flung the dress off before he could change his mind. His eyes were on her lacy bra. Her one sexy, black undergarment with panties to match, chosen for this possibility.

And it was happening. Mmm. Yes, it was happening! She lay back, his eyes still on her cleavage. That was good. He was not thinking. He was only feeling. And the moment her hands touched the bare skin of his chest, he was hers. He groaned again and his mouth was on hers, one hand undoing his pants and shrugging out of them while the other unsnapped her bra like a pro.

Suddenly they were both naked. He lay on top of

her and propped up on his forearms. "I can't resist you, Norah. I don't have *that* much self-control."

She smiled. "Good."

By the time he reached for the foil-wrapped little packet in his wallet, she was barely able to think for the sensations rocketing every inch, every cell, of her body. But she was vaguely aware that he'd brought a condom. Probably a whole box. Which meant he'd anticipated that something could happen between them.

Her husband *wasn't* lost to her behind that brick wall he'd erected between him and love, him and *feeling*. There was hope for them. That was all she needed to know. In that moment her heart cracked wide-open and let him in fully, risks be damned.

And then he lay on top of her and suddenly they were one, all thought poofing from her head.

Reed's phone was on silent-vibrate, but as a cop he'd long trained himself to catch its hum. He must have drifted off to sleep after two rounds of amazing sex with Norah. His wife. Sex that they weren't supposed to have. Not part of the deal.

He glanced over at her. She lay next to him, turned away on her side, asleep, he figured from her breathing. Her long reddish-brown hair flowed down her sexy bare shoulders. Just looking at her had him stirring once more, wanting her like crazy, but then his phone vibrated again on the bedside table. Then again. And again. What the hell could this be at almost one thirty in the morning?

David Dirk was what it was. A series of texts.

I owe u, man. Good talk we had earlier.

I'm lying here next to my gorgeous wife, feeling so lucky.

I might as well have won a mil downstairs, bruh.

I'm realizing the depth of my love for this woman means she comes 1st.

The selfish crap is stopping. I love Eden 2 death and I'm putting her needs above my own.

Double-date back in the Creek, dude?

Well, good for David Dirk. And Eden. The guy had flipped out, fled town in a spectacularly immature fashion, but had worked it out with himself and laid his heart bare to the woman he loved. And they'd both ended up getting what they'd wanted: each other—still with a hearty dose of legend on their side.

So why was Reed feeling so…unsettled? He put the phone back on the table and lay very still, staring up at the ceiling.

Because he wasn't putting Norah's needs above his own? She wanted the whole shebang—love, romance, snuggles while watching *Jerry Maguire*, a shared, true partnership. And what was he giving her? Just the partnership. Fine, he threw in some snuggles while watching the biggest date-night movie of all time.

And then made mad, passionate love to his wife of "convenience." His life-plan partner.

He shook his head at himself.

He got to feel like a better man than his father was when he was too much of a coward to marry and plan a family of his own. He got to have his ranch when his grandmother would be sorely disappointed at the "marriage" he'd engineered to have the Barelli homestead.

Meanwhile he was keeping Norah from finding what she really wanted. She'd agreed to the marriage deal; she herself had said she wanted nothing to do with love or romance or men. But something had changed for her. Because her heart had opened up. Somehow. Married to a brick wall like him.

Whereas he was still unbreakable and unblastable.

He turned his head and looked at Norah, reaching for a silky strand of her hair. Sex with her was everything he'd thought it would be; they fit perfectly together, they were in rhythm. But afterward, part of him had wanted to hit the streets and just breathe it out. He'd stayed put for her, like he was doing her some kind of big favor. Which had made him feel worse about what he could and couldn't give her.

There was only one thing to do, he realized as he lay there staring back up at the ceiling.

One way out of the mess he'd created by thinking this kind of marriage could work, could be a thing.

Yes. The more he thought about what he needed to do, the more he knew it was the right thing. He'd have to take an hour off work in the morning, but he'd make up the time and then some.

Decision made, he turned over and faced the beige-and-white-striped wallpaper until he realized Norah was a much better sight to fall asleep to. He wanted to reach out and touch her, to wrap his arms around her and tell her how much he cared about her, for her, but he couldn't.

* * *

Nothing about Reed Barelli escaped Norah's notice. So she'd caught on to his distance immediately. It had started in the hotel room when she'd woken up five minutes ago. All the warmth from the night before was gone, replaced by this...slight chill. He was polite. Respectful. Offering to run out for bagels or to call room service.

She sat up in bed, pulling the top sheet and blankets up to her chest. *Keep it light, Norah*, she warned herself. "All that hot sex does have me starving," she said with a smile, hoping to crack him.

Instead of sliding back into bed for another round, he practically raced to the phone. "I'll call room service. Omelet? Side of hash browns?"

Deep endless sigh. If she couldn't have him, she may as well eat. She hadn't been kidding. She *was* starving. "Western omelet. And yes to hash browns. And a vat of coffee."

He ordered two of that.

She could still feel the imprint of his lips on hers, all over her, actually. The scent of him was on her. He was all over her, inside her, with her. She felt like Cathy in *Wuthering Heights*—*"I am Heathcliff!"*

Maybe not the most hopeful reference for the Barellis of Wedlock Creek.

"Here you go," he said, handing her the fluffy terry robe, compliments of the Concordia. "Use mine."

Either he didn't want to see her naked anymore or he was just being kind and polite and respectful. She knew it was all the latter. Last night, everything he did had shown how much he'd wanted to see her naked, how much he'd wanted *her*. And now it was all over. Light of day and all that other back-to-Cinderella, back-to-a-pumpkin reality.

They ate on the terrace, making small talk. He asked how the triplets were, since of course she'd already called to check in on them. They were all fine. The Pie Diner was fine. The police station was fine. Eden and David were fine. Everything was fine but them. What had changed so drastically overnight?

He pushed his hash browns around on his plate. "Norah, we need to talk. Really talk."

Oh hell. She put down her coffee mug. "Okay."

He cleared his throat, then took a long sip of his coffee. Then looked out at the view. Then, finally, he looked at her. "I will stand by you, beside you, and be a father to Bella, Bea and Brody. I want to be their father."

"But...?" she prompted, every nerve ending on red alert.

"But I sense—no, I *know*—that you want more. You want a real marriage. And I'm holding you back from that. If you want to find a man who will be both husband and father, I don't want to hold you back, Norah. You deserve everything."

"I deserve everything, but you won't give me everything," she said, pushing at her hash browns. Anything to avoid directly looking into his eyes.

"I wish I could, Norah. I don't have it in me. I guess it's been too long, too many years of shutting down and out. My job made it easy. I swore off all that stuff, said 'no more,' and I guess I really meant it."

Crud. She wished there was something lying around on the floor of the terrace that she could kick. A soda can. Anything. "So I'm supposed to decide whether I want half a marriage or to let you go so I can find everything in one man."

He glanced out toward the Strip, at the overcast sky. "Yes."

Half of him or the possibility of everything with another? She'd take a quarter of Reed Barelli.

Oh, really, Norah? That's all you deserve? A man who can't or won't give more of himself?

He wanted to serve and protect the community and his family. Same thing to him. She shook her head, trying to make sense of this, trying to make it work for her somehow. But she wasn't a town. She wasn't a bunch of houses or people. She was his *wife*.

"And if I hand you the annulment papers to sign, you're prepared to give up the Barelli ranch? Your heart and soul?"

His expression changed then, but she couldn't quite read it. There was pain, she was pretty sure.

"Yes, I'm fully prepared to give it up."

God. She sucked in a breath and turned away, trying to keep control of herself. "Well, then. If you're willing to give up the ranch that means so much to you, I think we both know we need to get those annulment papers over to the courthouse."

She slid off her wedding ring, her heart tearing in two. "Here," she managed to croak out, handing it to him. "I don't want it."

He bit his lip but pocketed it. Then she pushed out of her chair, ran back into the room, grabbed her clothes off the floor and rushed across the hall into her room.

She sat on the edge of her bed and sobbed.

Chapter 13

"What? You're just gonna let him go?" Aunt Cheyenne said with a frown.

Norah stirred the big pot of potatoes on the stove in the kitchen of the Pie Diner. She'd asked herself that very question on the flight back home and all night in her bedroom at the ranch. Reed had packed a bag and had gone to the one hotel in town to give her "some privacy with your thoughts."

She'd wanted to throw something at him then. But she'd been too upset. When the door had closed behind him, she was just grateful the triplets were with her mother so that she could give in to her tears and take the night to get it out of her system. Come morning, she'd known she'd have to turn into a pot pie baker and a mother and she wouldn't have the time or the luxury of a broken heart.

"Not like I have much choice," she said.

"Uh, Norah, a little more gently with that spoon," her mother said from her station across the kitchen. "The potatoes aren't Reed."

Norah took a deep breath and let up on the stirring. She offered her mom a commiserating smile. "I'll be okay. The potatoes will be okay. The only one who won't be okay is that stubborn brick wall I married by accident."

"Fight for him!" Cheyenne said. "The man is so used to being a lone wolf that he doesn't feel comfortable having a real-life partner. He's just not used to it. But he likes being married or he wouldn't have suggested staying married—no matter what."

Norah had thought of that. Her mind had latched on to so many hopeful possibilities last night. But then she'd come back to all he'd said on the terrace in Las Vegas. "He's giving up the ranch to undo it," Norah reminded her aunt.

"Because he thinks you're losing out," her mother said, filling six pie crusts with the fragrant beef stew she and Cheyenne had been working on this morning. "He wants you to have everything you deserve. The man loves you, Norah."

She shook her head. "If he loved me, he'd love me. And we wouldn't have had that conversation in Vegas." Tears poked her eyes and she blinked them back. The triplets were in the office slash nursery having their nap and she needed to think about them. In Reed, they'd have a loving father but would grow up with a warped view of love and marriage because their parents' lack of love—kisses, romance, the way a committed couple acted—would be absent. They would be roommates, and her children would grow up thinking that was how married people behaved. No sirree.

The super annoying part? She couldn't even go back to the old Norah's ways of having given up on love and romance. Because she'd fallen hard for Reed and she knew she was capable of that much feeling. She did want it. She wanted love. She wanted a father for her babies. She wanted that man to be the same.

She wanted that man to be Reed.

He didn't want to be that man. Or couldn't be. Whatever!

Being Fabio was his fantasy, though, she suddenly realized. A man who *did* want to marry. Fabio had suggested it, after all. Fabio had carried her into that chapel.

Could there be hope?

A waitress popped her head into the kitchen "Norah? There's someone here to see you. Henry Peterfell." The young woman filled her tray with her order of three chicken pot pies and one beef and carried it back out.

"Henry Peterfell is here to see me?" She glanced at her mother and aunt. Henry Peterfell was a pricey attorney and very involved in local government. What could he want with Norah?

She wiped her hands on her apron and went through the swinging-out door into the dining room. Fiftysomething-year-old Henry, in his tan suit, sat at the counter, a Pie Diner yellow to-go bag in front of him. "Ah, Ms. Ingalls. I stopped in to pick up lunch and realized I had some papers for you to sign in my briefcase, so if you'd like, you can just John Hancock them here. Or you can make an appointment to come into the office. Whatever is more convenient."

Panic rushed into her stomach. "Papers? Am I being sued?"

Oh God. Was Reed divorcing her? Perhaps he figured they couldn't annul the marriage because they'd made love. *You're the one who gave him back your ring*, she reminded herself, tears threatening again. *Of course he's divorcing you*.

"Sued? No, no, nothing like that." He set his leather briefcase on the counter and pulled out a folder. "There are three sets. You can sign where you see the neon arrow. There, there and there," he said, pointing at the little sticky tabs.

Norah picked up the papers. And almost fell off the chair.

"This is a deed," she said slowly. "To the Barelli ranch."

"Yes," the lawyer said. "Everything is in order. Lovely property."

"Reed turned the ranch over to me? The ranch is now mine?"

"That's right. It's yours. Once you sign, of course. There, there and there," he said, gesturing.

Norah stared at the long, legal-size papers, the black type swimming before her eyes. *What?* Why would Reed do this?

"Mr. Peterfell, would it be all right if I held on to these to read first?"

"Absolutely," he said. "Just send them to my office or drop them off at your convenience."

With that, he and his briefcase of unexpected documents were gone.

Reed had deeded the ranch to her. His beloved ranch. The only place that had ever felt like home to him.

Because he didn't feel he deserved it now that they were going to split up? That had to be the reason. He wasn't even keeping it in limbo in case he met someone down the road, though. He was that far gone? That sure he was never going to share his heart with anyone?

A shot of cold swept through her at the thought. How lonely that would be.

She wasn't letting him get away that easily. Her aunt and mother were right. She was going to fight for him. She was going to fight for Fabio. Because there was a chance that Reed did love her but couldn't allow himself to. And if the feeling was there, she was going to pull it out of him till he was so happy he made people sick.

The thought actually made her smile.

Reed stood in the living room of his awkward rental house—the same old one, which of course was still available because it was so blah—trying to figure out why the arrangement of furniture looked so wrong. Maybe if he put the couch in front of the windows instead of against the wall?

This place would never look right. Or feel right. Or be home.

But giving Norah the ranch had been the right thing to do. Now she'd have a safe place to raise the triplets with enough room for all of them, fields to roam in, and she'd own it free and clear. She'd never have to worry about paying rent again, let alone a mortgage or property taxes—he'd taken care of that in perpetuity.

And he had a feeling his grandmother was looking down at him, saying, *Well, you tried. Not hard enough, but you tried and in the end you did the right thing. She should have the ranch, you dope.*

He *was* a dope. And Norah should have the ranch.

The doorbell rang. He had a feeling it was Norah, coming to tell him she couldn't possibly accept the ranch. Well, tough, because he'd already deeded it to her and it was hers. He'd even talked over the legalities with his lawyer; he'd married, per his grandmother's will, and the ranch was his fair and square. His to hand over.

He opened the door and it was like a gut punch. Two days ago they'd still had their deal. Two nights ago they'd been naked in bed together. And then yesterday morning, he'd turned back into the Reed he needed to be to survive this thing called life. Keeping to himself. No emotional entanglements.

And yet his first day in town he'd managed to get married and become a father to three babies. He was really failing at no emotional entanglements.

"I can't accept this, Reed," she said, holding up a legal-size folder.

"You have no choice. It's yours now. The deed is in your name."

She scowled. "It's your home."

"I'd rather you and the triplets have it. My grandmother would rather that, too. I have no doubt."

"So you get married, get your ranch and then give up the ranch, but the wife who's not really your wife gets to *keep* the ranch. That makes no sense."

"Does anything about our brief history, Norah?" An image floated into the back of his mind, Fabio and Angelina hand in hand, him scooping her up and carrying her into the chapel with its legend and sneaky, elderly caretakers slash officiants.

She stared at him hard. "I'll accept the ranch on one condition."

He raised an eyebrow. "And that would be?"

"I need your help for my multiples class. I'd like you to be a guest speaker. Give the dad's perspective."

No, no, no. What could *he* contribute? "I've only been a dad for a little while," he said. "Do I really have anything to truly bring to the class? And now with things so…up in the air between us."

Up in the air is good, she thought. Because it meant things could go her way. Their way. The way of happiness.

"You have so much to contribute," she said. "Honestly, it would be great if you could speak at all the remaining classes," she said. "Lena Higgins—she's the one expecting all boy triplets—told me her husband wasn't sure he felt comfortable at the class last week and might not be joining her for the rest because the class seemed so mom-focused. Poor Lena looked so sad. A male guest speaker will keep some of the more reluctant dads and caregivers comfortable. Especially when it's Reed Barelli, detective."

He didn't quite frown, so that was something. "I don't know, Norah. I—"

"Did you see how scared some of those dads looked?" she asked. "For dads who are shaking over the responsibility awaiting them—you could set their minds at ease. I think all the students will appreciate the male perspective."

Some of the guys in the class, which had included fathers, fathers-to-be and grandfathers, had looked like the ole deer in the headlights. One diaper was tough on some men who thought they were helpless. Two, three, even four diapers at the same time? Helpless men would poof into puddles on the floor. He supposed he could be a big help in the community by showing these guys they weren't helpless, that they had the same instincts—and fears—as the women and moms among them.

Step up, boys, he thought. That would be his mission.

Ha. He was going to tell a bunch of sissies afraid of diaper wipes and onesies and double strollers to step up when he couldn't step up for the woman he'd do anything for?

Anything but love, Reed?

He shook the thought out of his weary brain. His head ran circles around the subject of his feelings for Norah. He just couldn't quite get a handle on them. Because he didn't want to? Or because he really was shut off from all that? Done with love. Long done.

She was tilting her head at him. Waiting for an answer.

"And if I do this, you'll accept the ranch as yours?" he said.

She nodded.

He extended a hand. "Deal."

She shook his hand, the soft feel of it making him want to wrap her in his arms and never let her go.

"We make a lot of deals," she said. "I guess it's our thing."

He smiled. "The last one failed miserably." He failed miserably. Or had Norah just changed the rules on him by wanting more? They'd entered their agreement on a handshake, too. He wasn't really wrong here. He just wasn't…right.

"This one has less riding on it," she said. "You just have to talk about how you bonded with the triplets.

How you handle changing time. Feeding time. Bedtime. What's it like to come home from work and have three grumpy, teething little ones to deal with. How you make it work. How it's wonderful, despite everything hard about it. How sometimes it's not even hard."

He nodded and smiled. "I'll be there," he said. He frowned, his mind going to the triplets. "Norah, how are things going to work now? I mean, until you find the right man, I want to be there for you and the babies. I want to be their father."

"Until I find a father who can be that and a real husband?"

"Okay, it's weird, but yes."

She frowned. "So you're going to get all enmeshed in their lives, give a hundred percent to them, and then I meet someone who fits the bill and you'll just back off? Walk away? Bye, triplets?"

Hey, wait a minute.

"Look, Norah, I'm not walking away from anything. I want to be their father. I told you that. But I want you to have what you need, too. If I can't be both and someone else can…"

Someone else. Suddenly the thought of another man touching her, kissing her, doing upsie-downsie with his babies…

His babies. Hell. Maybe he should back off now. Or he'd really be done for. Maybe they both needed a break from each other so they could go back to having what they wanted. Which was all messed up now.

She lifted her chin. "Let's forget this for now. Anytime you want to see Bella, Bea and Brody, you're welcome over. You're welcome at the ranch anytime."

He nodded, unable to speak at the moment.

She peered behind him, looking around the living room. "The couch should go in front of the windows. And that side table would be better on that wall," she said, pointing. "The mirror above the console table is too low. Should be slightly above eye level."

"That should help. Thank you. I can't seem to get this place right."

"I'm not sure I want it to feel right," she said. "Wait, did I say that aloud?" She frowned again. "Everything is all wrong. I don't like that you left your home, Reed. That place is your dream."

"That place is meant for a family. I want you to have it."

She looked at him for a long moment. He could see her shaking her head without moving a muscle. "See you in class."

He watched her walk to her car. The moment she got in, he felt her absence and the weight of one hell of a heavy heart.

Chapter 14

Word had spread that Detective Reed Barelli, who'd become de facto father to the Ingalls triplets by virtue of marrying their mother at the Wedlock Creek chapel with its Legend of the Multiples, would be a guest speaker at tonight's zero-to-six-month multiples class. There were more men than women this time, several first-timers to the class who practically threw checks at Norah. At this rate, she'd be raking it in as a teacher.

She hadn't even meant to invite him to speak—especially not as a condition of her keeping the ranch. The sole condition, no less. But it had been the best she could come up with, just standing there, not knowing what to say, how to keep him, how to get him to open up the way she had and accept the beautiful thing he was being offered: love. She did want him to be a speaker in her class, and it would get them working together, so that was good. She couldn't try to get through to him if they were constantly apart now that he'd moved out.

They hadn't spent much time together in three days.

He'd come to the ranch to see the triplets every day since their return from Las Vegas. He'd help feed them, then read to them, play with them. Blow raspberries and do upsie-downsies. And then he'd leave, taking Norah's heart with him.

Now here he was, sitting in the chair beside her desk with his stack of handouts, looking so good she could scream.

"Welcome, everyone! As you may have heard through the grapevine, tonight we have a guest speaker. Detective Reed Barelli. When Reed and I got married, he became the instant father of three seven-month-old teething babies. Was he scared of them? Nope. Did he actually want to help take care of them? Yes. Reed had never spent much time around babies and yet he was a natural with my triplets. Why?"

She looked at Reed and almost didn't want to say why. Because it proved he could pick and choose. The triplets. But not her.

She bit back the strangled sob that rose up from deep within and lifted her chin. She turned back toward the class. "Because he wanted to be. That is the key. He *wanted* to be there for them. And so he was. And dads, caregivers, dads-to-be, grandfathers, that's all you have to know. That you want to be there for them. So, without further ado, here is Detective Reed Barelli."

He stood, turned to her and smiled, then addressed the class. "That was some introduction. Thank you, Norah."

She managed a smile and then sat on the other side of the desk.

"Norah is absolutely right. I did want to be there for the triplets. And so I was. But don't think I had a clue of how to take care of one baby, let alone three. I know how to change a diaper—I think anyone can figure that out. But the basics, including diapers and burping and sleep schedules and naps? All that, you'll learn here. What you won't learn here, or hell, maybe you will because I'm talking about it, is that taking care of babies will tell you who you are. Someone who steps up or someone who sits out. Be the guy who steps up."

A bunch of women stood and applauded, as did a few guys.

"Is it as easy as you make it sound?" Tom McFill asked. "My wife is expecting twins. I've never even held a baby before."

"The first time you do," Reed said, "everything will change. That worry you feel, that maybe you won't know what you're doing? It'll dissipate under the weight of another feeling—a surge of protection so strong that you won't know what hit you. All you'll know is that you're doing what needs to be done, operating by instinct and common sense, Googling what you don't know, asking a grandmother. So it's as hard and as easy as I'm making it sound."

A half hour later Norah took over, giving tutorials on feeding multiples, bathing multiples and how to handle sleep time. Then there was the ole gem: what if both babies, or three or four, all woke up in the middle of the night, crying and wet and hungry. She covered that, watching her students taking copious notes.

Finally the class was over. Everyone crowded around

Reed, asking him questions. By the time the last student left and they were packing up to go, it was a half hour past the end of the class.

"You were a big hit," she said. "I knew I called this one right."

"I'm happy to help out. I knew more than I thought on the subject. I'd stayed up late last night doing research, but I didn't need to use a quarter of it."

"You had hands-on training."

"I miss living with them," he said, and she could tell he hadn't meant to say that.

She smiled and let it go. "Most people would think you're crazy."

"I guess I am."

Want more, she shouted telepathically. *Insist on more! You did it with the babies, now do it with me. Hot sex every night, fool!* But of course she couldn't say any of that. "Well, I'd better get over to the diner to pick up the triplets."

"They're open for another half hour, right? I could sure go for some beef pot pie."

She stared at him. Why was he prolonging the two of them being together? Because he wanted to be with her? Because he really did love the triplets and wanted to see them?

Because he missed her the way she missed him?

"I have to warn you," she said as they headed out. "My family might interrogate you about the state of our marriage. Demand to know when we're patching things up. *If* we will, I should say."

"Well, we can't say what we don't know. That goes for suspects and us."

Humph. All he had to do was say he'd be the one. The father and the husband. It was that easy!

On the way to their cars, she called her mom to let her know she and Reed would be stopping in for beef pot pies so they'd be ready when they arrived. Then she got in her car and Reed got in his. The whole time he trailed her in his SUV to the Pie Diner, she was so aware of him behind her.

The diner was still pretty busy at eight thirty-five. Norah's mom waved them over to the counter.

"Norah, look who's here!"

Norah stared at the man sitting at the counter, a vegetable pot pie and lemonade in front of him. She gasped as recognition hit. "Harrison? Omigod, Harrison Atwood?" He stood and smiled and she threw her arms around him. Her high school sweetheart who'd joined the army and ended up on the east coast and they'd lost contact.

"Harrison is divorced," Norah's mom said. "Turns out his wife didn't want children and he's hoping for a house full. He told me all about it."

Norah turned beet red. "Mom, I'm sure Harrison doesn't want the entire restaurant knowing his business."

Harrison smiled. "I don't mind at all. The more people know I'm in the market for a wife and children, the better. You have to say what you want if you hope to get it, right?"

Norah's mother smiled at Norah and Reed, then looked back at Harrison. "I was just telling Harrison how things didn't work out between the two of you and that you're available again. The two of you could catch up. High school sweethearts always have such memories to talk over."

Can my face get any redder? Norah wondered, shooting daggers at her busybody mother. What was she trying to do?

Get her settled down, that was what. First Reed and now a man she hadn't seen in ten years.

Norah glanced at Reed, who seemed very stiff. He was stealing glances at Harrison every now and then.

Harrison had been a cute seventeen-year-old, tall and gangly, but now he was taller and more muscular, attractive, with sandy-brown hair and blue eyes and a dimple in his left cheek. She'd liked him then, but she'd recognized even then that she hadn't been in love. To the point that she'd kept putting him off about losing their virginity. She'd wanted her first time to be with a man she was madly in love with. Of course, she'd thought she was madly in love with a rodeo champ, but he'd taken her virginity and had not given her anything in return. She'd thought she was done with bull riders and then, wham, she'd fallen for the triplets' father. Maybe she'd never learn.

"Harrison is a chef. He studied in Paris," Aunt Cheyenne said. "He's going to give us a lesson in French cooking. Isn't that wonderful? You two must have so much in common," she added, wagging a finger between Norah and Harrison.

"Well, I'd better get going," Reed said, stepping back. "I have cases to go over. Nice to see you all."

"But, Reed, your pot pie just came out of the oven," Norah's mother said. "I'll just go grab it."

Norah watched him give Harrison the side-eye before he said, "I'll come with you. I want to say good-night to the triplets."

"They are so beautiful," Harrison said with so much reverence in his voice that Norah couldn't help the little burst of pride in her chest. Harrison sure was being kind.

Reed narrowed his gaze on the man, scowled and disappeared into the kitchen behind her mother.

And then Aunt Cheyenne winked at Norah and smiled. Oh no. Absolutely not. She knew what was going on here. Her mother and aunt realized they had Norah's old boyfriend captive at the counter and had been waiting for Norah and Reed to come in so they could make Reed jealous! Or, at least, that was how it looked.

Sneaky devils.

But they knew Reed wasn't in love with her and didn't want a future with her. So what was the point? Reed would probably push her with Harrison, tell her to see if there was anything to rekindle.

But as cute and nice as Harrison was, he wasn't Reed Barelli. No one else could be.

Every forkful of the pot pie felt as if it weighed ten pounds in his hand. Reed sat on his couch, his lonely dinner tray on the coffee table, a rerun of the baseball game on the TV as a distraction from his thoughts.

Which were centered on where Norah was right now. *Probably on a walking date with Harrison*, he said in his mind in a singsong voice. High school sweethearts would have a lot to catch up on. A lot to say. Memories. Good ones. There were probably a lot of firsts between them.

Reed wanted to throw up. Or punch something.

Just like that, this high school sweetheart, this French chef, would waltz in and take Reed's almost life. His wife, his triplets. His former ranch, which was now Norah's. A woman who wanted love and romance and a father for her babies might be drawn to the known— and the high school sweetheart fit that bill. Plus, they had that cooking thing in common. They might even be at the ranch now, Harrison standing behind Norah at the stove, his arms around her as he showed her how to Frenchify a pot pie. You couldn't and shouldn't! Pot pies were perfect as they were, dammit.

Grr. He took a swig of his soda and clunked it down on the coffee table. What the hell was going on here? He was jealous? Was this what this was?

Yes. He was jealous. He didn't want Norah kissing this guy. Sleeping with this guy. Frenchifying pot pies with this guy.

He flung down his fork and headed out, huffing into his SUV. He drove out to the ranch, just to check. And there was an unfamiliar car! With New York plates!

Hadn't Norah's mother said Harrison had lived on the east coast?

He was losing her right now. And he had let it happen.

This is what you want, dolt. You want her to find everything in one man. A father for her triplets. A husband for herself. Love. Romance. Happiness. Forever. You don't want that. So let her go. Let her have what she always dreamed of.

His heart now weighing a thousand pounds, he turned the SUV around and headed back to his rental house, where nothing awaited him but a cold pot pie and a big, empty bed.

* * *

"Upsie-what?" Harrison said, wrinkling his nose in the living room of the Barelli ranch. Correction. The Ingalls ranch. The Norah Ingalls ranch.

Norah frowned. "Upsie-downsie," she repeated. "You lift her up, say 'Upsie' in your best baby-talk voice, then lower her with a 'downsie'!"

They were sitting on the rug, the triplets in their Exersaucers, Bella raising her hands for a round of upsie-downsie. But Harrison just stared at Bella, shot her a fake smile and then turned away. Guess not everyone liked to play upsie-downsie.

Bella's face started to scrunch up. And turn red. Which meant any second she was about to let loose with a wail. "Waaaah!" she cried, lifting her arms up again.

"Now, Bea, be a good girl for Uncle Harrison," he said. "Get it, *Bea* should *be* a good girl. LOL," he added to no one in particular.

First of all, that was Bella. And did he just LOL at his own unfunny "joke"? Norah sighed. No wonder she hadn't fallen in love with Harrison Atwood in high school. Back then, cute had a lot to do with why she'd liked him. But as a grown-up, cute meant absolutely nothing. Even if a man looked like Reed Barelli.

"I'd love to take you out to a French place I know over in Brewer," he said. "It's not exactly Michelin-starred, but come on, in Wyoming, what is? I'm surprised you stuck around this little town. I always thought you'd move to LA, open a restaurant."

"What would give you that idea?" she asked.

"You used to talk a lot about your big dreams. Wanting to open Pie Diners all across the country. You wanted your family to have your own cooking show on the Food Network. Pot pie cookbooks on the *New York Times* bestseller list."

Huh. She'd forgotten all that. She did used to talk about opening Pie Diners across Wyoming, maybe even in bordering states. But life had always been busy enough. And full enough. Especially when she'd gotten pregnant and then when the triplets came.

"Guess your life didn't pan out the way you wanted," Harrison said. "Sorry about that."

Would it be wrong to pick up one of the big foam alphabet blocks and conk him over the head with it?

"My life turned out pretty great," she said. *I might not have the man I love, but I have the whole world in my children, my family, my job and my little town.*

"No need to get defensive," he said. "Jeez."

God, she didn't like this man.

Luckily, just then, Brody let loose with a diaper explosion, and Harrison pinched his nostrils closed. "Oh boy. Something stinks. I guess this is my cue to leave. LOL, right?"

"It was good to see you again, Harrison. Have a great rest of your life."

He frowned and nodded. "Bye." He made the mistake of removing his hand from his nose, got a whiff of the air de Brody and immediately pinched his nostrils closed again.

She couldn't help laughing. "Buh-bye," she said as he got into his car.

She closed the door, her smile fading fast. She had a diaper to change. And a detective to fantasize about.

Chapter 15

Reed kept the door of his office closed the next morning at the police station. He was in no mood for chitchat and Sergeant Howerton always dropped in on his way from the tiny kitchen to talk about his golf game and Officer Debowski always wanted to replay any collars from the day before. Reed didn't want to hear any of it.

He chugged his dark-brew coffee, needing the caffeine boost to help him concentrate on the case he was reading through. A set of burglaries in the condo development. Weird thing was, the thief, or thieves, was taking unusual items besides the usual money, jewelry and small electronics. Blankets and pillows, including throw pillows, had been taken from all the hit-up units.

Instead of making a list of what kind of thief would go for down comforters, he kept seeing Norah and the high school sweetheart with their hands all over each other. Were they in bed right now? He had to keep blinking and squeezing his eyes shut.

He wondered how long the guy had stayed last night. Reed should have made some excuse to barge in and interrupt them a bunch of times. Checking on the boiler or something. Instead, he'd reminded himself that the reason the French chef was there was because of Reed's own stupidity and stubbornness and inability to play well with others. Except babies.

He slammed a palm over his face. Were they having breakfast right now? Was Norah in his button-down shirt and nothing else? Having pancakes on the Barelli family table?

Idiot! he yelled at himself. *This is all your fault.* He'd stepped away. He'd said he couldn't. He'd said he wouldn't. And now he'd lost Norah to the high school sweetheart who wanted a wife and kids. They were probably talking about the glory days right now. And kissing.

Dammit to hell! He got up and paced his office, trying to force his mind off Norah and onto a down-feather-appreciating burglar. A Robin Hood on their hands? Or maybe someone who ran a flea market?

He's going to give us lessons in French cooking, Norah's mother had said. Suddenly, Reed was chopped liver to the Ingalls women, having been replaced by the beef bourguignon pot pie.

So what are you going to do about this? he asked himself. *Just let her go? Let the triplets go? You're their father!*

And he was Norah's husband. Husband, husband, husband. He tried to make the word have meaning, but the more it echoed in his head, the less meaning it had.

Husband meant suffering in his memories. His mother had had two louses and his grandfather had been a real doozy. He thought of his grandmother trying to answer Reed's questions about why she'd chosen such a grouch who didn't like anyone or anything. She'd said that sometimes people changed, but even so, she knew who he was and, despite his ways, he'd seemed to truly love her and that had made her feel special. She'd always said she should have known if you're the only one, the exception, there might be a problem.

So what now? Could he force himself to give this a real try? Romance a woman he had so much feeling for that it shook him to the core? Because he was shaken. That much he knew.

His head spinning, he was grateful when his desk phone rang.

"Detective Barelli speaking."

"Reed! I'm so glad I caught you. It's Annie. Annie Potterowski from the chapel. Oh dear, I'm afraid there's a bit of a kerfuffle concerning your marriage license. Could you come to the chapel at ten? I've already called Norah and she's coming."

"What kind of kerfuffle?" he asked. What could be more of a kerfuffle than their entire wedding?

"I'll explain everything when you get here. 'Bye now," she said and hung up.

If there was one good thing to come from this kerfuffle, it was that he knew Norah would be apart from the high school sweetheart, even for just a little while.

"Annie, what on earth is going on?" Norah asked the elderly woman as she walked into the chapel, pushing the enormous stroller.

"Look at those li'l dumplings!" Abe said, hurrying over to say hello to the triplets. He made peekaboo faces and Bea started to cry. "Don't like peekaboo, huh?" Abe said. "Okay, then, how about silly faces?" He scrunched up his face and stuck out his tongue, tilting his head to the left. Bea seemed to like that. She stopped crying.

"I'm just waiting for Detective Barelli to arrive," Annie said without looking at Norah.

Uh-oh. What was this about?

"Ah, there he is," Annie said as Reed came down the aisle to the front of the chapel.

Reed crossed his arms over his chest. "About this kerfuffle—"

"Kerfuffle?" Norah said. "Anne used the words *major problem* when she called me."

Annie bit her lip. "Well, it's both really. A whole bunch of nothing, but a lot of something."

Reed raised an eyebrow.

"I'll just say it plain," Abe said, straightening the blue bow-tie that he wore almost every day. "You two aren't married. You spelled your names wrong on the marriage license."

"What?" Norah said, her head spinning.

"The county clerk's temporary replacement checked her first week's work, just in case she made rookie errors, and discovered only one. On your marriage license. She sent back the license to you and Reed and to the chapel, since we officiated the ceremony. You didn't receive your mail yet?"

Had Norah even checked the mail yesterday? Maybe not.

"I was on a case all day yesterday and barely had

time to eat," Reed said. "But what's this about spelling our names wrong?"

Anne held up the marriage license. "Norah, you left off the *h*. And, Reed, you spelled your name *R-e-a-d*. I know there are lots of ways to spell your name, but that ain't one of them."

"Well, it's not like you didn't know we were drunk out of our minds, Annie and Abe!" Norah said, wagging a finger at them.

"I didn't think to proofread your names, for heaven's sake!" Annie said, snorting. "Now we're supposed to be proofreaders, too?" she said to Abe. "Each wedding would take hours. I'd have to switch to my reading glasses, and I can never find them and—"

"Annie, what does this mean?" Reed asked. "You said we're not married. Is that true? We're not married because our names were spelled wrong?"

"Your legal names are not on that document or on the official documents at the clerk's office," Abe said.

"So we're not married?" Norah repeated, looking at Reed. "We were never actually married?"

"Well, double accidentally, you were," Annie said. "The spiked punch and the misspelling. You were married until the error was noted by the most efficient county clerk replacement in Brewer's history."

I'm not married. Reed is not my husband.

It's over.

Her stomach hurt. Her heart hurt. Everything hurt.

Reed walked over to Norah and seemed about to say something. But instead he knelt down in front of the stroller. "Hey, little guys. I miss you three."

Brody gave Reed his killer gummy smile, three tiny teeth poking up.

She glanced at his hand. He still wore his wedding ring even though she'd taken hers off. Guess he'd take it off now.

"We'll leave you to talk," Annie said, ushering Abe into the back room.

Norah sat in a pew, a hand on the stroller for support. She wasn't married to Reed. How could she feel so bereft when she never really had a marriage to begin with?

"We can go back to our lives now," she said, her voice catching. She cleared her throat, trying to hide what an emotional mess she was inside. "I'll move out of the ranch. Since we were never legally married, I'm sure that affects possession of the ranch. You can't deed me something you didn't rightfully inherit."

She was babbling, talking so she wouldn't burst into tears.

He stood, giving Bea's hair a caress. "I guess Harrison will be glad to hear the news."

"Harrison?"

"Your high school sweetheart," he said. "The one you spent the night with."

She narrowed her eyes at him. "What makes you think we spent the night together?"

"I drove by the house to see if his car was there."

"Why? Why would you even care? You don't have feelings for me, Reed."

He looked away for a moment, then back at her. "I have a lot of feelings for you."

"Right. You feel responsible for me. You care about me. You're righting wrongs when you're with me."

He shook his head but didn't say anything.

"I should get back to work," she said.

"Me, too," he said.

She sucked in a breath. "I guess when we walk out of here, it's almost like none of it ever happened. We were never really married."

"I felt married," he said. Quite unexpectedly.

"And you clearly didn't like the feeling." She waited a beat, hoping he'd say she was wrong.

She waited another beat. Nothing.

"There's nothing between me and Harrison," she said without really having to. What did it matter to Reed anyway? His urge to drive by the ranch had probably been about him checking up on her, making sure she'd gotten back okay, the detective in him at work. "He did come over for a bit and was so insufferable I couldn't wait for him to leave."

He looked surprised. "But what about all the firsts you two shared?"

"Firsts? I had my first kiss with someone else. I lost my virginity to someone else. I did try sushi for the first time with Harrison. I guess that counts."

"So you two are *not* getting back together," he said, nodding.

"We are definitely not."

"So my position as father of the triplets still stands."

"That's correct," she said even though she wanted to tell him no, it most certainly did not. This was nuts. He was going to be their father in between semi-dates and short-term relationships until the real thing came along for her?

"I'd like to spend some time with them after work, if that's all right," he said. "I have presents for them for their eight-month birthday."

Her heart pinged. "It's sweet that you even know that."

"You only turn eight months once," he said with a weak smile.

And you find a man like Reed Barelli once in a lifetime, she thought. *I had you, then lost you, then didn't ever really have you, and now there's nothing.* Except his need to do right by the triplets, be for them what he'd never had.

"Time to go, kiddos," she said, trying to inject some cheer in her voice. "See you later, then," she said, wondering how she'd handle seeing him under such weird circumstances. Were they friends now?

"I'll get the door," he said, heading up the aisle to open it for her. He couldn't get rid of her fast enough.

Her heart breaking in pieces, she gripped the stroller and headed toward the Pie Diner, knowing she'd never get over Reed Barelli.

"Your grandmother would have loved Norah."

Reed glanced up at the voice. Annie Potterowski was walking up the chapel aisle toward where he sat in a pew in the last row. He'd been sitting there since Norah had left, twenty minutes or so. He'd married her in this place. And been unmarried to her here. He couldn't seem to drag himself out.

"Yeah, I think she would have," Reed said.

Annie sat beside him, tying a knot in the filmy pink scarf around her neck. "Now, Reed, I barely know you. I met you a few times over the years when you came to visit Lydia. So I don't claim to be an expert on you or anything, but anyone who's been around as long as I have and marries people for a living knows a thing or two about the human heart. Do you want to know what I think?"

He did, actually. "Let me have it."

She smiled. "I think you love Norah very much. I think you're madly in love with her. But this and that happened in your life and so you made her that dumb deal about a partnership marriage."

He narrowed his eyes at her. "How'd you know about that?"

"I listen, that's how. I pick up things. So you think you can avoid love and feeling anything because you were dealt a crappy hand? Pshaw," she said, adding a snort for good measure. "We've all had our share of bad experiences."

"Annie, I appreciate—"

"I'm not finished. You don't want to know the upbringing I had. It would keep you up at night feeling sorry for me. But when Abe Potterowski came calling, I looked into that young man's eyes and heart and soul, and I saw everything I'd missed out on. And so I said yes instead of no when I was scared to death of my feelings for him. And it was the best decision I ever made."

He took Annie's hand in his and gave it a gentle squeeze.

"I was used to shutting people out," she continued. "But you have to know when to say yes, Reed. And your grandmother, God bless her sweet soul, only ever wanted you to say yes to the right woman. Don't let her get away." Annie stood and patted his shoulder. "Your grandmother liked to come in here and do her thinking. She sat in the back row, too, other end, though."

With that, Annie headed down the aisle and disappeared into the back room.

Leaving Reed to do some serious soul-searching.

Chapter 16

"Not married?" Shelby repeated, her face incredulous as she cut up potatoes for the lunch-rush pot pies.

Norah shook her head, recounting what Annie and Abe had said.

"Oh hell," her mother said. "I really thought you two would work it out."

"You pushed Harrison on me last night!" Norah complained even though she knew why.

"Yeah, but I only did that because he was here when you called and said you and Reed were stopping in for pot pies. I wanted Reed to know he had competition for your heart."

"Well, he doesn't. Harrison was awful. He freaked the minute one of the triplets did number two in his presence."

"Norah, you and Reed belong together," Aunt Cheyenne said as she filled six pie tins with beef stew. "We can all see that."

"I thought we did," Norah said, tears threatening her eyes. "But he never wanted a real relationship. He wanted to save me. And he wanted the ranch."

"The ranch he gave up for you?" her mother asked. "You do something crazy like that when you love someone so much they come first."

"There's that responsibility thing again," Norah said, frowning. "Putting me first. Everything for me, right? He wants me to have 'everything I deserve.' Except for him."

"Coming through," called a male voice.

Norah glanced up at her handsome brother-in-law, Liam Mercer, walking into the kitchen, an adorable toddler holding each of his hands. Despite being in the terrible twos, Norah's nephews, Shane and Alexander, were a lot of fun to be around.

Liam greeted everyone, then wrapped his wife in a hug and dipped her for a kiss, paying no mind to the flour covering her apron. Norah's heart squeezed in her chest as it always did when she witnessed how in love the Mercers were.

You should hold out for that, she told herself. *For a man who loves you like Liam loves Shelby. Like Dad loved Mom.*

Like I love Reed, she thought with a wistful sigh.

In just a few hours he'd be at the ranch, which they'd both have to give up, and the wonderful way he was with the triplets would tear her heart in two. She could have everything she'd ever wanted if Reed would just let go of all those old memories keeping him from opening his heart.

Hmm, she thought. Since being around the triplets did have Reed Barelli all mushy-gushy and as close to his feelings as he could get, maybe she could do a little investigative detective work of her own to see if those "feelings" he spoke of having for her did reach into the recesses of his heart. She knew he wanted her—their night in Las Vegas had proved that, and she knew he cared for her. That was obvious and he'd said it straight-out. But could he enter into a romantic relationship with her and hold nothing back?

The man was so good at everything. Maybe she could get him to see that he could be great at love, too.

"Something smells amazing," Reed said when Norah opened the door. For a moment he was captivated by the woman herself. She wore jeans and a pale yellow tank top, her long, reddish-brown hair in a low pony-tail, and couldn't possibly be sexier. His nose lifted at the mouth-watering aroma coming from somewhere nearby. "Steak?"

"On the grill with baked potatoes and asparagus at the ready."

"Can't wait. I'm starving." He set a large, brown paper bag down by the closet. "Where are the brand-new eight-month-olds?"

She smiled. "In their high chairs. They just ate."

"Perfect. It's party time." He trailed her into the kitchen carrying the bag. He set it on the kitchen table and pulled out three baby birthday hats, securing one on each baby's head.

"Omigod, the cutest," Norah said, reaching for her phone to take pictures. She got a bunch of great shots. Including Reed in several.

"For the eight-month-olds," Reed said, putting a chew rattle on Bea's tray. And one on Bella's and one on Brody's. "Oh, I set up a college fund for them today. And got them these new board books," he added, pulling out a bunch of brightly colored little hardcovers. At first he'd gone a little overboard in the store, putting three huge stuffed animals in his cart, clothing and all kinds of toys. Then he'd remembered it wasn't even their first birthday and put most of the stuff back.

"Thank you, Reed," she said. "From the bottom of my heart, thank you. I can't tell you how much it means to me that they're so special to you."

"They're very special to me. And so are you, Norah." With the babies occupied in their chairs with their new rattles, he moved closer to their mother and tilted up her chin. "I'm an idiot."

"Oh?" she asked. "Why is that?"

"Because I almost lost you to that French chef. Or any other guy. I almost lost you, Norah."

"What are you talking about? I'm alive." She waved a hand in front of herself.

"I mean I almost lost out on being with you. Really being with you."

"But I thought—"

"I couldn't get the triplets gifts and not get you something, too," he said. "This is for you." He handed her a little velvet box.

"What's this?" she asked.

"Open it."

She did—and gasped. The round diamond sparkled in the room. "It's a diamond ring. A very beautiful diamond ring."

He got down on one knee before her. "Norah, will you marry me? For real, this time? And sober?"

"But I thought—"

"That I didn't love you? I do. I love you very much. But I was an idiot and too afraid to let myself feel anything. Except these little guys here changed all that. They cracked my heart wide-open and I had to feel everything. Namely how very deeply in love with you I am."

She covered her mouth with her hands. "Yes. Yes. Yes. Yes."

He grinned and stood and slid the ring on her finger. "She said yes!" he shouted to the triplets, then picked her up and spun her around.

"I couldn't be happier," she said.

"Me, either. I get you. I get the triplets. And, hey, I get to live in the ranch because the owner is going to be my wife."

She smiled and kissed him and he felt every bit of her love for him.

"So the Luv U Wedding Chapel?" she asked. "That would be funny."

He shook his head. "I was thinking the Wedlock Creek Wedding Chapel."

Her mouth dropped open. "Wait. Are you forgetting the legend? You *want* more multiples?"

"Sure I do. I think five or six kids is just about perfect."

She laughed. "We really must be insane. But you'll be in high demand to teach the multiples classes. You'll never have a minute to yourself."

"I'll be too busy with my multiples. And my wife."

"I love you, Reed."

"I love you, too."

After calling her mother, aunt and sister with the news—and Reed could hear the shrieks and cheers from a good distance away, Reed called Annie Potterowski at the chapel.

"So, Annie... Norah and I would like to book the chapel for an upcoming Saturday night for our wedding ceremony. We're thinking a month from now if there are any openings."

Now it was Annie's turn to shriek. "You're making your grandmother proud, Reed. How's the second Saturday in August? Six p.m.?"

"Perfect," he said. Norah had told him a month would be all she'd need to find a wedding dress and a baby tux for Brody and two bridesmaids' dresses for Bella and Bea. Her family was already all over the internet.

"And we'll spell our names right this time," he added.

A few hours later the triplets were in their cribs, the dishes were done and Reed was sitting with his fiancée on the sofa, stealing kisses and just staring at her, two glasses of celebratory champagne in front of them.

"To the legend of the Wedlock Creek chapel," he said, holding up his glass. "It brought me my family and changed my life forever."

Norah clinked his glass and grinned "To the chapel—and the very big family we're going to have."

He sealed that one with a very passionate kiss.

Epilogue

One year later

Reed stood in the nursery—the twins' nursery—marveling at tiny Dylan and Daniel. Five days ago Norah had given birth to the seven-pounders, Dylan four ounces bigger and three minutes older. Both had his dark hair and Norah's perfect nose, slate-blue eyes that could go Norah's hazel or his dark brown, and ten precious fingers and ten precious toes.

Norah was next door in the triplets' nursery, reading them their favorite bedtime story. Soon they'd be shifting to "big kid" beds, but at barely two years old they were still smack in the middle of toddlerhood. He smiled at the looks they'd gotten as they'd walked up and down Main Street yesterday, Norah pushing the twins' stroller and him pushing the triplets'.

"How do you do it?" someone had asked.

"Love makes it easy," Reed had said. "But we have *a lot* of help."

They did. Norah's family and the Potterowskis had set up practically around-the-clock shifts of feeding them, doing laundry and entertaining the triplets the first couple of days the twins were home. Many of their students from the past year had also popped by with gifts and offers to babysit the triplets, couples eager to get some first-hand experience at handling multiples.

Even the Dirks had come by. David and a very pregnant Eden—expecting twins without having ever said "I do" at the Wedlock Creek chapel.

"I've got this," David had said, putting a gentle hand on his wife's belly. "I thought I'd be scared spitless, but watching you two and taking your class—easy peasy."

Reed had raised an eyebrow. David might be in for the rude awakening he'd been trying to avoid, but Reed wasn't about to burst his bubble. They'd have help just like the Barellis did. That was what family and friends and community were all about.

Norah came in then and stood next to him, putting her arm around him. "The triplets are asleep. Looks like these guys are close."

"Which means we have about an hour and a half to ourselves. Movie?"

She nodded. "*Jerry Maguire* is on tonight. Remember when we watched that?"

He would never forget. He put his arms around her and rested his forehead against hers. "Did I ever tell you that you complete me?"

She shook her head. "You said it was nonsense."

"Didn't I tell you I was an idiot? You. Complete. Me.

And so do they," he added, gesturing at the cribs. "And the ones in the room next door."

She reached up a hand to his cheek, her happy smile melting his heart. Then she kissed him and they tiptoed out of the nursery.

But Dylan was up twenty minutes later, then Daniel, and then the triplets were crying, and suddenly the movie would have to wait. Real life was a hell of a lot better, anyway.

* * * * *

WE HOPE YOU ENJOYED
THIS BOOK FROM

SPECIAL EXCERPT FROM

◆ HARLEQUIN
SPECIAL EDITION

*Real estate developer Brittany Doyle is eager to
bring the mountain town of Gallant Lake into the
twenty-first century...by changing everything.
Hardware store owner Nate Thomas hates change.
These opposites refuse to compromise, except when it
comes to falling in love.*

Read on for a sneak peek at
Changing His Plans,
*the next book in the Gallant Lake Stories
miniseries by Jo McNally.*

He stuck his head around the corner of the fasteners
aisle just in time to see a tall brunette stagger into the
revolving seed display. Some of the packets went flying,
but she managed to steady the display before the whole
thing toppled. He took in what probably had been a very
nice silk blouse and tailored trouser suit before she was
drenched in the storm raging outside. The heel on one of
the ridiculously high heels she was wearing had snapped
off, explaining why she was stumbling around.

"Having a bad morning?"

The woman looked up in annoyance, strands of dark,
wet hair falling across her face.

"You could say that. I don't suppose you have a shoe
repair place in this town?" She looked at the bright red
heel in her hand.

Nate shook his head as he approached her. "Nope. But hand it over. I'll see what I can do."

A perfectly shaped brow arched high. "Why? Are you going to cobble them back together with—" she gestured around widely "—maybe some staples or screws?"

"Technically, what you just described is the definition of cobbling, so yeah. I've got some glue that'll do the trick." He met her gaze calmly. "It'd be a lot easier to do if you'd take the shoe off. Unless you also think I'm a blacksmith?"

He was teasing her. Something about this soaking-wet woman still having so much…regal bearing…amused Nate. He wasn't usually a fan of the pearl-clutching country club set who strutted through Gallant Lake on the weekends and referred to his family's hardware store as "adorable." But he couldn't help admiring this woman's ability to hold on to her superiority while looking like she accidentally went to a water park instead of the business meeting she was dressed for. To be honest, he also admired the figure that expensive red suit was clinging to as it dripped water on his floor.

He held out his hand. "I'm Nate Thomas. This is my store."

She let out an irritated sigh. "Brittany Doyle." She slid her long, slender hand into his and gripped with surprising strength. He held it for just a half second longer than necessary before shaking off the odd current of interest she invoked in him.

Don't miss
Changing His Plans *by Jo McNally,*
available September 2020 wherever
Harlequin Special Edition books and ebooks are sold.

Harlequin.com

HARLEQUIN

*Heartfelt or suspenseful,
inspiring or passionate, Harlequin
has your happily-ever-after.*

With new books published
every month, you are sure to find the
satisfying escape you know you deserve.

SIGN UP FOR THE
HARLEQUIN NEWSLETTER

Be the first to hear about great new
reads and exciting offers!

Harlequin.com/newsletters